I0754862

DOWN WITH THE SHIPMANS

ALSO BY MEG MITCHELL MOORE

Mansion Beach

Summer Stage

Vacationland

Two Truths and a Lie

The Islanders

The Captain's Daughter

The Admissions

So Far Away

The Arrivals

DOWN WITH THE SHIPMANS

A Novel

MEG MITCHELL MOORE

wm

WILLIAM MORROW

An Imprint of HarperCollins*Publishers*

HarperCollins books may be purchased for educational, business, or sales promotional use. For information, please email the Special Markets Department at SPsales@harpercollins.com.

hc.com

FIRST EDITION

Library of Congress Cataloging-in-Publication Data

Names: Moore, Meg Mitchell author
Title: Down with the Shipmans : a novel / Meg Mitchell Moore.
Description: First edition. | New York, NY : William Morrow, 2026.
Identifiers: LCCN 2025037629 | ISBN 9780063337015 hardcover | ISBN 9780063337039 ebook
Subjects: LCGFT: Domestic fiction | Fiction | Novels
Classification: LCC PS3613.O5653 D69 2026
LC record available at https://lccn.loc.gov/2025037629

ISBN 978-0-06-333701-5

26 27 28 29 30 LBC 5 4 3 2 1

To my favorite daughters: Addie, Violet, and Josie

SATURDAY

• • •

Mae Shipman stands on a secluded patch of grass outside a La Quinta in South Bend, Indiana, almost exactly halfway between Boulder, Colorado, and her final destination: Rye, New Hampshire. The temperature is ninety-one degrees. The humidity, at eighty-three percent, is nearly thick enough to see. The air is chewy. It is the fifth of July, afternoon.

Many of Mae's belongings are in her car, a twelve-year-old Subaru parked in La Quinta's lot. Her sister Jordan paid for the motel room. The Subaru bears the scars of hard, unlucky living. Just like I do, she thinks dramatically, but not inaccurately. The rest of what she owns is in a storage unit in Boulder that is costing her $139 a month, which is $139 per month more than she can afford. She imagines that one day in the near future her storage unit will be adopted by one of those people who scavenge through other people's abandoned detritus in hopes of finding a treasure. There should be a reality show about this, and she thinks there probably is. *Storage Scavengers. Locker Luck. Vacant Vultures.*

She's trying to coax some bathroom activity from Leo, a ten-month-old pit bull mix. Mixed with what? Who knows. Ninety-nine percent of rescue dogs, in Mae's experience, are pit bull mixed with something. This alarms a lot of people, but it doesn't alarm Mae.

Mae and Leo drove from just before noon the previous day until four in the morning, which is why she asked for, and received, a late checkout time, though she had to weigh the sleep time against the allure of the free breakfast. She and Leo had slept face-to-face on the same pillow, breathing each other's air. She'd been too tired to get the crate out of the car.

"What happens in South Bend stays in South Bend," she'd told him, and he seemed to understand. You are not supposed to allow a dog you are training into the bed. Leo is her first official board-and-train client. His new owner is an overworked computer programmer who's also named Leo.

"Sorry?" she'd said when her boss, Hal, had called to ask her if she was interested in meeting Leo. "This guy named his dog after himself?" (Hello, Narcissus!)

"No, no." Hal laughed. "Leo the dog came with the name from the rescue organization. It was pure coincidence! Leo the human felt bad changing it, since Leo the dog has already been through so much. He's a good guy, Leo the human, just too busy to give Leo the dog the initial training he needs. You know how it is."

Mae does, indeed, know how it is. The board-and-train is one of Hal's premium offerings; he charges $975 for a week. For her time with Leo, Mae will receive five hundred of those dollars. Passing on this offer was not an option.

This gig is a big deal for Mae, who will turn thirty next year. Thirty! When Mae was a little girl running along the wide stretch of New Hampshire's Jenness Beach, where this road trip will take her, trying, as ever, to keep up with her two older sisters, she would have considered thirty impossibly old. *Well, at least they lived a good long life!* she would have thought upon hearing about the passing of someone beginning their fourth decade on Earth. *What more could they hope for?*

Her father, Calvin Shipman, had sent an email to his three

daughters a few days ago, asking that they make haste to New Hampshire (he actually used the phrase "make haste"), and that they arrive on Sunday, when the last of the renters would be gone. He'd also used the phrase "family bonding." Perhaps to soften the imperative, perhaps because he didn't have his readers on and couldn't see exactly what he was doing, he'd added to his email a string of nonsensical emojis: a frog, a birthday hat, a "rolling on the floor laughing" face. A poop (he probably thought it was a mountain; Calvin loved to hike).

Can't, Mae had replied immediately. Need to work. She'd already committed to Leo. She is part of the gig economy! The new world order! She is an overeducated Gen Zer with holes in her ears (seven) and holes in her résumé. Holes in her heart, sometimes, especially now.

Technically she is a millennial, like her sisters, but she's right on the cusp, and she feels very Gen Z. The gig economy doesn't allow for paid time off, not for sickness, not for a mental health day, and certainly not for a thirty-hour drive to New Hampshire.

If her mother, Theresa, had been alive, she would have been horrified to think of Mae traversing two-thirds of the country alone (sorry, Leo, that's not fair, not really alone) and staying in a La Quinta, where she easily could have been murdered in the middle of the night, especially if the murderer knew enough to bribe Leo with a scatter of freeze-dried salmon. Leo will do almost anything for freeze-dried salmon.

Her father had replied all: I'm afraid it's not optional.

No emojis this time, not even the poop one. That's how Mae knew it was serious. That's why Mae began to make haste.

It has been just over twenty-six months since their mother's death, and communication has fallen quite silent since their father's mourning period ended abruptly and he married Kara, their mother's hospice nurse.

Do we have to go. This came from Natalie, the middle, about their father's recent petition. It's a rly bad time for me. The Shipman sisters maintain their own group chat, and this is where Natalie's text landed.

This was a typical reaction for Natalie; she and her husband are the queen and king of a social media empire, and they run a dairy farm, and it's always a bad time to do anything other than run the empire and the farm and raise their three children. The New York Magazine article is coming out, the next text elaborated. I'm going to get busier.

He hasn't asked us for anything for a long time, answered Jordan, the eldest, who usually has final say in matters of familial dissent. We need to go.

Fine, texted Natalie in a huff. (You couldn't hear a huff in a text, but it was implied.)

Jordan had then side-texted Mae to see if she needed money for a flight. Jordan is seven years Mae's senior and makes buckets of money in her job in crisis communications, managing the secret and sometimes sordid mistakes of New York's finest; she's also single and childless, so she's usually flush.

But, there was Leo.

Have to drive. Have to bring this guy. Mae had texted a photo of Leo the dog that she'd taken when she'd met with Leo the human for the initial assessment. In the photo Leo has his lips pulled back from his teeth in a way that makes it look like he's smiling, although he may well have been snarling. I wouldn't say no to a little cash for hotel tho.

Here, now, outside the South Bend La Quinta, Leo lifts his leg and unleashes the impressively voluminous contents of his bladder on an already dying shrub along the far edge of the parking lot. He looks expectantly at Mae, who reaches into her treat pouch and produces a reward. *Good boy, Leo.*

From across the parking lot a small boy approaches. He's maybe five—she's gauging his age, as she gauges the ages of all children, by comparing him with her sister Natalie's older daughter, Evangeline, who is almost six.

"I'm going to pet your dog," the boy announces, drawing closer.

Small children are one of Leo's triggers. Leo has come from the mean streets somewhere in Tennessee, and there's no telling what painful puppyhood memories are lodged inside his tangerine-size brain. One of them, Mae suspects, has to do with a cruel child.

"Sorry, we're working!" Mae says brightly, as she learned to do in her own training. "We can't say hi right now!" Usually this is enough to make a person turn back, if the obvious pit bull part of Leo's DNA hasn't done the trick. (People are so prejudiced against pit bulls! Many pits are very easygoing! Not Leo, but many others!) But the boy proceeds apace, hand outstretched.

Leo curls a lip. This is the first warning sign.

"I'm going to pet it," the boy insists. He has dark brown hair with a side part and navy-blue sneakers. He really is very determined.

Leo growls. Second warning.

"Nice doggy," says the boy.

Leo lunges.

"Move back!" Mae shouts to the boy. She keeps her grip on the leash, which is attached to Leo's harness, and braces herself. Mae is the smallest of the Shipman sisters and the second fittest (Jordan wins). Mae rock climbs and hikes and has been living at altitude for three years now. Last year, she ran a half-marathon to raise money for pancreatic cancer research.

The boy moves back, but not as far as Mae would like. Does this child have an adult with him? Yes, and here she comes, striding across the parking lot, all bleached-blond hair and quivering rage. She's holding a cell phone and a set of car keys; she's wearing a short pleated skirt that makes her look like a tennis player just off the court, but there are no courts at La Quinta. No doubt it's a fashion thing.

"Did this lady yell at you, Matthew?" she demands of the boy.

By this time Mae has pulled an emergency sow's ear (not a euphemism, unfortunately) out of her treat pouch and tossed it for Leo, who gives it his full attention and no longer cares about the boy.

Mae grits her teeth and says, "You should teach Matthew to ask before petting a dog he doesn't know." Matthew nods respectfully and his brown saucer eyes land on Mae's. Lesson learned! She feels momentarily accomplished.

"You don't have to be rude about it," says the mom, and now Mae feels chastised.

"I'm not being rude. I'm being careful."

"That dog should be put down."

Leo turns from his treat to look sharply at Mae. Dogs understand more than we give them credit for. She gives him a smile she hopes comes off as reassuring.

Out of the corner of her eye she spies a man near her car, looking in the windows. She sprints over, holding the leash tightly, away from Matthew and his angry mother. Leo, excited by the change in pace, unbothered by the humidity, sprints too. She has so many things in that car. Did she lock it when she got Leo's food out? She can't remember. It doesn't matter—the sight of Leo running toward him at full speed is enough to move the man along. Mae fills Leo's water bowl, watches as he gulps it, pictures his bladder filling up again, wonders how long they can make it before he has to stop again. A ten-month-old dog has the bladder control of a college girl in Boston on St. Patrick's Day.

"Ready, boy?" she says, when Leo is loaded into the back seat.

Leo seems to indicate with a tip of his head that he's ready.

"Because we've got miles to go before we sleep."

SUNDAY

• • •

Natalie's phone starts blowing up with notifications about two hours into the drive from Hillside Haven. She tries to glance at it surreptitiously, but Evangeline, always vigilant, catches her.

"No phone, Mommy," she says primly, then purses her lips and shakes her head.

"I wasn't," says Natalie, although she definitely was. (What if it's an emergency? What if something has happened on the farm—what if a cow has discovered a piece of broken fence and gotten out, or one of the farmhands had a big Saturday night in town and failed to show up to work? What if the barn has caught fire?)

Like a beacon of hope, along comes a sign for Natalie's favorite rest stop, two miles away. They left Shaftsbury with a full tank, and the car isn't on empty yet, but she'll pretend she needs gas so that she can check her phone; even Evangeline might not be sharp enough to cop on to that.

She signals and pulls off the highway and into the rest stop, which is built to resemble a Main Street of yesteryear, with a fifties-style diner, an old-fashioned doughnut shop, a roadside market.

Scarlett's eyes snap open, and from the third row she asks, "Are we getting out?" Scarlett is a sometimes-tempestuous four, a middle child through and through. Natalie, as the middle child herself, can say this. Caspian, the baby (so far), will be two next month. He's a man of few words, but those he does utter have particular meaning.

"Out," he says, and bangs on the window.

"I'm just getting gas," says Natalie. "Nobody needs the bathroom, right?" Scarlett and Evangeline shake their pretty heads (matching braids, ribbons at the ends).

"Meee," says Caspian, who can't possibly, because he still wears diapers. (He's also wearing his Carhartt bib overalls, a small version of those his father wears on the farm. Caspian is effortlessly casual.)

The dog, Cinnamon (golden retriever, red bandanna, long pink tongue), remains asleep between Evangeline and Caspian.

"Okay!" says Natalie. "Great. So we can all wait. We'll be at the beach so soon." They have almost an hour to go, but thankfully nobody asks how soon. As much as she loves a good rest stop when her husband, Austin, is with her, the thought of unbuckling and unstrapping everyone and trooping inside on her own, keeping track of all three children amid the racks of bright candy, the old-fashioned bottles of soda, the doughnuts, my god, the doughnuts, fills her with an unbearable sense of exhaustion. She'd rather put everyone in a diaper, herself included. Anyway, it's too hot to leave the dog in the car, even with the windows lowered pretty far down, and at some point you have to start to worry about the dog getting stolen.

While the tank is filling she leans against the Audi and checks her phone. There are notifications on all of her socials. Like, a lot of notifications. TikTok is going crazy. Instagram isn't far behind. Probably X too, but she doesn't open X. There are tags and links; there are alerts and dings and buzzes. There is a thumping inside her chest that she realizes is her heart, working overtime.

There's a text from Bethany, the freelance publicist she recently hired. Article is out.

The article is out. The article is out!

Photos are great!!

The photos are great! She's happy to hear this; the sun hadn't cooperated on their photo shoot day, but the children had, and if she had to choose one of the two, that's the one she'd pick.

Maybe don't look at it tho? says Bethany's next text.

Bethany follows this advice with a smiley emoji, so it's hard to know if she's serious.

Sorry, what, don't *look* at it? Don't look at the profile in *New York Magazine* for which a reporter spent an entire day at the farm at the end of May and for which Natalie bought new outfits for everyone, scrubbed her baby-blue range, made a batch of skillet biscuits to serve with homemade jam plus her signature peanut butter cookies? Don't look at her first big traditional media hit?

She clicks the link, and the article loads.

She barely glances at the photos, because the thing that takes up most of the page is a giant pull quote from Austin. It's in red, splashed across the first page of the article like a bloodstain.

The gas pump judders once, then stops. The tank is full.

The quote is awful—the exact opposite of everything she wanted the article to convey. Natalie's heart is beating too fast. It's so hot and hazy in the July sun, on the melting earth. Is she going to pass out? Her knees are wobbly. She can't pass out. She has three children and a dog with her. She doesn't have the luxury of passing out. She takes a deep breath and slides into the car.

"What's the matter?" says Evangeline. Evangeline always knows. She can read her mother like a text.

"Not a thing!" Natalie says, willing her voice into submission, telegraphing nonchalance. The greatest acting job, a wise man has never said (but should), is being a mother. "Not a single thing. Let's get to the beach, okay? Onward!"

"Onward!" repeats Evangeline dutifully.

Natalie drives on.

• • •

At 10 a.m. Jordan picks up the rental car, an impractical Porsche with a back seat so tiny it could scarcely fit a baby (not that she has one, or wants one), at the Hertz in Midtown because the one closest to her, on Eighty-Third, had no vehicles available at short notice. People have scattered from the city for the holiday.

Jordan had spent the Fourth of July alone in her apartment, reveling in the air-conditioning, watching the Boston Pops on television, and polishing off a Jersey Mike's Original Italian. Don't feel bad for her! She'd turned down three invitations, two to the Hamptons and one to the Jersey Shore, because she wanted a break. Work has been crazy.

If Jordan were to get a tattoo, it would say *Work is crazy.*

The Henry Hudson becomes the Saw Mill and her phone, plugged into the Porsche's aux cord, rings. Really? It's Sunday! Of a holiday weekend! But yes, really. Crises don't look at the calendar before they decide to happen. They just happen. Jordan's motto, which she adopted from her boss, Bernadette, is ABA: Always Be Accessible. She doesn't take a shower without propping her phone just outside the shower door so she can hear it if it rings. (And it rings! Oh, how it rings!) She's stood naked with shampoo dripping into her eyes taking a call from a newly disgraced US senator; she's stopped a ten-mile run at mile nine and a half when Bernadette has asked her to schedule a meeting with a Hollywood director. She's flown back from a long-awaited vacation on the Amalfi Coast to meet with the CEO of a major company (sorry, she can't say which one) whose son was involved in a hazing incident at a prestigious college's most prestigious fraternity.

But it's not Bernadette, and it's not a client who bypassed Bernadette to go right to Jordan, as more and more are starting to do, which is making Jordan wonder if she's not the only one beginning to question things about Bernadette. It's a voice as plaintive as it is familiar.

"Where *are* you?" she says. "Nobody's here but me."

• • •

The next fifteen hours for Mae and Leo pass as quickly as . . . well, as quickly as you'd expect fifteen hours in a car to pass, which is to say not very quickly at all. The check-engine light comes on outside of Buffalo. That's okay to ignore, right? The lights on her dashboard blink on and off like Christmas lights, giving visual pleasure and reminding one to donate to the Salvation Army.

Her father would not be happy to know the state of Mae's car.

Mae has loaded up on Red Bull and Spotify, and she's on Colorado time, which means she's able to drive without too much trouble, now that she has a solid night of La Quinta sleep behind her. She's a night owl by nature and also by lifestyle; the tattoo parlor where she works is open until 10 p.m., and often she and Tony go out after. She's rarely awake before eleven in the morning.

("How do you get anything done?" her sister Natalie has asked her. Natalie rises at five thirty and is in bed promptly by nine thirty every night. Shc won't hcar Mac's rcasoning that thcy'rc actually awake about the same number of hours, and therefore capable of being the same amount of productive. Not that they *are* the same amount of productive, but theoretically they could be.)

Time goes by, Ohio, Pennsylvania, New York. When Mae gets tired, she pulls into a rest stop on I-90 and sleeps for four hours with all the doors locked and Leo slumbering in the back seat, the windows cracked to give them air. She figures if anyone bothers them Leo will protect her. Despite his youth, Leo snores like a sixty-three-year-old man with sleep apnea, and, before she falls asleep, she can see one of his ears twitching by the light of the moon, filtered through the dark sky to her spot in the middle of the parking lot. She learned in her training that dogs dream about their daily life, which is a claim she finds a little questionable (who made this discovery, and *how did they prove it?*) but nonetheless charming. Maybe Leo is dreaming about her! Maybe he's dreaming about Human Leo. She hopes it's her. They did have that romantic night in South Bend.

They reach Massachusetts. Her home state. The Shipmans hail from Lenox, home to Tanglewood and Edith Wharton's The Mount. She's surprised, as she always is after time away, by how green New England is, especially after the dust bowl of a Colorado summer (they're in a drought; so many Western states are in a drought or under wildfire watch or, more commonly, both). Here, the trees along the highway, so tall and verdant, seem to be closing in on her.

Sometime around nine in the morning Mae and Leo make it to New Hampshire. They exit the highway into the dubious charms of Seabrook (sounds prettier than it is) and then finally, finally, they are on the coast.

North Hampton, and then Rye, up the long and curving stretch of Route 1A that leads to the house. It's the winding road of a fairy tale, of a buddy movie, of an untested future, with the ocean to the right, a great wide unbroken expanse of blue, and beautiful, spacious homes to the left. Legitimate mansions, many of them. She pulls off the main road and down the small access road that leads to Ruby on Rye and into the driveway. There's room for four cars, but only with a Tetris level of car management. Nobody has parked in the garage for as long as Mae can remember. She's the first to arrive.

The house, built in the late fifties as a summer cottage for Theresa Shipman's parents, Lewis and Roberta Perkins, but expanded, renovated, insulated, shored up, is two stories, with four bedrooms, two bathrooms, and an upper deck and a lower patio, both facing the water. Three steps lead down from the patio to the beach, and a stone wall sits to either side of the patio. Living room, small sunroom, kitchen, dining room. A little square of grass around the side, but the real yard is wide, bountiful Jenness Beach and the ocean beyond.

Theresa's parents had divided their kingdom among their own three daughters: the brownstone in Boston to Carolyn, the eldest; money to Dawn, the youngest (this was what Dawn wanted); and the house in Rye to Theresa, the middle. Both grandparents died within nine months of each other when Natalie was two, before Mae was born, so she doesn't remember a time when the house didn't belong entirely to the Shipmans.

It's not a mansion like the homes Mae just drove past, with their golf-course-green lawns, their turrets and gables, their location across the street from the ocean. Those houses observe the beach from a distance, while the Shipman house, and the houses on either side of it, a dozen or so altogether, inhabit the beach. They *are* the beach.

There's a woman bending over the outside spigot on the house. She straightens when she sees Mae's car, and a look passes over her face that could only be called—confusion? She's maybe in her late forties or early fifties, buttoned up, both figuratively and literally, in a pantsuit and square-buckle velvet flats (impractical beachwear, Mae notes).

Mae hesitates before getting out. Has there been a mistake? Has her father accepted a rental for the week and forgotten all about it? He *is* getting older—he'll be seventy in October. Maybe his memory is starting to go. (If there is a renter, if the family bonding week is off, if she needs to turn around and go back to Colorado, she will ask her father to pay her back for all of the gas she purchased so that she could make haste.) She lowers Leo's window a few inches and climbs out of the car.

She calls, "Hello!" She tries to make it sound merry but she hasn't spoken in hours and the word comes out with a dry, desperate croak.

The woman approaches, hand outstretched to shake Mae's. Very formal for a renter. "Hello there. I'm Nikoletta," she says. She looks at the window from which Leo's wide snout is visible. "Oh, what a nice dog," she says optimistically. "Can I say hi? I love dogs."

Leo shows his teeth.

"I wouldn't," says Mae. "Sorry. We're—training."

Nikoletta lowers her hand, clears her throat, and says, "You must be one of the girls. Your father thought you'd be arriving later."

Mae nods. But why would a renter know she's "one of the girls"?

"I think I've got the lockbox working now. You shouldn't have any trouble with it, but if you do, give me a call. I'll come right back. The code is four-three-seven-one."

"I have a key," Mae says, confused herself. They've all always had a key to the house; Mae keeps hers on her University of Vermont key ring, which she took with her when she moved out of Tony's place and commenced her month of couch surfing. Much less fun than actual surfing, which Mae and her sisters grew up doing on this very beach. Why would she need a lockbox code?

"Oh, but we changed the locks. Common practice."

Mae shakes her head. "Sorry?" In what universe is that? "The locks get changed every time a renter comes?"

Nikoletta tilts her head and considers Mae. She has kind brown eyes and the perfect amount of eyeliner, very much not smeared. She looks well-rested and organized. "I'm not—" She seems to reconsider. "Never mind," she says. "Sorry to bother you. I'm sure your father will be in touch with me later today, once you've all arrived."

"He'll give you a refund," Mae says. "If you're out any money."

Nikoletta is already walking quickly down the driveway. She

looks back over her shoulder. "What's that? Oh, I'm sure he will. Remember! Four-three-seven-one!"

Mae unloads Leo from the car and walks him on the patch of grass at the side of the house. She loops the leash around the railing, and he heaves himself onto the grass, panting like he's the third-place finisher in the Bolder Boulder 10K. "Be right back, Leo," she tells him. "Don't go anywhere." *As if I could,* says Leo with his eyes. *I'm attached to the railing.* Mae digs in the back of the car for Leo's food and bowls, fills his water, pours the kibble. "This is more brunch than breakfast," she tells him. "But it *is* Sunday, so we can make that work."

Where are her sisters? She doesn't want to be in the house without them. She doesn't want to face the ghost of their mother alone. She wants to see them, smell them, Natalie's flowery perfume, Jordan's expensively practical face wash. She wants to fall into their arms and tell them everything. She wants to say *Fix it, you guys. Fix it all for me.*

She calls Jordan. "Where *are* you?" she says, feeling very much the coddled youngest who is currently not being appropriately coddled. "Nobody's here but me."

• • •

The second they pull into the driveway the girls are asking if they can swim. They've invented a song too, which goes like this: *beach, beach, we want to go to the beach.* A songwriting Grammy is not, Natalie is afraid, in their near future, but the melody isn't bad, and the sound of their sweet little voices harmonizing almost brings her to tears. She's always been a sucker for the singing of children. Austin plays guitar and sings himself, and the kids seem to have inherited some of his talents the same way they inherited Natalie's blue eyes and unfortunate tendency toward sunburn.

("Christian rock?" Jordan asked sardonically the first time Natalie mentioned Austin's singing, and Natalie had said no, huffily, because she knew Jordan would make fun if she said yes, although the truth is that sometimes Austin does veer slightly into Matt Redman territory.)

Even Caspian is trying to sing along, his legs in the car seat pumping mightily up and down.

("Caspian, like from the sea?" Jordan had asked when Natalie called to tell her that her nephew had arrived, a perfect little boy to go along with big sisters Scarlett and Evangeline. And Natalie had said, "Caspian as in the prince from Narnia." The name was Austin's idea. "Noble, handsome, brave, and merry." She'd be too busy to put any more thought into it, Natalie knew. Jordan is always busy.)

Jordan loves her nieces and nephew, though, she really does. Both of Natalie's sisters are phenomenal aunts; she's so lucky. Even if her beloved mother won't get to see Natalie's children grow up, she knows that her sisters will be there. She just wishes that at least one of them would have babies so that her kids would have cousins on their side of the family. As it is things are very heavily weighted toward Austin's side. He's the youngest of four boys, and among them they have eleven children, enough for their own NFL team, as soon as the NFL goes coed.

Natalie sometimes forgets she's not technically a Shipman anymore; she's a Hanson. But she will always be a Shipman sister.

"Not now," she tells the singing army in the back seat, turning off the ignition. "Inside first, beach later. We have to unpack. We have to say hello to the house."

"Hello, house," says Evangeline.

Natalie takes a deep breath, trying to push energy into all parts of her body. She's so tired. Austin wants more children, and theoretically Natalie does too. But how will she ever have another baby, how could she handle four children under the age of seven, when three under six have her balanced on the knife's edge of sanity? Not that she's going to admit that to anyone but herself. That would be extremely off-brand.

Cinnamon lets out a low whine.

"Simanon needs the bathroom," announces Scarlett.

"Cinn-a-mon," says Natalie (the first rule of homeschooling is that every moment is a teaching moment), and Scarlett repeats, "Sim-a-non." She has articulation challenges that qualify as adorable right now but that might need intervention soon. Natalie adds it to her mental list.

"Out," says Caspian.

"Just a minute, buddy. Let me gather myself." She takes another deep breath.

There's one car in the driveway: Mae's old Subaru, the gently used one their parents bought her after college graduation. How did Mae make it here first when she drove all the way from Colorado, while Natalie has come only from Vermont? And why no Jordan yet, why no Calvin? She checks her phone. It's only eleven o'clock. It's going to be another thirty-four-hour day.

When she'd told Austin about her father's invitation-slash-order his face had crinkled up in a very Austin-like way, part sympathy, part kindness, and he'd said, "You have to go. Of course, go! Leave everything to me!" The "everything" did not include the children, of course. It rarely did, as per their unspoken agreement, except when Theresa was sick. Which is fine! It's mostly fine. Was she hoping Austin would break from tradition and suggest that she go on her own, have a little time with her family, lie on the beach, as she used to do when she was a teenager? Some of the best naps she's ever had in her life have been on that beach. But she knew better. Austin has a dairy farm to run.

"Out," says Caspian again, really quite pleasantly.

She sees a lot of Austin in her son right now, as she unbuckles him from his car seat while the girls unleash themselves from theirs. If the color of his eyes is Natalie's, the size and shape are Austin's, huge and round; both father and son seem to be always on the verge of a happy exclamation of surprise. This is how Caspian had looked at her the first moment she'd held him after birth: *Oh, hey!* his expression had seemed to be saying. *This is amazing! I was hoping it would be you!* Caspian has Austin's kindness too, his son-of-a-pastor way of putting others before him, which, for anyone who wonders how that manifests in a lightly verbal toddler, means that he's always thrusting his favorite slimy-eared bunny at his sisters or opening his chubby hands to reveal a smushed, damp graham cracker that he wants to offer to you, because even though he loves graham crackers and they are his favorite snack in the whole world, it would make him happy to see you happy so he'd like you to have it.

It's a euphemism, the son-of-a-pastor thing; Austin's family owns a commercial dairy farm in Montana. But he *is* kind! She cringes, thinking of the online comments she'd seen at the gas station. People are so quick to rush to judgment without having all the facts.

She reminds herself: out of sight, out of mind. The thing about the online world is that if you simply turn off your phone it all disappears. Right? *Pop. Whoop. Zoop.* Use any sound effect you like; it all disappears.

Her fingers itch, wanting to check her phone again.

If you take the love you have to be okay with the hate, Jordan will probably say when Natalie tells her the story, if she ever does. Or maybe Jordan will see it on her own. Maybe she already has.

But Natalie is *not* okay with the hate! She wants only the love.

The girls run up to the door, delighted. Caspian has never been here. He wasn't yet born when Theresa died, and only Calvin and his daughters made the trip to scatter Theresa's ashes. It's actually unlikely that Scarlett and Evangeline remember much, but they are obsessed with looking at photos of the Shipman sisters, and they've absorbed the house's memories into their own. Natalie had been fifteen the year the iPhone came out, so there is a healthy amount of digital documentation of her teenage years, for good and ill. ("Is that you, Mommy?" the girls ask wonderingly, scrolling through. "That's not you." Which makes Natalie wonder if the enormous amount of time and money she spends on skin care is worth it. On the inside, she still feels nineteen. In a mere five years she'll be twice that.)

With Caspian on her hip and Cinnamon's leash in her hand, Natalie and the girls enter through what is technically the back door; all of the houses that sit beachfront like theirs does have all of their best parts facing toward the ocean. And why shouldn't they?

She drops the leash and calls Mae's name; no answer. Then she hears her sister's voice from upstairs: "Leo, stay. I'll be right back."

Has Mae brought a boyfriend with her? Natalie tries to remember the last time they spoke and who Mae was dating at the time.

"Stay," Mae's voice commands.

Is this some kind of a dominatrix routine? *Not in front of the children, please.* Natalie had been hoping she could put one or both of the girls in with Mae so she'd have room to set up the portable crib for Caspian. He has a tendency to wander in a new place, so she doesn't trust him to stay in the bed with her. Caspian grabs a hunk of her hair and shoves it gleefully in his mouth. Cinnamon has ambled off, so Natalie uses her free hand to liberate her hair.

Mae appears at the top of the stairs. From behind Mae's bedroom, the Green Room, comes a collection of noises, whines and scratches and, what is that, a body banging against the door? Mae is wearing jean shorts with frayed edges and a fitted black tank, along with high-top Converse, also black. (They had always been a no-shoe household, but probably two years of renters had rendered that rule moot.) She makes her way down, and the noises intensify. Mae has new tattoos since Natalie saw her last, but if pressed Natalie wouldn't be able to point out which specific ones are new. There are so many.

Natalie puts Caspian down and stretches her arm over her head to release the tension in her hip while she hugs her little sister.

When they were kids, the three Shipman girls had their roles, as you do in a family. Jordan the problem solver, calm and capable. Natalie in the middle, a whirling dervish of emotions and plans and so many feelings she didn't always know what to do with them. And then there was Mae, the baby, so full of joy that if she burped, butterflies and rainbows came out of her mouth (not actually). And now look at her. Well, Natalie supposes you can be joyful and wear black Converse and armfuls and legfuls of ink. But Mae doesn't look joyful, hasn't really looked truly joyful, old-Mae joyful, since they lost their mother.

"Aunt Maeeeeee!" cries Scarlett, and for a second Mae does look like her old self, as she crouches and opens her arms and two nieces and a nephew tackle her until, in an exaggerated movement, she falls flat on the ground, her arms making a T. She sticks her tongue out of one side of her mouth and closes her eyes, pretending to be dead, and Evangeline bangs on her chest, maybe administering CPR. Maybe breaking a rib.

"Did you bring Cinnamon?" Mae asks, when she rises from the dead.

"Of course." Natalie whistles and Cinnamon comes, tail moving back and forth, heading straight for Mae, who buries her face in Cinnamon's neck and says, "Hello, gorgeous." Then to Natalie, "I was hoping you'd have left her back. No offense, Cinnamon."

A thread of irritation materializes somewhere in the side of Natalie's neck. She tries not to let herself pull at it, but she pulls a little.

"Well, I didn't. You love Cinnamon!" Mae loves all creatures great and small, and they all love her right back. She never babysat in high school because she ran such a thriving and lucrative pet-sitting business that she had all the spending money she needed.

Mae crosses one foot over another and stands in one single, elegant move, scarcely pushing off the floor. "I've got a trainee dog upstairs. He's a little reactive." Evangeline and Scarlett take hold of Mae's arms and examine her tattoos, tracing their fingers over a set of winding vines.

"What does that mean? Reactive to what?"

Mae clears her throat. "Most things. People. Dogs. A garbage can that looks at him the wrong way. It's okay, it'll be fine. I have a crate in the car. And you might have to leash Cinnamon when we're all here." Cinnamon looks offended. "I'll wear him, just in case," Mae goes on. "I should be doing that anyway."

"How do you wear a dog?" cries Evangeline, fascinated. Natalie imagines a dog in a BabyBjörn.

"I put a leash around my waist, and I attach him to it. That way I keep him safe, and I can teach him things as I go about my day."

"Attachment parenting at its best," says Natalie.

She's kidding, but there's Mae, nodding seriously and saying, "You know what? I'm glad you brought Cinnamon. She'll be a great practice dog. She's so mellow." Natalie doesn't know what a practice dog is but she figures it's all there in the context. *Bang bang*, goes the upstairs guest. *Scratch.*

"What is your trainee? Part elephant? All elephant?"

"Phant," instructs Caspian sternly.

"No, he's—" Mae glances at the kids. "Doesn't matter. He's a mix. He's a rescue. He's a good boy, just a little anxious. We're working through it. I'll go get him before he knocks the door down."

"I'll get our bags. Scarlett, why don't you help me. Evangeline, keep an eye on Caspian. Caspian, keep an eye on Cinnamon." (Cinnamon doesn't need an eye, but as she's said on her parenting Substack, it's important for the youngest member of the family to feel a sense of responsibility as early as possible.)

When she and Scarlett return with the luggage Mae is in the kitchen, filling a glass at the sink. Around her waist is some sort of belt, and clipped to the belt is a dog leash. At the end of the leash, sitting next to Mae with his eyes fixed on her, is a gray dog with short legs, a short snout, and a wide white stripe down the center of his face. His chest, which is also white, looks so strong he could have just come from a CrossFit gym.

"This is Leo," says Mae. "Don't say hi right now. I'm working with him. Leo, you're okay. Good boy. Stay." Leo whines and rolls his head toward Mae; Natalie can see the whites of his eyes. Mae puts down her water glass and feeds Leo a steady stream of small treats from a pouch clipped to her waist contraption.

"Um, Mae. Is Leo a pit bull?" says Natalie. She takes Scarlett by the shoulder and backs her up.

Mae turns and moves to the far corner of the kitchen, keeping Leo right next to her.

"Only part," she says. "Do you mind keeping your voice calm? "

"You brought a pit bull with aggression issues around my children?" Natalie feels her voice go up an octave or two.

Mae sighs. "He's not aggressive. He's reactive. They're not the same—"

Natalie cuts her off. "Where's Cinnamon? Where are Evangeline and Caspian?"

"I asked Eva to—"

"Evangeline," corrects Natalie. Natalie doesn't allow nicknames.

"—keep Cinnamon and Caspian in the living room. I didn't want to introduce the dogs yet. I thought that might trigger Leo." She's not looking at Natalie so she doesn't see how dramatically Natalie rolls her eyes at that one. "You know what? I'll grab the crate from the car."

"Uh, yeah," says Natalie, more snarkily than she means to. "Good idea."

As Mae walks away Natalie can see that there are new tattoos on the back of one of her calves too. Natalie thinks her mother might turn over in her grave if she saw Mae now. Of course she would never use that phrase. It's a ridiculous phrase, it defies logic (anyway, Theresa's body had been cremated), and Natalie is a logical person. She'd been captain of the speech and debate team in high school. They'd gone to nationals twice. She'd been told throughout her education that she should drop data science and go to law school; she'd even gone so far as to take the LSAT. She'd scored really high, especially on the logical reasoning section.

"Let's go find your brother and sister," she says to Scarlett. "Then we can bring our things upstairs and unpack."

Mae and Leo are back before she's made her way upstairs—packing three children for six days is not that different from packing an entire household to move across the country forever. Mae is carrying a folded-up dog crate with one hand and using her other hand to keep Leo at her side. If Natalie weren't so peeved about the whole situation, she might have been impressed.

"I just don't know why you brought a weird dog on a family bonding week, Mae," she says. "It's going to become a whole thing."

Mae unfolds the crate—she's like a magician with that thing—and scatters a handful of treats on the crate's padded floor. She whisks the dog inside, fastens the door, and turns to face Natalie.

"It won't become a thing," says Mae. "I have it under control. And he's not weird. He's just struggling with a few things. Who isn't, right?" Her voice starts to wobble and then her eyes fill. "Also, I didn't have a choice, okay?"

"Hello, sunshine!" their mother used to say when Mae toddled into the kitchen as a little girl, as an eight-year-old, at sixteen (not toddling, obviously, by that age). And Mae would smile her beautiful, sunny smile. They'd all babied her; it was impossible not to. Her terrible twos had been un-terrible; what was supposed to be her teenage angsty years were remarkably calm. Maybe she'd been saving up and was going to have all of her bad years now, in her late twenties, with no mother to help her through.

"Aw, Mayday," she says. She opens her arms and Mae steps into them; she's enough shorter that Natalie can rest her chin on top of Mae's head, right in her thick, glossy hair. Natalie is the tallest of the Shipman girls. Take that, birth order, she used to think during her own angsty teenage years, when she thought the world was against her (it wasn't) and that being the middle child meant she'd always be forgotten one way or another (it didn't). "I'm sorry," Natalie goes on. "I don't mean to be so cranky. I'm sure it'll be fine. It's just a few days. We can all pitch in to make it work. Dad and Jordan will be here soon, and unless there's something I don't know, they're not bringing any dogs!"

Jordan will fix everything, right? That's what she does for a living. She's a professional mess-cleaner-upper.

All they need is Jordan.

• • •

"Phones down, please. I want your full attention," says Calvin Shipman.

It's six thirty, and Jordan arrived at Ruby on Rye almost two hours ago. Weekend traffic had been brutal. One hour and forty-five minutes ago she made her first cocktail, just before her father pulled in. Now she's on her second.

Calvin is using his I'm-giving-a-lecture voice, and Jordan feels Natalie snap to attention next to her. They are sitting in the living room, lined up in a row on the couch like little girls waiting for their bedtime story. It's the sofa that, right before she was diagnosed five years ago, their mother refashioned with a plush vanilla-cream cover rather than replace.

Their father is in the easy chair, his back to the wall of windows. He has moved it to face them. The usual setup in this room is that every seat has a water view. The house is decorated in what might optimistically be called "cozy chic" but more accurately "jury-rigged haute." Rattan baskets hold magazines, throw blankets, the odd doll or toy left from Natalie's children's last visit, when Scarlett was only one. The kitchen, redone fifteen years ago, has the white cabinets and black granite countertops of the time, after white became the new brown but before gray became the new white.

There are absences now, for sure. The kitchen windowsill shell collections that had been there since time began, along with the wafers of old soap in the bathroom cabinets, always kept there "just in case," even though most of the world had transitioned to bodywash, are gone. Jordan, when she carried her Away suitcase in "coast blue" up the stairs to her bedroom, had been dismayed to find on her dresser a white sign with navy blue writing exhorting her to *SEAS THE DAY.* Definite HomeGoods vibes. Jordan had put it in one of the dresser drawers.

"Family bonding week has begun," says Calvin. "One, two, three . . . bond!"

Jordan laughs charitably. In his job as a professor of sociology at Williams, Calvin is known for his dry sense of humor, his specialty in social science theory, and his tie-under-sweater-vest professor look, though right now he's wearing a Red Sox T-shirt and a beleaguered hat from the local shop Summer Sessions. Calvin in summer casual. In a limited television series he might be played by a Harrison Ford of ten or fifteen years ago, handsomely lined, still mostly thick-haired. You loved him, and you knew he loved you, but he was not the one you were hoping to run into when you were trying to sneak in, tipsy, eight minutes past curfew, after a party in Nicholas Murphy's basement. Calvin, in the last year of his seventh decade, is not looking his age. He went gray in his late forties, so that's nothing new, and in his early sixties the gray began to turn to white, but his hair is as thick as it ever was, his biceps as strong, his eyes still sharp even if the skin around them has acquired lines over the years.

"Jordan has her phone," says Natalie.

Jordan's phone had been buzzing incessantly, so she put it on Do Not Disturb and is just keeping it handy. Jordan almost calls Natalie a tattletale but even here, in this familiar childhood locale, which is where people are known to revert to old habits and patterns, that's a bridge too far. Or too close, maybe, to their girlhood squabbles. She settles for a pointed glare, but Natalie is looking straight ahead, at their father. The Shipman girls are recognizable as sisters, with the small differences generated by luck and genetics. Natalie has the best profile, and Jordan the longest legs, though Natalie is half an inch taller. Mae has the thickest hair, with a natural wave, in a shade lighter than Jordan's (the shiniest) and darker than Natalie's (the closest to their mother's dark blond). They all have blue eyes, also their mother's, with some variation in shade and shape, from round (Mae) to almond (Natalie). It all evens out, except when it doesn't.

"No, I don't," says Jordan, sliding the phone under her leg, feeling, at age thirty-six, reluctant to get in trouble with her father. When they were growing up Calvin did the disciplining; Theresa was in charge of making you feel better after. She always said that as a second-grade teacher at Morris Elementary she did enough disciplining during the day.

"Do too," says Natalie.

"Come on Natalie, how old are you?" asks Mae.

Surprisingly, Natalie's phone is nowhere in sight. Jordan assumed she had been posting continuously throughout the day. Sometimes in her office Jordan will pull up Natalie's Instagram or TikTok account and watch her videos. There are videos of Natalie making biscuits in a cast-iron skillet, of her wearing overalls and milking a cow, of her cuddling with the children on an elaborately pillowed couch with a Christmas tree visible in the background, reading a picture book. When she watches the videos, Jordan can't help but think, Who is this person? She's so familiar, but she's also a stranger. Sometimes she reads Natalie's Substack (the free version, she's not a subscriber) and thinks, What? Are there actually people who depend on her sister—the girl who failed her driver's license test twice, who had a crush on her high school physics teacher so severe that her friends had to hold her back from delivering a letter she had written him, whose dwarf hamster had died from overfeeding—to tell them how to parent?

There are quite a lot of people who do, it turns out. Nearly one and a half million of them.

Mae has a dog attached to her; she's had a dog attached to her since Jordan arrived. Leo. The dog is lying down next to Mae, and every thirty seconds or so Mae delivers a tiny treat to him, right between his two front paws. In between treats he fixes Mae with an unswervingly devoted gaze.

"I can't tell you how happy it makes me to see the three of you together like this," says Calvin, as Natalie ignores Mae's question. "So grown up and beautiful." These would normally be sentiments Jordan would roll her eyes at—she's been told she's prickly, that she has a wall up, that it wouldn't kill her to be softer—but there's something really quite touching about watching her father express emotion. (Are his eyes damp?) Emotion had been Theresa's department, where Calvin expressed his love with acts of service and gratitude. And dad jokes, lots of dad jokes. Calvin used to bring Theresa flowers from Bella Flora after work every Friday. He made her the perfect dry martini each Saturday night before their date night. He pumped the tires on the girls' bikes and kept the garage organized and grilled a mean steak. He would have walked barefoot over a field of razor blades if doing so would have saved his wife.

Beyond the windows, of course, is the ocean, stretching on forever and ever and ever. At low tide, as it is now, it's the longest, widest, prettiest beach on the Seacoast. Maybe in the whole world. New Hampshire boasts eighteen miles of coastline, a length a state like California might laugh at, but each mile is a jewel. In another hour or so the sky will turn its famous pinks and purples and they'll have a front row seat to the show. Sunrise is even better, with the fireball rising over the water from the edge of the horizon.

Jordan takes a sip of her drink, a gin and tonic, Broker's London Dry; she'd brought it with her because she was worried there'd be no good gin in the house (correct). The cubes clink against her teeth as she tips the glass all the way back, emptying it. It would be rude to get up and get another. But she really wants one.

The children and Cinnamon have been banished to the upstairs, with the exception of Caspian, who's walking around the living room, placing a flat palm on any items whose name he knows and pronouncing them with authority and flourish, if sometimes without their first letter. *able. indow. ommy.* Caspian has been told to give the dog a wide berth but every now and then he circles a little too close and Leo shows the whites of his eyes.

"There's another reason I wanted you all here." Calvin clears his throat again and Jordan feels a pulse behind her left earlobe (this is where all of her concerns first appear). What's with all the throat activity? Esophageal cancer? She is not losing another parent. She refuses!

"I guess I'll just come out with it." Calvin frowns, like he's mad at the words that are about to emerge. "Okay, here we go. I'm putting the house on the market." They all stare at him, open-mouthed. "Tomorrow is Monday. We have an open house scheduled for Sunday. That gives us six days to say goodbye, to enjoy some time here, to complete some tasks. The Realtor expects it will sell quickly. I have a lot of details to manage, so I'm asking you girls to clean out the garage. I'll handle the rest. I want you to have enough free time to enjoy your last week here."

Natalie swivels her head back and forth between Mae and Jordan. She's the first to speak. "No," she says firmly, in her strict mom voice. "No. You can't do that. Sorry, but no."

"I knew that woman wasn't a renter!" cries Mae. "She was definitely giving Realtor."

Natalie and Jordan turn to Mae and together they say, "What woman?" at exactly the same time and in exactly the same tone. Sometimes, there's no arguing with the power of genetics.

"There was a woman outside when I got here. She was fiddling with the lockbox. I thought she was the renter, like maybe she'd come back because she forgot something. But it was suspicious; she was way overdressed for a beach vacation." Mae turns accusingly to her father. "Why didn't she say?"

"I asked Nikoletta if she happened to see you not to say anything until I'd talked to you."

"Nikoletta," says Natalie. "That's such a Realtor name."

"You can't sell Mom's house," says Mae. "You can't, this person Nikoletta can't, nobody can."

Calvin folds his hands and places them in his lap. He might have been praying, except the Shipmans don't pray. "It's already listed. It's done. I signed the papers. When Kara gets here on Tuesday—"

Natalie breaks in first, but they're all thinking it, ho, boy, they are all thinking it. "Kara's coming? To our family bonding week?" Her voice rises close to a shriek: "To the first time we've spent real time here without Mom?"

Calvin says, "Kara is—" and they take a collective breath, because they all expect him to say, *Kara is family*, and two of them have their mental fists raised, ready to pummel those words. "Kara is visiting her mother in Cincinnati," says Calvin. "She's flying back. She lands at two on Tuesday."

"That's a terrible idea," says Jordan, and her sisters turn toward her, surprised that she could be so bold. "What? She's flying into Logan at two? You'll spend the whole day in rush-hour traffic."

"That's not the terrible idea!" cries Natalie, going for it. "The terrible idea is that she's coming at all."

"She could take the bus," says Mae. "You could collect her in Portsmouth."

Calvin shakes his head. "She's not taking the bus. I'll pick her up."

Mae says, "It's a coach bus. It's not, like, a yellow school bus."

"You could put her in an Uber," says Jordan. "If she has to come at all."

"Uber's worse," says Mae. "She could get murdered in an Uber." Then, at her father's expression, "She could. You're not supposed to take an Uber alone for a long ride!"

"A young woman can't be too careful in this world," adds Natalie snarkily. Guns are blazing, thinks Jordan. Leave it to Natalie. (Kara is forty, only four years older than Jordan.)

"None of this is the issue. Why is Kara coming?" asks Jordan. "She's never been here, right?"

"Correct," says Calvin.

"Why not just keep it that way?" asks Jordan.

Calvin sighs. "She wanted to see the house once. And she is my wife, so, like it or not, she's part of this family."

Natalie huffs and says, "I call not liking it."

"You're all missing the point," says Mae. "The point is that selling the house is like selling Mom. Her ashes are out there!" She points to the ocean. Yes, it's true; on a cold gray October morning, just past dawn, six months to the day after Theresa died, they'd all donned waders and walked across the piles of seaweed cast upon the sand and flung handfuls of ashes into the sea.

"It does feel like you're selling Mom," confirms Natalie.

Calvin rubs his eye for many, many seconds. When he stops rubbing it, he says, "I understand your responses. Everything you're feeling is valid. But I'm not selling your mother. This is a financial decision, not an emotional one."

"All decisions are emotional," counters Natalie.

Calvin takes a breath so slow and deliberate they can all see his ribs expand. "This is a financial decision," he repeats. "You're all off in your own lives. This house is three hours away from Lenox. I needed to make a plan that makes the most sense."

"This house has always been three hours away from Lenox," Mae points out.

Jordan is annoyed—are her sisters being deliberately obtuse? "What he's saying, you guys, is that Kara doesn't want to come here."

"I'm not saying—"

"I knew Kara was behind this," spits Natalie. "I knew she was making you sell it."

"Kara isn't making me sell anything. But obviously we're not using it the way we did when your mother was alive."

"I thought you were renting it," says Mae.

"I was. But that's a lot to keep track of, from afar."

"You can hire a property manager," says Natalie.

"But if something breaks, I could lose the whole rental check on the repair. The roof needs replacing. The washer and dryer are on their last legs. The taxes are high. Flood insurance is through the roof. I'm just waiting for the day when the insurance company cancels it altogether. The cost of keeping a house we're not living in has become untenable." He clears his throat again. "I'm sorry. I know this isn't something you wanted to hear. But you all have your own homes now."

"Not me," says Mae softly.

"Yes, you do," says Natalie. "A rental is still a home." She pats Mae's knee, and Leo growls. Mae lets out a puff of air and doesn't answer. Natalie was four when Mae was born, and Jordan remembers how Natalie used to treat Mae like her own personal American Girl doll. She tried to help their busy mother change her diapers; she fed Cheerios, one by one, into Mae's little mouth as soon as she was old enough. She picked out her outfits and brushed tangles from her beautiful hair.

"Where'd all the pictures go?" asks Mae. Suddenly she sounds so young. "The family photos? Are they gone?" Her voice cracks.

"Same question," says Natalie.

"I put them away when we started renting it," says Calvin.

"If this is our last week here," says Natalie, "we need to put the pictures back."

"I'll put the pictures back," says Calvin. "Yes, sure, I can do that."

"I really thought this was family bonding week," says Mae. She looks really desolate. "Not selling-the-family-house week."

"I told the kids we'd go to the beach every day, and now we're cleaning out a garage," says Natalie.

"Of course we'll go to the beach!" says Calvin. "There are a lot of hours in a day."

"Not enough," says Natalie.

"I'm getting another drink," says Jordan, standing, picking up her phone. "Anyone want anything?"

Natalie and Mae shake their heads. "I'll take a double," says Calvin.

"A double what?"

"A double anything."

The living room bleeds into the kitchen. The sunroom is off to the side, with its own door. The sunroom is where, as kids, they were relegated with their card games and board games, their pre-technology forms of entertainment.

Jordan faces the sink and checks her phone. All of the calls and texts are from Bernadette. She finds a bottle of bourbon, plunks two ice cubes in a rocks glass, and pours her father's drink. She considers the gin but then fills her glass with water instead. It's going to be another long week; she'd better keep her senses about her before they've even had dinner.

She turns back toward the living room and sees someone running on the beach. The stride looks so familiar, the body, the bouncing blond ponytail. Is that . . . ? No. No, it can't be. *You're seeing things, Jordan. You're seeing the ghost of summers past.*

When she rejoins her family Caspian is still engaged in his resolute tour of the room. He points to the Summer Sessions cap on Calvin's head and says, "at." He squats to examine something on the floor but declines to give it a label. Then he makes his way over to Natalie and clambers into her lap. He puts his cheek against her cheek and his hand on her chest. "Heart," he says, kindly and fully. Unexpectedly Jordan feels her own heart constrict and her eyes spark with tears.

The ponytail runs by again, going in the opposite way. "Is that *Simone*?" asks Natalie.

"Who?" asks Jordan, playing dumb. Jordan turns her head away and tries not to remember her hands inside Simone's bikini bottoms, Simone's fingers in her mouth.

Calvin accepts his drink and goes on as if there'd been no break. "A house is just a structure. Family is not a structure. Family is people." He looks imploringly at Jordan.

"Jordan," Natalie demands. "Why aren't you saying anything? About the house?"

"Jordan!" Mae chimes in. *Fix it, Jordan, solve it, make it better.* What is adulthood, after all, thinks Jordan, but a reprise of our childhoods?

• • •

"So now what?" demands Natalie. They're in Mae's room, the Green Room, because this is where Leo's crate is. It's nine thirty. The children are asleep in Natalie's room; when Jordan is ready to go to sleep, Natalie will transport Scarlett from her room (the Flowered Room) into Jordan's (the Brown Room, or, more commonly, the Poop Room) to make more space. Scarlett is the deepest sleeper of the three and won't notice that she's been moved. Jordan is a deep sleeper too; deep sleeping has always been one of her talents. At some point Caspian will wake up and figure out that he's in a portable crib, which he will protest, and he will move into the bed with Natalie and Evangeline. Calvin has agreed to have Cinnamon in his room, until Kara arrives, to put more space between the two dogs.

All of the bedrooms in this house have queen beds, with the exception of their parents' room, which has a king. (Calvin insists on calling it the master bedroom still, even though they've all told him that he must call it the primary.)

They used to love coming here for a zillion reasons as kids, and one of them was that their rooms in Lenox all had twin beds, so it felt luxurious to spread out here on their own or have a friend for a sleepover or, sometimes, sleep with a sister, just because. Mae secretly loved sharing a bed with Natalie, loved breathing in the scent of her perfume, loved waking to find that Natalie's long hair had migrated over to Mae's pillow.

Mae is curled up on her side, which leaves room for Natalie to stretch out on the other side of the bed. Jordan is lying on her back on the floor, using one of Leo's dog towels draped over the arch of her foot to stretch her hamstrings. Jordan's phone is next to her, and it keeps buzzing.

"What do you mean, now what?" Mae asks Natalie.

On the night table is a bottle of Cabernet Jordan discovered in the back of the pantry, and she has poured some of it into three three-ounce Dixie Cups from the bathroom. Maybe a renter left the wine behind, or maybe one of the Shipmans did, years ago, but either way, it's theirs now. Tomorrow they will provision. Tonight, they will make do. Jordan is throwing the wine back like a series of shots, while Natalie is sipping hers slowly, holding her cup out to Jordan every so often for a refill.

"Do you mind?" Natalie asks Jordan with great exaggeration.

"Do I mind what?"

"Do you mind turning off your phone and being fully engaged in the conversation?"

"I'm not answering it!"

"But it's buzzing."

Jordan sits up and shakes her head. "I'll turn it face down."

"Did you take time off this week?" Jordan knows what Natalie really means: *unlike when Mom was sick.*

"I took the week. I'm engaged. I'm very engaged. Okay, what are we talking about? What do we do about what?"

"I mean, what do we do about Dad's plan? Do we have to, like, bow before the king and each declare our love for him before he'll reward us with a share of his kingdom?" (Natalie had toyed with the idea of being an English major in college, and her Substacks are rife with witty literary references. Even as a person with nothing in common with Natalie's target audience, Mae keeps up with her sister's Substack.)

"No," says Mae, who was an environmental studies major but did once date someone who played Edmund in an amateur summer theater production of *King Lear*. (Emphasis on the word *amateur*.) She'd sat through four long performances, and they'd broken up the next week. She remembers thinking, after the breakup, that she'd never get those hours back. "First of all, I don't want to get sent away. The youngest daughter in Lear gets sent away."

"True," says Natalie.

"I don't think you'll get sent away," says Jordan. "Aren't you the favorite?"

"I don't know," says Mae. "No." When they were growing up they were never sure who was the favorite, or, rather, they believed that Favorite Daughter Status was largely situational. As it probably should be. Their mother had even gotten them matching T-shirts one Christmas that said FAVORITE DAUGHTER in small caps across the front, with a red heart centered beneath the words. Mae still has hers; she wonders if her sisters do. They used to ask Theresa if she'd instruct each of them when it would be appropriate to put it on, and she'd throw up her hands and say, "Oh, come on, now. It's a joke. You're all my favorite daughter."

("You're each my favorite daughter," Natalie had corrected.)

"Cordelia was the favorite, and look how that turned out for her," points out Natalie now.

"Can you please stop with the Shakespeare references?" asks Jordan. "You're giving me a headache. I don't even know what you're talking about."

"Cordelia is killed in Act Five," Mae explains. "And a heartbroken Lear carries her lifeless body with him before he dies." The actor who played Lear in the production she'd seen four times had actually been very good.

"Okay, fantastic," says Jordan. "Thanks for the mood lift." She lies back down on the floor and tucks both of her knees into her chest, making her body into a little ball. Jordan is the most flexible of the three, owing to her devotion to very expensive Pilates classes. She carries herself like a dancer, even though she actually has two left feet. "Anyway. Moot point. I don't think there's a lot of kingdom to go around."

"When he sells the house, though," says Natalie. "I looked up the listing. It's jaw-dropping." She pulls the listing up on her phone and passes it around so they can all see. Obediently Mae and Jordan drop their jaws.

"Yeah, okay, but that's not our money. That's Dad's money," says Jordan. "When Mom died everything of hers went to him. And then, not to be cold-blooded and talk about an event that I'm sure is *extremely* far in the future, but when Dad dies . . ." Her voice trails off and they all look at each other, coming to the realization at the same time.

"Everything will go to Kara," says Natalie.

"Everything will go to Kara," says Mae.

"Yup," says Jordan. "Everything will go to Kara."

"I knew it!" says Natalie, half triumphant, half horrified. "I knew she was making him sell the house. Instead of waiting until she inherits it to do it. Why would she want something that holds all of our memories when she could have the money to spend on—on who knows what?"

"I don't know," says Mae. "She never seemed like a person who cares a lot about money. I don't think you go into hospice nursing for the money?" Her voice wavers uncertainly even though she's positive it's true: you do not go into hospice nursing for the money.

"We obviously never knew her the way we thought we knew her," says Jordan. "I mean, here we thought she deserved a nurse of the year award, when all along she was waiting her turn." It's not the first time the sisters have sifted through these thoughts, and it won't be the last.

"I don't think that's really true—" says Mae. She doesn't divulge her secret (one of many), which is that not only does she not dislike Kara the way her sisters do, she actively likes her. Her sisters would lose their minds.

"It's definitely true," says Jordan.

"I think if you looked at it differently . . ." Mae tries. Too far? Maybe she should pull back.

"I will never, ever change my views on Kara," says Jordan. "And that's that."

"Me either," says Natalie.

"Can't you buy the house, Natalie?" Mae asks, to change the subject but also because she's curious. "You're rich."

Natalie snorts. "Well, no. I'm not. And also, just no."

"But you are. You guys have an empire." Mae's favorite time of the year in Natalie's tradwife empire is autumn, when the foliage turns in Vermont and Natalie's social media is full of astonishing yellows and oranges framing the farmhouse and the dairy barn. There are (were?) lots of good things about living in Boulder, but the absence of a real New England fall is not one of them. In Natalie's October posts there's always lots of plaid flannel—even Cinnamon dons a plaid bandanna—and there are scarecrows and apples and videos of Natalie herself pulling a loaf of homemade pumpkin bread out of one of the two side-by-side ovens in the sixty-six-inch baby-blue Viking range. (After her first visit to Hillside Haven, Mae had googled the oven and learned that the range cost nearly forty thousand dollars. Not four thousand, which would have been enough to pay a few months of Mae's former apartment share in Boulder. Forty.)

The Christmas season is also something to behold. Sleigh bells ring (they actually do) and Scarlett and Evangeline wear matching red velvet dresses with white bows at the ends of their French braids as they hang ornaments on a Nutcracker-tall tree. Natalie herself always has a grown-up version of her daughters' dresses, with maybe one or two differences to give it a Hot Mom vibe, like a low V-neck where theirs have Peter Pan collars, or knee-high Stuart Weitzman boots instead of the girls' patent leather Mary Janes. It's a fine line, the line between wholesome and hot, and she walks it like a tightrope artist.

"Not sure we do anymore," Natalie says to her Dixie Cup. She'd been able to put a plug in her thoughts about the article for a little while, as her father's announcement took over, but wine and fatigue have loosened the plug, and it's all threatening to pour out, all of her anger and disappointment. She may not be showing it yet, but she's really rocked.

"What do you mean?" demands Jordan, sitting up.

"Nothing." She holds her cup out to Jordan. "Please, sir, I want some more."

Jordan refills Natalie and Mae. "I mean, I think he can make exceptions in his will or whatever if he chooses to, but, yes, when Dad dies, assuming he does not outlive his wife—" Natalie snorts. "Assuming he does not outlive his child bride," continues Jordan, "everything will go to her."

"Does forty count as a child bride?" Mae wonders.

"Yes," say Natalie and Jordan together.

"That's all fine," says Natalie. "From a financial standpoint. Who cares. We're adults."

Easy for you to say, thinks Mae. Her thoughts again go to the storage unit, the car, the bank account.

"But from an emotional standpoint, that's not fine at all," concludes Natalie.

Jordan undoes her body ball, floating her arms behind her head and her legs in front of her, and says, "Hold on. What if they have a kid? Then what?"

"Kara's too old to have a kid," says Mae.

"It's not out of the realm of possibility," says Jordan.

"Ew, that's so gross." Natalie covers her face with one of the pillows from the bed, then uncovers it enough to say, "To have a kid you have to have sex." She whispers the word *sex* as though she's at a middle school slumber party, as though she herself does not have three children and a husband.

"Well, obviously they've consummated the marriage," says Jordan. "More than once, probably." She pokes Natalie in the leg. "That's how that works, you know."

"*Ew*," says Natalie again. Her voice goes so high and strident that Leo lifts his head and stares at her.

"You're okay, Leo," says Mae. "You're a good boy. Settle."

"Leo's okay, but we're not," says Natalie.

"Has he ever mentioned kids with Kara?" asks Jordan. "That actually is such a horrifying thought."

"Kara could be pregnant right now, for all we know," says Natalie.

"Don't ever say that again," says Jordan.

"Would that be so bad?" says Mae. Her sisters turn on her, four blue eyes blazing at her. "What?" she says. "Don't look at me like that, it's a hypothetical."

"Of course that would be bad," says Jordan. "In so many ways."

"Well, maybe not to me. You guys already got to be older sisters. I never did. I only got to be the baby, always the baby."

"Being the baby is the ideal scenario," says Natalie. "Better than the middle!"

Jordan rolls her eyes and says, "It's good to know your middle child complex is alive and well." Natalie shoots her a look. "And Dad is not young, in case you haven't noticed," Jordan says to Mae.

"I noticed," says Mae. "But look at Steve Martin. And Robert De Niro."

"They have a kid together?" asks Natalie.

Jordan can't tell if she's serious. "No, dummy. They each became fathers at an unusually late age."

"I might have a hundred kids," says Natalie. "With my age-appropriate husband." She has momentarily forgotten about her fatigue from earlier in the day.

"Really?" says Mae.

"Well, maybe not a hundred," she concedes. "Maybe four. Or five."

"Five!" says Jordan. "Geez. What about overpopulation?"

Natalie goes on. "I love being pregnant. I pity men that they don't get to see what it's like, you know? Our bodies are amazing. They can do so much."

"Have fun with that," says Jordan, even though she loves her nieces and nephews with such fervor that she'd eat her own hand if they needed her to.

Natalie puts her Dixie Cup on the night table. If she doesn't change the subject away from Kara and her thoughts away from Austin and the article, she's going to lose it. She turns to face Jordan and sticks out her foot, tapping Jordan's elbow with it. "I know you saw her."

"Who?" says Mae.

"Simone," says Natalie. "Running along the beach. You didn't think I saw you, but I saw you see."

"I don't know what you're talking about," says Jordan.

"Yes, you do," says Natalie. "Do I need to tickle you until you admit it?" (Jordan went through a phase in her preteen years where the merest suggestion of this would send her into a panic.)

"No," says Jordan. "You do not need to tickle me. And, gross, get your dirty foot off my arm."

Natalie's foot is not actually gross or dirty; like everything about Natalie, thinks Mae, it's well tended to, matched to her aesthetic, camera-ready. Pumiced and moisturized. Currently her toenails are painted baby blue, the same color as that fantastic range, and her fingernails match. How does Natalie have time for this? There are days when Mae, who has zero children, no husband, and nobody expecting cast-iron skillet biscuits from scratch, feels like the world is asking too much to expect her to brush her teeth twice a day.

Mae closes her eyes and tries to drown out her sisters' voices, even though she's also reveling in them.

"I'm out of wine," says Jordan in her bossy big-sister voice. She lifts her Dixie Cup above her head like the Statue of Liberty hoisting the flame. "Who has the bottle?"

"You do," says Mae.

Natalie laughs. "The wine is gone. You drank it all, you psycho alcoholic."

Is now the time? wonders Mae. Is now the time to open up to her sisters, to tell them they must stop the sale at all costs, to confess that she needs to live here for a little while, until she sorts things out? Until she catches her breath, or maybe, who knows, forever?

"I will say that I kind of see Dad's point," says Jordan. She knows this is a controversial statement, but it's also true.

"About what?" say Natalie and Mae together.

"About cleaning out the garage storage room." She takes a deep breath. "Selling the house."

"You *what*?"

Jordan shrugs. "He refuses to hire a property manager. He's never here. We're never here. All of those repairs in the next few years—it's a lot. This house is old! Whatever isn't failing now is going to fail in the near future!"

"That," says Natalie, "is the most coldhearted of all of the coldhearted things you've ever said."

Now is not the time to bring up her situation, thinks Mae. Now is the time to be an adult, to train the dog she has committed her week to, to get to bed early and stay mostly sober and hydrated so she can wake up and be a productive member of the family tomorrow and the day after and the day after that. To bring the sunshine, the way they are expecting her to, have always expected her to.

"Right, Mae?" demands Natalie. "You're not saying anything, but you agree, right?"

Mae wants to say so many things, things that would take the conversation in a whole different direction. What she really wants to say is *see me, know me, help me.*

But she says, "I agree." Then: "I'll go downstairs and see if I can find another bottle."

"I'll go with you," says Jordan. "I need water."

Like magic, all the photos are back in their usual spots: the mantel, the hooks on the way up the stairs that earlier held nondescript beach scenes like you'd find on the walls of a midrange motel. Jordan appreciates that her father has gone to the trouble, especially since he'll have to undo all of it for the open house on Sunday.

There's a single photo—maybe the only one in the world—of Mae not looking cute, and that photo is now back on the wall. It's Christmas Eve 2008, and the girls are lined up in front of the tree in their Lenox living room in matching pajamas. Theresa bought them a new set every Christmas. They were allowed to change into whatever they wanted later, but they had to wear them for the photo.

Mae has come to stand beside Jordan.

"Oh my god," says Mae. "Look at this!"

"I'm dying at your face. What are you so grumpy about?"

Mae peers at the photo. "I think I just got my braces tightened the day before. Remember that feeling?"

"It's the worst," says Jordan. "I'm so glad that part of my life is over." She looks more closely. "Natalie's hair is on point. Even when she's ready for bed." In 2008 Natalie's hair falls in long sculpted waves, with a side barrette just over one ear, very Scarlett Johansson.

"She was probably going to sneak out and meet a boyfriend."

"Not on Christmas Eve!" Jordan chews her lip. "Or maybe yes."

"Probably yes."

"I just can't believe someone took a photo during the only two minutes you went through an awkward teenage phase."

Mae snorts. "Not true. I had the worst skin for half of middle school."

"I don't remember that. I don't remember you ever having even half a zit."

They both stare at the photo, their eyes growing uniformly damp. "She got us matching pajamas for so long," says Jordan. "I was a sophomore in college in this photo. I came home from, like, clubbing in Manhattan and had to throw on some L.L.Bean classic plaids."

"You loved it," accuses Mae. "You know you did."

Jordan's shoulders soften, and the air around them seems to soften too. "You're right. I did. We all did."

MONDAY

• • •

It's just after dawn, and Jordan's been awake for over an hour. Something kept her from a good sleep. This something could have been the Dixie Cups of wine on top of two gin and tonics, but it could just as easily have been the presence of Scarlett, who was not, as Natalie had claimed, a deep, motionless sleeper, but rather a thrasher, a cover thief, and an occasional whimperer. Scarlett didn't come as advertised at all.

Bernadette's voicemails and texts from the day before total seven. They all say basically the same thing, in a variety of ways: *Jordan, call me back.*

She will not! When she got the email from her father, Jordan put in for vacation time. She hasn't taken a proper vacation in years, not a full week—the last time she'd been out of touch for more than three days had been when Theresa died. She doesn't *want* to call Bernadette back. She's resisting! Ever since Memorial Day she's been wondering what her future is at the firm.

But Bernadette does have a hold over her that Jordan wishes she didn't. She's taught Jordan everything she knows about the business; she's paid her well; she's let her sit at her knee during some of the most interesting cases the firm has had. Jordan shudders. She doesn't actually want to think about Bernadette's knees.

A little while later Jordan slides out of bed, leaving Scarlett, who has her arms and legs starfished, her glorious dark hair spread out across both pillows. (For a slender little girl she really does take up a remarkable amount of room.) She dresses quickly in the bathroom, congratulating herself on being so quiet that neither dog stirs, then tiptoes down the stairs, through the slider, across the patio, down the three stairs to the beach, and onto the sand, still cool, for now, from the night. The tide is low, low, and the beach is absolutely enormous. It feels like the biggest beach in the world.

Jordan starts south, with the water to her left. A few early-morning dogs and owners are up, and so are a couple of solitary walkers, but this beach is so vast Jordan feels like they each have their own universe to themselves. The sun is newly risen over the water, which is a sight that never gets old, no matter how many times Jordan has seen it—and she's seen it a lot. In the distance, near the new public bathrooms (not so new anymore, but they still seem new, because the old ones were so *very* old), the majestic American flag is waving like a greeting. Surfers dot the water. Seaweed, flung by the tide, lies in clumps.

She faces the ocean, looking for strength and fortitude in its vastness, its—well, its relentless optimism, is one way to look at it. Those waves just keep coming back; no matter how many times they're sent away, they just keep coming and coming, not taking no for an answer. Sort of like Bernadette.

Maybe she'll just call Bernadette back to remind her that she's on vacation.

She'll just do it and get it over with. Bernadette will be up. Bernadette is always up! Bernadette operates a little like a dolphin, resting one hemisphere of her brain at a time while allowing the other to continue to function.

"Hello?" Bernadette's voice sounds . . . croaky. Almost like a person who has been . . . *woken up unexpectedly*?

But it's almost seven o'clock. On a Monday! The most important day of the workweek! Often crises pop up over the weekend, as sneaky as overnight dandelions, and people sit on them, stewing in them, chewing on them, enduring one or two dark nights of the soul, until Monday comes, and *bam*. The phone starts ringing.

"Oh my god, Bernadette, did I wake you?"

"No," croaks Bernadette. "Well, sort of. Not really. The family is still away, so I went out with a couple of girlfriends last night—"

Bernadette sounds almost like a regular person, a person who will let herself sleep in after a night out, a person with girlfriends! Jordan has known Bernadette for a long time now. She's heard her talk about colleagues, and journalists she has a good working relationship with, and politicians whose kids' birthday parties she might go to, but girlfriends? She's never heard about the girlfriends. She imagines Bernadette in college, out to breakfast with a hungover crew, reliving the shenanigans of the night before. Bernadette, brushing her teeth next to someone in a dormitory bathroom. Borrowing a dress for a semiformal. If she squints her mind's eye hard enough, she can almost see it.

Jordan hardens her heart. She cannot let Bernadette be too human. Since Memorial Day, Bernadette has owed her an apology. And even if she gives it, Jordan is not sure how she'll feel.

"You didn't return any of my calls or texts yesterday," says Bernadette, already playing offense. "That sort of lack of communication is unacceptable."

When Jordan started in crisis communications Bernadette imparted three rules. One: There are two sides to every story. If we judge our clients, we can't help them. Two: Communicate, communicate, communicate. And three: Your relationships with the press are sacred. Don't lie to the press.

"I'm using vacation days."

"Even so, you need to answer when I call you. If you want me to make you partner, there are no vacations."

"Ever?"

A pause. "Rarely."

Jordan starts to apologize, then sits on the word *sorry* until it goes back to where it came from. *When you need to apologize, do. When you don't, don't.* A Theresa-ism.

"Irina always answers her phone," says Bernadette.

Bernadette is baiting her. She may as well be loading bags of herring into a lobster trap. Irina is twenty-six, younger even than *Mae*, and has only been working for Bernadette for three years. Jordan will not take the bait. She knows her own value; she knows what she brings to the table. She knows the monsters that live under the table. She says, "You have me now. What's going on?"

She hears Bernadette gulping something—probably her first of many daily cups of coffee. Bernadette has been known to sip cold brew instead of water during a Peloton workout. In the afternoons, to relax, she switches to espresso. Someday, Jordan believes, this habit will catch up with her, but it hasn't yet. "I have a very important client that I want you to work with." Jordan's heartbeat picks up. A very important client! Bernadette usually takes the VIPs for herself. Last year the firm was approached by the family of a Qatari prince whose high jinks around the city were resulting in negative press for his family. Jordan never even got to sit in on a meeting with the Qataris.

"Who is it?"

"I need you to call Samantha Braddock from the *Times* about a client. You have a good relationship with her, right?"

"I *love* Samantha Braddock," says Jordan. Dammit! She feels herself getting pulled back into work, back into Bernadette's orbit. She wants to resist, she should resist, but she can't resist.

"I know you do. And Samantha loves you." Bernadette is flattering her, and Jordan, despite herself, is here for it.

"What am I calling Samantha Braddock about? Who's the client?"

Another pause, more gulping, and now Bernadette sounds fully awake. Mae has explained to Jordan that a dog shakes to release tension or energy, to reset itself. She imagines Bernadette shaking off the cobwebs of the night, morphing from a person with girlfriends to her regular professional, witchy self. "There's a story coming out that we need to get ahead of."

"By get ahead of it, you mean . . . ?"

"I mean, you need to make sure Samantha Braddock knows there's nothing to this story. So it doesn't run."

A common misconception about the crisis communications industry is that its practitioners do dishonorable things to protect dishonorable people. But much of the job is giving context to a story, managing an inevitable reaction rather than making sure the reaction doesn't occur. The best people in their business pride themselves on keeping their moral compasses pointing in the right direction.

Jordan clears her throat. In this case, it *almost* sounds like Bernadette wants her to kill a story. But that can't be right.

"*Is* there nothing to the story?" she asks.

There's a silence that, were you looking for a description, you might characterize as ominous.

"Correct," says Bernadette finally.

"What's the angle?" Jordan watches a sandpiper skitter across the sand, its little legs moving so fast. A brown Lab chases a ball joyfully into the water. A gull flies overhead, dips down for breakfast.

With her degree in political science, Jordan's first job had been working on a series of Senate campaigns. Nothing brings out the best and the worst in people like a political campaign. Jordan has watched candidates snap at a spouse and then, ten minutes later, bring a crowd to their knees with a story about an immigrant grandmother. She's found a box of tissues when someone was crying *literal tears of exhaustion,* and then helped that person reapply mascara so she could hit the Sunday-morning show circuit and talk Medicaid and Social Security. Many of those skills translated readily into crisis comms.

"If you're not up for it, I could ask Irina."

Jordan bristles. There is no way she's letting Irina pull ahead of her. Jordan can run crisis PR circles around Irina. She watches a surfer catch a beautiful wave, and he looks so otherworldly, so utterly free, that Jordan's heart lifts. No matter what, there is always the ocean. There are always the waves. "I didn't say I'm not up for it. I'm just trying to understand the situation."

"It's a hit piece."

"That can't be right," says Jordan. "Samantha Braddock doesn't write hit pieces."

"Well, in this case, she is. This client has been unfairly smeared by people who work for her. It's a disgruntled-employee-gone-rogue situation. Small things have been taken out of context, misunderstood." Bernadette's voice takes on a hard edge. "It's a disgrace, really, what this client is about to be accused of." Bernadette often gets angry on behalf of her clients, and they love her for it. That's why they hire her, for her passion and her fire. But she does not typically employ the passive voice with such recklessness. Something, Jordan can tell, is going on.

"If it's a VIP, why aren't you handling it?"

"Conflict of interest. And you know this client, so you can put the toxic thing to rest. Any statements would be more realistic coming from you."

"I do? They would?" Jordan combs the recesses of her mind, wondering who she has a better relationship with than Bernadette does. Bernadette's contacts are legendary; she's mystified. "Okay, who is it?"

The waves don't really crash into a crescendo at exactly that point, the Earth doesn't tilt, but it feels to Jordan like both of these things happen as her boss says, "The client is me. I'm the client."

• • •

Caspian is standing in the portable crib, banging his hands on the side, and saying, "Up!"

Natalie's eyes pop open and she glances at the clock. It's six thirty. "Shhh." Natalie tips her head toward Evangeline, who is sleeping.

Subtlety is not Caspian's specialty. He says, "UP!" even louder. Then: "Milk."

"Okay," whispers Natalie, a finger to her lips. "Okay, shhh."

A peek into Mae's room reveals that Mae and Leo are already up and out. Scarlett is alone in Jordan's bed, sleeping deeply. Calvin's door is still shut, which means Cinnamon is not yet up. She changes Caspian's diaper, then tiptoes down the stairs with him, as usual, on her hip.

She puts Caspian in his portable booster and as soon as she pours Cheerios onto the tray he begins shoveling them into his mouth. She hands him his sippy cup, which he immediately turns upside down to see how many drops of the precious Hillside Haven organic milk he can get onto his tray. (Natalie has brought two bottles with her, but she knows they won't last all week. Her children are voracious milk drinkers. As they should be. She'll have to buy milk from the store. She hasn't bought milk in a store in years!)

Natalie makes coffee in the ancient Hamilton Beach and sits at the island, staring at her phone, while the coffeemaker gurgles and hisses. She's not sure who she's most angry with—Austin for saying what he said, her father for putting the house on the market, Jordan for going along with it, or herself for drinking too many Dixie Cups of wine. Her stomach churns.

"Oh. Casp," she says, crouching down next to him. She runs her hand along his cowlick—appropriately named, considering where they live. "What are we going to do?"

He offers her a damp Cheerio and she accepts it. "Eat," he instructs, so she pops it in her mouth. She's eaten worse. Her quads complain so she rises, regains her seat at the island, and looks around the kitchen she knows so well, thinking about how she got here.

"You're a boyfriend person," someone once said to Natalie in high school.

Sure, okay, maybe. Yes, she had had a series of boyfriends since ninth grade, well, eighth grade if you're really counting, but did this technically make her a "boyfriend person"? Was that a good thing or a bad thing? She was captain of the speech and debate team, and she played middling basketball and decent soccer. She was the center of a loyal and popular friend group. But was "boyfriend person" her identity?

Partly to prove this person wrong she broke up with her last high school boyfriend the summer after graduation, and she entered Wesleyan resolutely single, remaining so for most of her college years, with a constellation of short-term relationships or non-relationships under her belt, and the best group of friends in the world. The Sisterhood.

After graduation the six members of the Sisterhood—a tight little knot, as beautiful and complex as a Celtic design—scattered: one to Washington to work on Hillary Clinton's presidential campaign; one to law school; one to a marketing job in Manhattan; one to toil away in a gene-sequencing lab at Massachusetts General Hospital; one to Montana to work for the state's Department of Fish, Wildlife, and Parks, where she got to wear a wide-brimmed hat and process applications for hunting mountain lions.

Natalie spent one summer at home while she conducted a job search. She had a double major in psychology and Gender and Sexuality, with a minor in data analysis. By August, she'd gotten an offer to become a data scientist at a wearable-tech start-up in Boston. Yes, please! With her new salary, she could afford a tiny one-bedroom on Commonwealth Avenue, a passable work wardrobe, and just enough going-out outfits. The brand was so new, she had equity. If they went public, she'd make actual money. She had two friends from college in the Back Bay, and it wasn't long before she met the friends of those friends and even the friends of friends of friends. She lived like Carrie Bradshaw, if the late nineties were 2015, Cosmos were Negronis, and words were numbers. After two years, she was promoted to head of analytics. She had her eye on going higher—she had her eye on, one day, the CTO role.

The Sisterhood got together when they could, which wasn't often. Everyone was busy, so it was more likely that two or three of them would see each other, sending photos to the others via the group chat. During Natalie's third summer in Boston, Chloe called to invite her to Montana. At a house party thrown by one of Chloe's colleagues she met Austin. He was from the south of the state, near Bozeman, but he was visiting friends up in Bigfork. That night, after they'd talked for ninety minutes straight sitting at the outdoor firepit, he told Natalie she had the most beautiful eyes he'd ever seen.

"And you fell for the line about the eyes?" said Jordan on the phone. "That's so corny."

"I do have nice eyes," said Natalie. "We all do."

"But you fell for it! Wasn't it dark by the firepit?"

"I wouldn't say I fell *for* it," said Natalie. "But I definitely fell." Austin himself had giant brown eyes with a rim of hazel around them. He had a degree from the College of Agriculture at Montana State and ropy forearms. He was about as different from Wesleyan guys as he could be. The first night she could tell that his humor was a little goofy, his faith was strong, and his heart was massive. She wanted to crawl inside his plaid flannel and stay for a week.

Austin invited her on a hike the very next day. They saw elk and bison. They jumped into Flathead Lake holding hands and screamed when they came out of the cold water. The day after that, he drove her to the airport for her flight home, went to the ticket counter while she checked in, and bought her a ticket to come to Bozeman in three weeks and meet his family on their dairy farm. It was the sexiest thing she'd ever had anyone do for her.

"His *family*?" said Jordan. "Already? On a dairy farm?"

"One hundred and ten head of Holsteins," said Natalie. She followed this statistic up with a bombshell of a statement: "I'm pretty sure this is the man I'm going to marry."

Three weeks had never passed so slowly. Natalie had fallen *so hard.* She'd never quite bought into the phrase "crazy in love" in the past, but now she did. Sex with Austin was better, different, somehow more profound, than it had been with anyone else, but it wasn't just that. I want to have his babies, she thought the third time they slept together. You weren't supposed to think that way, not when you came from a liberal family in Massachusetts and held a degree from Wesleyan. The Sisterhood might laugh her out of the group chat.

Soon enough, Natalie and Austin were on a speeding train they couldn't get off—didn't want to get off. They started planning the future on Natalie's trip to Bozeman. Natalie couldn't give up her job, not with the equity, the promise of mobility. Austin had lived in Montana his whole life. For Natalie, he was willing to make a change.

In Boston, Austin got a job in medical sales. He was so good! He had the personality for sales—he could talk to a dying houseplant and it would perk up like it had just been watered—but he didn't have the true temperament. Without putting too fine a point on it, he hated it.

"It'll get better!" said Natalie optimistically.

"Sure."

"It's just an adjustment."

In the next two years: proposal, bridal shower, wedding, two lines on the pregnancy stick that meant Evangeline was coming. A bigger apartment, double the rent. A coveted spot in a Back Bay day care. Little Evangeline, with her tiny pursed lips and her little waving fists, her milky eyes, her demands. Natalie's heart had never felt so big.

They loved their little family, but at work Austin was miserable. Tiny Evangeline was miserable too, constantly shuttled from here to there. Natalie wasn't miserable, but she was exhausted. They were tied to the drudgery of day care drop-off; the stress of one or the other of them always having to say no to staying late at work, to drinks with investors for Natalie, clients for Austin. They were stretched so thin. The winter sidewalks were so icy.

"All of this time inside is making my elbows itch," Austin told Natalie. "I'm allergic to the fluorescent lighting in conference rooms."

"I don't think that's something you can be allergic to."

"The sky is so small here. It's all hidden by the trees."

"Well, I can't change the size of the *sky*," Natalie said testily, scooping pureed carrots into six-month-old Evangeline's mouth. "I'm sorry," she said, shaking her head, willing herself to some equilibrium. "Do you want to quit?" She felt for him—she really did. She'd taken him out of his natural habitat, away from the wide Montana sky, and plonked him in the middle of asphalt and bricks. Of course he didn't fit here. Did *she* even fit here?

"And do what?" He was holding his big strong hands like a supplicant. His hands, so brown when she met him, had taken on an urban pallor. It was January, and outside the apartment window the trees were bare and stark, the winter sky a pale white-gray.

"Be my plaything? Station yourself in bed on satin sheets with a cocktail when I get home from work?" She was kidding, obviously.

They preferred organic cotton sheets, for one thing. For another, she was still pumping four times a day. A nightly cocktail was not in the cards. And, finally and most important, Austin did not want to be a plaything. He'd been working with his hands nearly as long as he'd been able to count his own fingers. Austin did not want to sit idle. Austin wanted to work.

Then, through a connection from a friend of an uncle, he heard about a dairy farm for sale in Vermont. "Let's just look at it," he said to Natalie. "We'll just look."

"I have equity," she said. "What if we go public? I can't imagine walking away from that."

"We're not walking away from anything," he said. "We'll just look." He fixed his baby browns on her, and she couldn't say no. The next weekend they packed up Evangeline and drove the nearly three and a half hours to Shaftsbury. They walked the farm with Evangeline facing out in the BabyBjörn, pointing at the cows.

In the hotel room in Bennington they talked long into the night while Evangeline slept. Natalie came to realize that if they didn't take this chance Austin would one day want to move back to Montana—and then what? She couldn't imagine being so far from her family, from the East Coast, from the beach house, from the ocean.

By the time they went to sleep themselves, they had a new life plan. That Monday, they put together an offer, subsidized by Austin's parents, who agreed to help them buy the farm with the understanding that Austin and Natalie would run it without additional help from them. On Tuesday, when Natalie was back in her office, the offer was accepted. Forty Holsteins, a farmhouse, a milking barn that would need renovation. Hillside Haven. Natalie set up a meeting with her manager and gave her notice.

Austin was so happy on the farm! He never complained about the early hours or the physical labor. He called the cows "the Ladies" and treated them with respect and reverence. He rarely needed an alarm; his body acclimated to the cows' schedule, as it had once done in Montana. They hired two local farmhands. Austin mended fences; he repaired the homogenizer when it broke; he sanitized the teat cups. He befriended the cranky old-timers in town, the ones who thought Natalie and Austin were city kids playing at farming. He proved them wrong the night the neighbor's heifer was in labor with a breech calf, the phone lines went down because of a storm, and he helped deliver the calf.

The Hansons had just moved to Hillside Haven when the pandemic hit. They felt removed from what they saw on the news. On the Sisterhood group chat, Leah talked about spending all day on Zoom calls for work. Kayla's toddler was going crazy in their San Francisco apartment. Amber, still working in a lab, barely took her mask off. Rachel and Mark had left Manhattan to move in with Rachel's parents in Connecticut; they worked for a Broadway producer, and of course the theaters were dark.

I'm spending all my time on Instagram watching sourdough bread videos, texted Rachel to the Sisterhood.

I made my own buttermilk, texted Natalie.

Leah weighed in with Ha ha, but Natalie actually *had* made her own buttermilk.

By summer she was pregnant with Scarlett. With her main jobs being caring for Evangeline, helping on the farm, and being pregnant, she threw herself into domestic life. She started an Instagram account: @hillsidemaven.

I feel like with every cake you bake you're betraying the Sisterhood, texted Amber. Ha ha.

Three other members gave it the exclamation points that mean *we agree!*

The Hansons applied for and received their organic certification.

They added ten more head of cattle. Natalie fell in love with it all: the meditative beauty of the early mornings, the intense clarity of the night sky, where every constellation she had heard of was visible. She fell in love with the cows' quirks and personalities, learning which ones were placid and forgiving and which were feisty or standoffish. She loved the paths they wore in the grass as they moved to and from the milking barn. She loved the way each day followed a rhythm and each year did too, with a portion of the Ladies always pregnant or calving and another portion "drying off"—resting from milking before giving birth. She loved the lined Carhartt pants and the muck boots and even the farm smells, which were so pronounced they had a texture. She loved the way each time a new calf was born it felt like a miracle, the head and front legs emerging in a dive position, then the rear legs, the big brown eyes, already open, already soulful.

She loved cooking in the kitchen, spending time she'd never had before, perfecting a loaf of bread or learning a new method for braising meat. She loved Austin's appetite for everything: food, sex, Heady Topper beer, the sky at 4 a.m. She, Natalie, who had struggled through honors biology in high school, did not flinch when she watched her first bovine birth, did not flinch when she assisted at her second. It was all so raw and beautiful. She watched the mother cow's rough tongue go at the calf to clean it off, watched the calf stand and nurse within the first two hours of birth. She loved the girl power at Hillside, the way dairy farms are by nature ruled by the ladies.

#allgirlband, she tagged an Instagram photo of the cows grazing with stunning autumn foliage behind them. #girlsrule.

When her favorite cow, Daisy, gave birth in their second year, she captured that video. Then Austin took one of Natalie herself, dressed in maternity overalls, her hair pulled back fetchingly in a red bandanna, milking Daisy for the first time after the calf had nursed. She started sending videos to her family, and Mae told her she needed to get them on TikTok and Instagram. She posted the videos to her account. Her followers grew. Scarlett was born. #motherhood.

The first time Natalie used the tradwife hashtag she did it ironically. Semi-ironically. Well, like a quarter ironically. She had baked Austin a cake for his birthday, a three-layer German chocolate number. It took her hours, and it was perfect. She put on an apron and made a video of herself with the cake. Yes, the apron would have been more helpful while she was baking, but better late than never. She took a deep breath; she posted it.

Made my hubby a cake. #tradwife!

She curled her hair, put on a pretty dress, and used it again a couple of days later when she made strawberry jam. *Tradwife* as a hashtag, as a movement, was growing, and she threw herself into it headfirst. If she wasn't going to be an executive at a wearable-tech start-up in Boston, she was definitely, definitely going to be the most successful dairy farmer's wife the internet had seen.

She lost the baby weight a second time. She was offered the opportunity for sponsored posts, affiliate marketing, brand ambassadorships. She was earning tens of thousands of dollars, then hundreds of thousands. Within a year, she was making more than the farm was. They renovated the milking barn, brought in a decorator, bought that gorgeous baby-blue Viking. She kept cooking, baking, posting, mothering. Theresa died; Caspian was born; Natalie's empire grew. She had two hundred thousand followers, then three, then four.

She researched curricula and applied to be approved for homeschooling by the State of Vermont Agency of Education. She took photos of Evangeline reading a picture book and Scarlett writing her name in giant block letters on butcher paper she spread out on the floor.

She pickled onions; she made her own granola. Eventually, she reached a million followers, then more.

Six months ago she hired a publicist, Bethany, who secured this article with *New York Magazine*, her first traditional media win. Her coming-out party, as it were.

Can this all be undone with one pull quote, a single caption?

She opens Instagram; she searches for tagged posts.

It's like a car crash I can't look away

Ladies, I hope you like driving in reverse. Girls like this set us back by 100 years.

If my husband said that about me I'd have the divorce papers drawn up so fast

WTF? Nice closet tho

She closes the app. She opens TikTok, where, oh god, it's even worse. She pushes the phone away. There's so much of worth in the article, so many pretty pictures of the milking barn and the addition to the main barn she uses as a schoolroom, with the vintage school desks and the bright white cubbies full of sharpened pencils and writing paper and coloring supplies. What about the photo of the three kids standing next to their favorite cow, Gretchen, who has the best eyelashes of all the cows? Why is nobody talking about Gretchen?

She tries to stay calm but the fury bubbles up. She pours more coffee, pulls the phone back toward her, and calls Austin. He'll be done with the morning milking by now, taking a breakfast break before he moves on to the rest of the day's chores, which will probably involves mending the fence by the south pasture. Nobody's going to call Austin's work ethic into question: he's the Energizer Bunny of Hillside Haven.

"Hey, babe!" says Austin. She pictures him in the kitchen, pulling out one of her labeled breakfast casseroles from the refrigerator and following the reheat instructions. (She'd put up a recent video on batch breakfasts, complete with affiliate links for the color-lock glass food storage bins.) "Buttercup has mastitis. You'll be happy to know Dr. George is on his way." The "happy to know" part is a joke between them—Dr. George is the hot vet, and Austin can joke about him because he knows that he himself is even hotter. The thought of Dr. George pulling up to the barn in his brick-red pickup does nothing for Natalie today. She doesn't even crack a smile. "How's it going there?" asks Austin.

"Not great," she says. Her voice is made of steel. "My dad is putting the house on the market. Kara is coming tomorrow. And, have you seen the article?" She tries to keep her voice from going up on the word *article* but up it goes.

"He's putting the house on the market? What article?"

"The house is a whole other thing. We're all devastated. Well, Mae and I are devastated. But the article—the link I sent you yesterday. *New York Magazine*. The one the reporter spent a whole day with us for? The big media hit?"

"Didn't get a chance." She hears the clink of a fork against a plate, the water running, the microwave door opening and closing. "Early to bed, early to rise, you know. How'd it come out?"

How did it come *out*? "Well, it's a disaster. It's a complete disaster."

"Oh, yeah? Why's that?"

He's chewing now. His unconcern is killing her. It is absolutely killing her! "Because of you!" she says. "Because of what you said!"

"What'd I say?"

"The thing about—"

She hears the chime of their fancy doorbell. "Sorry, babe, I have to run, okay? Dr. George is squeezing me in before another appointment. I'll look at it later, but whatever it is, I wouldn't worry about it. It's just an article. I'm sure it's fine. Love you."

"It is *not* fine!" she says. "I could lose hundreds of followers. Thousands! You know how it works! If there's a whiff of controversy I can lose the affiliates—" But she's speaking to nobody; he's gone.

Caspian says, "Ommy mad." She releases him from the portable seat and holds him against her.

"Mommy isn't mad," she says, even though, yes, Mommy is filled with an unspeakable rage so sharp she could slice a roast with it. She breathes in raggedly and says, "Should we go check on your sisters?"

• • •

Out on the patio, Mae buckles Leo into his harness and goes over her supplies. Dog? Check. Treat pouch? Check. Poop bags? Check. Long leash? Check. Small hangover from too many small cups of wine? Check.

Plus-size heartache? Double check. She can't *believe* her father is selling the house; she can't believe this piece of her mother will soon be gone, poof, as quick as you can say "purchase and sale." She can't believe Jordan isn't even upset about it. What treachery! And besides the emotional sting, Mae doesn't know how she's going to be able to pull herself out of her current hole with the disappearance of this, her last remaining safety net.

She can't believe how stupid she was to fall into her current hole in the first place. You hear about people getting scammed all the time. And you think, I would never fall for that. A little piece of you thinks, They got what they deserved, for not knowing any better. For being vulnerable, scammable. Yet here she is.

Even amid all this, with all these different thoughts and emotions crisscrossing in her mind, a dog needs to get out in the morning. This is how dogs work. Mae and Leo make their way to the cool morning sand. She lets Leo sniff around a little before they begin their training session. She's already impressed by the progress he's made around Natalie's kids and Cinnamon. Another few days of consistent training, and he'll be acting like a real member of the family.

("Consistency is key." —Hal Miller.)

Mae scans the beach. She'll go all the way to the left as she's facing the water, toward the rocks that line the northernmost edge of the beach and divide it from Straw's Point and Rye Harbor. This is the less populated section, where she's more likely to have space for herself and Leo, whose strong reactions to others could be construed as . . . well, negative. Even frightening, especially given the pit bull part of his DNA. This is what she told Human Leo during the assessment, which took place in the backyard of Hal's bungalow on Mapleton Hill.

Human Leo sucked in his breath. "Is he aggressive?"

Mae shook her head. "Reactivity is often misread as aggression. Usually a reactive dog is fearful, so when he's lunging toward a person or barking at another dog, what he's trying to do is drive the thing that's scaring him away before a perceived harm can take place." She was pleased with herself for this succinct explanation. She glanced at Hal to see how she'd done; Hal was beaming at her.

Human Leo nodded slowly, taking this in. "Okay. That makes sense. I really want this to work out. I really want to keep Leo."

"I didn't know you were considering not keeping him," Mae said sternly. She hates when people give up too easily on dogs. What did they expect when they took home a rescue? That they were rescuing something perfect? No. Perfect things do not need to be rescued.

"Nonono," Leo said, really fast. "I'm in it for the long haul. I want him to be my companion. I want to take him on road trips and everything."

"Like Thelma and Louise!"

"Exactly," said Leo. "With a happier ending."

Mae found herself thinking wistfully of taking a road trip with the Leos, then she immediately chastised herself. "I can help him," she said. "I know I can. Your fee will not go to waste." Hal frowned slightly at this; later he told Mae that he'd prefer the fee not be discussed during an assessment. Hal is a purist.

She held out her hand, and they shook to seal the deal. She saw Leo looking at the tattoos on the back of the hand, at the way they traveled all the way up her arm, disappearing into her tank top.

"I like what you have going on there," he said. "All the ink."

"Thank you," she said. "I apprenticed at Ink It." She considered her arm. Her favorite tattoo is the first one she got from Tony, the shooting star, an approximation of the one she saw the night Theresa died.

Now, on her own stretch of beach, she clips the long leash onto Leo and takes him through some warm-up exercises to focus him: some fist bumps (Leo's nose to her fist), some eye contact practice, a few sits and downs. Leo is smart and a quick learner, and his attention stays on Mae. He wants to do a good job, she can tell. He has a good heart. And if you have a good heart, Mae believes, everything else can be trained.

She gives Leo lots of leash—the long leash is fifty feet long—and steps back, her foot on the end, so she can call Leo toward her. They do this three times, and each time Leo performs perfectly. She rewards him plentifully. She takes a video. She'll send it to Hal so he can see her progress.

Then she sees an unleashed dog, a German shepherd, running along the edge of the water. The shepherd clocks Leo and Mae and heads directly toward them. The owner, a man in board shorts and a T-shirt, had been walking behind the dog, talking on a cell phone, paying no attention. Mae grabs the end of Leo's leash, but she's not in time to reel in the whole length of it. Leo pulls all the way out, straining toward the other dog. The shepherd stops and stands stock-still. She can almost see his dog brain working, trying to make a decision.

"Excuse me!" she calls to the man in board shorts. "Will you please call your dog?"

He can't hear her. She's yelling now. Leo is whining, and the whining turns to growling. "Call your dog! Excuse me! *Call your dog!*"

The man looks up, assesses the situation, calls the dog. He's too far away for her to hear what the name is. The dog looks back toward the man, ignores him, puts his attention back on Leo. The man calls again, then finally the dog makes the right decision, running toward his owner, who clips a leash on him. It takes all Mae's strength to hold Leo back as he strains against his own leash, barking, until the dog is farther away. It takes Leo several minutes to calm, and he's still breathing hard when he looks imploringly at Mae, as if to say, *I did a bad job, didn't I?*

"It wasn't our finest moment," she admits. "But we'll get there. Remember, we're all about progress, not perfection." Her heart is beating so fast.

Her phone pings, a text from Tony. You owe me for last month's rent. Can you Venmo me 1200?

It's not even five in the morning in Boulder—what is Tony doing up already? She sits down next to Leo in the sand, and he puts his big goofy head in her lap. He's spent. She looks back at her phone. Of course. Tony isn't up *already*—Tony is up *still*. Drinking, vaping weed, basically being Tony. She looks out at the water, finding the humps of the Isles of Shoals. Momentarily, they anchor her.

I didn't live with you last month, she texts back. Did you forget?

Her heart is beating almost as fast as Leo's, thinking of the credit card fees Venmo will hit her with if she pays Tony, in addition to the fees already accruing on the credit card itself. But she doesn't have the cash in her account.

You left with no warning. You still owe me.

She wants to call her mom, and with just the thought of that a lump rises in her throat. How did that lump get there so fast? What is *wrong* with her? She's letting grief over her mother consume her, more than two years after Theresa's death. When everyone else in the family—even her father, maybe especially her father—is emerging from the mourning period, she's still stuck there, and sinking, like a car in quicksand. But she doesn't know any other way to do it. "I don't know any other way to do it," she tells Leo. Her voice cracks. She removes his head from her lap, rises, bends to untangle the leash from his back paw.

Leo's tongue darts out and he licks her cheek. He doesn't know what's wrong, but he's trying to make her feel better. The way dogs learn human ways of living is astonishing, thinks Mae; the way we expect them to adapt to our ways of living instead of the reverse. We don't deserve their graciousness and goodwill, and yet the lucky among us receive both.

"Let's go, buddy," she tells Leo. "Time for breakfast." They walk back on the cool, wet sand, close to the water. Two broken people. Well, one broken person and one broken dog, searching for whatever can fix them.

• • •

Jordan walks the rest of the way in a state of intense agitation that even the beauty of her surroundings can't mitigate. Bernadette wants her to kill a story about Bernadette herself. If Jordan calls Samantha Braddock and says there's no truth to it, the story won't run, and Jordan will one day be Bernadette's partner at the firm.

She has Samantha Braddock in her contacts. They've worked on stories in the past. It wouldn't take much. She can say one sentence about how much she loves working for Bernadette and how disgruntled the unnamed employee must be (is it Irina?) to issue such untruths.

It's complicated. On one hand, Bernadette is a brilliant problem solver. Her instincts are unparalleled in the industry. She'll take a call from a client in distress anytime, anywhere, at the expense of pretty much everything else. On the other hand, Jordan has seen her belittle Irina for bringing up ideas in a staff meeting. She's publicly berated Tom for failing to get that actress (you'd know her if you heard her name) under contract when she was going through that situation on the movie set. She's condescending, she micromanages, she's definitely a narcissist. To deny any of that would be a lie.

And then there's Memorial Day weekend.

And *then* there's the fact that Jordan doesn't lie to the press.

On the other hand. If Jordan keeps her morals intact Bernadette won't make her partner. She'll still get clients, but they will be the bottom-feeders. Bernadette will start to punish her in ways large and small. Eventually, she'll have to leave the firm.

It's a Gordian knot she can't untangle, especially without coffee.

The sky is clear and the sun is all the way up as Jordan reaches the beach parking lot. All of the cars belong to the surfers right now, but soon enough the surfers will leave and the summer morning jockeying for a parking spot will begin, the moms with the young kids, the parents of the surf lesson students. She puts on her flip-flops and crosses the street to Summer Sessions, and the Sandpiper Cafe inside the shop. She would have killed for a place like this when she was a teenager, but the surf shop moved locations and expanded when Jordan was already launching into her adult life. At Sandpiper you can order a complete and healthy breakfast; you can choose from a full coffee bar menu; you can dress like a surfer or date a surfer or be a surfer, or whichever combination of all three feels right to you.

She orders a cappuccino and a smoothie from a beautiful suntanned girl in a Roxy T-shirt. She thinks about the cocktails and wine from the night before and adds a coconut water from the refrigerated case near the register. She repairs to the bench outside the pickup window, sipping the water while she waits for her name to be called. She woke this morning in near darkness, but now it's as if a curtain has lifted in a dark auditorium and in the center of the stage is a perfect summer day. She hears her name, and the beautiful suntanned girl slides the coffee and smoothie out to her through the pickup window.

Here is a conundrum: only two hands, but three drinks. Not the smartest thinking for a girl without a car. She sits back down on the bench to contemplate this, and—

"That's a lot of liquids," says a voice behind her.

Jordan turns and there is the ghost of Simone.

"Oh my god," she says. "It's you." So it was Simone she saw running the day before. She's a little older, yes (who isn't?), but with the same spun-sugar hair, the improbable tan layered over freckles, the soccer-player legs. Simone is wearing running shorts, a fitted tank top, and sunglasses, which she lifts to reveal the same eyes Jordan remembers, will always remember. Sea-glass green. Her heart beats extra fast. Her eyes were the rarest color in the world, seventeen-year-old Simone had informed Jordan. She was very proud of her eyes, as though she had somehow chosen the color herself.

"How are you going to carry all that?"

Simone was the first girl Jordan kissed—she was Jordan's first everything.

"I'm actually done with the coconut water," Jordan says. "So now I have two drinks for two hands."

"Well, that's good." Simone smiles. Her teeth are California perfect. "You look fantastic, Jordan Shipman. Look at you, all grown up."

"Ha," says Jordan "Yeah, I guess I am. You too."

"I look fantastic, or I'm all grown up?"

Jordan takes a few seconds with this, looking carefully at Simone. So she's still a flirt. "Both," she says finally.

God, Jordan was crazy for Simone. They'd met in the beginning of the summer before college. Simone was working as a lifeguard at the Beach Club and Jordan was a member, which right there tells you most of what you need to know about New England, because even though Simone's parents were loaded, it was time, connections, and family, not money, that got you a membership at the Beach Club. They were inseparable that whole summer.

Simone visited her once at NYU, freshman year. At a pregame the first night of her visit Jordan lost track of Simone for a little while, and when next she saw her she was making out with a guy wearing an Obama T-shirt. Jordan had left the party, stomped all the way down Mercer, leaving Simone to find her way back to the residence hall.

"Did you walk here?" Simone asks now, drawing Jordan back to the present. Jordan nods. "I could give you a ride home. I've got my car right here. I just finished my run and grabbed a coffee." Simone holds up her own cup for proof. There isn't a drop of sweat on her, but that's Simone for you. Her legs, which are quite visible, so please don't judge Jordan for looking, are the same lean, strong legs that all those years ago could rise effortlessly on a surfboard, race along the beach, wrap themselves around Jordan. She points to a Honda CRV in the small parking lot.

Simone had been angry when she finally got back to the room. "What's the big deal, Jordan, it was just a kiss, I always said I was bi."

But Jordan had been angrier, so angry she could barely talk. "Sorry," she spat, "but you never said you were bi. I thought you were here to see me." She'd been so shocked and hurt she felt like she had sunburned skin and Simone had slapped it.

"I was! I am! So what, it was just a guy at a party. It was just a kiss. It doesn't have to be so complicated, Jordan. Why can't we just have fun?"

But Jordan couldn't get past it. She couldn't, she wouldn't. If she couldn't have Simone completely, she didn't want her at all. They hardly spoke the next morning when Simone packed her bag, got in the cab that would take her back to LaGuardia. And they didn't speak again after. During the next summer Jordan avoided places she might run into Simone, even turning around on a run when she thought she saw her coming the other way.

"Or I could walk you home," says Simone now. "I can hold one of your drinks."

Simone's parents own one of the gigantic homes along Ocean Boulevard, across the street from the beach. Simone's father made his money in the early days of the tech boom. When Jordan knew her, all those years ago, when Simone's family had just bought and renovated the house, the money was new money. Jordan supposes it's older money now, or at least middle-aged money, with a couple of lines on its face and some extra weight around the hips.

The summer between sophomore and junior year of college she ran into Simone's mother on the beach, who told her Simone had a summer internship in California and wasn't coming back. Soon enough Jordan's visits were shorter too—an internship in the city before senior year, then graduation and her first real job. She blinked, and the endless girlhood summers were a thing of the past, and that was a wrap on Jordan's first love. If one of her sisters reported that they'd seen Simone or talked to her, she'd pretended that she didn't care. She had cared very much, until she made herself not care.

Now Jordan is full of mixed-up feelings—years-old hurt, and also nostalgia, and also genuine happiness at seeing someone she once truly loved, someone who turned her on, mentally, physically, emotionally. "Sure," she says. "Walk me home."

They cross the first parking lot, cross the street, cross the second parking lot. They cross everything they can cross and now they are on the beach. The early surfers are carrying their boards from the water, peeling off their wetsuits, packing their cars, and shaking the water out of their ears.

The tide is coming in now. Simone stops to take off her running shoes, and Jordan slips her feet out of her flip-flops. She can't believe she's here, with Simone, after so many years. Simone is a stranger! But also 100 percent familiar.

"Feet in the water?" asks Jordan. "Or stay dry?"

"Definitely in the water." They walk down, brace themselves, get their feet wet, brace themselves some more. This is how you have to do it on the Seacoast, where the water in the summer is almost always just the wrong side of welcoming. If you're lucky you might be able to wade in almost comfortably on a single hot day in mid-August.

"My parents told me about your mom," says Simone, and instantly Jordan's throat closes and she feels like she can't breathe. The grief is always right there on the edges, ready to pounce. "I'm so sorry, Jordan. Your mom was amazing."

"Thanks," she manages to croak. "Yeah, she was. I miss her. We all miss her." The word *miss* feels so inadequate; it seems like the loss of Theresa should have its own special word.

"We used to talk about books, your mom and me, that summer. Sitting out on your patio."

"Yeah," says Jordan, squinting toward the horizon. "I remember that. You were both reading *Water for Elephants*."

"We were! You're right. I can picture my paperback. I got it wet and it was so soggy and swollen. Your mom's was pristine." They start to walk, and Jordan can feel Simone looking at her, but she keeps her eyes straight ahead. "I wanted to reach out to you, but we weren't in touch so I didn't know if I could . . ." Her voice falters, then trails off altogether.

"Sure," says Jordan. "I get it." She hadn't really left an opening for Simone to get in touch with her. If she's remembering correctly, she'd said some irrevocable things. Can she revoke them now?

"I have been following your sister, though, I admit." Simone laughs. Her laugh sounds the same, like it's moving up and down a musical scale. "Well, I was. Until I couldn't take it anymore."

"What couldn't you take?"

Simone bends to examine a clamshell. "Empty," she says. "Nobody to rescue." She straightens again. "What I couldn't take was all of that heteronormative perfection. It's too much. It's unreal. I mean, I know that's an expression, but it literally seems like it can't be real."

"Yeah," says Jordan, feeling disloyal to Natalie but also agreeing. "I get it," she says again.

"Okay, so," says Simone. "Catch me up on your life in thirty seconds or less." They pass a man walking a German shepherd on a leash, and Jordan clocks Simone's double take. The man is very good-looking.

"Only thirty seconds?"

"You can have a little longer if you need it."

"Okay." Jordan takes a deep breath. "I live in Manhattan. I work for a high-end crisis communications firm, which means when people do something wrong that goes public—or even if they don't do something wrong, but the public perceives that they have—we manage the response."

"You're a fixer!" cries Simone.

"Not exactly. Sort of. More of a—buffer. A context builder. A handholder, sometimes. Does this count as part of my thirty seconds?"

"I forgot to look at my watch. Take as long as you need."

"Okay. Two years and two months ago, my mom died. Five months ago, my dad married her hospice nurse, who's twenty-nine years younger. My sisters and I boycotted the wedding. My dad is putting our house on the market. My sisters are up in arms about it, but I actually think it makes sense. Natalie has three kids, you've seen them online, I'm sure, and Mae lives in Boulder."

"Relationship?"

"Me or Mae?"

"You."

"I—no. Not currently. I was living with someone. Audrey. She moved out three years ago."

"Why?" Don't be so shy about getting right in there, thinks Jordan.

"She thought I was too focused on my work and that she'd never be the center of my attention."

"Was she right?"

Jordan chews her lip. "Maybe. I'm not sure." (She was right. And Jordan still misses her every day.)

"I can't believe your dad is selling the house! I can't believe you have an evil stepmother!"

"I do," says Jordan, even though she knows that's not true or fair. "It's very Disney-esque. She makes us sweep a lot." Simone snorts. "That was definitely more than thirty seconds. Now, you go."

"Okay. My parents are going to sell. They bought property on Kiawah, where the water is warmer. They stopped coming here regularly a few years ago."

Good luck with that coastal flooding, Jordan thinks, offended on behalf of Rye. Kiawah! It's not supposed to be easy to get in the water; you have to earn it.

"Really, I think they realized they were never going to get into the Beach Club. They would never say it, but they were *so jealous* of your parents." The Beach Club wait list is famously long, decades long, and money can't move you up. "My partner and I just broke up. We were living in Santa Cruz. There was cheating." Jordan tracks the passive voice. "It got ugly. I'm living in my parents' house while I get my yoga-and-smoothie place off the ground. It's something I've wanted to do forever, so—I'm doing it. I found a little space in Portsmouth. I plan to open in September."

Jordan should say *that's amazing!* She should say *I love yoga and smoothies and Portsmouth!* But a wire trips in her brain and instead she asks, "Was the partner male or female?"

They're walking side by side, but at this Simone stops, so Jordan stops too, and Simone gives her a long, long look. "Female," she says finally.

For some reason that frees Jordan up to say, "That's amazing. I love yoga and smoothies and Portsmouth." Simone smiles.

They walk in silence the rest of the way, and then, when they are adjacent to Jordan's house, Simone says, "That was the best summer of my life, when we were seventeen."

"I was eighteen," says Jordan. "Spring birthday."

"I'm lamenting my lost youth. Are you?"

"No," Jordan says. "I don't lament." She doesn't like when people talk about their lost youth. It's not lost, it's simply in the past. That's fine, that's the normal way of things, the only constant is change, etc., etc. "I like adulthood." She likes having money and a nice apartment and being the master of her own universe. She likes buying good bourbon and monochromatic Pilates sets and being a generous tipper and saying, "I'll have the Seven Stones Cabernet." She loves her job. She's good at it!

(She used to love her job.)

(She does love her job. Just not her boss.)

"But I will say," she adds wistfully, "life was uncomplicated then." Before she lost Theresa and gained Bernadette; before she even knew Audrey. When she had Simone. She hadn't lost anything yet.

"Oh, Jordan." Simone's smiling, but she sounds a little sad.

"What?"

"You think that, but you always made things complicated, even then." She squeezes Jordan's arm and Jordan's heart skips a beat. "It's like you're in a permanent defensive crouch." She laughs like this is some sort of compliment.

"No, I'm not," says Jordan defensively.

"It's okay. You are who you are, right?"

Jordan is stymied. She's not sure what to say, and she can feel herself starting to bristle, so she says, "I should get back to my sisters."

"Oh my god, your *sisters*," says Simone. "You have the best sisters. I was always so jealous of the three of you. I would have given anything for sisters! To be a Shipman girl!"

"Yeah," says Jordan.

"Text me, okay? I have the same number."

"I deleted it," says Jordan. "In 2008, I deleted it."

The skin around Simone's sea-glass eyes crinkles when she smiles. She never wore enough sunscreen, Jordan remembers. She always wanted to be so tan.

"So not right away?"

"No," admits Jordan. "Not right away."

"Well, I didn't delete yours. I'll text you, okay? Hang on, I'm doing it right now."

Simone's contact arrives on Jordan's phone with a buzz, they say goodbye, and Simone turns and goes back the way she came.

• • •

Natalie is wearing a giant sun hat and her new bikini, and she's thinking about corralling her children back to the house so she doesn't miss the window for Caspian's two o'clock nap. Miss the window, and the rest of the day goes south fast. She doesn't look too bad, maybe even pretty good, *Baywatch* meets MILF, and in the old days (last week) she would absolutely be making a post or a TikTok or both. Her followers go crazy when the Hanson family leaves the farm and ventures into the wild. *Watch us go apple picking! See us at the airport, on our way to Montana to visit the grandparents! Here we are visiting a museum in New York City, swimming in a lake, playing miniature golf.*

She understands, *obviously*, that the internet is addictive, capricious, potentially damaging to the psyche. She has prior experience with that damage herself. The previous fall, scrolling Instagram, Natalie saw a photo of four of the Wesleyan girls together on a getaway to Napa—everyone but her and Leah. Two-thirds of the Sisterhood. Immediately hot tears had pricked her eyes.

Leah had gone to law school and now works for a big firm in Manhattan; she and her husband, an oncologist, live in Connecticut, in commuting distance of the city. Two kids, two jobs, three rotating nannies. She and her husband never see each other. The kids hardly see them together. Every day, Leah once told Natalie, with an air of grievance but also a sort of pride in all she was managing, was a jigsaw puzzle into which they needed to slot one hundred and fifty pieces. Every. Single. Day. "No rest for the weary!" She laughed. It didn't seem so funny to Natalie.

"Why are you doing it?" Natalie asked her once, and then, into the silence, "No, really, Leah, I'm serious."

"Because how else am I going to do it? I went to law school! I'm not going to *not* practice law. Chris went to medical school! He's not going to not treat cancer so he can drive to soccer practice! Look, sorry if I don't make all of my salad dressings from scratch—" She broke off her sentence, and Natalie was silent. "Sorry, Nat, I didn't mean . . ."

The previous fall, Natalie captured a screenshot of the girls in Napa and texted it to Leah. WTF? she said.

Oh yeah, Leah texted back. Bummed we couldn't make it.

Couldn't make it? She hadn't been asked! She imagined the side text blowing up now as Leah realized her mistake. She hearted the photo anyway. It would have gone against her brand to make a big deal over something so trivial. But she understood that this was the cost of her new life. The Sisterhood no longer thought they had anything in common with her.

Now Scarlett and Evangeline are working on a massive sandcastle, using the buckets that Natalie unearthed from the garage storeroom. After she'd plucked them from an enormous pile of who knows what, she'd closed the door. Their father had given them only one job, but it's a doozy.

Caspian is walking around his sisters like a bull about to enter the ring, 100 percent unharnessed energy. It's clear from his expression that he wants to help but that he also wants to knock the whole thing down just to see what will happen. He looks so much like his father, with his strong legs (who knew a toddler could have visible quad muscles?) and the shape of his eyes—both Austin's and Caspian's are round as buttons and fringed with thick lashes. The male energy, always threatening to erupt. Caspian and Austin look most like each other when neither gets their way, which happens often enough with Caspian and really hardly ever with Austin.

Natalie observes as a little girl about Scarlett's age approaches her daughters. Long-sleeved rash guard, hat, zinc on her nose. When Natalie and her sisters were this age they ran around on this beach in almost nothing, which explains why Natalie has three moles on her upper back that the dermatologist is "watching." And who is she to judge? Her own kids are covered up too.

The girl clearly wants to join in but isn't sure how to approach, so instead she takes a swaybacked stance and watches from a careful distance, the knuckles of her right hand in her mouth. Evangeline and Scarlett pass a look between them, seeming to come to an agreement, and then Evangeline wordlessly hands the girl the small yellow shovel and the second-best bucket.

Who says homeschooled kids have no social skills?

A woman who is probably the girl's mom flops down next to Natalie, uninvited, and says, "My kid's so shy. She always waits to be included, you know?"

Natalie refrains from saying that this doesn't seem to be a genetic trait, and instead she smiles and says, "I get it."

"Ohmygod, Natalie, it's me! Rebecca Martin! From the Beach Club!"

Natalie looks and the face resolves into someone recognizable from her youth. The Shipmans belonged to the Beach Club because Theresa belonged, and Theresa belonged because her parents joined when they first built the house. The second a member turns twenty-five—actually, the second *before* they turn twenty-five—they have the option to get an adult membership, as Natalie chose to do. If you turn that down, as Jordan ("I'll never use it") and Mae ("Are you kidding? I can't afford that!") did, you can still visit the club with your family members who belong, but your only option to become a true member in the future is to join the decades-long wait list.

The question of what she will do with her membership is one Natalie hasn't been able to bring herself to ask yet. Will she retain it, without a house to use it from? Or will she let it go? The Shipman girls have the best memories of the Beach Club, with its swim team and white wooden lockers, its famous Third of July party, the comforting strictness of its rules. You can't set up for dinner before 5 p.m.! No entering the upper deck if you're under sixteen!

She does not, however, have fond memories of Rebecca. Rebecca was a boyfriend stealer and a snitch.

"Oh my god, *Rebecca*!" she says. "It's so good to see you!"

"If she knocks over that sandcastle I'll Venmo you fifty bucks. I'm kidding!" Natalie's annoyance radar is going off in a big way. (Obviously Natalie knew Rebecca was kidding.) She begins packing some of their things into her beach bag to indicate that Rebecca shouldn't make herself comfortable, and she's about to give a five-minute warning to her kids, when Rebecca says, "My friends and I all follow Hillside Maven. For, like, a lark, you know? We're, like, this is so nineteen fifties but we can't get enough of it!"

Natalie freezes.

"Thanks for following," she says carefully, even amiably. She's not feeling amiable, but she really cannot afford to alienate anyone else right now, *even Rebecca Martin.* She calls out the five-minute warning.

"The homeschooling stuff is really a hoot. I mean, just the fact that you have the time!"

A hoot? A hoot is not how Natalie would describe all the hours she puts into planning lessons for Scarlett and Evangeline. They can both already read! She'll have Evangeline at a sophomore-year French level by next year! It is the furthest thing from a hoot: it's honest work, and it's sacrifice, and it's for the good of her family.

(And her followers.)

(But mostly her family.)

"I'm glad you like the content," she says, smiling with just her mouth. Natalie calls a three-minute warning to the kids and begins to shake out the beach towels. Rebecca has parked herself on the corner of Natalie's beach blanket. Natalie doesn't want to shake the woman off like she's a bunch of sand, but she'll do it if she has to.

"I could never homeschool."

"It's not for everyone," says Natalie pleasantly.

"It's definitely not for me. I'm in finance; I'd never have the time. Plus, I don't think I could do what teachers have been trained to do. I like using my brain for my own work, you know? No offense."

"None taken." Natalie's voice is tight.

"Your husband, though, in that article—"

"Zero-minute warning!" calls Natalie. She can't lose her temper because even if this woman may not be a fan per se, she is a follower. She's waiting for Natalie to lose it so she can record it or tell someone or both. "Naptime for the little guy," she tells Rebecca.

Rebecca rises and wipes the sand off the backs of her legs, and Natalie reclaims her blanket.

"Thanks again for following," Natalie says, as sweet as the cherry pie she's finally perfected, right down to the braided edges of the homemade crust. "It was *so great* to see you." She's known that some people love her and some people hate her—that's the internet for you. She's known her life is full of contradictions—that's womanhood for you. But until this week, it's never felt so heavily weighted in the wrong direction.

As she's folding the blanket, she sees something change in Caspian, some alteration of his mood. It's subtle, and almost atmospheric, the way the air feels different the second before the first raindrop falls. But it's enough. She says, "Caspian!" but it's too late. He's got his shovel raised above the sandcastle, and, just as Rebecca grabs her little girl's hand and whisks her away, the shovel comes down and the sandcastle dissolves.

Scarlett stands still, utterly dumbfounded, but Evangeline raises her face to the sky and unleashes the most bloodcurdling scream;

she's protesting a grand injustice, maybe even screaming at God Himself. The grievances of the very young! They are every bit as legitimate to their owners as the grievances of the very old, Natalie knows this. But they are also sometimes very, very inconvenient.

Deep breath. In, out. Natalie snaps into action. She throws the rest of their things in the beach bag, scoops up Caspian (he has the gall to be smiling handsomely), and ushers the screaming Evangeline and the shell-shocked Scarlett across the sand and toward the house.

Away from the wet sandcastle sand, the dry sand is unforgivingly hot. Scarlett jumps from foot to foot, screeching at Natalie as though she can change the temperature. She steers them up the steps to the patio (also hot) and around to the outdoor shower, where she plops her bag on the bench and turns on the water. Too late she realizes she left the shovels and pails behind. She'll have to go back for them later.

"I'm sorry Caspian did that," she says, watching Evangeline's sobs subside. Evangeline wipes at her eyes, definitely rubbing sand into them. "He's little. He doesn't know any better."

"He does know any better!" says Scarlett. Natalie suspects that she's right. "He needs to apologize."

"Caspian, can you tell your sisters you're sorry?" There are two schools of thought on the efficacy of forcing children to apologize, and some days Natalie is not sure to which one she belongs. Whichever is easier, maybe, although she wouldn't tell anyone that. She is supposed to be someone with standards. She's supposed to have a plan!

"Orry," he says, grinning. She puts him down and he tries to escape the shower. She slides the lock, keeping them all safe inside, and takes her forty thousandth deep breath of the day.

"Rinse the sand," she commands the girls. "Caspian needs his nap."

"Do we have to wash our hair?" the girls ask in unison.

Scarlett and Evangeline have copious amounts of hair. It's fairy-princess hair, thick and heavy, with natural curl at the end. It's gorgeous, but it requires such maintenance. Natalie's second-biggest fear about her children (the first being something actually bad happening to them) is that lice will invade Hillside Haven.

Natalie is so, so tired suddenly. She's weak, she's hungry, she's thirsty. She's the poster girl for depleted. She won't make it to naptime.

She sets her shoulders back. She must make it to naptime. She will make it to naptime. And beyond. And beyond!

"No hair," she says. "Quick rinse, and we'll move along."

"I don't want to take a shower," says Scarlett.

"Well, you have to."

Scarlett says, "But—" and Natalie feels herself start to lose it.

"Quick rinse!" she says, and then repeats, yelling now, "I said QUICK RINSE!"

"You're yelling, Mommy," says Evangeline.

"I'm not yelling!" cries Natalie. "I am trying. To do. Gentle. Parenting."

• • •

Later that afternoon, Mae and Leo are in the sunroom, practicing Leo's settling. This means that as long as he's lying in a relaxed position, just chilling, he gets rewarded. Chilling is harder than it sounds for a reactive dog! But it's an important step in his training, so he can one day live comfortably in the world with Human Leo. She imagines them hanging out on Pearl Street on a busy Saturday, one Leo drinking a latte, the other lying next to him, watching the world go by. No, that's not right. Leo doesn't read like a latte guy. An iced Americano, or a nitro brew.

Mae didn't answer Tony's text, and he hasn't texted again, but she knows that he will. The money she owes Tony is another worry to add to her collection of worries, all of which she has folded up neatly and tucked away so she can concentrate on Leo.

She enlists Scarlett and Evangeline to help practice. Cinnamon and Natalie are upstairs getting Caspian up from his nap, so it's a good chance to work Leo in a controlled environment. She instructs them to walk past Leo, not too close, but close enough that he notices them.

"Pretend you're just out for a casual stroll," she says. "Just minding your own business, maybe having a chat."

Scarlett and Evangeline take this very seriously. Scarlett says, "How are you?" to Evangeline, and Evangeline gives a formal little bow and says, "Fine, thank you, how are you?" It's all quite civilized, very period-drama-with-parasols. Any minute now they may link arms and talk about which suitors they have their eyes on.

"Good job," Mae tells them. Leo watches them carefully, then, looking back at Mae to make sure there's no threat, relaxes onto one hip. "Good boy," she tells Leo. "That's perfect."

She's about to ask them to take another round when Calvin comes in. He's wearing his work jeans, which he's had probably since Mae sprouted her first tooth. They have dots and stripes of paint of all different colors, artifacts from every house project he's undertaken. He's probably been doing something to prepare for the open house on Sunday, but this Mae, the Mae who still *cannot believe* he's going to sell the house, will not dignify the situation by asking him what that was.

"Spackling," he says anyway. Mae nods crisply at him, as if to say *whatever you are doing to my mother's house you're about to sell is of no concern to me*, and continues working with Leo.

Calvin takes off his glasses, puts them on the coffee table, and rubs his eyes. He says, "Hello, ladies," to his granddaughters, and Leo rolls his eyes toward Calvin. "You're okay, Leo," says Mae. Leo has a harder time with men than with little girls. This is not uncommon for rescue dogs.

"Hello," say Scarlett and Evangeline pleasantly. Scarlett, still in character, full-on curtsies.

"Good boy, Leo. Scarlett and Evangeline, again, please. Stage right." They look at her blankly. She points. "Start over there."

They cross the room once more. If Mae were speaking to her father, she might ask him to take a video that she could send to Hal to show Leo's progress. Leo is already calmer even since yesterday! Imagine how much he'll improve by the end of the week. Evangeline and Scarlett cross the room again, and from the entryway comes a voice: "Yooo-hoooo! Anybody home?"

Leo starts, then growls, and Mae puts a hand on his side to let him know all is well.

"That's Nikoletta," says Calvin, rising. "She has some papers for me to sign." He calls, "In the sunroom! Come on in!"

Mae has a thought: If Leo bit the Realtor, would that cause her to give up the listing? (She's kidding! Mostly!) Natalie comes in just then, carrying Caspian, who is sleepy-eyed, his hair adorably mussed, and holding a sippy cup. At the same time the woman from yesterday comes from the entryway. She's carrying a manila folder and a cell phone.

"Ah, Nikoletta, hello! These are two of my daughters."

"We met," says Mae icily. *Under false pretenses,* she adds in her mind.

"Oh, right! You've met Mae. This is Natalie. And her children, Scarlett, Evangeline, and Caspian."

"Hello! What an adorable little boy!" Nikoletta exclaims, looking at Caspian. He grins and offers her his sippy cup.

"He wants you to have some milk," explains Scarlett.

"How nice!" says Nikoletta. "And I certainly would, but I'm vegan."

"What's vegan?" asks Evangeline.

Mae watches Natalie tense. She says, "Vegans are people who

don't eat any animal products." Mae can see her sister working out how far to take this instructional moment.

"Are we vegans?" Scarlett asks her mother.

"No, honey."

"Milk is an animal product," Mae explains.

Evangeline asks, "Why don't they drink it?"

Mae can see the Realtor warming to the topic. It's like they're on a roller coaster that is at the top of the hill and about to plunge down, and there's nothing anyone can do to stop it. "Well, people can be vegan for lots of different reasons," explains Nikoletta. "For me, it's because I believe animals have the right to their own uncomplicated existence, that they aren't ours to exploit for our own use."

Scarlett asks, "What's *exploit*?"

Mae clears her throat and asks, "Did you have some papers for Dad to sign?"

"We can talk about this later," says Natalie in an unnaturally tight voice.

"Oh, I don't mind!" says Nikoletta. *Blithe* would be a good, solid word to describe her tone. "I raised two children myself! Every moment deserves to be a teachable moment."

Natalie says, "Maybe not every—" But here goes Nikoletta, full steam ahead, sliding onto the couch so that she's closer to the girls' level: "*Exploiting* means using something or someone else for our own good."

"Girls, why don't you come help me in the kitchen." Mae hears the way the stridency in Natalie's voice shoots right to the core of Leo's anxiety. She watches his body tense.

Nikoletta holds up one finger to indicate she's almost done. "So a lot of vegans, myself included, don't think it's right to nourish our own bodies with something another mammal produces to feed her own offspring." The blank look from the girls again, then, "Her own babies."

Natalie cries, "Thank you! Girls, come on now!" The girls don't move.

Leo is over his threshold now. He grabs the closest thing he can find. Mae will congratulate him later, in private, because he self-regulates by focusing on an inanimate object in his environment rather than on a human or an animal. If this had been a stuffed toy, it would have been a perfect reaction. But as it is, he finds Calvin's glasses, which he bites swiftly and cleanly. They all hear the crunch.

• • •

"Resource guarding is common among dogs who missed the window for proper socialization as puppies," Mae is saying when Jordan comes into the very crowded sunroom. Natalie, all three kids, Mae, Leo, Calvin, and a woman Jordan has never seen before wearing ballet flats and a nervous smile. "Trade, Leo," Mae says optimistically, holding out a treat. Leo turns his head away and growls. To the room she says, "He's just learning this one. He's supposed to drop whatever he has with the understanding that what I have is better."

"I don't care about his socialization as much as I care about my glasses," says Calvin.

"Your glasses?" says Jordan.

"Leo took them," explains Natalie.

"Right off of Dad's *face*?"

"No," says Calvin, exasperated. "They were on the table."

"Got 'em!" says Mae triumphantly. She holds up the glasses. "Do you think you can wear these, Dad?" The left lens is cracked and one arm is hanging off at a rakish angle. The other arm has been amputated.

The unfamiliar woman turns to Jordan and says, "I'm Nikoletta, the Realtor in charge of the home sale." She offers her hand and Jordan takes it, but she can feel Natalie watching her, gauging her level of friendliness.

"Dad, I'm so sorry," says Mae. "Where's your backup pair?"

"They must be in Lenox."

"I could call Kara and ask," Mae suggests. "If there's a backup pair, she can bring them."

"But she's not coming from Lenox—remember? She's coming from Cincinnati," says Calvin.

For a moment they are stymied by this fact, and Mae looks at Natalie, and then Natalie looks at Jordan, and then Jordan looks back at Mae then down at her watch. "I'll call your home optician and see if they can email me the prescription before they close or first thing tomorrow. I'm sure there's a place in Portsmouth that can make a pair in a day. You might not have your choice of frames, and you might have to muddle through tomorrow. But you've muddled before. You can muddle again."

"I have muddled before," Calvin agrees. "Thank you, Jordan."

Mae realizes it first. "But if you don't have your glasses—"

"What?"

"Then you can't drive. And if you can't drive, you can't pick up Kara at Logan."

"Not it," says Natalie so softly that only her sisters hear, and Jordan echoes her, equally softly, "Not it." It's an old game of theirs: not it for the middle seat, not it for unloading the always-needing-to-be-unloaded dishwasher, not it for cleaning up the dog waste from the yard, back when they had a family dog. Mae, so much younger, always trying to play catch-up, never quick enough, got stuck with whatever "it" was more often than not.

"I'll do it," says Mae.

"You will?"

"Of course. It will be good for Leo to come along. I'm supposed to be exposing him to as many different environments as I can. I can walk him back and forth outside the arrivals area."

"Are you sure?"

"Positive."

"Thank you, Mae," says Calvin.

"Who's the favorite daughter now?" Mae asks.

Nikoletta looks back and forth. "You're all so *funny*!" she says uncertainly.

• • •

Natalie and Scarlett are looking at what may just be Natalie's favorite photo of all time. It's back hanging where it's always hung, in the sunroom, in a natural woven frame. Pottery Barn, circa whenever. It's the three Shipman girls, on the sand, facing the house, their backs to the ocean. Her mother must have taken the photo—except for the first day of school pose by the rhododendron, Theresa took all the photos. As a result, she was in far fewer than she should have been.

It's summer 2007. Fourth of July, the girls are holding unlit sparklers. Natalie knows she was fifteen because that was the summer she'd used her birthday money from the spring to buy a bikini, which she'd done with gusto, choosing a one-shouldered ruffled tie-dyed number that she'd now certainly caution herself (or anyone else) against. But how happy she'd been in it.

Natalie does some quick math. Yes, this was the summer of Simone! This was the summer Jordan got in trouble for staying out all night after a party at Simone's house; the battery on her flip phone (a flip phone!) had died, and she hadn't called.

"We thought you were dead!" Natalie remembers her father bellowing, and even her mother, who usually saved her disciplining for the classroom, had raised her voice.

"Well, I'm *not*," Jordan had snarled, eighteen, exhausted, stomping her way up to her bedroom, where she'd slept the rest of the day.

Mae is deliciously eleven, spindly legs, concave chest in her bright orange one-piece. (How Mae had *loved* that suit, even though orange was then, and would be forevermore, a terrible color on her.)

"Look at my butterfly clips!" Natalie tells Scarlett, pointing at her hair in the photo.

"Oooooh," says Scarlett appreciatively.

Natalie was in love, too, that summer, with an older man (sixteen) who had been visiting his grandparents for a week. Sean? Mark? She can't remember, but she does remember that he promised to call her once he got back to Michigan or wherever he was from and she never heard from him.

Talk about a cruel summer.

In the photo, Natalie is wearing the bikini, and Jordan, who had been flirting with a hair crimper that summer, with mixed results, is in shorts and a Cinnamon Rainbows T-shirt. She's looking slightly off to the left with a sly smile. Natalie is grinning straight at the camera, and Mae is jumping, both feet off the ground, like a kid in a commercial who's just been told she's going on a surprise trip to Disney World. Natalie puts her fingertips on the photo, touching each of the girls in turn. *Take me back*, she wants to say. *Just for a day, take me back*. She doesn't even realize she's crying until Scarlett says, "Are you crying, Mommy?"

"A little bit."

"What are you sad about?"

"I guess time passing. But that's what time does. It passes."

TUESDAY

• • •

After Leo's morning walk on Tuesday, Mae and Leo return to the kitchen, and Mae unhooks Leo's leash. He flops on the floor, tongue out, breathing fast in the satisfying way that a tired dog breathes. There's no sign of Cinnamon, but Natalie is sitting at the kitchen island, frowning into a coffee cup that says *I'M SILENTLY CORRECTING YOUR GRAMMAR*. They'd started getting these mugs for their mom years ago, the cornier the better, and they'd all ended up at the beach house. In Lenox, the cabinets hold a matching set of twelve light blue pottery mugs. Here they each drink from one of approximately nine ridiculous mugs.

"You like the coffee? I made a pot before I took Leo out," says Mae, pleased with herself.

"Thanks," says Natalie wearily. "It's on the weak side, but, yeah, thanks." Mae rolls her eyes—sisters can be so ungrateful.

"Then make it yourself next time," she suggests, not unkindly, but not kindly either.

"You asked if I liked it." Natalie rubs her temples. Her phone, next to her coffee, buzzes, and she silences it and turns it over, but not before Mae sees Austin's name on the screen. Mae fills the teakettle, sets it on the stove, and chooses a mug that says *MY BLOOD TYPE IS COFFEE*.

Leo raises his head, his ears go up, and footsteps approach. Mae grabs her phone, tells Leo to settle, and captures him watching Jordan enter the kitchen. He looks back at Mae for confirmation that this is okay, puts his chin on the floor. *Good boy, Leo.*

Jordan finds a mug that says *HOLD ON, LET ME OVERTHINK THIS*, and fills it nearly to overflowing. She opens the refrigerator door and stands there for way too long. "This house has no milk alternatives," she says. "Why didn't we get any when we went to the store yesterday?"

"Who needs alternatives?" asks Natalie. "You've got the finest, freshest milk there is right there. Organic."

Leo raises his head again, lifts his ears, and Caspian trundles into the kitchen. He's wearing pajamas with trains on them, and his hair is sticking up all over the place.

"Good boy, Leo," Mae says encouragingly, and Leo sighs and settles once again.

"Ommy?" says Caspian.

"How'd you get out?" Natalie asks, and Caspian grins.

"I got him out," says Evangeline, who comes in right behind Caspian.

Natalie hops off the stool and lifts Caspian, saying, "Wet diaper, mister." Caspian pats her approvingly on the head with a flat hand.

Next comes Cinnamon, who enters the kitchen halfway, and then, seeing Leo, halts, wags uncertainly, and backs up two steps. Four, if you're counting paws. Leo scrambles to his feet and emits a low growl. His tail is stiff. In an instant Mae has the leash back on him, her body in front of Leo to act like a shield, talking to him softly until she reads calm in his body language. When she does, she lets the two dogs sniff each other. She's ready to pull Leo back if needed, but he does just fine. It's a big moment!

"Hello, Dog Whisperer!" says Jordan. "Nice work."

"Thank you," says Mae. Next time, she'll be sure to record. She would have loved to show that recovery to Human Leo. "It's called counterconditioning."

MAE STARTS PREPPING for the trip to the airport long before she has to leave. She's going to set Leo up for success in the back seat with a couple of old beach towels and a Kong filled with frozen peanut butter. (She must remember to tell Human Leo about the wonders of the Kong, and about how licking is a calming activity for dogs; it's the canine version of meditation or yoga.) The Kong should keep him busy for most of the drive.

Her father comes out to the driveway as she's checking to make sure she has the collapsible water bowl and a full bottle of water.

"So you're off!" he says.

"Not quite." She checks her phone—she still has plenty of time. "I don't need to leave for a while. I'm just getting ready." She'd been rooting around for an extra blanket in her trunk but she slams it shut so Calvin can't see how many of her belongings are in there.

"Car holding up okay? You keeping on top of the oil changes and all of that?"

"Of course," she says, untruthfully, now wondering if she can move toward the front of the car to hide the outdated oil change sticker.

Calvin clears his throat, and Mae waits. Does her father have something important to say? Are they going to get into it about the house? "Mae—do you need gas money?" Mae exhales softly. The answer is, of course, yes. But which is the right play: Admit it, hide it, or inflate the amount so she can pocket the difference? She makes a noncommittal sound that could mean anything. "Well, here," says Calvin. "Why don't you take it anyway."

Mae straightens her spine, trying to seem un-needy and un-eager.

"I insist. You're doing me a favor." Her father opens his wallet and pulls out four crisp twenties. She had been anticipating Venmo or maybe, as in the good old days of high school and early college, the loan of a parental credit card. But here is cash! Dads are so old!

Also, eighty dollars is a lot of money, and way more than she needs to get to Logan and back.

"Thank you."

"Thank *you*," he says, with a little tip of his head that seems very formal. "For making the trip."

"No problem," she says, trying to convey with those two words all of the ambivalence she does not know where to put. She's still so angry about the house sale, but she's also feeling guilty about Leo destroying the glasses. She's looking forward to seeing Kara but doesn't want to look too forward in case her sisters notice.

She watches her father go back into the house—she tracks the stoop of his shoulders, the bellwether of aging.

"We're off!" she tells Leo later, but Leo, focused on his Kong, doesn't answer. Mae knows she's leaving earlier than she needs to, but she wants to take the long way. She checks the line at the Beach Plum as she passes by—long—and she reminisces about the Secret Spot, home of the most glorious smoothies, which never got rebuilt after the fire four years ago. She sees the place where Natalie got pulled over for speeding when she was a new driver with Mae in the passenger seat (she got off with a warning; Mae had helped her by bursting into very believable tears, requested by Natalie). She passes through Hampton Beach, home of the Casino Ballroom, where her parents used to go see a show every summer ("the theater of the has-beens," Jordan called it in her sardonic, late-teenage period, but her parents had loved their annual tradition, coming back flushed and happy, Theresa a little bit tipsy).

"What are we but our memories, Leo?" she asks, and she watches in the rearview mirror as he picks his head up, lifts his ears, and seems to be considering her question. It's not a bad quote. Somebody should put *that* on a coffee cup.

• • •

It is decided that Jordan will bring the kids to the beach while Natalie drives Calvin into Portsmouth to order his new glasses, waits with him for them to be ready, and drives him back home. At that point Jordan and Natalie will work on the storeroom while Calvin scrubs the tile grout in the upstairs bathroom. Jordan could have done the trip to the optometrist, but, if she's being honest, Natalie is sort of dying for a break from her kids. She loves her kids with all her heart and soul, but she is around them *all the time*—such is the life of a homeschooling mom—and the promise of a teeny-tiny break feels to her now the way the promise of a night out at the bars used to feel when she was single, that zing of anticipation, the first sip of the first drink hitting the back of your throat.

They had to wait for the optometrist in Lenox to open—they'd just missed the four thirty closing time the day before—and then to send over the prescription, so when they finally get on the road it's nearly time for Mae to leave for the airport.

They start off north, along the ocean, then turn inland.

"What did the dentist say to the molar when he had to leave the room?" Calvin asks.

"I give up," says Natalie. They pass the library, then the fire station, cutting west to pick up Route 1.

"You didn't even try to guess!"

"Sorry, Dad. I guess my mind was elsewhere." *Elsewhere* is an understatement. When she'd first learned that *New York* would be doing a profile, she'd imagined the days after its publication to be a victory walk of sorts. She'd planned the photo of herself holding the issue, standing in the milking barn in overalls, her hair in a careful messy bun. Maybe the children would be arranged adorably around her, maybe she'd be holding Caspian with a daughter on either side. But not only is she nowhere near her milking barn, she hasn't even considered looking for a hard copy. She hasn't posted a word.

What do I do? she'd messaged her publicist.

Stay quiet. These things tend to burn themselves out. In the meantime, I'll monitor your accounts. You spend time with your family.

She can't remember the last time she'd gone three days without tending to her accounts. Actually, she does remember: It was when Theresa died. She'd posted her favorite photo of sunrise at Hillside Haven and written a paragraph about her mother, announcing that she'd be offline for the rest of the week. Her followers had been so supportive; she'd gotten hundreds of thousands of likes and comments. She'd felt it, the kindness of strangers, flowing to her. How quickly people turn. Ingratitude, thou marble-hearted fiend, she thinks.

"I give up," she tells her father again. "Tell me."

"I'll fill you in when I get back." Natalie groans. He waits a beat, then says, "It's like pulling teeth to get you to laugh at my dentist jokes."

"Oh my god," says Natalie. "Dad!"

She needs more coffee. She's so tired! "Don't lose sleep over it," Theresa used to say when she saw her daughters worrying about something insignificant. But Theresa must have known this was impossible advice! Natalie thinks about all the sleep mothers through the ages have lost over one thing or another: a sick child, an unwieldy to-do list, a husband away at sea for months at a time or off to war. What if we could get those hours back, she wonders, all of us collectively? What if we could stitch them together into a great billowing quilt with which we could cover all of the other mothers, and let them sleep?

Let the mothers sleep.

The woman who works in the eyeglasses shop tells them they have two hours to kill. Calvin suggests they get lunch while they wait. He's a creature of habit, and he likes the burger at Popovers. Natalie isn't hungry, but she'll get another coffee.

I'm feeding Dad, Natalie texts Jordan. Feel free to start the garage without me.

Jordan texts back one of those memes of Jerry Seinfeld saying, *I tell ya, I don't see it happening.* I'm watching your kids, remember? Eva is going to make us lobster Thermidor.

Ha, ha, thinks Natalie. She texts back, Evangeline. Her sisters know how she feels about nicknames. Jordan doesn't reply to that text.

When they are settled at a table with Calvin's burger and Natalie's coffee, Calvin asks her about the farm. The farm equals the article and the article equals her marriage, but her father doesn't know that, so she tries to think of something to share. "Buttercup has mastitis," she says.

Calvin looks perplexed. "That's—too bad?" he says. "Or very good?"

"Bad," she says. "It's an inflammation of the mammary gland. If not caught early, it can affect milk quality and production. But Dr. George is on it; she'll be fine."

She knows that by talking about Buttercup they are skirting around the real issues—Kara's arrival, the house. The house is like a drumbeat in the back of Natalie's mind: *the house, the house, the house.*

"Listen, Natalie. There's something I didn't finish telling you all about the sale."

"Dad," she says. "I don't want to talk about the sale. Seriously, it's crushing me. I feel like I can't breathe when I think about it." Natalie watches her father take that in. She observes the grooves in his face, the familiar rasp to his voice, the bobbing Adam's apple. She remembers being seven and watching him lift little Mae onto his shoulders and wade into the Atlantic; she remembers him at the Beach Club, drinking a beer with his friend Joe (after 5 p.m.! club rules!), laughing so hard. She loves him so much, but she's got such a ball of anger inside.

"When Kara arrives—" he says.

"I don't want to talk about Kara either."

"Well, I do." This is his don't-mess-with-me voice. "I would appreciate it if, when she arrives, you'd make her feel welcome."

She says, looking at the clock on the wall, "The glasses should be ready soon."

• • •

At the beach, Jordan supervises Caspian, Scarlett, and Evangeline carefully. Nothing is going to happen on her watch! She helps Caspian build an approximation of a sandcastle. She walks with them to the edge of the water so they can all go ankle-deep, talk about how cold it is, and retreat to the blanket. She keeps a Goldendoodle, illegally on the beach outside of the sanctioned dog hours, from eating Caspian's homemade crackers. (When, she marvels, did Natalie have time to *make crackers*?)

"You're stingy with your time," Audrey once told Jordan. "It's like your time is a candy bar you're going to share but you always, always want the bigger half."

Look at me now, Jordan thinks. Look at me being a gentle, giving, loving aunt who isn't thinking about work at all!

Actually, she is thinking about work. She's thinking about Samantha Braddock, and about the three unanswered texts Bernadette has sent her just since breakfast, and about the fact that she hasn't yet decided what to do. She wishes she could talk to someone—but who? Audrey had been very good about listening to work stories, until she wasn't, which happened when the work stories started to take over everything. On their last vacation together, to Tulum, their first dinner at the resort was interrupted by a call from a university president with a campus crisis.

"What do you want me to *do*?" she'd asked Audrey (rhetorically).

Audrey had answered literally. "I want you to turn your phone off."

She reapplies the kids' sunscreen, she keeps Caspian from putting a large shell in his mouth, she congratulates Scarlett on her sandcastle with two turrets. Time passes. People are sunbathing and swimming and dragging surfboards to the legal surfing area. People are starting to unpack sandwiches and being very sly about pouring from bottles of rosé hidden in their coolers into Corkcicles.

"What's for lunch?" Scarlett says expectantly. She looks at Jordan like Jordan knows the answer to this question, or to any question. *Is* her father right to sell the house? What will it be like when Kara is here? What should Jordan do about what happened on Memorial Day? Should she call Samantha Braddock?

"Ah," says Jordan. "I didn't bring any lunch out here. Should we go back to the house soon?"

She expects some pushback, if not from Evangeline and Scarlett, at least from Caspian. But they are so compliant. Evangeline helps her put the towels in the bag, and Caspian feeds his crackers to the gulls, which at least makes their load a little lighter. Their beach neighbors give them the stink eye for encouraging the gulls to linger, but whatever.

"Don't tell your mom about the gulls and the crackers," she advises Evangeline.

In the kitchen, the kids eat the sandwiches Jordan makes for them. Well, *eat* is a generous term for Caspian, but he makes a nice design with the pieces and consumes some of them. She puts Caspian down early for his nap, but luckily nobody notices.

When Caspian is sleeping and Evangeline is reading *Ivy + Bean* out loud to her and Scarlett, all Jordan wants to do is lie down herself.

Aunting is exhausting! How does Natalie do this all day every single day? How does she make it all look so *pretty*?

"IF THIS IS what the summer-home storage room looks like I can only imagine what's in the attic in Lenox," says Jordan, after Calvin and Natalie have arrived home, and Calvin, spiffy in his new glasses, has gone inside to check on the to-do list.

"Ugh," says Natalie, coming to stand beside Jordan. Then she says, "Silver lining. The Lenox attic is not going to be our job. It's going to be Kara's."

"Natalie! What a morbid thing to say."

"What? It's true." There's a pause, then Natalie says, "Do you ever feel bad that we didn't go to the wedding?"

Jordan stares at her. "Are you insane? No, never."

"Yeah, me either."

"This is a terrible system," Jordan says, looking at the storeroom, which runs along the back of the garage. "You literally have to take out everything to get to the stuff on the far side. This thing should have a door in the middle. We'll get a dumpster and just put everything in it. I'll call today, have one here on Friday."

Natalie looks horrified. "We can't do that! With Mom's stuff!"

"Why not?"

"It's bad enough you're okay letting the house go! What if treasures abound?"

"I don't want any treasures. I live in an apartment. Do *you* want treasures?"

"Maybe," says Natalie. "Depends what they are. I want to see everything, everything that has to do with Mom."

Jordan sighs. But she knows she's already the odd man out among her sisters since she sees the logic of the sale in a way that they do not.

(Obviously, she's right.) And her mental space is heavily occupied; she can't turn everything into an argument. "Okay, then. If we're not dumping it all, we're going to need three piles. Keep, which means one of us or Dad has to take it. Donate; I'll find a place where we can bring everything on Saturday. And trash." Natalie nods. There is some discussion over whether or not they need handwritten signs to keep the sections straight, then Jordan decides they will be fine without signs: *trash* to the far right, *keep* in the middle, *donate* to the left.

"I'm going in," says Jordan. She straightens her shoulders, tips her chin up, and enters the storeroom, emerging with an electric roasting pan. "Item number one," she says formally. "Do you want this?"

Natalie glances at it. "I have one."

"You have an electric roasting pan?"

"Of course."

"Why?"

"I cook dinner for five people six nights a week. I have an extremely well-equipped kitchen."

"And on the seventh night you rest?" Jordan puts the roasting pan in the donate pile. It looks serviceable.

"Sort of." Natalie pulls a hair elastic off her wrist and uses it to put her hair in a high ponytail. She pulls a lip gloss out of the pocket of her shorts and applies it. "Every Saturday night Austin and I get a babysitter and have a date night in Bennington." Natalie sounds like she's auditioning for a role on *Father Knows Best*, which is a show Jordan has heard of only because she once dated a woman who loved to get high and watch old television shows that her own father used to like. (It was weird, but whatever, everyone has their thing.) "You would know that if you followed me on social media."

"Of course I follow you on social media," says Jordan. "I just don't spend a lot of time on social unless it has to do with work. You post a lot—it's hard to keep up!"

"Well, that's fine," says Natalie, and something sounds funny about her voice. "Have you been online a lot since we've been here?"

"Not even once. I'm technically on vacation. I'm just checking my calls and texts." Jordan pauses and looks more closely at her sister. "Natalie?" She touches her on the shoulder. "Is everything okay?"

"Why wouldn't it be?" Natalie turns away and goes into the storage room herself, returning with a garbage bag full of ancient beach towels. She looks through the bag and says, "These are a disaster. They're so threadbare they need a towel themselves. Trash." They keep going. Collection of warped sand toys, decades-old sand still trapped in them. Trash. A box of cloth napkins, zillions of them. Donate.

Kids' books are next, in a clear Rubbermaid with a bright blue lid. Natalie's kids have so many books already but she has to take a peek. Jordan imagines her mother packing these all away for grandchildren, and then forgetting that she'd done that. And then dying.

"*Bunbun*!" says Natalie. She holds up a book with a yellow cover and a long-eared bunny riding a scooter. It's called *Bunbun, the Middle One*. "I love this book. It's about a rabbit who's always getting in a muddle as the middle child." She begins to read. " 'This is Bunbun. Bunbun's big brother is Benny. His little sister is Bibi. Bunbun is the middle one.' "

Jordan pulls the book out of her hands. "Nope," she says. "We don't have time for reading."

"It's short!" protests Natalie. "It's *Bunbun*!"

"I said no," says Jordan sternly.

"Well, put it in the keep pile. I want it for Scarlett. It's hard being the middle child."

"I can't believe you still have a complex about that." Jordan rolls her mind's eye because Natalie would get mad if she rolled her actual eyes.

"It's not a complex! It's real."

"I call BS on that," says Jordan. "Being the eldest is much harder.

If you're in the middle you can play up or play down. You're never alone. And every road is at least partially paved for you. Where are the books about bunnies who are the eldest children?"

Natalie rolls her actual eyes and says, "I'll find one and buy it for you for Christmas." Then, as an olive branch of sorts, she says, "Being youngest is the easiest."

"One *hundred* percent," agrees Jordan. And harmony is restored. They keep going. A broken grill is back there, with a partial set of rusted tools. A fan with a broken blade. A vacuum from the 1970s—must have belonged to Theresa's parents—whose canister looks like a spaceship.

Jordan tries to introduce the next thing casually, as though she's simply making conversation about something that just occurred to her, even though she's been thinking about it since lunchtime. "Oh, hey," she says. "The girls are too funny. While you were in Portsmouth, after we were done with *Ivy + Bean,* they were playing house."

"Okay?" says Natalie. She brushes her hands on her shorts.

"It's just . . . I didn't know that was a thing kids still did."

Natalie laughs. "You didn't know kids still had imaginations?"

Jordan tries from a different angle. "Evangeline was the dad and Scarlett was the mom. She went looking for an apron! She told Evangeline to sit down while she brought him dinner!"

"What are you getting at, Jordan? That aprons are inappropriate? Aprons are a practical kitchen tool."

"Mom never wore an apron. The whole thing just seemed, I don't know—subservient." Natalie's shoulders tense. "Like, why weren't they pretending they were doctors, or journalists, or astronauts?"

"Sometimes they do," says Natalie. "They play all kinds of things. It sounds like today they decided to play house."

Jordan clamps her mouth shut because she's not sure what's going to come out of it if she leaves it open.

By the end of the two hours the storeroom looks better but the floor of the garage looks much, much worse. Jordan is torn between feeling completely overwhelmed and succumbing to nostalgia and emotion as she looks at the three piles. All of these things were once new, and were purchased with the hope and optimism that they'd be put to their intended use. Maybe some of them were, but certainly many of them were not. She imagines someone buying the picnic set with plates and cups tucked inside plastic sleeves. Had anybody ever even picnicked with this set? It suddenly all seems unbearably sad.

"I'm back to thinking we should just throw it all away," says Jordan. "Forget the donating. If we're getting the dumpster anyway."

Natalie crosses her arms. "Why are you so eager to get rid of Mom's stuff? Just like you're eager to get rid of the house."

Here we go, thinks Jordan. "I'm not eager," says Jordan. "I'm practical. We're not going to change Dad's mind, the house is going on the market, why torture ourselves going through dozens and dozens of things when nobody really needs more things? Why not just dump it?" She picks up a toddler booster seat and points it at Natalie to prove her point. "I mean, do you need more things in your life?"

"I don't need *that*. That thing wouldn't pass even a rudimentary safety test."

Natalie goes back into the storeroom and comes out with a cardboard box. They peer in together. It's full of old romance novels. She puts the box on the garage floor and pulls out one of the books. It's swollen and water-stained, like it went for a vigorous morning swim in the ocean twenty-five years ago and has been trying to dry out ever since. "Oh my," she says. "Do you ever remember Mom reading anything like this?"

Jordan shakes her head and holds out her hand for the book. On the cover, a bare-chested, dark-haired, suntanned man in jeans is pressed up against a woman in a flowing lavender gown with a lace-up bodice. The laces are half undone. "It's an actual bodice ripper!" she says gleefully. "Or at least a bodice unlacer." She studies the cover. "I'm trying to figure out the incongruity of the jeans with the gown. Like, what restaurant do they have a reservation at?"

Natalie studies the book. "I'm pretty sure they're skipping dinner," she decides. She turns her attention to the box. "Maybe these were Mom's secret guilty pleasure. Maybe she read them in the bathtub."

"Did Mom even take baths?" asks Jordan. "I think I remember her taking a bath, like, once, ever, when she strained her back. And yet we kept giving her bath salts and candles for Mother's Day as though she had all day to soak."

"Kids are the worst," says Natalie. "No awareness of context."

"Can't read the room," agrees Jordan.

Whether by accident or design all of the girls were late winter or early spring babies, so Theresa had them sleeping through the night in time for the first day of school in September. She never missed a year of teaching until she got sick. When Jordan thinks of Theresa she thinks of someone constantly in motion, buzzing from here to there, grading spelling tests at the kitchen table, carrying baskets of clean, unfolded laundry to each of their bedrooms, where she'd drop them on the floor with a *thunk* as if to say, *There. My part is done.*

"I never liked having to share her with her schoolkids," says Natalie. "I always wanted more of her." Jordan studies her sister. She remembers this about Natalie. The chaos of the house bothered her in a way it never bothered Jordan and Mae. She wanted quiet time, orderly meals, organized cabinets. "I think it's because I never got her all to myself. You had her when you were a baby, and Mae when we both left the house. But I never did."

Jordan doesn't know what to say to this, because it's true. She concentrates on a collection of plastic cups from Water Country, where they used to go once every summer, climbing the high ladders and skimming down the flumes.

Natalie stacks the cups into a tower and says, "What if we bought it?"

Jordan stops and stares at her. "What? No. With what money?"

"You make a ton of money."

"I make a good living," corrects Jordan. "But I live in an expensive city. I work long hours, every day. I wouldn't have time to come up here much." She pauses. "And maybe I'm saving for something."

"For what?" challenges Natalie.

"I'm not ready to talk about it. Why don't *you* buy it? With Austin's money."

"We don't live off Austin's money."

"I thought his parents were loaded."

"They are. But they're also big believers in self-sufficiency. They helped us buy the farm, but they don't give us regular money or anything. We live off what we make from the farm, which honestly is minimal, and the social media accounts."

"Wow," says Jordan. "I thought they were helping you. I didn't realize your accounts make that much."

"All of this stuff that never even got used," says Natalie, changing the subject. She holds up a metal rake–looking thing. "I mean, what even is this?"

Jordan examines the item, turning it this way and that. "Sand flea shovel," she says finally.

"I'm not sure I ever met a sand flea!" says Natalie. Then, quick as a wink, quicker even, she turns away from Jordan, and her shoulders begin to heave. She's crying.

"Nat! What is it? The sand fleas?"

Natalie shakes her head.

"Natalie." Jordan feels herself growing stern. "You can tell me." As the older sister, Jordan has seen Natalie through some sketchy times. Sophomore year of high school breakup with that kid Michael. The drunken prom night incident of junior year, 2009. The pregnancy scare freshman year of college. *Innumerable* friend dramas.

Natalie turns and wipes her nose. "Okay," she says. "Hold on. I'll pull it up." Natalie sits on a meditation cushion in the middle of the donate pile, scrolls through her phone, and holds the screen up to Jordan. Jordan sees an article on the *New York Magazine* website, with a photo of Natalie wearing a long flowered dress and holding a loaf of homemade bread. "Trad Dad wants her barefoot and pregnant," says the caption.

Jordan shoots her eyebrows up.

Natalie thought again of the Sisterhood Napa trip and how much the exclusion had smarted. She'd eased the sting by telling herself how busy she was, how fulfilled. If the Sisterhood wanted to exclude her, let them. She had Austin and the kids and the farm. She had nearly a million and a half followers. In April she caught the big kahuna. *New York Magazine* was going to write an article featuring five tradwives, and Natalie was one. In late May they sent a reporter and a photographer. The reporter was a sardonic twentysomething with a Brooklyn address, baggy jeans, and vintage brown boots she didn't want to get dirty. (Natalie offered her muck boots.) The photographer took pictures at milking time, pictures of the baby-blue stove, pictures of Evangeline and Scarlett doing schoolwork at the farmhouse table.

The reporter wanted to see Natalie's closet, which was not as strange a request as it might seem because Natalie often posted photos of her closet. It was full of flowered material and linens, and, yes, gingham. (She'd bought the gingham as a lark but it turned out she actually looked pretty good in it: #goodingingham.)

"When did you decide to become a tradwife?" the reporter asked her, when they sat at the farmhouse table with cups of tea and Natalie's famous peanut butter cookies.

"I didn't decide to be," Natalie corrected. "It's a hashtag, yes, but this is who I am. It's my most authentic self." She smiled a soft, feminine smile, like a woman in a vintage Summer's Eve commercial she had once seen on YouTube. She spread her arms wide to include the whole of the valley, and the mountains beyond.

Then Austin came in from the barn. Natalie hadn't planned on Austin being part of the interview; the photographer had gotten a photo of him and Natalie and the kids. He'd played his part. But Austin loved those peanut butter cookies. He sat down.

"What do *you* think of all of this?" the reporter asked Austin. "This tradwife empire."

Natalie saw Austin look uncertain, the half-bitten cookie in his hand. Austin has many, many positive qualities, but "polished" isn't one of them. Austin said, "I like . . ." He paused, and Natalie's palms started to sweat. Truth be told, Austin *doesn't* love the social media empire. He accepts it because it's important to Natalie, and because he loves his family, and because it provides income that feeds his true love: the farm. "I like all the things that Natalie does for me," he said, smiling his big, goofy, sunny smile. "I *love* these cookies."

Natalie tried to kick him under the table; his leg was too far away. "All of the things I do for the family, you mean," corrected Natalie.

"Sure," said Austin affably. "Same thing. I love being together in our lives. I love the family we've created. We're still creating. If I could have Natalie barefoot and pregnant forever, I would." He winked.

"He's kidding, obviously," said Natalie. She sent Austin a murderous glance. *She* knew this was an example of Austin's offbeat sense of humor, but how was anybody else going to know that if the reporter didn't understand it? Then she saw the gleam in the reporter's eyes. The damage was done.

"You have a degree in women's studies from Wesleyan University, is that right?" asked the reporter. She had changed out of the muck boots in the mudroom and was back in her Brooklyn boots. She tapped the heel of one against the toe of the other.

"I have a double major in psychology and Gender and Sexuality, with a minor in data analysis," said Natalie, sitting up straight. It felt good to say that again, because sometimes she forgot. "I worked for a wearable-tech start-up in Boston before we moved here."

"Interesting! Why'd you leave that job?"

What Austin probably meant to say was *We decided together to make a big life change.* But what he actually said was "She left for me." That part was in the article too.

"Oh my god, Natalie," says Jordan now. "Barefoot and pregnant? Why would he *say* something like that?"

"He didn't mean it in a bad way."

"Is there a good way to mean it?"

"He was *joking*," says Natalie. "It was part of a bigger thought, but the reporter only took what she wanted. You know Austin! He's a goofball. He didn't mean anything by it. He was just supposed to look good in the photos. He went off script."

"I'll say," says Jordan. "Wow. They made it the *caption*."

"And the pull quote," says Natalie miserably.

"There are thousands of comments on this article." Jordan clicks on one. She cringes. Another. She shudders. On and on they go, and on and on and on. "You could spend days inside the comments section."

"But you've seen worse, right?" Natalie is desperate now, desperate for her sister to make her feel better. "You've seen some really bad stuff, and you've fixed it."

"I've seen some things," says Jordan, her expression unreadable.

"You have to help me, Jordan. I can't have this happen."

"You can't have what, exactly, happen?"

"*This.*" She gestures toward the phone. "Any of it." Jordan is still looking through the comments. "I can't have the wave of public opinion turn against me. I can't lose all of my sponsorships. *Please*, help me."

Instead of saying what Natalie wants her to say, which is *of course I'll help you*, Jordan asks, "What did Austin say?"

Natalie crosses her arms. "We haven't had a chance to talk it through. But I'm sure he'd say I'm overreacting."

Jordan blows out a puff of air that, if it were 2004, the year of Jordan's Bad Bangs, would have raised said bangs and settled them back down. "I think you need to figure out what he was doing, Natalie. I think that's your first step, before you figure out how to handle it."

"I told you! He was joking. He made a bad joke."

"I don't know, Nat," she says. "This seems bigger than a joke. This seems like—I mean, is this really what he thinks, maybe? And that's the real issue?"

Natalie's ire rises as swiftly as a river with a broken dam. "Oh my *god*, Jordan. Are you serious right now?"

"Yeah?"

"That's not what he thinks."

"If you say so."

"So you'll help me, right?"

Jordan says, "I don't think I can."

• • •

For what is probably the one time in the history of the universe, the second half of the ride to Logan is smooth as whipped butter, and Mae and Leo are at the arrivals pickup area well ahead of time. She chooses a spot that she hopes is out of view of airport security (those guys are famously scary), unloads Leo from the car, and takes him through his warm-up exercises.

Leo does beautifully, considering this is a new and potentially stressful environment with all manner of people coming in and out of the doors. A wheelchair, a woman on crutches, small, shrieking children, rumbling luggage carts. Through all of this, Leo keeps his attention on Mae. He's amazing! Should she record? Hal should see this. There's nowhere to prop her phone that makes sense but she does her best to hold it in one hand and capture the highlights. *Good boy, Leo.*

But.

After that.

It's while she's trying to manage the phone and the treat pouch and the leash that she takes her eye off the environment. ("Never, ever take your eyes off the environment." —Hal Miller.) This means that Leo sees a small white fluffball about thirty feet away before Mae does, and by the time Mae clocks it Leo is deep into his reaction. Like, really deep.

He stiffens. He looks like he wants to murder Fluffball. He lunges, pulling so hard on the leash that it takes every ounce of Mae's strength to hold him back; there is a split second when she thinks he might actually pull her over. People are staring. Children are backing away.

"Sheeee-it," says a bystander.

Fluffball's owner is a man a little younger than Calvin. He scoops up Fluffball and backs away, yelling, "You shouldn't have a dog like that out in public!"

Mae's face is flaming. Her heart is beating so fast she feels like she just hiked Gregory Canyon to the Amphitheater, one of Boulder's hardest hikes. She starts to say *I'm just—* but the man yells, "Security!" so loud that her voice is drowned out.

Mae blocks Leo's sight line with her body and gets him back into the car as swiftly as possible. He's over the threshold now; all she can do is remove him from the situation and allow him to calm down.

Mae gets in the back seat with Leo, locks the doors, and puts up the windows except for a three-inch gap. Leo's paws are scrabbling at the windows. He barks and whines until the other dog is completely out of his sight. His tongue is long, and his breathing is frantic. It takes a long time for it to become un-frantic. She waits, and when Leo's breathing starts to slow she strokes him along his side until his tongue returns to his mouth, until his heartbeat slows. Finally, hers does too.

"I'm sorry, buddy," she whispers. "That was my fault. I wasn't paying attention. I'm the worst." She feels terrible. She should never have trusted herself to take on a board-and-train. She's not ready. She's twenty-nine years old, and she's not ready for anything. She has nothing to show for the seven years between college and now. No home, no money, no real job, no prospects. No partner. No mom.

She breathes in and out, but when she exhales what comes out is not a breath but a shuddering sob. Suddenly she's ugly crying, and she can't stop. Mae is wearing a tank top, so she doesn't even have a sleeve with which to stem the flow of tears. She rummages on the floor, and under the driver's seat she finds a napkin from In-N-Out Burger. It's hard to tell if the napkin is actively dirty or merely crumpled, but it will have to do.

She blows her nose exuberantly. Theresa used to tell Mae she could summon the angels from the gates of heaven with how loudly she blew her nose, and remembering this almost makes her cry harder. It was a funny expression for somebody who never went to church.

When she leans with her back to the window, legs out across the back seat, spent, Leo puts his big, funny, square, offensive to some-but-not-to-her head in Mae's lap. He's spent too. She strokes his cheek and closes her eyes. Then she snaps them open because in all the excitement she has forgotten to check the status of Kara's flight on her phone.

The plane landed nineteen minutes ago.

She takes one more swipe at her face, removes Leo's head from her lap, lays it on the seat of the car, and opens the car door just enough so that she can squeeze out and Leo can't. She scans the crowd exiting the baggage claim area and sees a familiar woman wearing a blue flowered sundress and carrying a light blue shoulder bag. Kara! Kara has cut her dark blond hair since the wedding. It was longer and wavier then; now it falls to her shoulders, and it's blown stick straight. Minimal makeup, clear skin, a familiar smile, with a space between her two front teeth that would have been corrected if she'd grown up like the Shipman girls.

Mae steps into Kara's arms and they hug. It's a long hug, a hug of friendship and comfort, and now Leo, at least, knows one of Mae's secrets: She doesn't hate Kara. She actively *likes* Kara. Kara likes her. Kara and Mae are friends. *Don't tell anyone, Leo.* But also, tell everyone, because Mae is an adult, and she's allowed to make her own decisions, separate from her sisters. She is allowed to choose her own friends.

"I'm so happy to see you, Mae," Kara says. "Have you been crying?"

"I'm so happy to see *you*," says Mae, ignoring the question. It's not like Kara has never seen her cry before—Kara saw the Shipman family during the darkest of their days. She's seen them all cry and snipe at each other and laugh maniacally and sit quietly, all energy drained from them—but there's something humiliating about crying now, more than two years later, in the arrivals area of Terminal B. She tries to pull herself together and says, "Oh! Let me introduce you to Leo. Kara, Leo. Leo, Kara." Leo, exhausted now, accepts this visitor amiably (*good boy, Leo*).

Kara hesitates.

"Is your door locked?" asks Mae. She presses the button on the key. It's unlocked, but Kara is still standing there. "You're not scared of dogs, are you?" Would she have had reason to know this? The last beloved Shipman family dog, Coco, had died when Mae was a junior in college, and she hadn't been replaced, so there had been no dog around during Theresa's illness. Is Kara one of those people who assumes all pit bulls are evil? Mae will have to set her straight on that. Kara will love Leo once she gets to know him! Wait until she sees him roll over and play dead; wait until she sees how he can spin on command. He can't do those things yet, but Mae is going to teach him.

"Your father didn't tell you?" asks Kara.

"Tell me what?"

"I can't believe he didn't tell you. I'm allergic to dogs."

"Ohhh," says Mae. "No! No. Really?" How could her father have neglected this piece of information when he saw not one but two dogs in the house?

"Really and truly. I can take medicine, but . . . it's not ideal."

"Shit," says Mae. "I'm so sorry. What do we do? Natalie's dog is at the house." She thinks of Cinnamon's copious shedding. She found a golden tumbleweed in her sneaker just before she left; you could knit a sweater from what Natalie swept up from the sunroom yesterday.

Kara shrugs. "I'll pick up some antihistamines and hope for the best. Should we put this in the trunk?" She indicates her bag.

"No," says Mae. The trunk is where the rest of her life lives. "I'll squeeze it in back with Leo." She takes Kara's bag from her and wedges it in the back footwell, under the pile of pillows and blankets.

Kara slides into the passenger seat and cracks the window. Mae hears her sisters' voices in her head. *If you're allergic to dogs, don't come!* they would say. *Go back to Lenox! Better yet, go back to Ohio!* But Mae doesn't want Kara to go back. She wants her right here.

They're off! They pass Logan's long-term parking options and the giant white cross that sits atop Orient Heights; they pass budget hotels and strip malls galore. If there are few beaches as pretty as the ones you get on the Seacoast, thinks Mae, there are few drives as un-pretty as the route to get there from the airport. They are comfortably silent for the first part of the ride.

"How was the visit with your mom?" Mae asks as they merge onto Route 1.

"Not great," says Kara. "It was her birthday, that's why I went out—but it's never great."

"I'm sorry," says Mae. "Do you want to talk about it?"

"No. Maybe. I don't know. We have a lot of baggage, the two of us, and we spend most of our time tiptoeing around it, pretending everything is okay." Mae knows the barest outlines of Kara's story—single mom; alcoholic, absent dad; free school lunches; a scholarship to study nursing at Ohio State, where she maintained a 4.0 and graduated with distinction. But of course Mae doesn't know how that felt, what Kara's life looked like from the inside. "It's exhausting. Honestly, she needs to do something about her drinking, but I couldn't bring that up on her *birthday.*"

Mae and her sisters have been so well cared for, so carefully tended, like hothouse flowers, their biggest complaint being—what? A curfew earlier than they thought was fair? Having to share a bathroom? She's embarrassed for them, thinking about how they must look to Kara. She wants to put her hand over the ache in Kara's heart.

"I'm sorry," Mae says again.

"It's okay. It is what it is. I'm happy you all had some time with just your dad, and now I'm really happy to be here. I can't wait to see the house."

"I can't believe you've never seen it."

"Your dad and I only reconnected in September, remember?" Mae hears Natalie's voice in her head, calling *reconnected* a euphemism.

(*Be quiet, Natalie.*) "He came out here a couple of times over the winter, to check on it, get it ready for renters. I never asked to come. I thought maybe it was a place he needed to go to think about your mom."

THEY'RE MAKING THEIR way past the shopping centers, the gas stations, the iconic hulk of Kowloon Restaurant.

"How'd it go when he told you all about selling? From your point of view?"

"Well," says Mae carefully. "Natalie and I are more upset than Jordan. You know her, Miss Practicality. She sees how it makes financial sense. Natalie and I want to keep it forever. And I—" She almost starts to cry anew, thinking about the little dream she had of living in the house indefinitely. "I'm sad," she says finally. "Yeah, I'm sad about it, for sure."

"I'm sorry," says Kara. She squeezes Mae's hand. After a beat she asks, "Are they blaming me?" Mae doesn't want to lie, so she pretends to be very busy checking the GPS and remains silent, but they've left Route 1 and they're traveling north on the highway, so there's nothing to check. "I know they are," says Kara. "I get it. It's all part of the package."

"I'm sorry," says Mae.

"Don't be. I'll be fine. I'm tough! I've handled worse." Kara turns her face toward the window, and her blown-out hair swings. Softly, like she's just telling the outside world, she says, "Much worse."

To give Kara the full experience Mae exits the highway in Salisbury, and before long they're crossing the causeway leading to Hampton, with water on both sides of them, and then, finally, into Hampton proper, with the sandy beaches to their right. They may as well be on a whole different planet from where they started their journey. Mae lowers the back right window enough to let Leo stick his snout out, and Kara lowers hers too.

Kara can't get enough of it. She squeals at the wide sandy beach, points out the people on the deck of Bernie's, the stands selling fried dough, the cat walking on a leash. Even The Wall that hides a section of Hampton Beach from the road delights her, especially when Mae tells her that this is where you'll find the biggest number of surfers on any given morning.

"But this beach is nothing," says Mae, even though this beach is definitely not nothing. "Wait until you see our beach." Jenness won't be their beach after this summer! Probably not even after this week! Someone will put in an offer at the open house; that's how things go in today's market.

Everything is so sad, to Mae. The mom holding the hand of a little girl to cross the street is sad, because someday that mom will be gone and the little girl might be living out of her car, training dogs for a living. The young couple with their arms slung across each other's shoulders is sad, because they might break up tomorrow, and one or the other will have a broken heart, because breakups are rarely mutual. The old lady in a wheelchair, being pushed by a man in a hat who's bending over the woman, saying something that's making them both laugh—sad! They may be laughing, but it's still sad.

Kara must have caught something in Mae's expression because she says, "I'm sorry. I'm really sorry about the house."

"It's not just the house," says Mae, before she can check herself.

Kara's face, turned toward her, is so full of kindness and concern. The crosswalk empties, and Mae drives on. Should she tell Kara? If she unburdens herself, will she feel better or worse?

"What is it? You can talk to me." Kara's hands, folded in her lap, are so familiar to Mae—except for the simple gold wedding band she now wears; of course that's a change. Mae can see Kara's hands holding a cup of water so Theresa could drink from it, pulling the bedsheets taut, shaking pills into Mae's hand so Mae could help her mother swallow them. Checking Theresa's pulse, checking her temperature, checking on all of them.

Mae shakes her head. "It's okay," she says. "It's not a big deal. I'm having some money troubles. It's so boring." She hears her voice catch, and she swallows down the accompanying lump. She will not cry again, and she will not elaborate. But then what will she do? *What is your plan?* as Jordan would say. Jordan likes there to always be a plan.

"Can you tell your sisters or your father? Can they help you?"

"No. Maybe."

"I think you should."

They are entering Rye and the scenery takes over the conversation for a moment. "Welcome to paradise," Mae says.

"Wow," says Kara. "I mean. Wow. This is even prettier than I imagined." Mae feels proud, like she created the scene herself, as the road curves and curves again and the magnificent mansions come into view, and across the street from them, the endless expanse of ocean, just a small froth of whitecaps, a single gull flying above, a runner moving along the rock-bordered path. It's a picture-perfect summer day.

They pass the beach parking lot, and Summer Sessions, and The Carriage House, and, as they're about to pull into the driveway, Kara says, "Talk to your family, Mae. If there's anything my work has taught me, it's don't waste time keeping things to yourself that people can help you with."

WHAT REALLY RUINED things in Boulder for Mae was the same thing that Theresa had kindly called Mae's "willingness to see only the best in people." More roughly translated, her naivete.

"You're always so happy," a guy she'd dated in college said to her once. "I don't get it."

"What's not to be happy about?" asked Mae. "I mean, look." They were seniors at the University of Vermont, and Mae lived with three roommates in a third-floor apartment on South Willard. The view downhill to Lake Champlain, with the Adirondacks in the distance, was stunning. They were about to embark on their own, which was exciting, but for the time being, they were still dependent enough on their parents to keep real-life troubles at bay, which was comforting. Really, what *wasn't* there to be happy about?

Of the three Shipman girls, Mae had a reputation as the "most chill." Within her friend group at Lenox Memorial she was known as the one to whom others could bring their problems because her own were so light that they barely registered on the scale. She was the diplomat, the mediator, the calm in the chaos.

Mae and the college boyfriend did not last past the holiday break of senior year, and anyway, soon after graduation, Mae and her friend Alice moved to Boulder, to begin their young adult lives. It was a natural progression from Church Street to Pearl Street, from the Green Mountains to the Flatirons, from vodka tonics at Nectar's to margaritas at the Rio.

She got a job working for the National Oceanic and Atmospheric Administration, one of the many institutes that call Boulder home. She put her degree in environmental science to excellent use. She spent most of what she made on rent, on ski weekends at Keystone and Copper, on cocktails and dinners out and life in general. Four and a half years went by, easy peasy. She got her second tattoo, a mountain, on her hip, to go with the infinity sign she got on her ankle in college.

Then Theresa got sick. Toward the end Mae took a leave of absence from her job and went home to Lenox. While she was gone, Alice got a job at a tech start-up in the Bay Area and began plotting her move farther west. Mae should come! They'd take San Francisco by storm! They'd get millionaires to buy them drinks until they invented something that turned them into millionaires themselves!

But Theresa got sicker and sicker, and was one day gone.

How could this be? How could life feel so different almost overnight? Since college Mae had seen her parents only three times a year on average: on her annual visit to the beach house; when she returned to Lenox at Christmas; and the one time each year her parents flew out to Colorado. This usually happened in springtime, during the Massachusetts school break, when their home state was a mud pit formed from melting snow or driving rain but the sun was shining in Boulder and the hiking trails were dry and open for business. She was an adult now, launched, a separate being from her family. How could the absence of someone she hadn't seen on a daily basis for years hurt like this, every single day, multiple times a day?

Mae didn't have the energy a move with Alice to San Francisco would require. Where her joy had been, her zest for life, there was now only a void; where purpose, a gaping uncertainty. Alice left for San Francisco without her.

Mae, unable to afford the rent for their apartment on her own, knew she had to advertise for a roommate. She kept putting off this task, not wanting to share her grief with a stranger. She started to eat through the meager savings she'd accumulated, not just on rent, but on burritos, on the tattoo of a shooting star she got at Ink It from a man named Tony. A couple of roommates came and went, but nobody was dependable, everybody was transitory.

Each time she talked to her sisters she was astonished at the speed with which they seemed to be processing the loss of their mother. They were sad, yes, even devastated, but they were also busy, and being busy was a blessing. Their lives were ordered, their futures clear.

She began to resent the fact that her sisters had had more time with Theresa than she had. They were further along in their adult lives when she died, while Mae still felt like a baby. Theresa had seen them all the way through their twenties while Mae was stuck, unmoored, untended to, in what nobody told you was one of the most difficult and most confusing decades.

Why didn't Mae stay busy? Natalie suggested. Get a second job! Join a club!

"Like, a knitting club?" Mae was incredulous that her sister would suggest this.

"I was thinking more like rock climbing."

Mae did the opposite. She quit her job, the one with the health insurance and the government wage that, if not high, was at least steady.

"Sounds like self-sabotage to me," said Jordan.

"Maybe it is," said Mae, challengingly.

It seemed so effortless for everyone else, including her sisters, to acquire the accoutrements of adulthood—pajama sets, espresso makers, responsibility—seemingly without doubt or suffering. As a kid she'd thought (if she'd thought about grown-ups at all) that this happened naturally. But now she saw that there is a series of arduous steps you must climb, one by one, and that she missed a few. She had stumbled on the staircase, and she wasn't sure how to right herself.

Stillness hurt the most, so she moved. She went on hikes: Green Mountain. Doudy Draw. Chautauqua to the Arch. It was beautiful up there, of course, but also lonely. With such unfiltered views Mae felt small and a little bit scared.

Alice met someone out in San Francisco; in short order, *really very quickly*, she was engaged. Thankfully she chose as her bridesmaids her sister, her future sister-in-law, and her best friend from high school, saving Mae the tremendous expense of bridal party membership. But she couldn't say no to the bachelorette party in Nashville, nor the destination wedding weekend in Savannah, both of which required hundreds of dollars in plane fare and hotels. The allure of Afterpay became too strong to resist.

She went back to Ink It for another tattoo: the one of her mother's handwriting on her wrist.

While Tony was tattooing her they got to talking. Tony had an extra bedroom in his place in Gunbarrel, an older condo off Twin Lakes Road, he was looking to fill. He'd give Mae a rent reduction if she worked the front desk at the tattoo parlor two nights a week. She was living off the fumes of her savings; she gave notice on the apartment she used to share with Alice and headed for Gunbarrel.

"Don't start sleeping with him," said Jordan when Mae called to report this development. "It could get messy."

Mae said, "Thanks for the vote of confidence." (She was already sleeping with Tony.) She'd need more than two nights of employment, though. She started delivering for Uber Eats. She added in one night as a barback on Pearl Street. By the one-year anniversary of Theresa's death she was officially part of the gig economy—overemployed and underinsured.

Then a friend of a friend told her about a dog care and training center that was looking for a dog walker. The guy's name was Hal Miller; the place was called Dog On It. (Mae wasn't sure about the name, but okay. She'd call. She loved dogs!)

Hal was not what she expected a dog trainer, or a person named Hal, to look like. She'd expected—from the name, but also from a certain gravelly character to his voice—a weathered man close to her father's age, one of those old-timers you sometimes see in Colorado, wearing an old Rockies hat and muttering about what the city was like in the eighties, before the trust-funders came in. But Hal was not so much older than Mae! Thirty-four, he told her. He looked even younger, with a baby face and an almost obscene amount of hair, or so said Tony when he met Hal. (Tony had started balding at twenty-two so he shaved his head religiously and tattooed a snake above his eyebrow to draw attention away from his hairline.)

Hal was actually quite famous in the Boulder dog world. He was always fully booked for private training sessions at least a month out. He had worked for a long time at a variety of shelters, taking in dogs from all over, and almost nothing fazed him. His demeanor was calm and professorial. Also somehow sexy.

Hal was sparing with the details of his personal life, although Mae knew that he'd been married and that he and his ex-wife shared custody of their four-year-old son, who lived most of the year with his mother in Denver. Hal had retained custody of their dog, a basset named Angela, pun intended, and he had a constant stream of other dogs boarding with him, either for his sought-after board-and-train program, or because people who could afford it would rather have their dogs stay in Hal's bungalow on Mapleton Hill, with its little square of fenced-in yard, than in an actual kennel.

With Hal, Mae started walking one dog at a time, then two, then, when her dexterity improved, three. "You have gorgeous leash skills," Hal told her, and Mae, batting her eyes in a way she hoped was fake-coquettish, said, "That's what all the boys tell me." Were they flirting? Mae couldn't tell, but she knew she was starting to feel a little better, or at least a little more distracted, around Hal, which felt pretty much the same as better.

Tony suggested that if Mae gave up her bedroom and shared his they could rent out the one she was in, thereby reducing Mae's share of the rent even further. It made financial sense, and she was lonely, so she said yes.

Six more months went by like this. Tony gave her her next tattoo and the next one after that, and after that. He gave her an extravagant vine that curled around her right arm (for free), and he rubbed the healing ointment on it every night in a way that could only be described as erotic. But he was *emotional*, fickle, confusing, leading Mae into loud, dramatic fights over the silliest things, and this made her feel like they were characters in a Tennessee Williams play.

"Fine!" Tony screamed at her one night, over something she can no longer remember. "*Go*, then!"

"I *will*!" she screamed back, feeling like a stranger to herself (what had happened to being the chill one?). She had nowhere to go, so she drove her Subaru around the block and returned to Tony's. She wanted her own room back, but she couldn't afford to pay for it. What strange bedfellows hath the rental market wrought, she thought grimly.

From dog walks Mae progressed to accompanying Hal to clients' homes for private training sessions. She hung in the background and watched Hal take the owners of new puppies through the basic commands: *sit, stay, heel, come.*

At the tattoo parlor she rang up customers and presented them with a clipboard of waivers to sign. She checked IDs. Wherever she went she was always an apprentice, never a bride. She was no longer putting her degree in environmental science to excellent use, or any use whatsoever. She was flailing, she knew this, but she didn't know how to un-flail.

At night she scrolled through TikTok and Instagram, sometimes watching videos or reels of Natalie on the dairy farm, in muck boots and mascara. She wanted to talk to her more often than she did, but there was the difference in time zones, and she knew (from those same videos and reels) that Natalie and Austin had a strict nine thirty bedtime because their mornings started so early. She imagined Natalie in a long white nightgown with elastic at the wrists, like something Emily Dickinson would wear, though she knew that in fact Natalie wore a ragged Wesleyan Cardinals T-shirt and a pair of short-shorts to bed.

After a time Hal let her move on from observing to actually taking part in the training sessions. It turned out that Mae had a knack! She had a knack for working with the most troublesome dogs, the ones with reactivity or fear-based aggression; the ones who needed not just a few basic training sessions but hours of one-on-one attention so they could live comfortably in the world.

She might have gone on like this forever, balanced on the knife's edge between debt and solvency, if she hadn't gotten that box in the mail a month ago and lost all of her money. She asked Tony if she could pay him the next month's rent a little later. "You know I'm good for it," she said, although the truth was she wasn't.

Tony said no. She packed up her half of the bedroom, made two trips to a storage unit she couldn't afford, and began the no-fixed-address portion of her young adulthood. A situation that would once have seemed inconceivable was now her reality. Hal offered her the chance to take on Leo for the board-and-train session right before she got the email from Calvin, and that's when she picked up Leo and set off east. Family bonding time sounded lovely. And also, so did a soft place to land.

• • •

Jordan and Natalie have turned the garage storeroom inside out and somehow this seems significant, like they've turned out their own emotions, leaving them sitting in three piles. Keep, donate, trash. But it's hard to know which emotion to put in which pile.

Jordan puts the Natalie situation in the mental container of things she doesn't know what to do with, along with Bernadette on Memorial Day, along with Samantha Braddock. She goes into the house to wash her hands and face, and she returns to the garage just as Mae's car comes down the driveway. The garage door is open, and part of her wants to close it, to shield herself and Natalie from what's coming next. If they can't see Kara approaching their mother's house, maybe it isn't actually happening.

"Ready for this?" she asks Natalie.

Natalie shakes her head but doesn't say anything. Natalie is angry with Jordan, it's clear. Natalie wants her to say, *Do these three things, Natalie, and all of your troubles will vanish.* But the situation feels bigger than that. Austin's comments don't seem so much like a joke to Jordan as a deeper statement about Natalie and Austin's marriage, and how is Jordan supposed to solve a problem with her sister's marriage? If there is a problem? Austin and his pack of brothers alternatively fascinate and mystify Jordan, but she's never had any reason to think anything but the best of him. This comment, though.

"How are we going to play it?" Jordan asks Natalie. For certain situations in life there is a basic rulebook, but Jordan has never read the one about what to do when your father's new wife, who was once his first wife's hospice nurse, comes to see the first wife's family home the same week the home is going on the market.

Natalie adjusts her ponytail and sighs. Jordan thinks if she waits a minute without saying anything Natalie might answer. "Cordial but cold," Natalie says finally.

Jordan tries not to sound too eager. "Like, arctic cold?"

Natalie thinks about this and adjusts. "Cool."

"Copy that." Then: "Is she going to hug us?"

Natalie turns to her. "*Is* she? I hope not. What do we do if she wants to?"

"Present with straitjacket arms," Jordan advises. "Very effective." She folds her arms across the front of her body, between her chest and her pelvis, to demonstrate.

There's still tension, and Natalie's smile is reluctant, but it's there. Mae's Subaru tries to find a space in the crowded driveway behind Calvin's and Natalie's vehicles. Mae parks at a slant, somehow blocking both cars in at once. Natalie is holding the baby monitor, and just then they hear Caspian making the first waking-up-from-a-nap noises.

"Shoot," says Natalie. "Rotten timing! I'd better go up."

"No," hisses Jordan. "Don't leave me here alone."

"Duty calls."

"He's not crying! He sounds quite happy up there."

"Sorry not sorry," says Natalie, and just like that she's gone.

Karma really is a bitch, Jordan thinks.

An exorbitant amount of car activity follows: Mae emerges first. Then she opens the door for Leo but instructs him to wait.

"This is part of his training," she calls to Jordan. "It's a safety thing, and I'm working on his impulse control."

When she releases Leo, he shoots out like the car is a cannon, stopping only because Mae is holding the leash. Then the passenger door opens, and out comes Kara. Jordan hasn't seen Kara since Theresa's funeral but she looks the same. Her hair is a little shorter, a little straighter. When she smiles, as she does uncertainly, she has the same space between her front teeth.

"Jordan," says Kara. "Hi. It's really good to see you." Jordan has the straitjacket arms ready, but Kara, probably reading the body language, doesn't go in for a hug. Jordan had vowed to remain stoic, even stiff, so she's surprised and offended by the rush of emotions that hits her. Kara is a reminder of the worst time of their lives, but she's also a link to the days when Theresa was still with them, to some of the last best days too. She was someone who cared for Theresa but also cared for the rest of them, who explained to them what they could expect at each stage, all the way until the end. Jordan can't encapsulate all of this into words, nor does she want to, because the emotions feel too raw and close to the surface, so she says, "Hi, Kara," and turns away before any dampness in her eyes gives her away.

This is when Calvin comes out of the house in his new glasses. He and Kara embrace, but they are mindful of their audience, and the embrace is short. It's tight, though, definitely tight. Calvin takes Kara's bag and says, "I'll give you the tour."

"I'm going to walk Leo over near the patio," says Mae.

Jordan follows her sister and watches Mae guide Leo away from the beach, where he really wants to go, and to the small grassy area. After he does his business she has him sit, then lie down, then sit again.

"How was it? Was it awful?" Jordan asks.

Mae looks up, startled. "What? Well, there was this one guy, and Leo—"

"Not *Leo*. Kara!"

"Oh! Sure, yeah, pretty awful. I mean, I survived."

"But barely?" asks Jordan hopefully.

"Right. Barely."

Then Natalie is there, holding Caspian, who has her ponytail in his fist. "I snuck down when they were in Mom and Dad's room. The girls are in the sunroom. I don't think I prepped them enough. What do I call her? 'Your new grandmother?'"

"Definitely not," says Jordan.

"What, then?"

"Your grandfather's child bride."

Natalie rolls her eyes. "Much better." She releases her hair from Caspian's hold and sits on one of the loungers. Caspian, still sleepy, lays his head on her chest. Mae sits in one of the regular chairs, holding Leo's leash, and Jordan hovers, full of confused energy.

"They were so young when Mom died," continues Natalie. "Only Evangeline has any real memories. It breaks my heart to realize they didn't really know her. Or she, them." Jordan watches her sit with that for a moment, then Natalie says, "Did she do anything egregious yet? Anything we can complain about?"

"Not yet," says Jordan. "Frankly, it's annoying."

"How about on the drive, Mae?"

"Hmm. Nope."

There's a long silence while all of the Shipman girls look out at the beach. The beachgoers are like characters in a play, and the Shipmans are the audience, in their own private box. Families, young couples, people walking alone, the occasional runner.

"You know," says Mae. "I don't think it was having no glasses that made Dad look vulnerable."

Jordan turns to her. "What do you mean?"

"I thought he looked like not himself without his glasses, but I don't think that was it. I think it was solitude."

"Oh, please, Mae."

"What?"

"Where's your *loyalty*?"

"It's not about loyalty."

"Of course it is," says Jordan. "Dad marrying Kara is disloyal to Mom. It's that simple. And if you're okay with that, you're disloyal to Mom too."

She almost says *and that's that*, and makes a motion like she's dusting off her palms, because Mae is so much younger and has always listened to Jordan. So she's surprised when Mae meets her gaze and shakes her head.

"I disagree," she says. "I think there's more than one kind of love. I think Dad has found another kind, and maybe that's okay."

It's a wise thing for Mae to say, and it may even be true, and these things make Jordan even more angry, just the way the rush of feelings when she saw Kara made her feel confused. "Well, there shouldn't be," she spits. "There should only be one."

From the upper deck, the one outside the primary bedroom, Kara sneezes.

• • •

Natalie offers to make dinner for everyone and disappears into the kitchen with Caspian. Mae goes in search of Leo, who'd been so tired from the airport adventure that he'd conked out in the sunroom.

This is where she finds Evangeline sitting on the couch. Her spine is as straight and her bearing is as pleasing as a debutante's. In front of her are two sleeping dogs. Cinnamon lies on her left side and Leo on his right. Cinnamon's black lip is trembling with each exhale. Neither wakes when Mae comes in.

"Shhh." Evangeline lifts a finger to her lips, so Mae does an exaggerated tiptoe over to her and sits beside her on the couch. This is what she likes about being an aunt: being able to do silly things like exaggerated tiptoes and getting a good satisfying laugh from her audience.

"How long have you been sitting here?" she whispers.

"Awhile. Leo woke up when Cinnamon came in, then I sang them to sleep."

"You did? What'd you sing?"

"'Tomorrow.' From *Annie*." Without shame or embarrassment Evangeline opens her mouth and unleashes a verse: "*When I'm stuck* . . ." Her voice is high and clear and lovely, perfectly in tune, and Mae is mesmerized. None of the Shipman girls can sing. Where did Evangeline get this voice? Can Austin sing? She thinks back to Natalie and Austin's wedding at the Wentworth by the Sea hotel. She has a vague memory of Austin holding a microphone, but that's it. It had been a giant party of a wedding, and everyone had been tipsy or downright drunk, Mae included. "They settled down, and then they fell asleep."

"Amazing," says Mae, legitimately impressed. "Look at how they're lying. See? When a dog lies on his side like that it means he's completely relaxed. Dogs don't go into that position unless they feel really safe and protected. You're officially hired as my assistant dog trainer!"

"Really?"

"Definitely. Unfortunately, it's an unpaid position. But it's prestigious."

"What's that mean?"

"Important."

"Okay."

Then she asks Evangeline if she can video her singing to the dogs. She imagines sending the video to Human Leo, showing him how relaxed Leo is around another dog, how well cared for he is during his week with Mae.

"Okay," says Evangeline.

"I won't post it or anything. I might just send it to Leo's owner."

"I thought you were Leo's owner."

"Alas, I am not. I'm just Leo's trainer for the week."

"And then what?"

"And then I have to give him back to his real owner."

"Are you sad to do that?"

"I am. I'm very sad to do that." Again comes the pull on her heart.

Evangeline repeats the verse, and Mae captures it. "You can post it if you want." Is there something world-weary in this, or has Mae imagined it?

Evangeline leans against Mae like it's the most natural thing in the world. Her hair smells like strawberry shampoo and her hand is just a little sticky. Is this motherhood? wonders Mae. This deep and abiding sense of peace, the connection with another person—is this it? Could she do it one day?

She remembers Natalie's all-consuming fatigue the summer she was pregnant with Scarlett and Evangeline was still so little. Mae had stayed on the farm with the family for two weeks. She remembers how Natalie had to keep dragging herself from task to task because, well, she had no choice. To the barn, to the house, the crib, the kitchen. "Go rest," Mae had told her. "That's why I'm here." Natalie had said, "This is resting."

"I have to tell you something," whispers Evangeline.

"I'm all ears."

"I lost a tooth."

She unrolls her fingers to reveal the white nugget in the center of her palm. With her other hand she pulls down her lower lip to show Mae a hole in the center of her bottom row of teeth.

Mae says, "May I?" When Evangeline nods she picks the tooth up and studies it. It's so small! How did it possibly do any chewing or biting? "Wow," she says reverently.

Evangeline nods. "My first one."

Mae sits up straight, almost throwing Evangeline off of her. "Your first one?" Should Mae get Natalie? What is supposed to happen next? Evangeline nods and then confesses, "All my friends already lost their first ones. I've been wiggling it with my tongue."

"As you should!" says Mae. "The wiggling of a tooth is a rite of passage." Then she says, "Should we get your mom?" Evangeline considers, then shakes her head. "Are you going to put it under your pillow tonight?" Evangeline shakes her head more vehemently. "Why not?"

"Scared," she whispers.

"What are you scared of?" Mae hands the tooth back to Evangeline, who puts it down on the coffee table, where it looks even smaller, like a piece of rice that spilled out of somebody's take-out container.

"I don't want a little fairy flying around me."

Mae thinks about this. She doesn't blame Evangeline. *Grimms' Fairy Tales*, Santa coming down chimneys to bring presents, creatures flitting near pillows while you slumber. What outlandish scenarios we paint for children! It's a wonder, thinks Mae, that anyone comes out of childhood even remotely sane.

On the other hand, Evangeline has seen some real shit. She's seen a cow die in childbirth, another from pneumonia. She's witnessed stillbirths. Evangeline understands that a glass of milk is not just a beverage but a stop on the life-death continuum. With this vast life experience, shouldn't she be okay with a small money-dropping fairy?

"Did you?" asks Evangeline.

Mae snaps herself back to the conversation. "Did I what?"

"Did you used to like when the Tooth Fairy came?"

Mae squeezes her eyes shut, brings herself to their house on Galway Court, her twin bed with the light pink comforter. She used to have a little heart-shaped cushion with a small pocket on the front of it to hold the tooth. The pillow had belonged first to Jordan and then had been passed down to Natalie, then down again to Mae. By the time Mae started losing teeth, of course, her sisters were all done; Jordan was already in braces, her adult teeth established enough to need straightening, always so far ahead of Mae. "I liked the money, sure. Who doesn't?" Two dollars was the going rate then. Five for each front tooth. Mae remembers Jordan complaining that she used to get only a dollar and Theresa had said, "Inflation strikes even the fairy world." She probably had a wink in her voice, but Mae was too young, or simply too much of a believer, to catch it. She had believed so long in the Tooth Fairy, the Easter Bunny, even the St. Patrick's Day leprechaun, which should have strained even her stalwart credulity. Her family is right about her. She is too naive. And that's why she is where she is now—pretty much penniless, quite literally unhoused, and without a plan for how to get back on track.

Evangeline sucks on her bottom lip and says, "Yeah, I guess. I guess the money would be good."

"What would you buy with it?"

Evangeline thinks about it, really thinks, and then says, "A present for Mommy. A diamond necklace."

This kid is too good to be true. "Okay!" says Mae, encouragingly. "That's really nice." She won't pop the bubble of Evangeline's dream with an economics lesson. Instead she asks, "Do you miss your cows when you're gone, or do you like having a break from the farm?"

"Both."

"What's your favorite thing about them?"

"Their eyelashes," says Evangeline instantly.

"Nice!" says Mae. "Eyelashes. Love it. What about them?"

"They're long. And pretty. Sometimes they're blond and sometimes they're brown but they're so, so pretty."

"I'll have to look more closely next time I visit you."

The dogs begin to stir. Cinnamon stretches her front legs all the way straight, which is a signal that she's waking up. Evangeline slides off the couch and gets right down on the floor to pet her. "Shh, you can go back to sleep," she tells Cinnamon, like a miniature mother, but now Leo is stirring too.

"You're so good with animals," Mae tells her. "Do you want to live on a farm when you grow up?"

Evangeline nods and says, "I think I want to be a large-animal vet."

Mae says, "Like a large person who is also a vet, or a vet for large animals?"

Evangeline giggles. "A vet for large animals." She tells Mae about the vet who comes to their farm to give vaccinations, help out with births, check on new calves hours into their existence. They call him Dr. George, and he drives a red farm truck. ("Dr. George is superhot," Natalie once told Mae. "Like, he'd be July in a vet-of-the-month calendar.")

"I think that sounds like a noble pursuit," says Mae. "I really do. And I don't think you should wait until you grow up either. I think you should be a very small large-animal vet. You could be that as soon as today." Evangeline giggles again. Mae is killing it with this crowd!

Two things happen next.

Cinnamon rises and gives one of those full-body shakes that means she's ready to rock. Then, before either Mae or Evangeline can stop her, she flicks out her tongue toward the coffee table, faster than a lizard. The tooth is gone.

• • •

In the sunroom Jordan finds Evangeline sitting on the floor between the two dogs. They're both waiting and watching while Evangeline lines up tiny treats on the table. "Wait," Evangeline says to Leo, and then to Cinnamon, "Wait." She sounds exactly like Mae, commanding and patient. Then she releases them: "Okay!" And the dogs go crazy, snuffling along the table for the treats.

"Where's Auntie Mae?"

"She went to get me a tissue."

Jordan looks closely at Evangeline. Her bottom lip starts to wobble. "What's going on?"

Evangeline slaps her hand over her mouth like there's a creature in there she doesn't want to let out. "Nothing," she whispers into her hand.

"Are you sure?"

Her eyes fill, and she says, "Cinnamon ate my first lost tooth." She points to a hole in her mouth.

"Oh, no! How'd that happen?"

"It was on the table. She stuck her tongue out. And now I can't leave it for the Tooth Fairy even though I didn't know if I wanted to."

"I think we can write a note," says Jordan, "explaining what happened. I can help you." Evangeline is bringing out a gentleness Jordan didn't know she had.

"Okay," whispers Evangeline from behind her hand, "if you think that will count."

"It definitely counts. I have it on good authority. Do you want to go find your mom?" Evangeline nods. "Go ahead. She's in the kitchen with Caspian. Where's Scarlett?"

Evangeline removes her hand and then says, "Upstairs on the iPad."

"Ah." Jordan knows that Natalie is very strict about the kids using the iPad. This goes with her homeschooling-farm-rearing-family-first persona. Scarlett must have spotted a loophole and decided to dive right into it, like a proper middle child, no different from what Natalie herself would have done if iPads had existed when they were kids.

(*What comes around goes around,* Theresa might have said, had she been here, and a sharp pain hits Jordan somewhere—her soul?—when she realizes that she isn't.)

Just after Evangeline exits the room, Mae enters. The dogs rush up to Mae, maybe eager to share the tale of what she missed in her absence. She's holding a tissue in one hand and her cell phone in the other. "Evangeline went to find Natalie in the kitchen," Jordan explains.

"Okay," says Mae. She's looking at her phone. Jordan looks more closely at Mae. Mae wears an expression that, for lack of a better description, Jordan might call grouchy. "What's going on with you?"

"Nothing is going on. Why do you ask?"

"Because you look like a dog ate *your* first tooth."

Mae makes an annoyed face.

Jordan remembers Mae, at twelve, getting her period for the first time three days before Christmas. Jordan had been home from college for the holiday, and she'd been the one to pick Mae up from school because Theresa had been teaching her own class and Natalie had been in school herself. She'd felt very important and motherly, showing Mae the corner of the bathroom cabinet where all the supplies were kept, giving her Advil and a heating pad in case she had cramps. But she knew the real mother would be home in just a few hours. Now she's not the backup, she's the main event.

"I wish Dad wasn't selling the house. I was hoping to stay."

"Not that again," says Jordan.

"Yes, that again. To anyone with a heart, this is a big deal!"

"I have a heart, thank you very much. I just have a brain to go with it." She pauses. "How long were you hoping to stay?"

"I don't know. Until I save some money. Or forever."

Mae flops on the couch, and suddenly she's the defiant version of Mae. This version doesn't show up very often, but when she does, watch out. Mae was the baby who was chill until she wasn't, easygoing until she wanted (or didn't want) one thing, just one single thing, and then she dug in her heels so hard she simply could not be budged. They used to call it the Storm. *The Storm is brewing. The Storm is on the horizon. Hope the Storm passes quickly.* (Mae hated the Storm joke, it made her furious, so Jordan is careful not to bring it up now even though she's really tempted.)

Only Theresa could negotiate the Storm; she'd put on her metaphorical Hunter boots, zip up her waterproof jacket, and wade right in. Sometimes she'd get batted away, but more often she'd get Mae to see reason. *You can't wear a bathing suit to school because it's January, but you can wear it in the bathtub tonight. We are not having chocolate for dinner because I made roast chicken but I'll make chocolate pudding for dessert.* For the zillionth time in the past two years, and at least the thirteenth time today, Jordan wishes her mother were here.

Jordan looks at the tattoos on Mae's arms. She had started so small and innocuously—a hip, an ankle, the small shooting star on one forearm—but now she has dozens, and that seems to Jordan to be a whole different direction than adorable. She looks more closely and sees something on Mae's right wrist. She reaches for Mae's hand and holds it, opening the wrist out so she can see it. Mae doesn't pull back, she holds her arm steady, and when Jordan meets her eyes they're both tearing up. "When did you get this?" Jordan whispers. "How come I didn't notice it before?"

"This was one of my early ones," says Mae.

Jordan traces the tattoo with the index finger of her other hand. *Love, Mom,* in Theresa's distinctive handwriting, a precise cursive, the same cursive she wrote her grocery lists in, her thank-you notes; the same cursive she lamented over and over again that kids were no longer taught with regularity.

"There's a whole section on the website," says Mae, her voice catching. "Handwriting tattoos. It's really popular as an *in memoriam* thing." Jordan nods, too affected to speak. Several seconds pass, and then Mae takes her hand back, says, "I really, really wish I could live right here forever."

Instead of going through all the reasons why this makes no sense, Jordan says, "That sounds really lonely. Especially in the winter." In the winter, she'd see only surfers and dog walkers on the beach. Portsmouth remains lively, but life on the waterfront shuts down. Most of these houses are summer homes.

Mae takes a deep, shuddering breath and for a moment it seems like she's not going to say anything at all. Then she stands and walks to the window, looking out at the water. The tide is in, so the beach is smaller, but it's still bigger and wider than most beaches around. It's still the best beach. Mae says, "To me it sounds less lonely than the rest of life feels now."

"Mae!"

She turns. "It's true."

"I thought you loved it out there in Boulder."

"I did. I used to. Sometimes I do. But it feels different now." The last time Jordan visited Mae in Colorado was before Theresa got really sick. They'd all gone as a family for a long weekend. Even Natalie, who'd left the farm for two nights. They'd all loved the way the sun set behind the mountains; the way people were so much more laid-back and friendly than they were on the East Coast; the way you could witness the country's western expansion in the hard-packed hiking trails; the land beyond the city, which went all the way to the horizon, unbroken by the thick woods that line the highways in New England.

Has it really been that long since Jordan has been out there?

"What's different?"

Jordan's phone buzzes and she flips it so she can see the screen. It's Bernadette, of course. She flips it over. It feels important that she give Mae her full attention.

"It got different after Mom died. It turned out to be a really hard place to grieve, you know? It's so—dusty." Jordan moves closer to Mae so that their hips are touching. Poor Mae, all lonely and dusty and sad. "Everything there feels transient. People are always moving in, moving out, working all these small jobs to try to get them to add up to one job. Me too. Next year I'll be thirty, and I don't even have health insurance."

In retrospect, Jordan realizes this is not the hill to die on, but before retrospect arrives she says, "Hold up. You don't have *health insurance*?"

Mae bristles. "Jesus, Jordan. That is so not the biggest of my worries right now."

"Does Dad know?"

Mae's voice rises. "I don't know if Dad knows!" The Storm is coming back.

Jordan's voice goes louder to match Mae's. "You *have* to have health insurance, Mae!"

"*God*, Jordan. Get off my back."

They both stop, because Evangeline is there, as unobtrusive as a butler, saying, "Mommy wants to know if Auntie Mae can help her in the kitchen."

• • •

Natalie doesn't actually need help with dinner. (From Mae? *Please.*) But she heard Jordan's and Mae's raised voices so she'd sent Evangeline as a small emissary.

"Did you forget that I can't cook?" Mae asks, sulking her way into the kitchen.

"If you can chop, you can cook." Natalie sets Mae up with an onion, a cutting board, and a knife. "Careful you don't cut yourself," she says. "The knives in this house are so dull. They're a disgrace to knives. I don't think they've been sharpened since before Mom got sick." Mae sets to work on her onion. Natalie clears her throat and says, "Hey, have you looked at any of my accounts since you've been here?"

Mae shakes her head. "I'm sorry. I usually keep up. I guess I got busy with Leo. Is there something new I should see?"

"No," says Natalie quickly. "Nope, nothing new. I haven't posted any new content since I've been here, actually. I'm sort of taking a little break." She's popped online a couple of times to check the comments on her accounts, and then she's popped right back off with her insides churning, her stomach tied in knots. Nobody is talking about the lovely photos of the farm in the article, and how adorable her children are, and what a beautiful family she and Austin have created. Nobody cares that she can milk a cow and that her children are growing up virtually screen-free and that Evangeline has assisted at a calving. *Everyone* is talking about Austin's quote.

She crouches down and looks in the lower cupboards, the ones with all of the random items like the giant lobster pot and the little ramekins they use only for lobster butter. It's been years since they've cooked lobster here!

"What are you looking for?"

"A lemon zester. There's no proper lemon zester here. I'll just use a cheese grater. It'll do. Now, chop, please."

Her phone rings: Austin.

Mae says, "Are you going to answer that?"

"No," says Natalie.

"Want me to answer?"

"No," says Natalie.

Mae gives her a funny look. "Everything okay?"

"Of course!" She makes her voice as chipper as can be. If Natalie gets into it now with Austin, she will never get this dinner on the table. She may start screaming and never stop. She'll call Austin later, or tomorrow, when she can scream in peace.

"Nat?"

"Yes?"

"Can I ask you something?"

"Sure."

"How do you know all of this?"

Natalie, the cheese grater in hand, looks at her little sister. "Know all of what?"

"All of *this*—" Mae's gesture includes the whole kitchen. "Like, what a lemon zester even is."

"Doesn't everyone know what a lemon zester is?"

"Well, sure, okay, maybe that's self-explanatory. But all the rest of it, all the stuff you do online, the food you make, the kids, all that stuff. How'd you go from where I am to where you are, and how'd you get there so fast?"

With great care and kindness, Natalie doesn't say, *I was never where you are.* By the time she was Mae's age she already had a husband, a farm, two kids. "How'd I become a real grown-up, you mean?"

"Exactly! Yes, that. How'd you become a real grown-up?"

"Well. I guess it happened little bit by little bit, but also sort of quickly. I learned as I went. It was sort of the snowball effect, you know; once we started a family, once we had the farm, there we were, and we just kept going. Rolling down the hill."

"But did you know, ahead of time, that you'd end up here?"

Natalie thinks about this. "No," she says. "Not really. I mean, I hoped, I guess, but I didn't *know* any of it ahead of time."

She thinks some more, letting the thoughts really pile up on each other while she rubs the lemon against the grater, making sure not to hit the pith. There are so many things you don't know about motherhood until you become a mother. You don't know about the physicality of all of it. First, there is labor, of course—shocking, violent in its way, rife with fluids and tearing and other savage acts. Then comes the nursing, the sharing of one's body that is in many ways more intimate than sex. Your body, on demand, for the purposes of keeping a tiny human alive. Eventually the nursing ends, yes, but still you have not reclaimed your body as your own. And perhaps you never will. Children use your body as a jungle gym. They put their sticky fingers on your face, your arms, in your hair, your mouth. They follow you to the bathroom, sometimes into the bathroom. They cannot get enough of you! They curl their bodies, shrimplike, into yours. They want to sleep near you, on you, practically in you.

And when they've loosened their grip on you, there's your partner, patiently waiting his turn—because his body is lonely, and it longs for connection with yours, which is not lonely, which may never be lonely again. The world feels free to comment on your body. The world has earned this right. *You've lost the baby weight! You haven't lost the baby weight!* Things move and jiggle and loosen and tighten; hormones surge and abate; hair sheds then grows thickly back—wavy sections crop up where the hair used to lie flat and smooth. It's past your shoulders now, and the next day it's down your back. Your skirt is too long, it's too short, it's indecent, it's puritanical. You're not doing enough, wait, slow down, you're doing too much, you're going to hurt someone, probably the very children you have been doing all of these things for.

But there's more! These children expect that you can provide answers to all of their questions, even though, when nobody is looking, you must subtly google: How many people are in the world? Why is there fog? How does your heart work? Can a worm think? Do I see the same red you're seeing?

She cannot say all of this to her sister; she can say none of this, when it comes down to it, because she doesn't know how to encapsulate it. So she says, "Let me show you a better way to chop that onion."

Mae's mouth twists. She doesn't want to be shown a better way! "What's wrong with this way?" she asks.

"Less efficient. And see how much you're wasting?"

Mae looks down and says, "Not really."

Natalie takes the knife out of Mae's hands, slides the cutting board over in front of her, and demonstrates how to cut with the grain of the onion.

"Wow," says Mae, looking at Natalie with such wonder that Natalie feels a surge of pride. "I never knew that." She reclaims the knife, takes up the second onion, and goes to work on it. She's clumsy at first—and to be fair, the knives *do* need to be sharpened—but soon she gets the hang of it.

"Okay, Food Network star," says Natalie approvingly, and Mae grins.

After she had her children Natalie saw her own mother in a different light, and she had so many questions for her. *Did you go through this?* she wanted to ask her mother. *Did you feel all of these things?* But of course she must have! Theresa had given freely of her own body in all the ways Natalie was now doing and had never said a thing about it, about how she had navigated the vast canyon that lay between the warmth of motherhood and the sheer exhausting physicality of it all.

Natalie had waited too long to talk about all of this with Theresa, and then Theresa was sick, so she didn't ask her, and then she was gone, and it was too late, and now she will never know what her mother thought about any of it.

In the winter, Lenox kids went sledding at Gould Meadows in Stockbridge. Natalie is looking at her adult baby sister now, but she's seeing Mae all bundled in her snowsuit at age four or five, barely able to walk because Theresa had put so many layers on her. She's watching the three of them in age order on their bright orange family-size sled: Jordan in the back, her long legs extended; Natalie in the middle, always in the middle; Mae cross-legged in the front. An invisible push from behind, and off they went. Mae used to laugh so hard the whole way down that the entire hill could hear her. Now here she is, standing in front of Natalie, looking for someone to tell her it's all going to be all right.

Mae looks down. She says, "I just wonder what Mom would say, seeing what a mess of things I've made. Seeing where I am."

"You haven't made a mess—" Natalie is interrupted by Calvin, breezing into the kitchen, saying, "Hello, ladies! Any snacks around?" He takes a carrot slice and pops it into his mouth. From far away, Kara sneezes. "I heard," says Calvin, "that Cinnamon ate Evangeline's tooth."

• • •

"Natalie, this looks beautiful," Kara says. They are all in the dining room, ready to sit.

Scarlett and Evangeline have set the table, without complaint, in a way Mae doesn't ever remember doing herself at such a tender age. With two working parents their dinners on Galway Court were often chaotic; the older girls would have homework spread over the dining room table right up until it was time to eat; then, as soon as everything was cleaned up, Theresa would work on lesson plans or grade spelling tests and Calvin would read through student essays. Natalie's table, by contrast, is gorgeous. Who even knew they had matching linen napkins in this house? Who knew they had candles; who knew you could snip a couple of hydrangeas from the bush on the garage side of the house and, *bam,* instant centerpiece?

"Thank you, Kara," says Natalie, icily at first, and then more generously, "Mae and the girls helped." All Mae did was chop an onion, and now that the dinner is complete, Mae can see that there's a tiny charity sprinkling of onions on the salad, but otherwise Natalie was giving her busywork, no different from the coloring books she pulls out for the girls when they're at a restaurant or the waiting area of an airport.

Natalie brings down Caspian's portable crib and sets it up in the dining room. Calvin opens a bottle of sauvignon blanc and walks around the table like a fine-dining waiter, filling glasses. "I'll get a second bottle from the kitchen," he says.

When he's gone, Kara stands uncertainly—not quite guest, not blood relation, she's somewhere in the no-man's-land in between. The only unclaimed chair, they all realize at the same time, is Theresa's. "She can't sit there," Jordan says to no one in particular. "That's Mom's chair." Then to Kara, "Sorry, it's just . . ."

"No, I get it," says Kara. "So where should I sit?"

Mae is desperate to save Kara. (What is taking Calvin so long?) "Switch with me," she says. She picks up her water glass, the napkin she's already unfolded, and prepares to move around the table. Then Calvin comes back, assesses the situation, and says, "Kara, you sit here." He indicates his own chair. "I'll sit there." Theresa's.

The lemon pasta is gorgeous, with ribbons of fresh basil on top and shaved Parmesan on the side. There's a homemade dressing to go with the salad. Croutons from scratch, which Mae watched Natalie make by cubing a partial loaf of bread, tossing the cubes with olive oil and spices, and baking them. Mae didn't even know homemade croutons were a thing. Mae puts Leo's leash on and loops it around the leg of her chair. She has a pocketful of treats to reward him for nice dinnertime behavior. Natalie offers to serve the pasta from her seat since the bowl is heavy, but says she'll pass the salad and the cheese and the bread around the table. She passes to her left first, to Jordan.

Jordan passes the cheese without taking any.

"Please don't tell me you're vegan now too," says Natalie.

If this family were a string diagram, thinks Mae, with each string representing a source of tension between one person and another, they'd have quite a design by now. She'd start with whatever is going on between Jordan and Natalie; that would be one string. Jordan and Kara: a permanent string. Ditto Natalie and Kara. Who would Mae's string attach to?

Jordan says, "Too?"

Evangeline is watching closely with the observance of a person small enough to fit into the corners of the world and witness from there. "Like the lady Mommy doesn't like."

"Who?" says Natalie.

"The lady with the brown hair."

"The Realtor," deciphers Mae.

"I didn't say I didn't like her!" Natalie protests.

"You called her an idiot," says Evangeline.

Mae sees the color rise to Natalie's cheeks.

Mae waits for Natalie to Houdini her way out of this, but while there is a lot a person can argue with, there is very little arguing with the Venus flytrap memory of a smart young girl. Mae places a slender string between Evangeline and Natalie.

"Nikoletta comes highly recommended," says Calvin. "I didn't realize you had a problem with her."

"I don't," says Natalie. "I have a problem with selling the house. As you know."

Caspian yells, "Bah!" and beats the side of the portable crib. Natalie fed him while she was cooking, so he's chewing a board book for dessert.

They eat in silence for a while. "The dinner is phenomenal," says Kara. She sneezes. Mae peeks under the table and sees that Leo is lying on Kara's foot. She tries to give him a hand signal to move him closer to her but he doesn't see, or pretends not to.

"I don't think I'll ever be able to eat a store-bought crouton again," Mae says, digging into her salad. "These are incredible."

"We grew up on store-bought croutons," Jordan points out.

"Me too," says Kara. Jordan ignores this attempt at solidarity.

"Sure, but homemade is always better," says Natalie primly.

"If you have time to make them. Mom didn't."

"Easy, girls," says Calvin warningly.

This odd little altercation is not about the croutons, obviously, but Mae can't figure out what it is about. The string between her sisters is growing thicker.

Calvin drops his napkin and bends over to get it. It's just out of reach, and the display of his bald spot as he tries for it makes Mae sad. She wonders if her sisters notice it too. Throughout his fifties and into his sixties Calvin had had famously thick hair. The Lion of Lenox, Theresa used to call him. Scarlett cries, "I'll get it!" and jumps out of her seat.

Jordan says, "Dad can get his own napkin." Her voice is sharp.

Scarlett freezes.

Natalie shoots Jordan a look and says, "No, go ahead, Scarlett, thank you, that's very kind."

Scarlett reaches down slowly, like the napkin might bite her.

"*Natalie*," Jordan hisses.

"What?"

"Your *daughter* is *waiting on the man.* Do you not see a problem with this?"

"My daughter," says Natalie, "has manners, and she's being helpful to her grandfather."

Jordan shakes her head. "This is why you're where you are right now."

"Where is Natalie right now?" Mae wonders.

"Nowhere," snaps Natalie. "I'm right here."

"Can we get a puppy?" ask Evangeline. Kudos to Evangeline, thinks Mae, if she's trying to change the subject. If it's just your garden-variety non sequitur, well, then, props to that too, because it pulls Natalie's attention away from Jordan.

Caspian says, "Uppy!"

Natalie puts her hand to the side of her neck, where she once told

Mae all of her tension resides. "You have a puppy," she says. "You have Cinnamon."

"You said when we get to two million followers we can get a puppy," says Evangeline. (Mae clocks the first use of *we*.)

"We haven't gotten to two million," says Natalie.

"Cinnamon is *old*," accuses Scarlett.

Cinnamon, hearing her name a second time, raises her head and looks offended.

"She's not old," says Natalie. "She's younger than you are."

"She's not a puppy," says Evangeline.

"She has a puppylike attitude," says Natalie. "That will have to be good enough for now. Is everybody done? Good. Girls, let's clear the table." She stands and begins whisking the salad bowls away, making a tower of them. "When everything is in the kitchen, you can go play on the iPad."

Scarlett and Evangeline exchange a look at this unexpected bounty. "For how long?" asks Evangeline.

"Until I say you have to stop. Hurry, go, before I change my mind."

"Calvin and I will wash the dishes," says Kara. "In fact, I'll clear what's left."

"I got it," says Natalie. Kara is trying to get the last mouthful of pasta in before Natalie takes her plate too.

"Well, Natalie," says Calvin, when she returns from the kitchen, "thank you for making dinner. I give you credit for everything you're doing. Little kids are a lot of work."

"Confirmed," says Natalie.

Calvin continues: "I forgot how tiring this stage of parenting is. I must say, watching you, I'm glad it's behind me."

"Is it?" challenges Jordan.

"Geez, Jordan," says Mae, adding a string between Jordan and her father.

Jordan turns to Mae. "What? It's not like we all haven't been wondering. All three of us, not just me. I'm just the one with the nerve to ask."

"To ask *what*?" Calvin looks truly bewildered.

With a dramatic flourish of the wine bottle, with which she's refilling her glass, Jordan says, "To ask if you and Kara will be attempting to produce a male heir."

"Oh my god," says Mae. "Jordan! Too far."

Jordan fixes Mae with her fiery gaze. "I'm only saying out loud what we said in private." She casts a glance around the table, her eyes locking onto Mae's. "What we *all* said in private."

"I didn't," says Mae quickly. "I didn't say anything." She glances at Kara, willing her to understand: she is not her sisters.

"If you and Kara have a child, you'll be eighty-eight by the time that kid goes to college," says Jordan.

Natalie joins in. "But the kid may one day have a nice little nest egg tucked away from selling this house. So that's something."

Kara stands up so fast she almost knocks her chair over. They all turn toward her. "That's not why your dad is selling," says Kara.

"It's okay," says Calvin, and slowly Kara regains her seat. "We don't need to get into it."

"I think we do," says Kara.

"Why else, then?" challenges Jordan.

"He's selling to pay back the loans he took out to pay for your mother's treatment."

They all turn to Calvin, shocked. Jordan says, "*What*?"

"You never told us that!" Natalie says, her voice full of sound and fury.

"What treatment?" says Mae. "Like, was there a treatment we didn't know about?"

Calvin's face has turned somber. He says, "There was. About six months before your mom died, we flew to Switzerland for her to receive a treatment that wasn't available in the US. It was very expensive and very experimental. None of it was covered by insurance. We took out a second mortgage on the Lenox house to pay for it. And it wasn't successful, obviously."

"*When*?" cries Jordan.

He takes a deep breath. "The time we said we were taking a bucket-list trip to Paris."

"How come you didn't tell us?" demands Natalie.

"She didn't want you to know. She didn't want you to get your hopes up."

The Shipman sisters absorb this. Mae imagines her parents boarding the plane, checking into some Swiss hotel room, lying quietly together either before or after the treatment. She doesn't know what to do with this image.

Kara says, "And the answer to your original question is no. We aren't having kids. I can't carry a child."

Jordan's head swings back and forth between Kara and her father. "You can't?"

"Apparently I have an inhospitable womb," says Kara. Jordan blanches. "It's an outdated term, but it just means that . . . Well, never mind the details. I've known since my first marriage. I just—"

She doesn't get to finish. "*What*?" say Mae and Natalie and Jordan at the exact same time, and then, elaborating on that, Jordan says, "I'm sorry, *what*? You were married before?"

Kara folds her napkin. "I was married when I was in my mid-twenties. We were married for two years, together for three, and he died in a car accident."

"You never told us that!" Jordan turns again to Calvin, again accusingly. "Dad?" This is yet another thing Calvin has been keeping from them, and, somehow, fair or not, another strike against Kara.

"It's not my past to tell," says Calvin neutrally.

"That's awful," says Mae. "Kara, I'm so sorry." Jordan kicks Mae under the table, and once again they are seven and fourteen. "Ouch," says Mae irritably.

"Thank you, Mae. It was a long time ago."

"Does anybody else have any secrets to share?" Natalie asks, sort of sarcastically, but also sort of not. Mae clears her throat, wondering if this is the time, but nothing comes out. She feels Jordan shift.

"No, but I have something to say," says Kara.

"Fantastic," says Jordan, and now Mae kicks Jordan.

"You're not just upset about the seat, you're upset that I'm here at all, in your house, in your lives. I get it. I do. But I have a place here, too, now. And I'm not going to apologize."

This is where a Shipman girl might have made a dramatic exit. Mae remembers Natalie storming off after a fight with Theresa over the length of her skirt; Jordan screaming at Calvin, "*Those classes are a waste of time*!" after she got caught skipping out on SAT prep; Mae herself dissolving into tears and slamming the door of her room on Galway Court when her phone was taken away after a curfew infraction. She thought the world had ended; they each had thought that, so many times, while all the time the world kept spinning.

But Kara, stranded but also safe in her no-man's-land, neither Shipman girl nor Shipman parent, rendering the sisters silent, looks like she understands this intuitively. On and on, the world will keep spinning.

WEDNESDAY

• • •

In this picture—on the end table, living room—the three Shipman girls are lined up for the requisite first-day-of-school photo. The first day of school was always so hectic! Everybody needed a lunch. A button might pop off a brand-new shirt. Theresa had her own case of nerves. New classroom, new group of students, sometimes a bigger change in the school like a new principal or different colleagues. For these reasons, Calvin took the photo before he went to campus to teach his own classes, which had begun at least the week before so he was much less fraught.

Each year they stood in the same place, by the rhododendron in front of the house. They always stood in age order, with Jordan farthest to the left, and Jordan often had a look on her face like she was running late for a congressional budget meeting—too important and busy to stay for long, but understanding that the formality of the occasion required her presence.

Natalie was beginning sixth grade, which means Jordan would have been a freshman in high school. In Lenox the middle and high schools are combined so she and Jordan would have been in the same building once again for the first time since they were at Morris Elementary. Sometimes, in certain moods, they could pass in the upstairs hallway of their own house with scarcely an acknowledgment, but Natalie remembers now how comforting a glimpse of her older sister had been in those early days in middle school. Jordan would be traveling in a small knot of friends, all of the high schoolers tall and exotic; it had felt like sighting a herd of gazelles on the savannah, and she might wave at Natalie or even say her name. Inside Natalie would swell with pride, even if she'd never admit it.

The only makeup Natalie was allowed at that time was an innocuous lip gloss, although her friend Shay Thompson was already enthusiastically clumping on mascara. How Natalie had applied her gloss, with strength and fortitude! As though her entire middle school experience depended on it!

Natalie picks up the photo and examines it. She's smiling in the photo, of course (Natalie always knew how to look good in a photo), but she's sure her insides are roiling with the anticipated stress of changing classes and operating a locker for the first time.

(Will her kids never learn to use a locker? She and Austin have talked vaguely about "integrating them into the school system" at some point but that point seems so far in the future, hazy and distant.)

These girls. With their careful hair, their agonized-over outfits, their stiff new backpacks! There was so much ahead of them. The poignancy of this strikes her particularly hard right now. What would she do if she could go back in time, visit the Natalie of this photo? What would she tell her?

She would tell her never, ever put a tank top over a shirt with sleeves, for one thing. But what else?

• • •

In the early afternoon on Wednesday the doorbell rings. Leo loses his mind and, perhaps suffering from canine FOMO, Cinnamon joins in. The dogs run back and forth from the door to the window, looking at each other as if to say, *Can you believe it? The doorbell? I can't believe it. Can you believe it?*

Someone is here!

Natalie huffs her way down the stairs and hisses at Mae, "What the hell is going on? I just got Caspian down for his nap. What's all this barking?"

"Bad word," says Evangeline gleefully.

"Evangeline," Natalie says sharply, "I wasn't talking to you."

Natalie isn't doing gentle parenting right now.

"*I'm* not ringing the doorbell," Mae hisses right back. She's all done taking the blame for things she isn't responsible for. As the youngest, she's been the dumping ground for other people's mistakes her whole life. Enough! "And one of the dogs is yours. Don't yell at me."

"I'm not yelling," yells Natalie, although, to be fair, the dogs are barking so loudly that yelling is the only way to go if one wants to be heard. The doorbell rings again. In a slightly quieter voice Natalie asks, "Are you going to answer it? I'm not expecting anyone."

This makes Mae feel more affronted than she already feels. She could *just scream*. But she won't. She'll take a deep, cleansing yoga breath (she can't afford yoga classes, but whatever, breathing is free). She says, "I'm not expecting anyone either. Why don't you answer it? I'll take the dogs to the kitchen."

"Fine," says Natalie. She lets out an irritated sigh. Mae happens not to have her magic treat pouch on her, bad form on day five of a board-and-train, but she rummages in the pocket of her shorts, and, yes, reliable as the sunrise, she finds a handful of freeze-dried salmon. She calls the dogs to her; they stop barking and come immediately. This is a big win! She heads toward the kitchen.

"Nice," says Evangeline approvingly. "Cinnamon never listens like that."

"Cinnamon never had a professional dog trainer working one-on-one with her," says Mae modestly, but not that modestly, because she's proud that she's made progress.

In the kitchen, feeling a little show-offy, Mae gives both dogs the hand signal for *down*. They lower themselves, Leo with a graceless plonk as his ribs hit the floor. They stare at Mae with such attention, such adoration and love. Or probably they just really like freeze-dried salmon. Either way, she'll take it. She slides her phone to Evangeline and asks her to take a video. "I feel like the saint that commanded the animals," whispers Mae. She rewards the dogs for staying down, placing treats at intervals between each set of front paws so neither dog is tempted to get up before she releases them. "Was that Patrick?"

"Patrick was snakes," says Evangeline. "You probably mean Saint Francis."

• • •

"Look who's here," says Natalie. This time the Realtor is dressed for the beach, in a striped cover-up, flip-flops, and a straw sun hat. She smells like Sun Bum and has a little strip of white near her ear, where she didn't rub it in completely. She's carrying a big HomeGoods bag with a white frame sticking out of it.

"Hello!" she says brightly. "Excuse my casual wear. I'm technically not working today."

"I can see that," says Natalie frostily. Nikoletta had really thrown Evangeline into a frenzy on Monday, making her worry about the ethics of the milk industry—it had taken a while for Natalie to talk her down, and even after Evangeline had fallen asleep Natalie had lain awake for a while, thinking about the harrowing cries of a baby calf on the first night it's separated from the mother. She and Austin can never sleep on that first night; they lie awake holding hands. Her children have been brought up to think milk is good for you. Not to think it, to believe it, because it's the truth. Milk *is* good for you!

This is obviously too much to explain to the Realtor right now so she settles for a stern look.

"I just wanted to drop off a few things for the open house that I'd promised your dad—"

"He's on the patio," says Natalie. "I think he's fixing the latch on the door."

Obviously the Realtor knows where the patio is but Natalie leads her through anyway.

Calvin has moved on from the latch to examining a small bit of wood rot on the house's exterior. Jordan is sitting on one of the loungers, tapping out an email on her laptop, brow furrowed.

"Hello, Nikoletta," says Calvin.

"Hi! Excuse my casual wear."

"What have we got here?" Calvin asks, indicating the bag.

"Ah." She puts the bag on an empty lounger and looks inside as though she herself is curious about that. "A few things for the open house. You'll want to take down all personal photos, of course, so I've brought you a few more impersonal beach scenes you can hang to hide any nails or picture hangers. Then, let's see, here's a nice throw blanket for the living room—"

"We have a throw blanket," says Natalie.

"Right. But it's a little battered. This one's just nice and fresh. And, oh, a couple of matching hand towels for the bathroom. Aren't these pretty? They have seashells." She beams. "These little touches can really make a difference in how a house shows."

"Thank you," says Calvin. He has a small pad of paper and a pen tucked inside his back pocket—Calvin is *such* a professor—and he takes it out to show Nikoletta his to-do list. "Here are the things I've done, and here are the things I'm hoping to do. Could you help me prioritize? Since time is flying, and I'd like to take care of what you think is most important and then spend as much time with my daughters as I can before the big day."

"I love an organized seller!" Nikoletta beams harder. She takes the notepad and studies it, then holds her hand out for Calvin's pen. "These, I'd definitely get done." She goes down the list, circling. "And these, I wouldn't put any time into. Like the latches on the windows? Not a big deal. Fan in the upstairs bathroom? Same thing. Things like that, a buyer isn't going to worry about at this point."

At this point? Natalie looks to meet Jordan's eye, but Jordan is still staring at her phone, so she searches for and finds Mae, newly arrived from the kitchen. "What do you mean, at this point?" asks Mae.

"Well, because . . ." says Nikoletta, but her voice trails off when she sees Calvin's expression, which Natalie could only describe as *warning*. "Oh, I see!" says Nikoletta. "You haven't had this discussion yet. No, that's fine. Why don't I leave you this bag, and we'll catch up tomorrow, okay, Calvin? No need for me to go through the house. I'll just walk around this way." She takes the three steps down to the beach, then scurries around the side of the house.

"Dad?" says Natalie. "What was that about? Why doesn't she care about the window latches? Or the bathroom fan?"

Calvin clears his throat. He sits on the lounger beside Jordan's, feet planted on the ground, hands on his knees. "The structural things don't matter . . ." he begins, but the words seem to get stuck in his throat. He tries again, and eventually they loosen. "They don't matter, because the buyer will most likely be building from scratch."

"Building from scratch?" asks Natalie. "What does *that* mean?"

Jordan puts her phone down, raises her sunglasses, and regards her sisters. "Come on, Natalie. You're smart enough to know what he's saying. Whoever buys this house is going to demolish and rebuild. Right, Dad? Isn't that what you're saying?"

Calvin nods. "I'm saying that's the most likely scenario."

"What?" screeches Mae.

Natalie turns to Jordan. "Why do *you* know that and we don't?"

"I didn't know," say Jordan. "I just figured. Because it makes sense, from a practical point of view."

"*Practical*," spits Natalie, like she's saying *rat poison*.

"Dad?" says Mae in a quavery voice. "I don't get it. What's going on?"

"What's going on," says Calvin, "is basically our old friend climate change. FEMA has adjusted the flood maps of areas like this, so when a home changes ownership, and the new owner plans significant renovation, they must bring the home up to code. For a house this old—it's almost as old as I am—it makes much more sense to demolish and rebuild than to try to get up to code."

"You're going to *tear down Mom's house*?" cries Natalie.

"*I'm* not going to—"

"Wait!" says Mae. "If that happens only when a house changes hands, why aren't we keeping it for as long as we can? And *using* it, just as it is?"

"I bet it's not that simple," says Jordan, and Natalie and Mae turn on her so fast that it feels like they're each flicking a forked serpent's tongue at her.

"Oh, yeah?" spits Natalie. "Why don't you explain why it's not that simple?"

"The money, for one thing," says Jordan. "As discussed. Duh."

"I'll explain," says Calvin. "Jordan's right. If we were to do that, never mind all of the reasons we've already discussed about not being able to use it, and yes, needing the money, chances are that sooner rather than later we'd sustain damage from a major storm, and without flood insurance, which we can no longer get, we'd be left with nothing. This way, we get the value of the house and the land, and whoever buys and rebuilds can rebuild to current code, raising it above the tide line to withstand inevitable tidal issues."

"See?" says Jordan. "Practical."

"I'm sorry, girls. I should have explained this when I first told you about the house. But I figured, all in good time. I thought we'd get to it."

"We got to it, alright," says Natalie. "I can't believe this."

Kara walks up the stairs from the beach right then, a pair of binoculars swinging. "Hey, everyone! What's going on out here? Should I grab a bottle of rosé and some glasses?"

"CAN WE CALL Daddy?" Scarlett asks Natalie, when they go upstairs to get Caspian from his nap.

"Sure," says Natalie, ungently. She's already feeling combative, but the kids want to talk to their father. "Of course we can call Daddy." She looks at her watch. "Maybe we'll catch him in the house before the evening milking."

"I want to call Daddy too," says Evangeline, popping out of Mae's room, closing the door quietly, presumably so Leo doesn't wake from his own nap. Natalie bends down to pick up a tuft of Cinnamon's fur, then, remembering that Mae said Kara is allergic, decides to leave it. It's a childish gesture, and it's also satisfying.

She dials their home number and hands the phone to Scarlett while she changes Caspian's diaper. Scarlett tells Austin about a starfish with a missing arm she found, about the smoothie she'd had from Sandpiper, about her sandcastle with two turrets. Evangeline takes the phone next, puts it on speaker, and goes into a long story about how to teach a dog to spin.

"To spin, like, a web?"

Evangeline giggles. "No, Daddy, to spin around in circles." Caspian, freshly changed, holds out two hands for the phone and Evangeline gives it to him. He licks it.

Finally it's Natalie's turn. She asks Evangeline and Scarlett to help Caspian down the stairs, sits on the bed, and says, "You didn't answer my last text about the article. Did you read it?"

"Hello to you too, babe," he says.

"Sorry, I mean hi, but did you read the article?" On Austin's end she hears water running in the sink, the tick of one of the burners on her baby-blue stove coming on.

"I saw it! The photos came out great."

Is he really so oblivious?

"But did you *read* it? Did you see the 'barefoot and pregnant' thing?"

"Sure, yeah. Nat—I don't think it's a big deal."

"Bethany thinks it's a big deal! She's been tracking the responses online. People are backlashing hard. My follower number has dropped every day this week. The comments are awful."

"Who's Bethany?"

"The publicist I hired six months ago!" She definitely told Austin when she hired Bethany. "She says that one quote ruined the whole article. You must see that?"

"I've been busy here, Natalie. I haven't really thought about it that much. One of the Ladies has a prolapsed uterus—"

She can't reach him. It's like they're on opposite sides of a giant lake, whispering at each other. "But have you thought at all? Have you thought about what you said? Or why?"

Something metal clatters into her farmhouse sink (nothing, she hopes, that will scratch it). "I mean, when that reporter was here, I opened my mouth and that's what came out." She can picture him shrugging his infuriatingly strong shoulders. "It was a joke. I didn't think it would be anything."

"Well, it is something! It's *the whole story*!" Her voice is raised now, and they might be able to hear her on the patio, but she can't stop. "People think I'm some kind of—*childbearing machine.* And seriously, Austin, *barefoot*? What the hell? Our brand is about traditional families, and raising our children with care and consideration, and not, like, randomly spitting out *babies*! " She's so angry she could scream. Everything she's cultivated, all of the care she's taken, and he can't see how it's ruined. How he's ruined it!

But then there is a pause, and in that pause a great uncertainty blooms. "Our *brand*?" says Austin. His voice sounds different now, not breezy, not carefree.

Natalie swallows hard. "Yes."

"I thought we were a family, not a brand."

"You know what I mean. Of course we're a family."

Austin sighs, and it's a sigh that contains a little bit of everything: hurt and confusion and disappointment and maybe a little bit of fatigue. "Nat, I have to get ready for the 5 p.m. milking. Tell the girls it was great to talk to them. I love hearing their voices."

"Wait!" she says. Her heart is in her throat. "Wait, Austin!"

But he's gone.

LATER THAT EVENING, after they've eaten the burgers Calvin grilled, after Natalie has *not* said out loud that two burgers in two days might be a lot for someone her dad's age, after they've cleaned up, Natalie puts Mae in charge of Caspian and walks the girls down to the water to look for shells. She feels terrible about so many different things that she's not even sure which one is taking the lead. She turns and sees her father standing next to her, his arms crossed, his chin lifted, his eyes closed. It's the posture of a sun worshipper, but behind them the sun is going down, and the sky over the water is beginning to change color.

He's appeared like a ghost, and maybe he *is* a ghost: the ghost of summers past.

"Dad?" She almost expects to see Theresa standing next to him in the navy-blue one-piece she had for at least ten years, and over it a long-sleeved gauzy white shirt, the sleeves rolled up. The girls are a little way down the beach; she can see the curve of their pale necks as they search the sand. They know when they get to the yellow house they must turn around, and she sees Evangeline look up to make sure they haven't gone too far.

Calvin starts, as though surprised to find her there, to find himself there.

"Oh, hello. Listen, Natalie, I was thinking—"

"Dad, I can't do this now." It's killing her to think that her daughters won't be doing this walk into their teen years and beyond. It's double killing her to think of the house itself not existing as they know it, replaced by some hulk of a thing that will strain against the property lines and have no character, no memory of the Shipman family, no association with the Beach Club or Theresa's parents or any part of the past.

"No. No, it's not about the house. I was just talking to Kara, and we were wondering if the three of you might want to go out on the town tonight."

"The three of us . . . ?" This is so unexpected for a few immediate reasons—she's angry with Jordan, she can't imagine her father watching her kids without Theresa, and also, she is no longer a person who "goes out on the town," unless you count her weekly dinner dates with Austin—that she finds herself needing to make a joke instead of answering seriously. "Scarlett and Evangeline and me? I mean, I could ask, but I don't think they brought their fake IDs."

Calvin blinks at her, then, after a beat, he chuckles: when you dad-joke a dad, sometimes it's confusing. "You and your sisters. Kara and I would be delighted to watch the kids."

"*All* of them? Even Caspian?"

"Yes, of course even Caspian. Especially Caspian. He gives me a much-needed dose of male energy."

She snorts. "If that's what you want to call it. But his diapers are something else. Are you sure you're up for it? Should we check with Kara?"

"Kara sent me out here to ask you."

This stymies Natalie. "She *did*? Does Kara know about the diapers?" Even as she says this she realizes that's not the smartest thing she's ever said. "Right," she says. "Kara's a nurse. I don't think bodily functions are a thing of horror to her."

"Exactly. And, it would make me happy to see you girls have some time together. If nothing else, do it for me."

It helps to think of saying yes as doing a favor for her father, but in fact Natalie is starting to come around for other reasons too. She and Austin have their Saturday-night dates, yes, but she doesn't have a group of girlfriends in Vermont. She hasn't seen the Sisterhood together in one place since Theresa's funeral. Until this week she and her sisters haven't all been in the same place since the Christmas after Theresa died. Maybe it will be good for them to leave the house and to go somewhere they aren't accosted by ghosts at every turn.

• • •

They take Mae's car to Portsmouth because Natalie's car seats are a pain to move and Jordan's rental car is blocked in by Mae's car—and it's too small anyway. It's a reverse of their teenagerhood, when Mae was forever a passenger, never a driver. The driver gets to choose the music, and Mae sings along to her Spotify playlist.

"When did you go country?" asks Jordan from the passenger seat. "Was it when you got the tattoos?"

"Zach Bryan is so mainstream," says Mae. "Anyway, I *do* live in the western half of the country. It's not a stretch."

"Feels like you actually live in your car," says Natalie from the back seat. "There's so much stuff back here. Is this a *baking dish*?"

"It might be," says Mae, without elaborating. "Where are we going?"

"Portsmouth."

"Duh. But where specifically?"

"We'll figure it out when we get there," says Jordan. She clears her throat. She wants this to go well, she really does, but she knows that her sisters are holding against her the conversation with the Realtor. If she can just get them to see the logic of the situation, they might all be able to relax into the evening and enjoy being together. "Listen, you guys," she says. "About the house—"

"Nope," says Natalie, and Mae says, "Uh-*uh*."

"Wow. Did you guys choreograph that or something?"

"No," says Natalie. "But I'm sure we're both ready for a break from talking about it."

"We are," confirms Mae.

"Got it," says Jordan. "Definitely noted."

They luck their way into a parking spot on Congress Street. Back in the city, on a night out, Jordan might just be getting into the shower right about now. The street is buzzing; some of the shops are still open, and people are pouring in and out of the restaurants. There must be something on at The Music Hall, because there are swarms of people walking through the big metal arch and toward the iconic pink building. It smells like the summers of Jordan's youth, the heaviness to the air, the sense that, even though you can't see it, the ocean is not so far away. It smells like nostalgia and heartache.

"Is there still a wine bar here?" She could go for a very cold, very good champagne. One glass, maybe two.

"Let's go here!" Natalie leads them to the door of The Goat and pauses to read the sign outside. "It's Portsmouth's only country bar."

"Were we looking for a country bar?" wonders Jordan.

"We weren't *not* looking for a country bar."

"Looks good to me," says Mae, and Jordan says, "Well, yeah, it would," and Mae rolls her eyes and says, "Sorry, Jordan, would you rather go to the bar at the Wentworth?" (The Wentworth is the fancy Gilded Age hotel in New Castle, just a few miles east, where Austin and Natalie had their wedding reception.) Yes, *of course* Jordan would rather go to the bar at the Wentworth, where they could look at the fancy pleasure boats in the harbor and drink good wine, but she zips her lips. She's with her sisters! They're already mad at her! She can do a country bar!

Lucky again, two people are vacating the bar, leaving three empty stools in a row. The Shipman girls slide into the seats. It's been a long time since Jordan has been out with both of her sisters—she'd forgotten how they make sort of a spectacle, a triangle of genetics and DNA. They look like each other, yes, but each with her own distinctive differences. Natalie's hair is longer, Mae's face rounder, Jordan's eyes a deeper blue, almost navy. "Here come the Shipman girls," the hostess at The Red Lion Inn used to say when they arrived for their Christmas dinner reservation each year. The receptionist at the dentist would say the same thing. Jordan used to roll her eyes at the latter—Mae was so much younger, couldn't Jordan have her own dentist appointment?—but secretly she'd loved it; it had felt like being a member of a very exclusive club.

All of the female servers and bartenders at The Goat are wearing cutoff shorts and cowboy boots, and Jordan is put in mind of the weekend she and Audrey once spent in Nashville. Drinking on Broadway, long mornings in bed at The Hermitage Hotel. She'd summarized Audrey so quickly for Simone, but they'd been together for nearly four years, and when Jordan thinks about her she still experiences a deep pang of regret and loss.

On the wall behind the bar, above the painted American flag, are the words *WHISKEY THE PEOPLE.*

"That's my kind of wall painting," Jordan says.

"Because you're a patriot?" asks Mae.

"No, dummy, because I'm a whiskey drinker."

She's sitting between Natalie and Mae, and to Mae's right is a guy by himself, maybe in his early forties, who might or might not be eavesdropping.

"I can't do whiskey." Mae wrinkles her nose.

"I can," says Jordan. "I can do whiskey all day long." She peruses the bourbon selection—it's actually pretty good! Okay! She sees Buffalo Trace and Woodford Reserve and even Blanton's.

"Sisters?" says the guy, leering, and Mae nods and tilts her body slightly so that a little bit of her back goes toward the guy. *Good job, Mae,* says Jordan in her head. She forgets sometimes that Mae has been out in the world for many years now. She knows how bars work.

"Should we start with a shot?" Natalie suggests.

"Whoa," says Jordan. "I didn't know earth mothers did shots."

Natalie rolls her eyes. "I never called myself an earth mother. *Earth mother* to me implies ill-fitting outfits." Jordan snorts, delighted. The funny Natalie has come out tonight. Mae's phone buzzes and she glances at it and turns it over, but not before Jordan sees that the text is from someone named Hal.

"Who's Hal?"

"My boss."

"Which boss?" Jordan can't keep track of all of Mae's jobs. She seems to be at once underemployed and also quite overemployed.

"Dog boss." She chews her fingernail and says, "What should I get? I'm driving. I can only have one drink; I have to make it a good one."

"We could Uber," suggests Jordan. "And pick up the car tomorrow."

"I'll get a ticket," says Mae.

"If you do, I'll pay it," says Jordan.

"You promise?"

"Promise."

"Yes!" says Natalie. "Okay, so let's do shots. Bartender!" This is how Jordan knows Natalie is already tipsy from the wine they had with dinner. Sober people just signal for the bartender or catch their eye; nobody actually calls out the word *bartender*, just as nobody in New York actually yells "Taxi!" as they're signaling for a cab.

"Sisters?" asks the bartender, and they nod. "I love that. Sisters are the best. I always wanted a sister."

"I like your tattoo," Mae tells her. The bartender has a small goat tattoo on her wrist, just like the goat brands on the burger buns here. "It shows real workplace commitment."

"Thanks." She smiles. "I like all of yours."

Jordan presses her lips together; respectfully, she disagrees. She hates that Mae has so many tattoos now. She hates that she looks like—well, like someone she is not. Or never used to be. Their mother would be so upset to see Mae's pretty skin marked up like this, like a dark, angry costume that doesn't really fit. "We can't do whiskey shots," says Jordan. "That's not very sophisticated."

The bartender shrugs. "No judgment. We'll pour anybody a shot of anything."

"Tequila?" asks Natalie hopefully.

"Who *are* you, Natalie?" asks Jordan.

"It's been a long week."

"It's only Wednesday!"

"Exactly."

"How about no shots," says Jordan. "How about cocktails?"

Natalie sighs and says, "Fine." She orders a Goat-a-Rita, and Jordan deliberates between a Golden Hour Spritz and a bourbon, neat. She chooses the bourbon. (They are beyond golden hour by now.) Mae gets The Red Door, with espresso, vodka, Irish cream, and cold brew—named, they speculate, after the bar that closed a decade ago. Jordan would be up all night if she drank that. Oh, to be in her twenties again!

It's fun to be out with her sisters. The first hour passes so fast, the way time used to pass in college bars, when you look up from hanging out with your friends and the night is nearly over, the bar about to close. Natalie brings up the summer Jordan babysat for the family with triplets; they spend a good long time speculating about what white-collar crime the father got investigated for. The summer a pipe bomb washed up on the beach and Calvin was the one who called the authorities. The time Natalie dared Mae to eat a whole Seafood Platter from Petey's by the end of the day and she ate the last bite at 11:57. Every single Third of July party at the Beach Club.

Jordan feels the joy of this night like an ache in her heart, like nostalgia for something that isn't yet over. Natalie seems to have put her worries about the magazine article on the back burner, which means that for tonight she's not asking Jordan for something Jordan doesn't want to give, and Jordan doesn't have to deal with the messy truth that while she would hang from her fingernails for Natalie and Natalie's family, she would not do the same for Natalie's "brand." If her sisters don't want to talk about the house, that's okay by Jordan. She's not going to let herself think about Bernadette; she's stuck to her vacation guns and ignored her calls both yesterday and today. She's feeling almost . . . calm and balanced. Jordan doesn't believe in heaven, but if she did she knows Theresa would be there, looking down at her three girls together and smiling.

She would also tell Mae not to drink coffee so late in the day.

When there's a lull in the conversation Natalie says, "Do you think Dad is doing gentle parenting with the kids?"

"Definitely not," hoots Mae. "Definitely not."

"What is gentle parenting?" asks Jordan, mystified.

"It's a parenting fad," explains Mae.

"It's a parenting *style*," corrects Natalie. "Not a fad."

"Give me the sound bite."

"Well," begins Natalie. "The idea is that you focus on empathy, understanding, and healthy boundaries. So, if you're trying to get out the door and your kid is throwing a tantrum, instead of screaming, 'Put your shoes on!' like an old-school parent, you'd explain why the kid needs to be on time to school and how you, the parent, need to be on time to work, and the tantrum is making you feel anxious, so maybe you can talk about why the kid is upset and both get out the door together."

"Oh my god," says Jordan. "That sounds really time-consuming." She does not point out that Natalie's kids don't go to school and Natalie doesn't go to work. Does she have to rush them to the milking barn? "Does anyone ever actually get out the door that way?"

"Sometimes," says Natalie, chewing her lip, considering. "Not always."

"Don't you read Natalie's Substack?" Mae says. "She did a whole piece on it. 'The Ungentle Part of Gentle Parenting.' It was really good! Natalie, you're such a good writer."

"Thank you," says Natalie. She looks expectantly at Jordan, as if for her to corroborate.

"I don't always have time to read. My job keeps me really busy."

"I have noticed you're not a subscriber."

"Really? You check who *doesn't* subscribe?"

To her drink Natalie says, "Sometimes I forget that you only have time when it suits you."

The air stills. "Whoa," says Mae. "Major mood shift."

"What's that supposed to mean?" asks Jordan. She looks at Natalie's glass. It's empty, and she's looking again at the cocktail menu.

"Another round, please," Natalie tells the bartender.

Mae says, "But I'm not—" and Natalie says, "So drink the first one down, sister."

When they have their second drinks Jordan repeats, "What did you mean, Natalie?"

"Nothing. Just that sometimes you have time, and sometimes you don't have time." Natalie shrugs. "That's how it is."

"What did you *mean*?" she repeats. Natalie shakes her head, still bowed over her glass. "What did you *mean* that sometimes I have time and sometimes I don't? Natalie?"

When Natalie looks up her eyes are blazing. "I mean that you don't have time to help me with what I'm going through. Right now, today."

"Hang on," says Mae. "What am I missing? What is Natalie going through? What do you not have time for?"

"I didn't say I didn't have *time*—" What she doesn't have, Jordan thinks, is desire.

Natalie cuts her off. "And how about when Mom was dying? How much time did you have then?"

"*Whoa*," says Mae, shocked. "Natalie!"

"I was *there* when Mom died!" cries Jordan. "We all were!" She's not crazy, right? They were all there! Calvin, Kara, Mae, Natalie—the gang was all there. *They heard the death rattle.*

"She was dying for longer than just two days, Jordan. Until I was too pregnant to travel often I was there a lot more than you were."

This is so unfair Jordan can hardly believe it. "You live an hour away. I was three hours away, with a demanding job."

"I was pregnant, with two little kids, and I made it work. I went to her appointments."

"Being pregnant isn't a *job*, Natalie."

Natalie laughs meanly. "Well, it sure isn't a leisure activity."

Mae is looking back and forth as though her sisters are playing pickleball. She keeps opening and closing her mouth like a koi, saying nothing.

"Where is this coming from?" But Jordan doesn't really have to ask this; she knows where it's coming from.

"You may hate my traditional view of motherhood—"

"I don't hate—"

"But at least I was there for our own mother!" Natalie has too much composure to yell in a bar, but she's close.

"*What*?" Jordan can't believe those words just came out of Natalie's mouth.

"Yeah. And not only did you put work ahead of her, now you're just fine with tearing down her house!"

Okay, thinks Jordan. "Oh my *god*," she says. "You both need to stop talking like I'm standing outside the house with a bulldozer. None of this was my idea!"

"But if we all *agreed*," says Natalie, "if we were all *united*, maybe we could do something about it. If you cared."

Now the gloves are well off. On the inside Jordan is seething and shaking, but she knows from years of experience that the antidote to Natalie getting too emotional is to remain cool herself. It was the same with Audrey. Maybe we purposefully find in the outside world the patterns we grew up with because we think we know how to manage them. She draws herself up with as much dignity as she can summon, and, keeping her voice steady and even, says, "Well, Natalie, you may think your memory is pretty good—"

"My memory is *very* good," snaps Natalie.

"—but one thing you're definitely forgetting is that you aren't the only one with things going on. As usual, you think you are. I'm going to the bathroom." And with that, she pushes in her barstool (because even as angry as she is she doesn't want anyone to trip) and heads to the back of the restaurant.

• • •

"Oooooh," breathes Mae once Jordan is gone. Natalie rattles the ice in her glass. "What was *that* all about?"

Natalie gives Mae the CliffsNotes: the article, the backlash, Austin's refusal to see any of it as a problem. Mae winces and nods at all the right times, and Natalie is grateful for that.

"I hate that reporter," Mae says loyally.

"Me too," says Natalie. But she's mostly angry and scared about Austin. She's scared that she's taken this beautiful part of their life and broken it. In all the time she's known him, Austin has never gotten off the phone without a goodbye, without saying *Love you.*

Natalie considers. "To be fair, maybe it was the editor or the designer who decided to highlight the quote and write the caption," she says.

"Then I hate them too." Mae takes the last, exuberant sip of her drink. Natalie tells her about her hope for Jordan to fix it, and Jordan's refusal.

"But Jordan fixes everything!" explains Natalie. "She's being *so weird* about this."

"Jordan does fix everything," Mae agrees. "She used to fix my American Girl doll when the leg kept falling off. Grace? The one who baked? That girl's leg would *not* stay on."

"Tough to be a one-legged baker," observes Natalie. Then she says, "She always untangled my necklaces."

"She organized the drawer that held the food containers, like, once a month."

"No, *I* did that," says Natalie.

"That was you?"

"Definitely. I always wanted them to be matched with their hats but nobody ever put them away properly. It drove me crazy, all those orphans." In Natalie's kitchen, her beautiful, grown-up, endlessly photographed kitchen, every container has a lid and every lid has a container. There are no orphans.

They're quiet for a minute. The bartender comes by and says, "Another round?"

"Yes," says Natalie, at the same time that Mae says, "Probably not."

The bartender raises an eyebrow and waits. "We'll decide when our sister comes back," says Mae.

"I'll be over there when you do."

"She's taking, like, a year in the bathroom," says Natalie. Then, "Was I too harsh with her?"

"Well," says Mae diplomatically. "That depends on your definition of *harsh*."

"Ouch."

"I mean. You're angry with her about being okay with the house sale. I get it. I'm angry about that too."

"The Realtor pretty much said the next owners are going to tear it down!"

"I know. I know! I can't believe it. I can't even really let myself think about it or imagine it. But the stuff about when Mom was sick . . . *I* wasn't there as much as you were either, if we're keeping score."

"You live in Colorado. You took a leave of absence from your job!"

"A short one."

Natalie can't decide if she's being too hard on Jordan or too easy on Mae. "Okay, okay, *fine*. What do I do?"

"You could start by apologizing."

Natalie thinks about this; she thinks long and hard. Apologizing is not her favorite thing to do. "I don't know if I'll apologize. But I will order a round of shots, and that's sort of the same thing."

• • •

Of *course* Simone is sitting at a table in the back of the restaurant, and of course she looks up and sees Jordan at the same time that Jordan sees her. Simone's face breaks into that warm, beautiful smile—summery, if a smile can be seasonal—and Jordan, who's so angry at Natalie that she could shake her fist at the gods, if she believed in the gods, sees the smile and feels like she's eighteen again. Unmarred. Simone is wearing a long gauzy white skirt and a fitted coral tank top. Minimal makeup, suntanned face, those freckles. This, Jordan realizes, is exactly who she wants to see at this moment. Simone.

Simone stands and hugs Jordan, introducing her to the woman she's sitting with: "Jordan, this is Marnie, my partner." Jordan raises her eyebrows—Marnie is at least fifteen years older than Simone, and hadn't Simone said she was single?—and Simone hurries to say, "My *business* partner. For the yoga and smoothie bar. Marnie's taught yoga all over the Seacoast area."

"Nice to meet you." This Marnie does have a certain taut, flexible look to her. "I'm here with my sisters," Jordan tells Simone. "Girls' night out. My dad and his new wife are babysitting."

"Fun!" says Simone.

"Well," says Jordan, "sometimes."

To Marnie: "Jordan has the *best* sisters."

"Sometimes," repeats Jordan.

"You weren't even here the last time I saw them. You were working. Did they tell you we saw each other on the beach a few years ago?" Jordan nods. Simone tells Marnie, "Jordan has the most interesting job."

Jordan thinks about Memorial Day and about Bernadette's hand on her leg. "Sometimes," she says for a third time, and they all laugh. Jordan isn't in a mood to make small talk with someone she doesn't know, so she excuses herself to use the bathroom. Washing her hands, she looks in the mirror and replays Natalie's words—*sometimes I forget that you only have time when it suits you.* How dare she. Jordan has been the older sister as long as Natalie has been alive. Natalie has no idea of the responsibilities placed on the eldest! Hold your sisters' hands crossing the street. Help Mae with her homework. Pick up Natalie from speech and debate. Give, give, give, and who's giving back? When she comes out, Simone is standing there.

"You okay?"

"Of course." Jordan knows that just under the surface of the words is the truth, and if Simone were to scratch ever so gently it would be uncovered. Bernadette. Samantha Braddock. Natalie. The presence of Kara and the absence of Theresa. The Realtor. The house. Each thing is piling up on top of the next like stacking cups, and the stack is about to tumble. "Why wouldn't I be okay?"

"You look upset."

"I'm fine."

Simone laughs, not unkindly. "Classic Jordan. You always used to say you were fine even when you weren't." Jordan doesn't know what to say to this, so she says nothing. "You can talk to me, you know. If you ever need an ear. I can be an ear." This, thinks Jordan, is just what she'd been wishing for the day before, an ear! And now here's Simone, fixing her sea-glass eyes on Jordan and offering it, her words like a jump in the ocean on a hot day.

"Natalie just got all over me for some ancient history, and I've got this thing with my boss . . . Never mind, though." She could go on and on, but she won't. "I shouldn't get into it. It's really not just-ran-into-you material."

"I was always scared of Natalie," Simone admits. "All the way back when she was—what was she that summer? Fifteen? *I* wouldn't have wanted to cross her." Even if Simone is exaggerating (and she probably is), this makes Jordan feel better, like her corner is not empty. "Listen," Simone goes on. "The offer for the ear stands, okay? I'm around."

"Thank you."

"Hey, I want to say hi to your sisters! Is that okay?"

"Sure," says Jordan. "I believe they are glued to their bar seats. What about Marnie, though?"

"She left. She wanted to check on her cat. She's really attached to her cat."

"Fair enough," says Jordan, leading Simone back to the bar. She's glad Simone is there to diffuse some of the tension with Natalie. Greetings, hugs, etc.

"We're doing shots!" Natalie tells her.

Jordan says, "Not this again. We're not twenty-two, Natalie." She's torn between her anger and her desire for her anger to be gone.

"Who cares. There's not a maximum age. Simone, will you do a shot with us?"

Simone assesses the Shipman girls and asks, "How're you getting home?"

"Uber," they say together.

"I have my car," says Simone. "I'm not drinking tonight. Do your shot. I'll be your Uber."

"Yay!" say Natalie and Mae together.

Jordan sighs. "Just one teeny-weeny shot before we go," Natalie says to Jordan.

"Fine," Jordan agrees, knowing it's a bad idea, because one shot before you go is always, always a bad idea and it only ever makes you feel better for about four minutes. "But make it bourbon, okay?"

"Bartender!" calls Natalie, and Jordan cringes, but the bartender comes over, and she says, "That's what I'm talking about, ladies!" when Natalie orders a round. The shot burns going down, because you aren't supposed to shoot bourbon, you're supposed to sip it, but if that's the biggest mistake Jordan makes this week she can live with it.

"Should we do another?" asks Natalie.

"*No*," says everyone, and Jordan adds, "Oh my god, you're drunk on two drinks and a shot; when did you become such a lightweight?"

"Do you think we'll be in trouble with Dad if we come home drunk?" asks Natalie, ignoring Jordan's question.

"Uhhhh," says Mae. "Is that a thing that happens to adults?"

"I think you're safe," says Simone. "I'm sure your father has been drunk before."

"Actually, I've never seen Dad drunk," says Natalie.

Mae says, "At Dad and Kara's wedding—" and then claps her hand drunkenly over her mouth.

Natalie and Jordan turn on her. "I'm sorry, *what*?" cries Jordan.

"Nothing."

"No, not nothing. You said something about the wedding."

"No wedding," says Mae, speaking in the space her fingers leave as they part.

Jordan and Natalie exchange a glance, confused. Jordan, who feels instantly sober, says, "Mae? Were you *at* Dad and Kara's wedding?"

Mae removes her hand and says, "Possibly."

Everything shifts then—everything.

"This seems like a good time to call it a night," says Simone.

"It's only ten o'clock," says Natalie. Her eyes are shooting daggers at Mae. "I think we can stay a little longer."

Simone catches the bartender's eye and says, "These three are ready to settle up."

Jordan pays the bill, waving away Natalie's credit card. Mae, that little traitor, who isn't meeting her or Natalie's eyes, doesn't even offer to pay.

• • •

They have to walk two blocks to Simone's car, and during those two blocks Mae starts at least a dozen sentences.

"You guys, it wasn't—"

"I was only—"

"It's just because—"

Natalie and Jordan walk ahead of her. They don't want to hear anything Mae tries to say. When they're in the car, with Simone in the driver's seat, Jordan beside her, and Natalie and Mae in the back, Jordan turns around and says, "So, you were at the wedding?" Classic Jordan—she wants the answer, but on her own time. Simone, to her credit, simply drives. The streets are dark, mostly quiet; the moon is full. The water, in glimpses behind the rock walls, glows.

"I got invited, so I went."

"We all got invited," says Natalie. "We agreed as a group to boycott."

Mae inhales, exhales on the answer. "I changed my mind. I called Dad and told him I wanted to go. He bought me a plane ticket, and I went." She can hear the uncertainty in her voice, and she doesn't like it.

Natalie says, "This is unbelievable. And you didn't tell us?"

"I didn't tell you because you would have reacted exactly the way you're reacting now."

Natalie snorts. It's the snort that gets to Mae. "You know what? I don't have to explain. I don't have to apologize."

"Yes, you do," says Jordan. "You have to do both."

Even Mae doesn't recognize the steeliness in her own voice. "I don't. I think Kara is *nice.* I *like* her. I think you're both too hard on Dad and Kara, okay?" Each emphasized word feels like she's delivering a punch.

"We're not hard enough," says Natalie.

"I miss Mom as much as you guys do—"

"Apparently not," says Jordan, under her breath, but still Mae hears her, and is infuriated. She tries to hold her voice steady.

"Of course I do. You know I do. But I think Kara is *good* for Dad. And Dad is good for Kara. If you took even a second to get out of your own heads and get to know her you'd see that too. You're not even *trying.*"

"I don't want to get to know her," says Jordan.

"Me either," says Natalie.

"Well, who cares? Who *cares* what you want? This is not about *you.*" They both stare at her, at this person with a very un-Mae-like tone of voice, these harsh words.

Then she softens. "I wanted to go to the wedding. I *wanted* to go. I wanted us all to go, but I knew you wouldn't. I was happy to be there." She pauses and then says, "It was a really nice wedding. I'm not sorry I was there. I was lonely, and I felt less lonely being there."

In the moonlight she sees something shift in Jordan's posture.

Simone clears her throat and they all startle, as though they've forgotten about her, as though they thought they were being transported by a driverless car. "If I may," she says. "I know this conversation is none of my business, but I just want to say, you guys had an amazing mom."

A great silence falls. Mae is the first to speak.

"Yeah," she says.

"Yeah," says Jordan.

"We did," says Natalie.

"I know that. *You* know that. But tell me about her as though I'd never met her."

"Now?" asks Jordan.

"Here?" asks Mae, glancing at Natalie.

"Now," says Simone. Her hands are shadowy on the steering wheel. There is the quiet tick of the turn signal, the glow of the moon. "Here. Natalie, you go first."

"Well," says Natalie. She appears to be thinking about it, and then to come to some internal resolution. She shakes her head quickly the way she used to do as a kid when she got ocean water in her ears. "Okay. The first thing is . . . she was constitutionally sound."

"Great!" says Simone encouragingly. "Say more."

This is what Natalie chose? thinks Mae. But then Natalie goes on, and they all start nodding along, because it's true. "I mean, she was healthy. That's it! Maybe her immune system was built up from being around kids all the time, at school and at home, but she never got the colds the rest of us got. Never got the flu. Always took care of us when we got sick. Honestly, I don't remember her being in bed a day in her life. Do any of you?" They all shake their heads. "That's why it was such a shock when she got Sick with a capital *S*."

Mae's eyes are moist.

"That was lovely, Natalie," says Simone softly. It's as if Simone has turned into a pastor and they are all part of her congregation. But it's working, the pastor vibe. "Mae?" says Simone.

"She had beautiful handwriting," says Mae, looking at her wrist, just visible from the streetlights and the moon.

Jordan goes next: "She had gorgeous legs, but she hated her stomach."

"She always knew who the shyest kid in the class was and she never called on them without warning. She was allergic to humiliating people."

"She hated rodents as pets but she let me have one anyway."

"Until you killed it."

"Right. Until I killed it."

"She never went to Italy."

"Or apparently Paris."

"Her pancakes were not great."

"But her French toast was amazing."

"She always pulled over for little kids selling lemonade."

"*Always.*"

"She couldn't knit. She tried to learn but she was terrible at it."

"She made the best brownies."

"Her hands were always cool and dry."

"She cried if an animal died in a movie but not necessarily if a person did."

"She was always awake first."

"Her coughs were loud but her sneezes were quiet."

"She reminded us to look at the sky."

That's the best one, so they all look at the sky through the windshield and out their respective windows. They're doing that just as Simone pulls into their driveway, and they understand that Simone has given them not only a ride home, but a gift: the gift of focusing on Theresa and letting their squabbles go, if only for a moment.

"Out you go," says Simone. "Water and Advil, ladies. Water and Advil."

Inside, Mae wonders if her sisters notice that the lights are just as their mother always left them at night, with a single table lamp on in the living room, like a ghost light in a theater.

Calvin is in the kitchen, drinking a cup of tea and reading something on his laptop. He looks up when they troop in. His face, bathed in laptop light, looks happy and relaxed. "There they are, the Shipman girls!" he says. "Have fun?" He sounds so hopeful that they all nod and say yes, yes, so much fun that they got a ride home from Simone, so much fun that they have to go back for Mae's car in the morning. They do not say *we're barely speaking to Mae,* and they do not say *we can't believe she went to your wedding.* They do not say *we still cannot believe you had a wedding for Mae to go to.*

"Okay," says Calvin. "I can take you back in the morning. Kara went to bed after the kids were settled."

"The kids settled?" asks Natalie. "All of them?"

"To a man. They did play a little bit of musical beds. Evangeline wanted to sleep with Leo, so she's in Mae's bed. Mae, I took him out for the bathroom and put him in his crate. Evangeline came with me and held Cinnamon's leash. Scarlett and Caspian are in Natalie's room. Kara changed Caspian's diaper. Everybody did great."

"Wow," says Natalie. "Thank you, Dad."

When Mae goes to her room, she finds that Evangeline is really spread out in Mae's bed. How can someone so small take up so much room? Mae tries to move Evangeline but she's dead weight.

"I'll sleep with you, Jordan," says Mae, appearing at Jordan's door like a hallucination.

"I don't think so," says Jordan. "I'm still pissed. Also, you had all that coffee. You'll never sleep again."

Mae climbs into Jordan's bed anyway and says, "I'm asleep already." And somehow, against all odds, she is.

• • •

Natalie can't sleep. Scarlett has pushed her all the way to the edge of the bed, and her drinks and her thoughts and her worries are roiling around in her stomach and in her head. She's thinking about Mae telling her and Jordan they've been too hard on Calvin, and she's wondering if Mae might be right. She's picturing her father's face lighting up when they all came in together. She's wondering what Austin is doing right now. But she knows what Austin is doing. She knows he's sleeping because he has to be up in just a few hours, and if he's not sleeping then he's worrying about the cow with mastitis, and running through his endless to-do list in his mind. The to-do list on a farm is constantly growing. There is always something to repair or call about or buy or put on the list for next year.

Scarlett makes a little grumbling sound and pulls the covers off Natalie. That's it. She's not going to sleep. Natalie swings herself out of bed and peeks at Caspian, asleep in the portable crib. He's so big for that thing. This is probably the last week he'll be able to use it. She tiptoes down the stairs. In the kitchen she pours a glass of milk. It's such a cliché, the farm wife with the glass of milk, but so what. She likes milk; she believes in the nutrients it provides. She believes in the dairy industry at large. She thinks milk is a very natural way for humans to nourish themselves. (It also helps absorb alcohol, if you believe some people on the internet.)

If Natalie is up in the night at the farm she likes thinking about the cows slumbering in the fields in the warm weather or the barn in the winter, unbothered by all the worries with which humans consume themselves. Most of what we worry about, thinks Natalie, is so futile, unworthy of the brainpower we grant it, and yet, here we are. When she's up in the night in Rye, it's the presence of the ocean that comforts her, almost within arm's reach, waves coming in and receding, constant, ominous, reassuring.

She hears a tread on the stairs, and now here's Jordan, in a set of expensive pajamas, black, edged with white piping. She startles when she sees Natalie and says, "I didn't know anyone was up. Mae snores like a truck driver."

"Night milk?" Natalie holds out her glass. "Or I could pour you your own. I could even make yours chocolate and warm it up!" Natalie had been so angry with Jordan at the bar, she's been angry at her since they cleaned out the storeroom, but then Mae dropped her own bombshell and Natalie isn't sure who to be mad at. Everybody? Nobody?

Jordan winces and shakes her head. "No, thank you."

"Oh, that's right, you don't drink milk."

"Well, that, and I can't have chocolate at night. Do we have bourbon?"

"You want *more* bourbon?"

"Just a tiny bit."

"Good man." Natalie locates the bottle and finds a rocks glass for Jordan. She pours, considers, pours herself a tiny bit too, like an eighth of a finger, and puts the glass of milk in the refrigerator. She'll give it to one of the kids in the morning; that milk is far too hard-won to waste. They each take a seat at the island.

"What's keeping you up?" Natalie asks. "Besides the snoring."

A look passes over Jordan's face and then disappears. "Generalized dark night of the soul," she says. "Some work stuff. And, my god, Mae was at the wedding? And nobody told us?"

"I know," says Natalie. "I'm flabbergasted. I don't understand. How could she not tell us? How could she"—she lowers her voice—"how could she *like* Kara, and keep it a secret? It's like she's been having an affair with Kara behind our backs!"

Jordan sips her bourbon, then stares into her glass, letting a puff of air out of her pursed lips. "I mean, she wouldn't be wrong to think that we wouldn't be receptive to it."

"Preach." Natalie rattles the ice in her glass. "I'd say that's an understatement."

"Is that what's keeping you up too?"

Natalie sighs. "That, and . . . I don't know."

"The internet trolls?"

Natalie nods; suddenly her eyes are full and she doesn't trust herself to speak. When she's gained a shred of composure she whispers, "I wish I didn't care so much. Why am I letting a bunch of strangers crawl under my skin and stay there?"

Jordan is silent for a moment, like she's really thinking about it. "I think what may have happened," she says, "is that the world held a mirror up to you, and you didn't like what you saw."

"But that's not fair," says Natalie.

"Not fair of me to say, or them to do?"

"The latter, mostly. We're just living our lives, and no matter what we do, everybody hates us for something." She pauses. "Is this how Harry and Meghan feel?"

Jordan snorts. "Maybe." Then, "Yeah, probably." Then, "Aside from the article, what do people hate you for?"

Natalie thinks about it and begins to tick her list off on her fingers. "Let's see. The hardscrabble Vermonters hate us for being organic. We have to create a buffer between our land and theirs, you know, to make sure that whatever they're fertilizing can't get on our land. They hate us for creating a buffer. They hate us for selling off some of our stock so we could repopulate with organic cows; they thought that was disrespectful to the former owners, who were their friends. They hate us for selling our milk for so much more, but it's really expensive to run an organic farm so of course we have to sell it for more. That's just economics. They think that we think we're too good for the public schools—"

"Do you think that?" asks Jordan.

"Sort of. I mean, other way around. We think the public schools aren't as—well, aren't the same as they are in Lenox, let's put it that way." Lenox has excellent public schools. All three of the Shipman girls are products of them, of course.

"Diplomatic," says Jordan.

"The people in the feed store laughed the first time I bought Carhartts, and I could feel them getting ready to hate me too. But I need Carhartts! Lined Carhartts! I do actually milk the cows. It's cold out there in the early morning."

"Fair," says Jordan. "Lined Carhartts don't seem unreasonable."

"I could tell they thought I was buying them to look cute."

"You do look cute in them."

"Well, thank you." She smiles briefly. She's running out of fingers. "And now these people online! The vitriol. The judgment. I didn't ask for any of this." She massages her temples.

Jordan clears her throat.

"What?" says Natalie.

"Didn't you, though?"

"Didn't I what?"

"Ask for it."

"No." How *dare* Jordan. "Who asks for vitriol?"

Jordan rubs at an imaginary spot on the island with her thumb and, without looking up, says, "Didn't you open yourself up to it the first time you called yourself a tradwife? Or called yourself anything, and wanted people to pay attention?"

"What? *No*." Natalie hurries to explain, to make it right. "That's just a hashtag. To get more views. But the beliefs behind it are real. It's a movement back toward tradition. Traditional doesn't mean bad. But people get it all mixed up. I mean, even you—you don't hate me, but you don't like me enough to help me."

"Of course I like you. I even love you. By law, I have to. We're sisters."

Natalie laughs and says, "I don't think that's a law. Plenty of sisters hate each other."

Jordan's voice goes level, and she's not meeting Natalie's eyes. "I just don't believe in everything you're doing, I guess is what I've been trying to say. And that makes it hard for me."

Natalie can't believe this. "Oh, I'm sorry. You don't believe in what *I'm* doing? What about that guy from Congress you helped, the one who waved his dick around at his intern? You agreed with what he was doing?"

"*Natalie,*" says Jordan.

"What?"

"First of all, no, of course I didn't agree with what he was doing. And second, that's not how we phrase it in the industry."

"How do you phrase it, then?"

Jordan clears her throat again as if she's making room for her professional voice. "We say, 'Representative So-and-So was going through a challenging personal time and is now seeking professional treatment. He fully owns the consequences of his actions and has expressed to Intern So-and-So his deep sorrow and regret. He hopes to move forward from here and continue to serve this great country as his constituents have trusted him to do for the past twelve years.'"

Despite herself, Natalie is impressed with Jordan's smooth tongue, her facility with language. "Not bad. So why does it matter if you believe in me? Why can't you pretend I'm a client like that guy?"

Jordan takes a long time before answering, like she's really thinking about it. "Maybe it's different because I know you. I can tell what's authentic and what's not."

Natalie tries to take this in, but something isn't tracking. "It's all authentic."

"Is it, though?"

"Of course." Then: "Wait a second," Natalie says. "Is it because of Jesus? That you won't help me?"

Jordan makes a choking sound. "Excuse me?"

"Jesus, Jordan, the guy with the—"

"No, I know who Jesus is. I mean, is that actually what you're asking me?"

"I think that *is* what I'm asking you. Is this really about religion? Because Austin is Christian. And because I'm Christian now too, and my kids are Christian. You're embarrassed by our faith."

"Your faith?" asks Jordan. "*You* don't believe in your faith! That's just the thing. That's what I'm struggling with. You believe for show. You do so many things for show now."

Tears prick Natalie's eyes anew. "How can you say that?"

Now Jordan is looking straight at her. "I've known you for a long time, Nat. And you weren't ever this person. Not until you met Austin. Not until you went hard on social media."

"That's not true. I've always wanted faith. I just didn't know where to get it. These may not be the beliefs we were raised with, Jordan, but I came by them honestly."

Natalie's elementary school best friend, Ursula, was the most religious person Natalie had known growing up in Lenox. Ursula's family attended St. Ann's devotedly, every Sunday plus each holy day of obligation. If Natalie spent the night on a Saturday the family would tote her along to the 9:45 a.m. Mass the next day. Ursula, newly First Communioned, would cast an apologetic look at Natalie as she rose and followed her parents and older brother down the aisle to receive the sacrament. In a hushed, reverent voice, Ursula would explain to

Natalie the significance of the colors of the priest's robes, and the locked box ("the tabernacle") that held the consecrated host ("the body of Christ"). Natalie loved it all.

"Can't we go to St. Ann's?" Natalie suggested one Christmas, when her friendship with Ursula was at its height (at that age, best friendship can look a lot like love).

"We're not Catholic," Theresa said.

"What are we?"

"We are lapsed Episcopalians."

(For years Natalie thought that was a proper-noun descriptor, Lapsed Episcopalians being somewhat equal to Roman Catholics.) "What does that mean?"

"It means we sleep in on Sundays."

Ursula moved to St. Louis in the fourth grade. Until she met Austin, Natalie equated God almost entirely with ceremony and recitation, robes and secrecy, with the standing and kneeling and sitting that seemed like a special kind of choreography reserved for the lucky. Austin's family, members of the Journey Church in Bozeman, were altogether different. They talked to Jesus not only like he was in the room with them but like he was an actual friend of the family. ("Jesus, bro," Natalie once heard Austin's brother begin a prayer.) Austin's family opened another doorway into faith, and Natalie at first wasn't sure how to walk through it.

Then Theresa got sick, and Natalie began to pray in earnest, all the time. She believed someone was listening to her, even as Theresa got sicker. She believed and she believed and she believed, and she continued to believe, because if she didn't, there was only a void.

But Jordan doesn't get this. "Look, it honestly all just seems . . . performative," Jordan says now. "And on top of that, a lot of it seems unfair. That you tell women how to live their lives. Making it look like it all comes so easy, when really you have a lot of advantages not everyone has."

"Like what?" challenges Natalie.

Now it's Jordan's turn to tick a list off on her fingers. "Well, you're really pretty. And you're naturally thin. Thick hair. Effortlessly fertile. Good-looking husband who's obviously devoted to you. There's a lot to envy there. So when you tell people how to live their lives, they tend to listen."

Natalie touches a lock of her hair. (Her hair *is* very thick, though not as thick as Mae's.) "I'm not telling anyone else how to live their lives. I'm just sharing mine. Nobody has to follow me or do anything I'm doing."

"Respectfully, I call bullshit on that," says Jordan. "You're ex*actly* telling people what to do. You're offering yourself up as an example. As something to aspire to."

"An example of *one* way to live! Not of the *only* way!"

"Tens of thousands of young women, probably way more, who are trying to figure out their lives and their futures are looking at you and wondering if they should be yoking themselves to a man—"

"I'm not yoked! I'm *married*. It's not the same thing. Geez, Jordan."

"It doesn't have to be the same thing, no. But you've got to see those two things look pretty close from where I sit."

Natalie can't take it another second. "Oh, yeah? Up on your high horse? Is that how they look from there?"

"Burn," says Jordan softly. But she doesn't look ready to give in. She looks like she's still got important things to say. "What about your daughters? What are they taking from your example?"

Natalie's eyes widen, dry now, flashing. She's incredulous. If Jordan brings up that dropped napkin she's going to lose it. "What are they *taking*? I hope they're taking an example of what a happy family looks like! I hope they're seeing the power of dedicated, concentrated parenting. I hope they're seeing love! So one day when they—"

"When they become breeders?"

"Too far," snaps Natalie. Her blood is nearly boiling.

Jordan concedes with a tip of her head. "Sorry," she says. "You're right. Go on."

For a minute Natalie feels too angry to go on, and then too sad—she blinks at the ceiling the way people do when they're trying to keep a fresh flow of tears from coming out. "What I'm saying is, of course my daughters can make their own choices. Caspian can make his own too. Like I started to tell you yesterday, my accounts make way more than the farm brings in. I'm actually showing them an example of working motherhood."

"Go on," says Jordan.

"It's really hard to make a profit on a dairy farm. We count on that income. Austin's family isn't handing money out all the time. Most of Austin's family money is in a trust as long as his parents are alive. Does that make a difference to you?"

Jordan thinks about it. A-ha! thinks Natalie. I've got her. But then Jordan says, "I think that might be worse, actually."

"Worse? Why?"

"Because you're telling women that financial independence doesn't matter, that they should focus their time and energy on their families, when you're actually financially independent. Don't you see what you're doing?"

"I'm not doing anything!"

"You have a million and a half followers, Natalie. Yes, you are doing something." Jordan sounds remarkably like their mother used to sound when she scolded them—which wasn't so often, but it did happen. The time Natalie took the car out by herself when she only had her learner's permit; Mae's failing algebra grade in high school; the summer of Simone, when Jordan stayed out all night without checking in. "You know, it's been more than a century since the first women got the right to vote."

Natalie bristles at this. "I'm not suggesting women don't vote, Jordan. God, I'm pretty sure you know me better than that!" She's so angry she can feel her words coming out like little bullets from her tight pursed lips. But Jordan is angry too, Natalie can see that. Jordan is blinking so rapidly Natalie fears she'll lose a contact, if she has them in.

"Then what," Jordan says, "are you suggesting? Please explain it to me."

"We made a choice that's right for our family, together, Austin and I did. Of *course* I know what the naysayers say. I know what some of my own friends say, friends who are stressed out all the time and arguing with their spouses over who 'gets' to focus on work and who 'has' to take care of the kids. But I'm doing what I believe is right. And that actually takes guts."

"It's just not how I thought you'd turn out, Natalie. Under someone's thumb." Jordan stands as though she's about to leave the kitchen. Jordan has always been a fan of a grand gesture, of delivering a zinger and departing. But Natalie won't let her do it, not this time! Why does Jordan get to be so certain, so bulletproof? Why does she get to make the rules?

"What about you, Jordan?"

"What about me?"

"Why aren't you ever the vulnerable one?"

"I'm sorry?"

"You heard me. Why's it all black-and-white for you, no questions, no equivocation, no doubts about who you are and how you've set up your life?"

Of the barbs they've been tossing back and forth—tonight, for sure, but also, more quietly, maybe all week—this is the one that hits. Natalie can almost see it land, and when it does Jordan's eyes fill, then the tears spill over.

"Jordan!" says Natalie, moving to get a box of tissues from the counter and slide it toward her. "Oh my god, I'm sorry! I didn't mean to make you cry! What is it?"

"I'm not certain at all," says Jordan. "About anything."

Natalie is an idiot: in the excitement of seeing Simone, in the shock at Mae's revelation, she had forgotten what Jordan said at the bar: *You aren't the only one with things going on.*

Natalie gets them clean glasses and fills them with ice water. She sits beside her sister. "Tell me," she says. "Tell me, Jordan."

• • •

It was the Sunday of Memorial Day weekend, and Jordan was invited to go with Bernadette to a party all the way out in Sagaponack, at the home of a VIP client. We won't say who. You'd know the name, and, had Bernadette not worked her magic, you'd know a lot of other stuff about this person too.

Jordan was invited as Bernadette's plus-one. Typically Bernadette's husband, Jed, would serve as Bernadette's plus-one, but Jed and the two children (ages nine and seven) were visiting Jed's parents in South Carolina, as they do twice a year, whether they like it or not. (Bernadette doesn't like it. Too much downtime, and Jed's mother gets offended when Bernadette checks her phone during meals.)

Despite these constrictions, Bernadette was supposed to go with the family. Then she got the invitation to Sagaponack. In their business there are some parties you just don't turn down, no matter who is waiting for you on the golf course at Wild Dunes. So she called Jordan and enlisted her. A car would come for her at three o'clock. Dress for success, Bernadette told her.

Jordan chose a white pantsuit. She felt like a suffragette.

"They're better off without me," Bernadette confessed to Jordan in the town car, as though they were continuing a conversation they had begun earlier. It took Jordan a moment to realize Bernadette meant her husband and children. "Jed's mom thinks I'm A Lot."

"Oh, I'm sure that's not true," said Jordan. It was probably true. Bernadette *is* A Lot. But that's why she's so good at her job. Like Tom Petty, she won't back down; like Destiny's Child, she's a survivor. Bernadette is forty-six; she looks thirty-five and acts, alternately, twenty-four and fifty-seven. Depending on the situation. She has the sort of long, thin legs that look good in a tennis skirt, brown eyes set just a smidge too close together, and lips you keep looking at because you can't decide if she uses filler or not. (Jordan still doesn't know, but her money is on yes.)

She started her firm at thirty and plans to sell it when she's fifty, at which point she will "sit on a beach, doing nothing." There's no way the "doing nothing" thing is going to happen, Jordan knows. Bernadette is incapable of this. She barely sleeps, scarcely eats, completes a forty-five-minute Peloton bike workout every morning before sunrise.

For the first hour plus change of the drive, they were on the Long Island Expressway and there wasn't much to look at except expressway, so when Bernadette picked up her phone, Jordan set her thoughts free to roam and wander. The invitation to Sagaponack was a big deal. The last time Bernadette brought someone from the firm as her plus-one was five years ago, when she invited Jordan's former coworker, Michael, to a Christmas party on the Upper West Side. Michael had three too many peppermint martinis and invited one of their clients to engage in a push-up contest with him. He didn't even have the good grace to let the client win, and this is why Michael is Jordan's former coworker and not her current coworker.

Jordan resolved she would self-monitor her drinking in Sagaponack. One cocktail or two glasses of champagne. No showing off. No push-up contests, not even a plank contest. (She would definitely win a plank contest, unless The Rock himself was at this party, which, come to think of it, was not out of the question.)

Except for Sheila in accounting, Jordan was the person who had worked for Bernadette the longest. Bernadette considered Jordan her right-hand man. Woman. She trusted Jordan with tasks she wouldn't dream of delegating to the younger and greener Tom or Caitlin or Irina, and Jordan had become Bernadette's first call when Bernadette herself receives a call.

This is not to say that all was perfect in Bernadette-land. Bernadette could be a bully. Jordan had heard her on the phone with her nanny, her chiropractor, her eyelash esthetician, even her own husband, speaking in a tone any of the Shipman girls would have been roundly scolded for had they ever dared to introduce it with anyone.

There were times when Bernadette's response to a crisis was so aggressive that even Jordan, who had never been known for her soft touch, balked. And yet! Bernadette was no longer simply a rising star in the field. She was the star, and she had risen. Rolodexes don't exist anymore—they've never existed in Jordan's professional life, though she's seen them in movies—but if they did, Bernadette's card would have prime placement on more desktops than you could count.

They exited onto the two-lane Sunrise Highway, and traffic began to build. Who were all these people, heading to different parts of the Hamptons on day three of the holiday weekend? Bernadette and Jordan were traveling with the parasites, the hangers-on, the day-trippers.

The start of the summer instilled in Jordan a sudden, intense longing for the summers of her youth. There were summers when she played the brat, of course, when she longed to be back in Lenox, working at Tanglewood with her friends, waitressing at the Pittsfield Country Club, but there were many more summers when there was no place else in the world she'd rather be than Ruby on Rye.

"We're going to be fucking late," said Bernadette, and with a wallop Jordan came back to the present. Jordan thought she saw the driver's ears twitch. She thought that maybe she saw his soul twitch.

Did Jordan ever have second thoughts about having tied her cart to such a—well, to use a euphemism—powerful horse? Were there times when she thought that Bernadette's moral compass may have skewed slightly off, and did that frighten her? Perhaps. But not so many times that she needed to worry about it. It was the nature of the crisis communications business to come out swinging, to react quickly, to move fast so that you controlled the narrative. If Bernadette wasn't who she was, she wouldn't be so good at doing what she does.

They arrived.

When their car pulled up to the house, joining the other vehicles that were variously parked or letting people out, Jordan tried not to gape openly. But in her mind, very quietly, she gaped. Lenox had its share of beautiful homes, of course it did, and so did Rye, and Jordan had lived in Manhattan long enough that this was not her first trip to the Hamptons, but, wow, this house was something else altogether. It must have been worth thirty million dollars. The front was entirely glass. Visible inside and perfectly lit to show off every straight line, every geometric cube of furniture, was a winding, floating staircase.

She cast a subtle glance at Bernadette to see if she was equally impressed, but Bernadette was once again looking at her phone and barely seemed to have noticed that they were here.

"Whoa," Jordan said experimentally.

Bernadette glanced up and says, "I heard this house has seventeen bathrooms. Does that seem excessive to you?" She didn't wait for Jordan's answer (which is, of course, *yes*—how could there be any other?), but slid out of the car. She said not one word to the driver, so Jordan thanked him, because if there was one thing her mother taught her, and there were many more than one, it was that you always thank a person who has done something for you, whether or not they have been paid to do it.

In the perfect light of an early summer evening, they followed the curvy path that led around the house and toward the sounds of the party. Jordan imagined that with a drone's-eye view the paths would spell out something like WE'RE IMPORTANT AND WE HAVE A LOT OF MONEY, HOW ABOUT YOU?

Nothing felt off yet.

On the endless, Gatsby-like lawn, the party, like the interior of the house, looked as artfully arranged as a stage set. Beautiful people in beautiful clothes. Flutes of champagne, a string quartet dressed in red, white, and blue, and playing all the holiday favorites. Copland, Gershwin, Bernstein. A raw bar, of course. There was always a raw bar, the rawer the better. Lanterns floating in the pristine rectangular pool, servers moving around as unobtrusively as moths. Much of the outdoor furniture was built into the patio itself, and around the pool are at least thirty lounge chairs, so fancy that they didn't even have frames.

Bernadette took a flute of champagne from a server, downed its contents, then took another before Jordan had even had two sips of hers. The server, who reminded Jordan of Mae, young, with creamy skin and bright eyes, averted her gaze as though Bernadette was undressing in front of her. Jordan imagined that you saw all sorts of things working at parties like this. Designer drugs, high-end hookers, wild infidelities. The bigger the stock portfolio, she has learned, the bigger the taste for risk, and the stronger the feeling that you'll skate away from your transgressions.

"I've got to go say hello to someone," said Bernadette, and just like that Jordan was alone in the crowd. She should have known, when asked to be Bernadette's plus-one, that this would mean being an only one, a stranger in a sea of people who all seemed to know each other.

She drank her champagne until it was gone. She accepted another glass from a different server, and walked around the perimeter of the party, sipping, until that one was gone too. She spotted someone she knew tangentially from the city and she briefly joined a clot of people, then made her excuses when she realized she didn't know anyone they were talking about.

She wished, as she did at least once a week, that Audrey were here with her. That would be ironic, Audrey at a work party, since one of the main reasons they broke up was Jordan's "toxic workaholism."

They'd arrived at the party just before six, and now it was close to seven thirty. Maybe forty-five minutes from sunset. The light was beginning to peel back from the edges of the sky, revealing the oncoming darkness. Jordan was looking at the sky when yet another server approached, this time with a tray of cups. Each cup contained a single oyster and a mini bottle of Tabasco sauce. A traveling raw bar! The mini Tabasco sauce was probably the cutest thing Jordan had ever seen, so she accepted one, even though she's not an oyster girl. She slipped the Tabasco bottle into her bag, left the cup on a tall table, and realized that she needed the bathroom. Off she went, then, toward the glass house. There was a joke here about throwing stones, but there was nobody to tell it to. She'd workshop it in her mind, maybe tell it later.

Finding a bathroom was harder than it seemed like it should be in a house that purportedly had seventeen of them. (The Shipman house in Lenox has three, which on the surface seemed like plenty, but only one has a shower so there was almost always one sister standing outside it, exhorting another sister to hurry up.) In this house, seventeen bathrooms strong, all of the doors blended into the walls and Jordan was too nervous to open any of them. What if behind one of them was, say, an opium den? Or a den of iniquity? Or some other kind of den? Also, why did Jordan feel like she was the only person in this house? Had nature called to no other party guest? Where were the caterers?

She admired the floating staircase for a moment. Even up close, she couldn't figure out the mechanics. An architect, she was not. She wondered if anyone outside was observing her, the same way she'd looked in when they first arrived. Then she found another staircase, going down this time, and not white and floating but gunmetal gray and anchored industrially to the wall.

Jordan descended.

Success.

She came out of the bathroom and saw that behind one wall was a full movie theater complete with giant plush seats. Next to that, a home gym, glassed in like the gym in a hotel, with a Peloton treadmill, bike, and rowing machine, *and* a Pilates reformer. She'd never seen a Pilates reformer out in the wild, in somebody's house! She inched closer, practically drooling, her feet itching to try out the straps. They looked pristine, not like the ones at her studio that saw many pairs of feet a day. A voice behind her made her jump.

"Hello there, young lady. Looking for something?"

Jordan whipped her head around. "Jesus! You scared me, Bernadette." Bernadette was standing on the last step of the staircase, smiling at Jordan in that half-mocking way she has, as though she is the middle school queen bee and she has your number. "I was looking for the bathroom," Jordan explained. "Took me forever. But I found it. One down, sixteen to go."

Bernadette descended the final step and stood level with Jordan. "There's one in the pool house. That's the one guests are using. I saw you walk over here so figured I'd track you down and tell you."

Jordan's face burned. No wonder the house was empty. "Ohmygod," she said. "I'm not supposed to be in here, am I?"

"Strictly speaking, no."

"Am I going to get in trouble?"

"Are you going to *get in trouble*?" Bernadette tilted back her head and hooted. She must have been a nightmare in high school. Jordan felt foolish. "I guess you can take the girl out of Western Mass . . ." said Bernadette. She laughed some more, then said, "I won't tell anyone that we're in here if you won't."

This was when Jordan realized that Bernadette was drunk. Really drunk. Many-glasses-of-champagne-on-an-empty-stomach drunk. Ho, boy. Bernadette plopped down in one of the plush movie seats and patted the one next to her. Reluctantly, Jordan sat, but she looked around while she did, as though the usher was going to come and ask for their tickets.

"I've been thinking," said Bernadette. "I want someone to be partner. I'm thinking about succession planning."

"Really?" Jordan sucked in her breath and her heart started to beat faster. "Really, do you mean it?" This is what she'd been hoping for—to beat out Tom and Caitlin and Irina! To be partner! To be in the right position when Bernadette is ready to retire!

"I mean it." Then something unexpected happened. Bernadette's hand was *on Jordan's thigh*, resting as casually as if it was on her own thigh. This couldn't be right. There must be a mistake. Jordan returned Bernadette's hand to her, placing it on the armrest between their seats.

The hand came back almost immediately, resting on Jordan's crotch, the heel against her pubis. Jordan froze. She couldn't move or think. What should she *do*? Her voice sounded like it was coming from the corner of the room when she said, "I don't think you mean to do this." She squirmed, tried to shift away, but Bernadette's hand held her fast.

"It's okay, nobody knows we're here," Bernadette said, undeterred. She turned slightly in her seat so she was facing Jordan. "Why don't you loosen up, Jordan? Have a little fun?"

"Loosen *up*?" repeated Jordan. "Bernadette—"

Bernadette leaned in, her breath hitting Jordan's neck, and whispered, "If I were you I'd think carefully about what choice you make here, Jordan. I'm about to make some big decisions."

Jordan was breathing hard, and she could feel her face flaming. She twisted her body completely away and stood, leaving Bernadette sitting, looking up at her. Her crotch was still burning where Bernadette's hand had been. Her eyes were smarting from Bernadette's dragon breath. She said, "Bernadette. You're drunk. You don't know what you're doing."

Bernadette snorted and said, "*I* don't know what I'm doing?" She hooted. "We'll see about that!" She rose, gave Jordan a long, inscrutable look, and stalked up the stairs. Jordan stood next to her theater seat for a good long time, her knees shaking just a little. She waited before following Bernadette, and right when she emerged from the house and into the night the fireworks show began. *Pop pop. Pow pow pow.*

It took Jordan forty-five minutes to find an Uber that would make the $295 trip from Sagaponack back to the city. The Uber driver was cranky and quiet, the way Uber drivers often get when they accept a really long trip and then regret it. She was glad for his silence—she didn't want to talk.

When she was back in her own apartment, she poured herself a nightcap—WhistlePig, neat, in one of the Glencairn glasses she bought herself the previous Christmas, for no reason other than she wanted them.

Her hands were shaking a little as she poured.

She put on her pajamas and climbed into bed, setting the glass beside her on the nightstand. The WhistlePig was so smooth and flavorful (notes of cocoa and cured leather) that just holding it made her feel calm. She took a small sip, then another, set the glass down again, picked up her phone.

Nothing from Bernadette, not that she'd really expected anything.

She drank the rest of the WhistlePig in one gulp. If Glen Cairn were a person (he's not, right?) he might be disappointed in Jordan for her gracelessness. She settled herself on her pillow for a long summer's nap.

She would deal with all of this in the morning. Or not.

• • •

"Oh my god, Jordan," says Natalie. "Is that why she's calling you all the time? To apologize? Is she worried you're going to complain to HR or something?"

"Actually, there's been no apology. There's been no acknowledgment."

"But Memorial Day was, what, six weeks ago? What's happened since then?"

"She's traveled a lot. A client in LA, a client in London. I was in Atlanta for a week when she was back. She was on vacation over the Fourth . . . so it's kind of been business as usual. But it's not. She's been calling me because she wants me to lie to a reporter who's working on a story about her, about her being a 'toxic boss.'" Jordan makes air quotes with two tired fingers. "She's trying to make sure I'll do what she needs me to do to make it go away."

"Why would you do that?" asks Natalie, horrified. "She's definitely toxic—and threatening. She put you in a terrible situation."

"I know." Jordan tents her fingers and lays her head gently in them. "But she's my boss. And it was just that one time. And, like, it's easy to talk myself into the possibility that I'm making it a bigger deal than it was. If I'm on her side here, she'll make me partner. I've been working toward this for *ten years*. I know I'm capable of running that place one day."

"So what are you going to do?"

"I don't know," says Jordan. "And I only have tomorrow to figure it out. She wants me to talk to the reporter by Friday."

"Is there any more of whatever you're drinking?" says a voice from the Great Beyond—or the doorway of the kitchen. "I know you're both mad at me, about the wedding thing. But I can't sleep."

"We're drinking water," says Jordan.

"You can't sleep because you had, like, nine shots of espresso," says Natalie, her voice chilly.

"I know," says Mae. "I fell asleep right away and then all of a sudden I was wide awake, feeling like it was nine a.m."

"Well, try again," says Jordan, without sympathy. To both of them Mae is eight years old in a peach-colored two-piece Carter's pajama set with ruffles at the shoulders, refusing to go to bed because she wants to hang out with the big girls and their friends in the kitchen. Except now she is a twenty-nine-year-old traitor who forgot to remove her mascara before bed, which is now giving her the look of a restless racoon.

"I can't," says Mae softly. She rubs her eyes, smearing the mascara further. "There's something I need to tell you guys. It's been weighing on me, and I need you to know what's going on."

Unrelenting, Jordan says, "Is it another amazing example of disloyalty?"

At the same time Natalie says, "Oh, Mae, are you *pregnant*?"

Mae shakes her head. "Neither of those. It's worse. Or maybe better, I don't know. But I don't know what to do, and I need you guys, okay? I really need you."

"Okay," says Natalie finally, glancing at Jordan.

Jordan pulls out the stool next to her. "Sit down. Tell us."

• • •

Mae can't find a delicate way into the story, there's no easy on-ramp, so she tells the ending first, and quickly, without any verbal punctuation. She says, "I fell for a stupid scam and I lost most of my money and I'm living out of my car." Then, seeing the shocked faces of her sisters, and guessing what might come next, she says, "You don't need to berate me. I've berated myself enough already."

Jordan speaks first. "Whoa, Mae," she says. "You're going to have to back up."

"Back *way* up," says Natalie. "We can't berate you if we don't even know what happened."

"Okay," says Mae. Deep breath, filling her ribs, big exhale. Then she tells the story. "Last month, a box came for me at my apartment. Well, Tony's apartment. Inside the box was a Bluetooth speaker."

She hadn't ordered any speakers, she explains, so obviously she was confused. "I thought maybe it was from one of you!"

"I would have sent you a speaker if I knew you needed one," Jordan hurries to say.

"Me too," says Natalie competitively.

"No, that's just it, I didn't need one. I have a speaker! I have a great speaker. It's in the back of my car right now. So I . . . I don't know, it made me think of Mom, you know? How she used to send us silly gifts, in college and stuff. She did that for you guys too, right?"

"Holiday socks," Natalie and Jordan say together.

"Exactly! Who even knew Thanksgiving socks were a thing?" This is Jordan.

"Turkeys wearing Pilgrim hats," confirms Natalie. "Or a coloring book . . ."

"Not even an adult coloring book," says Jordan, nodding and

smiling at the memory. "Just a regular children's coloring book with, like, puppies to color in, and a box of eight fat Crayolas."

"Jumbos," says Natalie. They're all quiet for a few seconds, remembering, and then Natalie says, "Anyway, go on. Box. Speaker."

"Okay, so, I know Mom wasn't actually sending me a speaker, duh, but I guess part of me somehow thought she was. You know how we used to dance around the kitchen sometimes—"

"Hold up," says Jordan. "Hold right up. What *family* did you grow up in, Mae? Mom never danced in the kitchen."

Mae looks back and forth between them, confused. "Yes, she did."

"When Mom was in the kitchen," says Natalie, "she was doing forty things at once and she was rushed. She certainly wasn't *dancing*."

"Only sometimes," says Mae.

"To *what*?"

Mae considers. "Elton John," she says finally.

"Elton John isn't danceable," says Natalie decisively, as if this settles it.

"'Crocodile Rock,'" says Mae. "You can dance to 'Crocodile Rock.'"

Jordan thinks about this. "Awkward dancing, maybe."

"I didn't say she was a *good* dancer," says Mae. "I just said she danced. But now that I think about it, this was after you two were out of the house. Remember, I was there for all those years without you, Jordan, and for four years without either of you."

"I never had her to myself," says Natalie. "Not on the front end and not on the back end."

"Not the point of the story, Natalie," says Jordan. "The point is—Go ahead, Mae. What's the point?"

"The point," says Mae, "is that when I saw the speaker I thought about Mom and me, and I really did believe for a second that it was from her."

"Oh, Mae," says Jordan. There's so much pity in her voice that

Mae cringes. "So who was it from? I can't figure out where this could possibly be going."

Mae takes a deep, shuddering breath. "This is the bad part." Inside the box was a slip of paper with a QR code. It looked like something you'd get inside a box from, say, Amazon, with Mae's name and address printed on it, along with the code and a message that said *SCAN HERE FOR A MESSAGE ABOUT YOUR GIFT.*

"So I scanned the code." Then, uncertainly, "Like anyone would, right?"

"Right," say her sisters agreeably. And, "Of course, we'd scan it too."

"But it was a scam."

"A scam?"

Mae nods sadly, and her eyes fill. "A scan scam."

"What do you mean?" Jordan's brow is furrowed.

"I mean, when I scanned it, all that appeared was a message that said *ENJOY!* But it must have also gotten, I don't know, some malware on my phone, and somebody got into my online banking accounts and got my passwords and everything, and over the next week or so my debit account was wiped out. And that was all I had."

"What account?"

"My debit—"

Jordan says, "You keep all of your money in your debit account?"

Natalie turns on her. "Oh my god, is that what you're focusing on?" To Mae she says, "Did you report it?"

"I closed that account."

"Did you tell the bank people why you were closing it?" Jordan asks. Mae shakes her head. "Why not?"

"I was embarrassed," whispers Mae.

"You were a *victim*," says Jordan. "You should be advocating for yourself, not be embarrassed."

"I changed my passwords. I took my phone to my friend Chip and he got the malware off."

"You have a friend Chip who's an electronics expert?"

Mae nods. "He works for a data recovery service." Then, small grin. "Ohhh, yeah, I get it. Chip." The grin doesn't last long, but it's nice to see a flash of the old Mae come out of the rubble. "I didn't know who to report it to."

"The bank, for starters. The FBI. I think the FTC?"

Mae shakes her head. "I was too exhausted to figure that out. And ashamed. It's humiliating, to think someone sent you a present—your dead mom!—and then you're completely wiped out. What I had in there would probably be nothing to you guys, spare change or whatever, but it was all that was keeping me from basically not having a place to live."

"The shame is common," says Natalie. "I've read about people being extorted right in front of their family members but not telling anyone because they're so far in it. I read an article about a lonely rich lady who lost, like, fifty thousand dollars when someone called pretending to be her grandson needing to post bond."

"But I'm not a lonely rich grandmother," says Mae. "I should have known better. I shouldn't have fallen for it."

"I might have fallen for it too," says Natalie soothingly, even though there's something in her expression that makes Mae think that she doesn't really believe she would have.

"And besides that," says Jordan, "you never should have been teetering on the edge like that without telling us!"

Mae realizes she's feeling comforted by this, by the familiarity of the kitchen and her sisters' voices, the strangeness of the late hour, the relief of having shared the thing she's been carrying around. But the real problem is still there.

"None of this is the point, okay? All my rent money, everything

I had, was in that one account. So it's gone. Now I owe Tony twelve hundred dollars." Mae can feel it rising again, the sense of panic that has been with her for the last month, the feeling like she's always on the verge of hyperventilating.

"We can lend you rent money," says Jordan. "We can *give* you rent money. You should have asked."

Mae puts a hand on her chest to try to slow her jackhammer heart. "It's not just that, though. I mean, that would help get Tony off my back. But I have nowhere to live, nothing to start over with. I was going to live *here*. I thought I could ask Dad to let me stay here for the fall, while I figure things out, maybe get a job and save some money."

"Ohhhh," says Natalie.

"I moved my stuff out of Tony's, and I can't even pay the storage fees. I don't have a security deposit or recent landlord references. I don't have anything. I'm literally without a home. I don't know what to do, you guys. I don't know what to do." She's looking into the future, and all she sees is a dark, scary void, a black hole she will get lost in.

"It'll be okay," says Jordan.

Mae turns on her. "How's it going to be okay? Like, specifically?" Her voice rises. "I know you want to be helpful but if you were, you wouldn't just say it's going to be okay and then be fine with Dad selling the house." She screws her face up.

"Uh-oh," says Jordan. "Uh-oh, here comes the Storm," and something about this, about her perfect sisters with their put-together lives, their offers of help that aren't really a solution, their *complacency*, so enrages Mae that she just can't take it anymore. She slides off the stool, and, as much as a barefoot young woman in pajamas can stomp, she stomps upstairs.

• • •

"I'll go," Natalie says.

Jordan is half off her stool. "Should we both go?"

"Let me try first."

Mae had always moved through the world as if with a gentle breeze at her back, Natalie thinks as she climbs the stairs. But she hasn't been like that for a long time, maybe not since Theresa's death. Even the fact that she'd gone home to their father and Kara's wedding without telling them, which just a few hours ago Natalie and Jordan considered to be an impeachable offense, was a sign, a plea. A cry for help. Mae needed her family.

Natalie used to scroll through the comments on her videos, and if she saw one from Mae (*slayyyyy*, Mae might comment, or *love this so much!*) she'd smile and heart it, but did she wonder what Mae was doing right then, how she was feeling? Did she wonder if anyone had broken her heart or stolen her money, left her blowing in the wind like a sheet on a clothesline?

Mae is lying in Jordan's bed, her eyes open. The lights are off, but she can see her sister's face because of the moon. Natalie smooths Mae's hair back from her forehead and pulls the sheet up and tucks it in along the sides, the way their mother used to when they were little. Mae watches her.

"Mae," says Natalie. "So what. You made a mistake."

"There's something wrong with me."

"There's nothing wrong with you! Mistakes are what your twenties are for."

"How come nobody told me that?"

"We don't talk about it enough. Your twenties can be hard. You have so much collagen still, and that's a blessing, but in every other way, these years aren't always so great."

Mae doesn't say anything, but Natalie can see that she has her attention, so she goes on. "You're used to traveling along the same path as your peers, because you've been doing it forever, and then, *boom*, you're all going at different paces. You feel like you're the only one who isn't engaged or hasn't found your career or bought a house."

"I literally cannot imagine ever buying a house," says Mae. "That seems so complicated."

"It is and it isn't," says Natalie. She considers. "Actually, it is pretty complicated. But the point is, this shitty thing that happened to you, it sucks, but you'll recover from it. You'll move on. You'll grow up. When I was twenty-two, twenty-three? I was a *hot mess*. I was having fun, sure, but it was messy."

"No you weren't."

"I swear. Burning hot."

"But I'm so much older than twenty-three."

"Okay, so when I was your age? We were one year into owning a *dairy farm*! I was covered in *manure* most days. No social life, no friends, a barn that needed rebuilding, a mud season that wouldn't quit, a baby and a toddler. No idea what I was doing. Do you think I didn't have days when I woke up and wondered what the hell had happened, what path I was on? Nobody teaches you how to be a grown-up, Mae. It's trial and error. Lots of error."

Mae closes her eyes. "That makes me feel so much better," she says softly. "To know that you were once a hot mess."

"Many days," says Natalie, "when the cameras are off, I still am. Now, let's get some sleep. In the morning, we'll figure all of this out."

When she opens the door she sees Jordan standing there, taking in every word.

They tiptoe back down the stairs, and in the kitchen, they consider each other.

"You did a good job," Jordan says. "You were great in there."

Natalie shakes her head. "We've done a terrible job as big sisters," she says. “It’s not just the recent money thing. She’s been struggling for a long time.”

“Terrible,” agrees Jordan. “Mom would be crushed.”

“Absolutely crushed,” Natalie says. “I get so caught up in my own life—”

“Me too,” says Jordan. “Definitely me too.”

“I told her to join a *club*!”

“At least you told her something.”

“We should have known something was going on when we saw all the tattoos. That’s nothing against tattoos in general, but such an abundance is very un-Mae-like.”

“Yeah.” Jordan shakes her head. “What do we do?”

“I don’t know.”

“One of us has to take her home with us, right?”

“Like a rescue dog?”

“Very similar to a rescue dog. But a little better on the leash.”

“I would have scanned that code too,” Natalie confesses. “Especially if it was a really nice speaker.”

“I don’t think I would have,” says Jordan. Then, reconsidering, “I don’t know. Maybe I would have. I definitely would have reported it immediately when all my money was gone, though.”

“Wait,” says Natalie. “That’s your bed that I just put Mae into. Should I have tucked you in with her?”

Jordan shakes her head. “I’ll find somewhere else to sleep. It’s not just the snoring. I think I’m going to sleep outside. On the patio.”

“Ooooh,” says Natalie. “Under the stars.”

“Want to come?”

“I do,” says Natalie. “But I’d better go back to the kids.”

“We used to sleep on the patio once a summer, remember?”

Natalie nods. “Always in August. But we had to wait until Mom and

Dad went to bed because Mom thought we'd get kidnapped." There's *nothing* like falling asleep to the sound of the waves. "Kidnapped from a patio! In Rye! You can't even see the patio from the street."

"She also thought we were going to get roofied any time we went out."

"Upon reflection," says Natalie, "I guess a person can get kidnapped from anywhere." Now that she has kids of her own she's much more understanding of her parents' fears. There is *so much to be afraid of.*

"And then we'd have to wake up early and sneak upstairs to our rooms."

"But we'd wake up early anyway, because of the sunrise."

The sunrises at Jenness are absolute stunners, throwing prisms of color over the water, backlighting the really early surfers in red-gold, shining a spotlight on the humps of the Isles of Shoals, six miles out to sea. You can't sleep through that, and there is absolutely no better way to wake up.

The sisters are quiet for a minute, remembering the long-ago mornings, the sandpipers skittering across the sand. They never slept as well as they thought they would on a patio chair so they'd crawl into their actual beds and sleep for a few more hours, emerging when the rest of the family was well into their day. "Morning, lazybones," Theresa might say to them, and they'd let her think that so the night could remain their secret.

Natalie helps Jordan gather blankets from the basket in the sunroom and carry them out onto the patio. She helps her wipe the dew from the cushions, and when Jordan is settled in one of the loungers, she covers her with the blankets. This is the second sister she's tucked in tonight! It's just past two o'clock by now; first light is less than three hours away. The stars are bright and close, and the moon, one day away from full, is mighty.

THURSDAY

• • •

"Do you think I'll have a ticket?" Mae and Calvin are driving to pick up Mae's car. It's nine o'clock in the morning. Calvin takes the scenic route, up 1A. Mae feels like a preteen again, getting picked up from a sleepover with scratchy, tired eyes. But not exactly like a preteen, because she has a solid hangover, respectable but manageable. She'd woken up at seven in Jordan's bed with no Jordan. When she'd taken Leo for his morning training Jordan was fast asleep on one of the patio loungers. Mae laid another blanket on top of her and kept Leo from sniffing her. She took him to the far end of the beach, videoed him coming back to her five times in a row as she'd backed up a little farther each time. The long leash was there, but she'd never needed to reach for it. Leo's recall is really improving. By the time she'd returned, the household was waking up.

"Sorry?" says Calvin. "Did you ask if I think you have rickets?"

Oh my god, thinks Mae, is he losing his *hearing*? But she glances at him and sees the smile playing at his mouth. She rolls her eyes, but she laughs a little bit too. "Is it actually illegal to park overnight in Portsmouth?"

"I don't know," Calvin muses. "I've never tried it. But if you do, it won't be much. They wouldn't tow."

Mae hadn't even thought about the possibility of an expensive tow. She pretends that her father's answer is a soothing one. She doesn't want to tell Calvin that anything, anything at all, would be too much for her right now. The constant worry about a place to live is a little knot that will never loosen. She felt better in the middle of the night, after she told her sisters, but then it tightened right up again—because they were concerned, and they listened, but listening and concern do not equal a solution.

They pass a sign for Petey's and Calvin says, "It's been ages since I was at Petey's. Remember how often we used to go?"

"Of course," says Mae. "Cups of chowda all around."

They turn inland and continue on, passing a cemetery, a playground, an auto center. Her phone buzzes with a text. She looks surreptitiously and sees that it's from Human Leo. It's long! She's dying to know what he thinks of all the videos she's been sending, but she doesn't want to be rude to her father. Is Human Leo impressed? Disappointed? Does he think that the board-and-train has been a good investment? Does he regret letting Mae take Leo so far away? Her fingers are itching to tap the screen and read the text, but her dad is asking her a question.

"So you three had fun last night?"

"Sure," she says. Then, because her voice quavered a little, sounding uncertain, and she thought that would make him sad, "Definitely."

"Natalie seemed a little—subdued this morning. If that's the word."

Mae laughs. "That's *a* word."

"What's another word?"

"Hungover."

"Ah."

"Natalie doesn't get out much. I think it was good for her." Then: "I told them I was at the wedding."

Calvin glances at her. "I thought you didn't want them to know."

"I didn't, and then I did. Well, I didn't, and then I still didn't and then I sort of accidentally told them anyway."

A deep sigh issues from the driver's seat. "Ho, boy. How'd they take it?" They turn onto State Street.

"Not well," says Mae. She reflects on this, and then adds, "Not well at all."

"I'm sorry, Mae." Mae looks over and sees his worried-dad face. It's the face of a man who would rebuy the ice cream that slipped off a daughter's cone (a cliché, but it happened to Mae more times than it should have); a man who practiced parallel parking with Natalie fourteen days in a row so she could (finally) pass her driver's test; a man who barely left his wife's side to go to the bathroom or eat when she was dying. A man who wants everything to be okay for everyone, always.

"It's okay. They have to deal in their own way. I think it's all right now. And even if it's not, I'm an adult now. I can make my own decisions."

"Even if you're the baby." He's smiling for real now.

"Even if I'm the baby. I'm an actual live adult baby." Calvin laughs, and Mae realizes it's good to hear him laugh, because he's been doing his best this week, but she hasn't really heard him *laugh*, not the way he used to when Theresa was alive. They're on Congress Street now, pulling up behind Mae's car, and sure enough, an orange ticket is blazing on the windshield. "Oh, noooo," moans Mae. She hops out of the car and grabs the ticket. Thirty-five dollars. The time on the ticket is 9:21. She looks at the sign, then back at the ticket. "I didn't even get this for parking overnight! It's just from not paying at nine a.m.!" She could cry. But hadn't Jordan said she would pay if Mae got a ticket?

Then her dad is beside her, out of his car, and he's taking the ticket from her, folding it, putting it in his pocket. "Dad, no," says Mae, without much conviction. "I'm a baby adult, remember? I can pay that."

"This one's on me," he says. "Belated Fourth of July gift."

She can feel how gigantic her smile is. "I mean, I was going to say, I hope Dad gets me something really good for the Fourth this year."

Calvin has a funny look on his face.

"What?" she asks.

"What what?"

"Why are you looking at me like that?"

"Your smile," says Calvin. "You look exactly like her right now."

She feels something inside her open and turn toward the sun. "I do?"

"You do. Your smile is full of light just like hers was."

"It *is*?" Their mom had the best smile.

"Don't lose that, okay?"

"Okay."

"Listen, Mae? I wanted to talk about the house, to explain—"

She feels her smile fall away. "Dad. Thank you for the ride and everything. But I don't want to talk about the house. When I think about someone else buying it, that's bad enough, strangers living in Mom's house. But when I think of it not even *existing* anymore . . ." Her voice trails off. She's too sad to be angry. "I can't."

He looks at her for a long moment, then nods slowly. "Noted," he says. "I seem to get that response from everyone. But at some point, we should all talk about it." He taps twice on the hood of her car with his knuckles and returns to his own car without looking back. Mae wants to call to him to turn around; she wants to say *let's talk about her smile some more!* But the moment is gone. It's amazing how quickly you can change the mood of someone you love. The power we have over other people's emotions is formidable.

Mae texts Jordan: You should take Dad to Petey's.

Immediately the reply comes: Why me?

I think he'd like to go with you.

Before she starts driving, she reads the text from Human Leo. Human Leo has loved seeing all of the videos Mae made. The transformation Leo has undergone has been truly amazing. But he has decided he won't be able to have a dog after all. He got an offer to move out of the country for work. The job is in Dubai! He's always, always wanted to live in Dubai. It's a dream come true, really. Of course he'll still pay for the board-and-train! But he will no longer be able to be Leo's owner. Should he contact the shelter to initiate a return, or is there any chance Mae wants to keep Leo? They seem to have developed a real bond!

On Dog Leo's behalf Mae is both sad and irate. *Initiate a return?* Leo is not an Amazon purchase! Human Leo can't drop him off to be scanned at the closest UPS Store!

Mae's fingers hover over her phone screen. She's not sure what to say.

She thinks about Leo's big square head, and the way he looks like he's smiling when he's panting really intensely. She thinks about how hard he tries in his training sessions, and how much of his inauspicious beginning he's already overcome. Does she want to keep Leo? Yes. No question. But she can't afford him. There would be food bills and vaccinations, chew toys and treats and poop bags and license fees. Never mind the cost of an apartment that would allow her to keep a dog. It's bad enough to live out of your car; forcing a dog to live out of your car with you is a bridge too far.

Oh, Leo, she thinks. I don't want the world to fail you again. But how can she stop it from doing so? She eases her car onto the road and points herself toward home.

• • •

While Calvin and Mae go to get Mae's car Natalie checks the weather on her phone. Sunny in the morning, clouds rolling in in the afternoon. Rain tomorrow! Did they know this? They have had such a perfect string of days so far that they all imagined it would go on like this forever, but they are, after all, in New England, where all good weather must come to an end.

Nikoletta has left them a punch list of tasks to complete prior to the open house. The dogs have made a mess of the stair risers, so those will need a good scrub. The bookcases have somehow cluttered themselves since the photos for the listing were taken. They need to clear the kitchen countertops of extra appliances, fill the paper towel roll, put out fresh kitchen towels. But these things can't really be done until Saturday; if begun too early, they'll only need to be redone.

Natalie's head is pounding and her eyes are scratchy from lack of sleep. She downs four Advil and finds her middle child in the living room, lying on the couch in her nightgown.

"Are you ill?" asks Natalie. "Are you dying of consumption?"

Caspian pats his sister on the leg and says, "Lett."

"I don't think so," says Scarlett, but she sounds uncertain. "What's consumption?"

"Doesn't matter," says Natalie. "I don't think you have it. Move over a smidge." She sits next to Scarlett.

"What are we doing today, Ma?" Scarlett asks, suddenly cured, sitting up expectantly. She has recently taken to calling Natalie Ma because Natalie has been reading the *Little House* books to the girls. Natalie doesn't care for being called Ma, but she really loves the books. She believes she would have made a fantastic frontierswoman.

"What *are* we doing?" repeats Natalie, stalling for time. She's too tired to think. "We can do something fun in the morning," she says, "but then Aunt Jordan and Aunt Mae and I need to finish sorting out the garage. The dumpster is coming tomorrow. Beach?"

"I'm tired of the beach." Scarlett sighs.

"I think Evangeline and Caspian want to go to the beach."

Agreeably, Caspian says, "Beach!" He clambers into Natalie's lap and pushes his nose into her neck. It feels sort of nice. Damp, but nice.

"They always get to pick," says Scarlett. "I never do. It's not fair." She sits up and stomps her unshod foot for effect.

Natalie considers her middle child. She gets where Scarlett is coming from, this unarticulated rage, this sense of injustice. Her sisters made fun of her for it, but it's real.

"Thus it shall always be," she tells her daughter.

Scarlett says, "Huh?" and knits her brows together.

"Nothing," she says. "Never mind. I just mean, I get it. I get why it feels unfair. Look, I found a book for you." She finds *Bunbun* where she has set it on a shelf and brings it to Scarlett.

"That's a baby book," says Scarlett disdainfully.

"But it's full of wisdom," says Natalie.

Kara comes in then, holding a mug that says *MY HUSBAND IS HOTTER THAN MY COFFEE*. Natalie winces. Did Kara not read the mug? Did Kara not read the *room*? Then comes Jordan, who looks much better than someone who slept only half the night, and most of that in a lounge chair, deserves to look. Her mug says *BUT FIRST, COFFEE*. Basic, but a classic.

Natalie begins reading *Bunbun* to Scarlett anyway, and Scarlett pretends not to listen while actually listening. Soon enough they're interrupted by Calvin and Mae, back with Mae's car.

"I know!" says Natalie. "We can go to Strawbery Banke." Strawbery Banke is a living history museum in Portsmouth made up of a bunch of buildings that preserve the Puddle Dock neighborhood through its many iterations over the past three hundred and fifty years, from the Abenaki people to the present day.

"I don't want to go to the museum," says Evangeline. "I want to go to the beach."

Natalie is sure Caspian would also choose the beach over a museum, but she doesn't want to disappoint Scarlett.

"Why don't Kara and I take Caspian and Evangeline to the beach, and you and Scarlett go to the museum?" suggests Calvin.

"Really?" asks Natalie.

"Yesss!" says Scarlett. She's picked up a miniature fist pump somewhere (Mae?) and she employs it now.

"Actually," says Kara, "I'd love to go to the museum with Natalie and Scarlett."

"You *would*?" says Natalie. She would?

"I would. I really would. I was reading up on the sights of Portsmouth. I want to see the role-players." The role-players portray people who lived in different historical periods related to the buildings. You can engage them in conversation, but they can only answer in character. It's fun to try to trip them up.

This conversation is presenting Natalie with a true conundrum. On one side is her natural instinct, which is to find a moderately polite way to say *absolutely not, no way* to Kara. What right does Kara have to home in on Natalie's special day with Scarlett? On the other side is the memory of her father just two days ago at the optometrist. What had he said? *I would appreciate it if, when she arrives, you'd make her feel welcome.*

"The role-players are pretty great," says Natalie finally. Kara smiles, and Calvin is positively beaming.

"*I'd* like to take them to the beach," says Mae.

"You would?" Natalie is incredulous. Such a bounty of offers! "Are you sure? Caspian is a lot at the beach. You have to watch him every second."

"I know that," says Mae. "I didn't just meet him yesterday."

Caspian wipes his nose on Natalie's shoulder.

"What about you, Dad? Care for some role-play?" Natalie cringes, realizing that this came out wrong. "I mean, care to go to a museum?"

"I have a few things I need to get done around the house—" he starts to say.

That's when Jordan comes in and says, "I call Dad. I'm taking him to Petey's for lunch today."

• • •

If you're a Rye resident in search of seafood, especially chowder, you are either a Petey's person or a Ray's person. The Shipmans are Petey's people, though they understand the value of being Ray's people too. Riding past Rye Harbor, with her father driving, Jordan feels special the way she used to as a kid when she went along on certain errands with Calvin that the other girls were either too young for or not interested in. The hardware store was one of these. Jordan would always go to the hardware store. There was something about the organized shelves, the knowledgeable salespeople (just try to stump them; that's right, you can't), the wide assortment of unrelated items that made her feel happy and complete.

They snag the last spot in the parking lot, which is usually full ten minutes before the restaurant opens. Jordan has so many happy memories of going to Petey's, but most of them involve Theresa. She has to pause before getting out of the car, because she's picturing her mother ordering her favorite meal, whole fried clams, and suddenly she can't breathe.

Calvin orders a cup of chowder and a lobster roll. Jordan studies the salad menu, then she chastises herself for being an idiot and turns her attention to the fried portion of the menu (clam strips, oysters, lobster tails, crab cakes). She lands exactly where her father landed.

Without conferring with Jordan, Calvin then orders two beers. Okay! thinks Jordan. We're doing this! He carries them to a picnic table and sets one in front of Jordan. Jordan can't remember the last time she had a beer. But this beer in a plastic cup brought to her at a picnic table by her father, it tastes so good. It tastes like college and that feeling where you don't know what's going to happen next but all possibilities are on the table. It tastes like youth! They sip the beers while they wait for their number to be called.

"I know you're upset with me, Jordan. For you it's not so much about selling the house—"

"Make no mistake," she says. "I'm upset about selling the house too. I just see where it makes sense."

He nods, accepting this. "But what you're really upset about is Kara."

It's been five months since Calvin married Kara, but they haven't had this conversation yet. None of the Shipman sisters have had this conversation with their father. Well, apparently *Mae didn't need to.* But it's been lurking for Jordan and Natalie, like a monster in the closet, like the stranger on the dark corner. The thing you want to pretend isn't there. "What I'm *also* upset about is Kara," she corrects. "I mean—Dad!"

Calvin tents his fingers, holds them in front of his face, and looks at her over them. It reminds Jordan of how he used to look at her or her sisters if they got in trouble. Their parents were traditional in that the father did the disciplining. The mother, when asked, listened to the complaining about the disciplining, or clattered pans loudly in the kitchen to pretend it wasn't happening. Calvin was the master of the stern silence, the disappointed gaze. Natalie scraping up the side of the car pulling out of a parking spot where she'd parked too close to a cement wall. Mae coming home drunk sophomore year of high school, which even Jordan thought was too young to come home drunk. Jordan throwing the one rager of her life senior year and getting caught for it.

She waits for him to say something but he doesn't, so she continues. "I mean, do you ever think about what Mom would say?" Her voice gets smaller, more choked. "Do you ever think about Mom at all anymore?"

She watches her father's face go through a series of emotions: sorrow, bewilderment, a hint of defensiveness. "Of course I do. All the time. All the time, Jordan. Every single day. Before she died—"

Jordan cuts him off. "I swear to god, Dad. If you're going to tell me that before she died Mom handpicked Kara to be her successor and begged you to promise her that you wouldn't be alone . . ."

"Then what?"

"Then I'm going to throw up. That stuff only happens in Hallmark movies."

Good timing: their number is called. Calvin rises to get the food, and, though Jordan knows she should help him, she remains where she is, stewing in her indignation. She wasn't prepared for this conversation—she has come to Petey's under false pretenses!

Then she feels bad so she keeps an eye on Calvin walking from the counter. If he's struggling, she'll get up and help. Okay, fine, she'll get the napkins and the spoons for the chowder.

When they have their chowder and their lobster rolls, and while they are busying themselves opening the little packets of oyster crackers and scattering them across the creamy surface, Calvin continues as though there's been no break in the conversation.

"I suppose that's true. Although I've never seen a Hallmark movie."

"Well, don't," says Jordan. "You'd hate them." (She herself, in times of loneliness or heartbreak, especially during the holidays, has been known to quite enjoy them.)

"Anyway, that's not what I was going to say. Your mother never decreed any such thing to me. Whether she thought it or not, I don't know. But she didn't say it. What I was going to say was, before your mom died, I never, ever, ever thought I'd want to be with someone else. Never in a hundred years would I have imagined it." This, from her father, is an extreme amount of hyperbole, even though most people would have said *never in a million years*.

"So what happened?" She can hear it in her voice, the way she's challenging him. She should be giving her father the gift of curiosity, but she can't.

There's a really long pause next, long enough that Jordan isn't sure if he's going to answer or not. She blows on her chowder to cool it and takes a bite of her lobster roll.

"What happened," he says, "is a fairly simple thing." He pauses again, and she waits, confident that he's going to keep going. "What happened is that the afternoons and early evenings became insufferably long. Longer even than I'd ever imagined they could be." Jordan tries to absorb this. She can't relate. She finds each day to be far shorter than she needs it to be. She has dozens and dozens of things to fit into each day, especially during a work crisis, and by four o'clock in the afternoon the thing is never to figure out how to fill the next six or seven hours but rather to decide which tasks to complete before bed and which to push off to the next morning.

She's never thought of this as a blessing. She thought it was just life. But here is her father, telling her something different. Experiencing the opposite. She gives him an expression that she hopes conveys *go on*.

"I'd wake up every morning, alone. I'd try to stretch everything out as long as I could. My coffee. The reading of the *Berkshire Eagle*. I'd read every word. And as you probably know, very few people read every word of the *Berkshire Eagle*. I'd do all that, and it would be only nine o' clock, time to head in for my first class! I'd have twelve more hours to fill."

"But you have work. You have friends! Where did all of your friends go? Don't you still golf?" She knows her father was still golfing after Theresa died because every Sunday, when they did their family FaceTime, one of the girls would ask, "Done any golfing lately, Dad?" And the answer was always yes!

They thought he was doing okay, because he was golfing.

Calvin pauses to drink from his beer cup. "I have friends. Yes, yes, of course I do. I still golf. But friends and golfing don't fill every minute, especially when your friends have their spouses." She's quiet, taking this in, and eventually Calvin continues. "I just . . ." He trails off. He seems like he's thinking about what to say next. "Life was always so busy and full, with you girls, and then when you went off into your own lives, we were busy then too. Working still, and traveling, you know. Then your mom got sick, and there was no time to be lonely because there were appointments and treatments to arrange and drive to, and meals to cook, and medications to track. So many medications, they were practically a full-time job. I never thought of loneliness as a real affliction before. I suppose I should have, but I didn't. I thought of it as a choice. Find something to do to fill your time! I would have told a friend in my position: Volunteer! Work more! Work less! Go to the movies! Get a dog, get a gerbil, learn a language. Get something!"

"But it's not that easy," says Jordan. She's beginning to understand.

"It's not that easy at all. You can do all of those things, and there are still so many hours in the day to fill." He grows quiet and pensive. "Still so many hours, and days, and weeks. Just sitting there empty, staring at you."

Then, he explains, along came Kara.

(Along came a spider, thinks Jordan.)

When they bumped into each other at the Apple Squeeze, Calvin had been so happy to see her. She'd been a part of the worst time of his life, but at the same time she felt like a link to an era when he'd been okay, because even though Theresa was so sick she was still alive, she was still there. They chatted for, oh, maybe fifteen minutes or so, and then they'd exchanged phone numbers. Kara had suggested that they do this, and it was Kara who then texted him to see if he wanted to meet for a drink at Brava.

"And the rest . . ."

"Is history?" says Jordan.

"The rest happened quickly, is what I was going to say. I'll spare you the details."

"Thank you," says Jordan. "I accept your sparing." Her beer is gone, and her father's beer is too. They're almost done with their lobster rolls. Only the dregs of the chowder remain.

"I wanted you to hear all of this from me. You can be upset with me, you and your sisters. That's your right. If I were in your position I'd be upset with me too. I just want you to understand."

Jordan nods.

"When you're staring down the road of the rest of your life, and you don't know how long or short that road is going to be, and someone appears who you think you might be able to love, not in the same way you loved before, but in a new and different way, and the afternoons no longer seem endless, and there's someone to come home to, or someone to come home to you, well, then, you don't take that person lightly. You learn how to treasure that person. Even if it's not the same person you thought you'd be treasuring forever."

Jordan sits with this and, okay, it starts to make sense to her, from her father's point of view, that it's possible to love two people consecutively, especially if you are loving each in a different way. It's possible to think everything good leaked out of your heart and then to discover that the fissure sealed itself up and you can grow more because love is a renewable resource. It's possible to have hope.

"Wow," she says finally. It might just be beautiful, everything Calvin has just said. Still, something isn't clicking. "But Kara . . ." she says. She can't form the rest of the sentence because she's not sure what she wants to ask, or, more accurately, how to ask it.

But her father knows. Father knows best. "What's in it for her?" Calvin supplies. Yes. That's exactly the question. Jordan nods slowly. "I've asked myself that many times. I've asked her that."

"You have?"

"Of course. Any sane person would. Someone with her whole life ahead of her, and an old guy like me . . ."

"Oh, Dad. You know you're young for being old." This is true; she's not merely flattering him. He's a very young sixty-nine-year-old. But still, he's sixty-nine. So the question is a fair one. "But, yeah. I guess I'm wondering that. What is in it for Kara? Not to be indelicate but she's still working, right? This isn't a Logan Roy situation, where you sort of see why the young ladies . . ."

"Who's Logan Roy?"

"The really rich guy on *Succession*," she explains. "The patriarch."

"Ah," he says. "What's *Succession*?"

"Never mind," she says, waving her hand at him. "If you don't know that much, you're hopeless."

He nods as if to say *fair enough.* "I suppose," says Calvin, "if you really want to know the answer to that question you'll have to ask Kara directly."

"Yeah?" Jordan isn't sure if he's kidding or not.

"Kara knows that while I'm her second husband, I probably won't be her last. Maybe not even her best." He smiles wryly.

"Dad!" cries Jordan, shocked. "Don't say that."

Calvin chortles. "Why? It's true. And I'm perfectly okay with it. I say it to Kara all the time."

"You do not." Calvin shrugs and smiles mysteriously. Maybe he does and maybe he doesn't.

Things are really getting going at Petey's now, as the height of lunchtime approaches. There are kids spilling out of cars and dumping ice cream on themselves and pointing at the dozens of bright lobster buoys hanging from the sign and from the railings. There are parents who look like they might just have one of the signature cocktails, because the children are driving them crazy, and they're on vacation, so why not? One young boy, most likely a new reader, is sounding out the words on the sign that says *LIVE LOBSTERS*. He turns to his grown-up and says, with horror and wonder, "People eat alive lobsters?"

Calvin begins to gather their detritus, saying, "We should probably give up our spot." Jordan helps him, stacking the plastic cups, balling up her napkin to place it inside her chowder cup. She agrees that they should go, but she doesn't want to leave without asking one more question: "Why'd you decide to talk to me about this? And not Natalie?"

What she means is, *Is it because I've been such a bitch?*

Calvin doesn't hesitate. "I thought you'd understand the most. I thought maybe if you got it then Natalie would too. Or that maybe you'd help her understand."

"I see." She nods. "I think I do. I think I will."

He's being kind here, she can see that. It's not so much that Jordan can help Natalie understand; it's that Jordan has had the hardest time with Kara.

It occurs to Jordan that Kara is not just Kara. She's the symbol of all of Jordan's erroneous judgment. If she has judged Kara so wrong, what else has she judged wrong? Natalie? Mae? Bernadette?

No, not Bernadette. Definitely not Bernadette. But she's willing to concede the others.

"Dad?"

"Yes, Jordan?"

"Does this make me the favorite daughter?"

The first rule of Favorite Daughter Status, they all know, is that you do not talk about Favorite Daughter Status. Her father merely raises his eyebrows at her and grants her again that mysterious smile.

• • •

Natalie, Scarlett, and Kara meet a millworker from the 1800s, a shipbuilder from the 1700s, and a homemaker from 1950. They visit all nine houses at Strawbery Banke that are open to the public. They admire the wallpaper in Governor Goodwin's house; the fireplace frieze in the Chase House, home to a successful Portsmouth merchant; and the tools that Samuel Kingsbury used in the 1800s. They watch a cooking demonstration on an open hearth where a woman in a bonnet makes a meat pie.

I could rock an open hearth, Natalie thinks. I could kill this assignment.

They visit the 1940s general store, the tavern, the live demonstration of coopering (which, they learn, is the production of casks and barrels). Each time Natalie thinks Scarlett will get bored she finds something else to marvel at. In the olden days, last week, Natalie might have taken a video of Scarlett wandering through Strawbery Banke, hashtagged it with #homeschool, and written a caption about every experience being a learning experience, even in summer. #yearroundeducation. She would have tagged the museum too, and her followers would have liked and shared it, and overall visits would have risen by some percentage. It might have become A Thing. But today her phone is in her bag, and she will only reach for it if Mae contacts her with a question about Caspian or Evangeline.

Natalie can't believe Scarlett's endurance or her attentiveness to the past. Natalie is pretty sure that if her mother had marched her through The Mount, Edith Wharton's home, one of the jewels in Lenox's vast crown, when she was Scarlett's age, she wouldn't have taken such interest. She would have wanted to repair to the gift shop. (Natalie has always been a shopper.)

Then again, maybe she would have loved to go to The Mount at that age with her mother. Maybe, like Scarlett, she would have been happy for any time with Theresa, away from her sisters, the rare only-child day for the middle child, and she, too, would have soaked up every second, would have done anything to make the day go on forever.

Tears form immediately in her eyes as she thinks this. Maybe Theresa did take her to The Mount, and she's forgotten! Maybe she's forgotten many important things. Early childhood memories are capricious; we don't capture everything from those years, even as so many parents do all they can to enrich us, expose us, form us, mold us. Most of it, we won't even remember. This is suddenly unbearably sad to Natalie. Nothing of Ruby on Rye will remain in Caspian's memory—he's too young.

In the heirloom garden, Scarlett finds a hoop and a stick to try her hand at—yesteryear's version of the iPad, but much more difficult to maneuver, and with no battery limitations. Natalie and Kara watch her, watch another little girl, maybe a year or so older, approach and stand shyly, waiting her turn.

Natalie is content with the silence, but then Kara breaks it to say, "Your father is really sad."

"We're all really sad," says Natalie immediately, hotly. How *could* Kara?

"I know."

"You don't know."

Then Kara says the very worst thing of all, the very worst thing she could say. She says, "I loved your mother too."

If Scarlett were not just a few feet away, doing what's actually a passable job of rolling the hoop with the stick, Natalie might have raised her voice. But instead she hisses, "Don't you dare. Don't you dare say that."

"I can say it, because I did. Not like you all did, of course not. But I got to know her, and I loved her. She was a lovely woman. She was beautiful and gracious and honest and funny, all the way until she died." Natalie wants Kara to stop talking and at the same time she wants her to keep going. Even though she'd been there herself, she wants more; she's like parched earth soaking up every extra thing she can learn about Theresa. Close to the end it had gotten harder to make the trip back and forth from Vermont to Lenox—she was nearing the third trimester of her pregnancy with Caspian, and he weighed nearly nine pounds at birth, so Natalie was enormous. And there was always a lot to do at Hillside Haven. Evangeline and Scarlett were so young; every time Natalie got in the car she knew she was leaving Austin with the lion's share (the cow's share) of both farm and family life. Austin hadn't complained, not even once.

She thought she'd be able to bring the baby to meet Theresa. She'd take a photo of their hands together, Theresa and the baby's. She's always been a sucker for those old hands/young hands photos. Not to post it! Of course not! Just to have it. To treasure it.

She thought there was time.

But there hadn't been enough time.

Natalie considers calling Scarlett over as a distraction, but now Scarlett and the other little girl have found a second hoop and a second stick and they're playing together so nicely. (You worry about social skills as a homeschool mom; you rejoice in every "normal" interaction you witness. Like there's any such thing as normal.) Scarlett is a little better than the other girl at managing the stick and the hoop, but Natalie tries not to notice that.

"I've seen a lot of ends, and some of them are awful," says Kara. "A peaceful one is a blessing."

Oh, no. No, she did *not*. "Death is not a blessing," says Natalie, continuing to hiss. "Losing your mother is never a blessing." She thinks suddenly of the calves again, those guttural, haunting cries, slicing through the night air.

"You're right."

"And I suppose now you're going to tell me that with her last breath my mom managed to wheeze at you that you should marry my dad?"

Kara looks like Natalie slapped her.

"Of course not. That's not how it happened. It was much later, long after, when Calvin and I reconnected. I'm not trying to take her place."

Natalie does not like the word *reconnected*, so she gets even meaner. "He's almost seventy, you know."

"I know. Of course I know. I'm married to him! I know how old he is."

"Well. Don't you think that's weird?"

Kara shakes her head and says, "No."

"Why *not*?" You should! she thinks. Everyone else does!

"I always thought I'd marry an older man if I married again."

"You did?"

"Not this much older. But, yeah. Older."

"Why?"

"It always made sense to me."

"But why?"

"I didn't grow up with a dad. My mom was—is—*problematic*, to put it generously."

"So you married your dad?"

"*No.* I married *a* dad. I always thought I'd want someone who offered me a chance to step into his life and his family. Someone who was willing to say *Here's where we live. Here's our favorite restaurant, our favorite Cabernet, our favorite way to read the newspaper.*" (Not from front to back, thinks Natalie, if you ask Calvin. Sports first, then News, then Lifestyle.) "Someone who would say *Here is our life. And here's how you fit in it.*"

"But didn't you want to do all of those things with someone your own age?" asks Natalie. She thinks about how she and Austin have been growing up together for the past eight years.

"I did that," says Kara. "My first husband was my age. But we couldn't have kids, and now, a ready-made family is more appealing to me than any kind of family. And if you're waiting for an apology, Natalie, I'm not going to give you one. I'm sorry your mom died, but I'm not sorry your dad's not alone now. I love your dad, and he's good for me, and I'm good for him."

Her voice is steady, and her eyes are clear. Kara isn't asking permission or forgiveness. She's stating facts. "When I said he's really sad, I didn't mean about your mom. I meant about you and your sister. How he feels that by choosing any happiness for himself, any at all, he's lost you and Jordan. And that's not fair, Natalie. He shouldn't lose you two. He doesn't deserve that. He brought you all here to try to make it better."

Even hearing this, even acknowledging, in some ways, the validity of it, Natalie still clings to the vestiges of anger that she feels are rightfully hers. "He brought us here to sell our mother's house! To someone who's going to tear it down!"

Kara inhales deeply, then blows out a puff of air. "That's the tangible reason, sure. But also, he wanted to see you all together and he knew you wouldn't come if he didn't force you into it. The cleaning out of the garage, getting the house ready, those are things that had to be accomplished. But they're also excuses. Seeing you all here together, that's the reason."

Scarlett comes up to them, breathless, red-cheeked, happy, and says, "I love it here!" before she runs back to her new playmate.

There it goes. The ice begins to thaw, the stranglehold to ease. Natalie softens. Maybe it's the hundreds of years of ghosts she feels around her that are helping her to do that. There are three centuries' worth of history and life and death in this very spot, this neighborhood that changed and changed again and again throughout time.

"I thought I'd feel grown-up enough for this," she says finally, as though Kara is her therapist. "I thought maybe I'd be ready to lose my mother, when the time came."

"Nobody's ready," says Kara, as though she *is* Natalie's therapist. "I'm around grief every single day. There are various stages of being not ready, but nobody is ready."

"Nobody? Really?"

"Nobody," repeats Kara. This sort of makes Natalie feel better, like she's not worse than anyone else at having her mother die.

"That's why I try not to say no to joy, because it's fleeting. You could easily turn it down and it doesn't come around again."

Natalie thinks about life being dim sum on a lazy Susan at a Chinese restaurant. You might fail to take a spring roll as it spins by and then suddenly they're all gone. You might grab the last egg tart, leaving none for the next person. Joy might seem like a renewable resource, but it's finite, just like everything else.

"You missed some time with him, you and Jordan. You shouldn't miss any more."

The other girl successfully does the hoop and stick and Scarlett cries, "Good job!" just the way Natalie says it when she or Evangeline does something skillful with the cows. The Ladies.

"I didn't know you couldn't have kids," she tells Kara. "I'm really sorry."

"Why would you know that? It's okay." Kara smiles. "I came to terms with it a long time ago." She has a lovely smile, even with the gap between her front teeth. Maybe because of the gap! It's a smile that really transforms her face. Natalie had forgotten about that, about Kara's smile.

Then just like that, she is not their father's new wife but the woman who helped her family through the awfulness of two years ago, the woman whose smile sometimes managed to lead them out of the darkness, and who is still leading Calvin, step by step, out of a lonely place.

Mae was right the other day, when they talked after Kara's arrival. There's more than one kind of love. When they get home, maybe she'll even admit that to Mae.

It's past lunchtime now, and Natalie is getting hungry. She will offer to take Kara and Scarlett to Popovers, which Scarlett loves, and Natalie will let her pick out anything she wants from the baked-goods case, and she won't even check with anyone at home to see if they want anything because this is Scarlett's special day.

Okay, *fine.* She'll let Kara pick out something from the bakery case too.

She is definitely the Favorite Daughter now.

• • •

Family is too much! This is what Jordan is thinking as she power walks the beach on Thursday afternoon. The expectations, the history, the nostalgia, the longing, the failing. How are you supposed to keep your balance with all of these living creatures, these blood relations, pulling at you? How are you expected to remain sane, remain calm, continue on the straight path in your own orbit that you have set out for yourself? She must be nicer to Kara to keep her father happy. She must keep a better eye on Mae, who's been drowning while nobody noticed. She must continue to grieve the loss of her mother without grieving too much or too little, and that's a scale she's incapable of balancing. For Natalie—for Natalie, what? Does Jordan need to be more understanding of Natalie's perplexing choices? Or more strident in her beliefs to see if she can bring Natalie around to Jordan's way of thinking? She must be a good sister, a good aunt, a good daughter. She must finish clearing out the garage storeroom because that will put her father's mind at ease, and she owes him that.

And. She must figure out what to do with the other part of her life, her work life. She must decide what to do about Bernadette and Samantha Braddock. On one side of the scale, the possibility of making partner, with its attendant respect and title change and, yes, money. The culmination of her hard work. Her name on the company shingle! (They work in Manhattan; there's no shingle. But having her name on the sign near the elevator counts too.) On the other side, her integrity and . . . what else? Just her integrity, really. How much does her integrity weigh—is it enough to tip the scale?

She wants to talk about this with someone, someone who will really listen, someone who will tell her what to do. She'd told Natalie the outlines of it the night before, but then Mae had come in and they'd never finished. Now Natalie is reading with Scarlett and Evangeline while Caspian naps, and Jordan doesn't want to pull her away. Mae has gone who knows where. Anyway, Jordan still thinks (will always think) of Mae as the baby and herself as the wise elder sister. You can't ask a baby for advice, especially if that baby has recently lost all of her money in a QR code scam.

Her father? They've already had one heart-to-heart today. Two might be pushing it. Kara?

No. Definitely not. She'll offer an olive branch to Kara, but she's not ready to lay bare her heart and soul to her.

She pulls up the contact info for Samantha Braddock from the *Times.* It would just take one call, one declarative sentence. The story would either die there, or, if it is published, Jordan's quote would be enough to throw the thesis out of balance.

My boss has never treated me with anything but the utmost respect. We have a perfect working relationship.

She pictures the floating staircase in Sagaponack, the in-home movie theater, Bernadette's hand, her scornful face.

Why don't you loosen up, Jordan? Have a little fun.

My boss has never treated me . . .

If I were you I'd think carefully about what choice you make here, Jordan. I'm about to make some big decisions.

There's one person left. She looks back at her texts from Monday—only Monday? not ten years ago, as it feels?—and finds Simone's contact info.

Hey, she texts. Thanks so much for the ride home last night. Have time to grab a drink? Her fingers hesitate over the phone's screen, but not for long. She hits send.

Immediately the reply comes, arriving with a *zing.* Yes! Upstairs at The Carriage House.

Okay, thinks Jordan. This is happening. When?

Now.

Whoa. Jordan has forgotten about this quality of Simone's. It's not impulsiveness, exactly—it's more of a lack of hesitation. A gung-ho-ness, if you will. And she will. She gives Simone's text a thumbs-up.

"Where are you going?" Natalie asks from the kitchen when Jordan zips in for her sunglasses.

"Out," says Jordan. She makes a beeline for The Carriage House. It's just a short walk from their home—the only sit-down restaurant in walking distance. The Shipman family used to eat there once a summer, as a special-occasion meal, and they've watched it go through iterations. At one time you might take your relatives there for cracker-crumb-covered New England cod, and now it's a proper destination restaurant, with oysters, a wine list to die for, and creative, upscale entrées. Downstairs, the restaurant is giving coastal grandma, with white walls, simple dark brown tables, a gorgeous stone fireplace. Upstairs, where the bar is, there are grays and browns and more tables, plus a bar that's big enough to feel welcoming but small enough to feel intimate. A picture window looks across the street to the sandy beach and the ocean beyond. And at the bar, in a white sundress that shows her tanned shoulders, laughing at something the bartender is saying, is Simone. Jordan slides into the seat next to her.

"Hey!" says Simone, with real delight. She squeezes Jordan's hand. "I'm so happy you texted."

"Hey," says Jordan. "Look at you, all in white."

"I'm the Ghost of Summers Past." Simone laughs and gestures toward the bartender. "This is Hector," she tells Jordan. "He's a magician."

"Like an actual magician, or really good at making cocktails?"

Simone giggles. "I'm going to have the Never Have I Ever or the I Wish There Was More Communication." Jordan stares at her: Is Simone speaking in code or are these actual cocktails? Simone slides her the menu. They are actual cocktails. Jordan considers ordering the To Be Frank, because that seems most fitting, but she doesn't like rum, so she orders the We Are All Busy Mate, which also feels somewhat appropriate and has the advantage of gin.

It's quiet in the bar in the late afternoon; only a couple of the tables are occupied, and one other bar seat. Hector gets to work on the drinks, and Simone tells Hector, so casually, "Jordan and I used to date. We're exes!" Maybe this is what they're going to do: they're going to talk to Hector instead of to each other. Jordan can play that game too.

Hector glances up briefly from his magic bartending and says, "Cool."

"From a really long time ago," says Jordan to Hector. She thinks of Audrey as her real ex—Audrey is the one she almost built a life with. Does a pre-college summer love count officially as an ex? Maybe, if it was your first! And Simone was Jordan's first.

"In fact," Simone goes on, "Jordan broke my heart. We saw each other once during college, and then never again."

Jordan whips her head to the side so she's looking at Simone. "Uh," says Jordan. "Sorry, what? I'm pretty sure it was the other way around. I'm pretty sure you broke my heart." Then she remembers they're talking through Hector so she tells him, "Simone came to visit me at college and we went to a party and the next thing I knew she was making out with a guy in an Obama T-shirt."

Simone shrugs and says, "It was just a kiss." Jordan snorts. She feels the old ire rise up, the sense of betrayal, and she's about to say—

But then Hector is placing their drinks in front of them and saying, "Enjoy, ladies!" and the drinks are so beautiful, like works of art, indeed like magic, that Jordan makes the executive decision to let the past be the past.

"Bygones," says Simone, lifting her glass, as if she read Jordan's mind.

"Bygones," agrees Jordan. They clink. They each take a sip. Hector really is a magician; the blackberry-sage preserve and the gin are perfect together. Jordan takes another sip and says, "I'm looking for advice from a friend."

"I can be a friend," says Simone. She smiles at Jordan, and she's not this Simone, today's Simone, with the yoga-and-smoothie business and the ex in Santa Cruz, but the Simone Jordan remembers, who excelled at beer pong and who once took Jordan's hand at a party at a house on the beach and said, "She's with me." And just like that, Jordan was.

Sometimes the past is like that. Eighteen years can be forever and it can also be no time at all.

Jordan starts talking, and she doesn't stop until she's finished with the whole story. She tells Simone about the party in Sagaponack, and about Bernadette in the in-home movie theater, and about her phone call the other day. About the chance to be partner, and the necessity of selling her soul to do it.

"Wow," says Simone, when Jordan stops to take a breath, a sip, another breath. "Geez, Jordan."

"So what do I do?"

Simone taps her fingers on the side of her cocktail glass and says, "The first thing you need to do is, you need to say it out loud. What you're describing is one hundred percent harassment."

"I wasn't sure—"

"One *hundred* percent, Jordan. You have to say, 'My boss sexually harassed me.'"

"Okay." She'll say it later, maybe?

"Say it, Jordan. Say it now."

Jordan takes a deep breath. "My boss sexually harassed me."

"Good job. Perfect. Now you need to decide if you want to continue to work for someone who has sexually harassed you, and maybe not just you."

"I don't." The answer slides right out of Jordan, as though it's been available the whole time. She's been agonizing all week, and the answer was right there!

"There you have it," says Simone. "There's your answer."

Jordan chews her lip. "It's not that simple."

"Why not?" *You always make things so complicated, Jordan.*

"Well. This is my job, Simone. This is my career. My income. This is what I've been working for since college."

"Wouldn't someone else snap you up? Another firm that does what you do?"

"Bernadette's tentacles reach far and wide in our world," says Jordan. "She knows how to bury people. If she wants to destroy me, she can."

"But if you want to destroy her, *you* can do that," Simone points out. "You know all the tricks she knows. And you can call this journalist right now and tell her everything." They both look at Jordan's phone, lying face down on the bar between them.

"I don't think I'd do that."

"Doesn't even matter if you do," says Simone. "It matters that she knows that you can. You have her over a barrel the same way you think she has you." Jordan imagines Bernadette, in wide-leg trousers and a stretch-linen waistcoat, her arms jacked from the time she spends in the upper-body section of the Peloton app, holding Jordan over a barrel.

Simone is right!

"But maybe you don't want to go to another firm anyway," says Simone. "Maybe you want to start your own. Be your own boss."

This has always been a dream of Jordan's, as tender and precious as a new plant shoot, so fragile she's never even said it aloud. It's like Simone has peered into her soul.

"I want to do that," she whispers.

"So do it!" Simone slaps the bar, flushed and triumphant. "Do it, Jordan. I know you can. You've always had this drive and ambition, always. Don't waste it. Use it."

"Yeah?"

"Yeah."

There's a long, long pause while all of this sinks in: Simone's kindness toward her, her belief in Jordan, and, in turn, Jordan's burgeoning belief in herself. "What are you thinking?" asks Simone eventually.

"I'm thinking that I'm hungry," Jordan realizes. "I'm so hungry!" She thought she'd never want to eat again after lunch and beer at Petey's, but suddenly she's ravenous.

"I know exactly what you need," says Simone. She calls over Hector, who has had the nerve to turn his attention to new customers at the far end of the bar, and says, "One order of Parker House rolls, please, Hector."

"You got it."

When the rolls arrive, Jordan decides they are the best things she's ever, ever tasted, so soft and buttery, with flavors of garlic and rosemary: heaven in a basket.

"Simone!" says Jordan as they're making short work of the rolls. "I'm such a jerk. I've only talked about myself. Let's get one more. I want to hear what's going on with you."

Simone looks at her watch. "I'd love to, but I'm meeting someone."

"But I want to hear more about your business! Your life!"

"We'll talk about me next time, I promise. And you have to get home for dinner, right?" Jordan has told her that they only have two family dinners left. On Saturday, to keep things looking good for the open house, they're going to go to a restaurant. Maybe they'll come here! She imagines Caspian knocking over the delicate cocktail glasses or squishing the buttery rolls in his chubby hands. Maybe they'll go to Flatbread in Portsmouth instead.

Then it hits Jordan like a sack of rocks: What next time? Calvin is selling the house. All at once she feels as desolate as she knows her sisters have felt all week.

"We'll probably get an offer on Sunday, Simone. I'm not sure I'll ever be back here."

Simone slides off her barstool. "You'll be back, Jordan Shipman. The state of New Hampshire isn't going anywhere."

Outside, at the edge of the parking lot, they stand close to each other. "Do you need a ride home?" asks Simone.

"It's, like, a two-second walk." Jordan laughs. "I think I can make it." But she doesn't move. "You smell the same," she tells Simone. "Like limes."

"You know, smell is the most nostalgic of all the senses."

"Right." Jordan inhales one last time, so deeply that she hopes to save the scent forever, and then she says, "Thanks for this, really. It helped me so much. Seeing you, talking it out—it all helped."

"I'm glad," says Simone, all smiles.

Jordan looks at Simone, at her blond hair and her freckled skin and her sea-glass eyes. She feels like she's seeing her more clearly than she's ever seen her before—and that Simone is seeing Jordan clearly too.

"I'm sorry I kissed the guy in the Obama shirt," says Simone. "He was cute, though. Do you remember how cute he was?"

Jordan shakes her head.

"Well, he was really cute."

Jordan laughs. "I'm sorry I couldn't get past it." She wonders how things might have been different, if they would have stayed together longer or if they would have broken up over something different but equally silly and dramatic.

"My problem," says Simone, "is that I like everybody."

"That's funny," says Jordan, her heart full of nostalgia and longing. "I have the exact opposite problem."

• • •

When Mae comes down the stairs before dinner Kara is looking at a photo of Calvin and Theresa's wedding. "Look how puffy these dresses are!" she says, holding out the photo to Mae.

"Is it strange that my dad put this one back out with the rest of them?" Mae wonders aloud.

"I think it would have been stranger if he hadn't," Kara says. "It's your family history."

"You're not insisting all of these photos be removed and then burned?" she asks Kara.

"I'm not really an evil stepmother," says Kara. "I only play one on TV." Mae smiles.

She takes the frame from Kara. She's seen this photo a thousand times, but she'll never get enough of it. It's 1984, early May, and her mother and father are standing with their wedding party in front of the showy star magnolia in the Boston Public Garden. The bridesmaids—Theresa's two sisters and her two best college friends—are in peach. Lots of peach. Here's Theresa in capped sleeves, full skirt, a train that went on for days. It might be the hair and the puffy dresses, but every woman looks a little like Princess Diana, and the men, with their side-parted, slightly feathered hair, could all be John Travolta.

They'd been married at Trinity Church, and somewhere in their house in Lenox, Mae knows, are photos of the ceremony inside the rough-textured stone walls of the church, surrounded by the famous stained-glass windows.

Her parents are so young and so beautiful that it takes Mae's breath away. In this picture Theresa is three years younger than Mae is now. Mae looks, trying to read something in her eyes, in her wide, imperfect smile. Her mother had lived almost four decades after her wedding day, and yet died too young.

FRIDAY

• • •

The photo Jordan finds on Friday morning is in the top dresser drawer in her room, maybe put there in a hurry to clean up for renters, maybe forgotten about altogether. It's a shallow drawer, made for lingerie or socks, and Jordan hasn't unpacked anything into it. She recognizes the Beach Club immediately, the white railings between the deck and the rocks, then the sand and ocean beyond, the place where the tide pools formed and the kids used to go crabbing, finding regular crabs, hermit crabs, sometimes even an eel or two.

If she could pan out and show the rest of the scene, she knows she'd see the bright blue of the club pool, with the colored flags around the perimeter. Three lifeguard chairs on three sides of the pool. She can almost taste the chlorinated water, feel the sensation of it in her nostrils as she somersaulted. She can almost hear the laughter of the adults, which would grow more raucous as long summer days turned to long summer evenings.

And here, leaning against the white railing, shielding her eyes from the sun, is her mother. Jordan slides the photo out of the frame and turns it over. Before digital cameras—and later, of course, smartphones—pushed analog photography out of the way, Theresa used to note on the back the month and year a photo was taken after she had them printed.

August 1995. Theresa must be pregnant with Mae, and perched next to her (dangerously, Jordan thinks, but apparently they all survived) on the railing is Natalie. Just visible behind Natalie is a sign reading *PLEASE STAY OFF THE RAILINGS.* Standing next to Natalie in a navy one-piece, a signature ruffle at the neckline, is Jordan herself. (She hated that ruffle.) Pointy elbows, pointy chin, looking out at the water. Thinking about what? She wishes she knew.

• • •

On Friday they wake to rain. Lots and lots and lots of rain. Mae, sleeping in the Green Room, wakes thinking that Jordan is there beside her. Jordan sleeps the way she lives (self-contained, efficient, productive), and while Mae also sleeps the way she lives (chaotically, a little bit behind), when Jordan was in the bed with her she was so careful to move as little as possible, and enjoy the feeling of the warm body beside her. She didn't want to jeopardize losing her bedmate.

Now she sits up and peers into Leo's crate. He's slumbering on his back, with his ears splayed out and his front legs bent at the knee, one floating in the air as if tied to a string hanging from the ceiling. Soon enough he senses that Mae is awake and he flips over, immediately alert, looking at her with his beautiful eyes. His body language says, *Do you need me for something? I'm here and I'm ready!*

"Hey, buddy. Top of the morning to you." A warm feeling spreads through Mae. Is she falling in love with Leo?

Ugh, but the rain. It's really hammering the roof.

"There's only one solution to this," says Jordan in the kitchen, once Mae has taken each dog out in turn, when Natalie is holding a wriggling Caspian and staring somberly out the window.

"Down!" shouts Caspian. She obliges. Natalie notes that Jordan looks unaccountably cheerful and has since dinnertime last night.

That's classic Jordan: to cheer up just when the rest of the world becomes despondent.

"What's the solution?" Natalie asks warily.

"Breakfast!" cries Jordan. "Let's take the kids to The Friendly Toast!" The Friendly Toast is the all-day brunch place in Portsmouth where chicken waffles mingle with avocado toast and steak-and-cheese sandwiches and forms of eggs Benedict you didn't even know existed.

"That's not a terrible idea," Natalie acknowledges. "Except that everyone in the Seacoast area will have had the same one."

"Then let's go now. Maybe everyone else on the Seacoast is sleeping in. Scarlett, Evangeline, get dressed as fast as you can. We're going to breakfast paradise!"

"What does that mean?" inquires Scarlett.

"Trust me," says Jordan, beaming. She's so chipper! What, wonders Natalie, the heck is going on?

"What about Dad and Kara?"

"You snooze, you lose," says Jordan, shrugging, and Natalie says, "Fair."

• • •

A big party has just left, and they are seated with menus within ten minutes of arriving: this must be some sort of record.

"Should we get cocktails?" asks Jordan. The bar menu is killer: Mimosa Flights, spicy Bloody Marys, an espresso martini that reads like a dream. It would be sort of a shame not to take advantage of it.

"Oh my god," says Mae. "When did you become an alcoholic, Jordan?"

Jordan shrugs. Yes, she has been drinking more than usual this week. And she hasn't seen a Pilates reformer for days. "It's temporary," she says. "We're on vacation. Come on, Mae. Drink with me! What else is there to do on a rainy beach day?"

Mae thinks about it, then says piously, "I don't think so. I can't afford it." She waits to see how this news will go down now that she's told her sisters her situation. Caspian drops a fork on the floor, and Evangeline retrieves it. Then, yes, here it comes: Natalie and Jordan fall all over themselves saying they'll pay for the whole breakfast, drinks included.

"Fine," says Mae, as though she's doing them both a favor. "I guess one Blood Orange Aperol Mimosa won't kill me." Natalie declines because she's driving; they had to come in her car because of the car seats.

It's time to choose the food! Jordan, to balance out her alcohol intake, wants a garden omelet; Natalie, a breakfast burrito, plus pancakes and scrambled eggs that she will split among her kids. When it's Mae's turn she chews her lip, furrows her brow, and says, "What happened to the Guy Scramble? It's not on the menu." The server doesn't know about the Guy Scramble, or what happened to it. Mae settles on the Berries and Cream Waffle, which is topped with cheesecake buttercream and powdered sugar.

"Isn't that a toddler meal?" asks Jordan.

Mae shrugs. "I'm reverting."

Carefully, like the question is made of glass, Natalie says, "Have you thought any more about what you plan to do, Mae? Sunday is two days away."

Mae shakes her head so rapidly she does in fact look a little bit like a toddler, one who's refusing naptime.

"We'd both be happy to have you come live with us."

"But Leo," says Mae.

"And Dad and Kara would have you too, you know that."

"But Leo," says Mae again. "Kara is allergic."

Natalie and Jordan pass a sisterly look between them, and Jordan says, "We can table that for now." But not for long, she thinks. For, like, hours, not days.

When the food comes Natalie busies herself cutting and divvying the kids' food, moving cups of milk out of the way of errant elbows, positioning Evangeline next to Caspian, where she can put single, innocuous bites of pancake onto his tray one at a time. She puts Scarlett on the other side with a pile of napkins. For a few moments, the children are completely occupied, making a game out of feeding Caspian. The world is at peace. Around them is the hustle and bustle of the restaurant, and outside on Congress Street it's raining sideways, which makes them feel even cozier, especially with the bright green of the walls and the warmth of the hanging lights.

Jordan clears her throat and says, "Today is the deadline. This is the day I'm supposed to call the reporter."

"Oh geez!" says Natalie. "Today. What are you going to do?"

Mae says, "What reporter?"

"Didn't I tell you?" Jordan could have sworn she'd told Mae. Didn't she tell her the day after she told Natalie? No, wait, that was Simone.

"Nobody ever tells me anything," says Mae.

Jordan, making sure the kids are occupied enough that they aren't listening, fills Mae in on the situation—she's getting good at it, now that she's told it twice; she knows when to deliver a dramatic flourish and when to keep her voice calm and steady. For the grand finale, she tells them that Simone suggested she go out on her own, and that she thinks she might do it.

They both say different versions of "Jordan, yes!" and "You have to!" And "Do it! Definitely, definitely do it!" Caspian celebrates the news by knocking over the rest of Scarlett's milk, and they all spend a few minutes grabbing for napkins and sopping and wiping.

When all is calm(ish) Jordan says, "Yeah? You really think so?"

"We know so," say her sisters, again and again. "Definitely."

On the way back to Rye, Mae looks over Scarlett's head out the window at the driving rain and says, "Mom would have loved a day like this."

Jordan's head whips around from the front seat and she says, "*What?* No, she wouldn't have. She was such a sun worshipper. She hated the rain."

"But she loved a summer storm."

"Not at the beach, she didn't," insists Jordan. "At the beach, she wanted sun."

"Natalie? I'm right, aren't I?" It's very important to Mae that Natalie agrees with her.

Natalie, taking care on Sagamore Road, where the car has to drive through deep puddles that splash up against the sides, feels a rising panic. Whose memory is correct, Jordan's or Mae's? "I don't know," she says worriedly. It scares her that she can't remember. There are days when she can't call up in her mind Theresa's voice, or her laugh, or certain expressions she thought would be with her forever.

They merge onto Ocean Boulevard south of Petey's. "I'm worried we're forgetting her," says Mae. "Are we forgetting her?" Evangeline, who, Mae is learning, is *always listening,* pats Mae's hand. It's such an adult gesture, so full of care and understanding, that Mae's eyes mist.

"Of course not," says Jordan, though she feels it too: the fear, she can almost hear it, like a faraway drumbeat. What if they are? What if they do?

Mae thinks about how she and her sisters were each spokes on Theresa's wheel, and how they might have had a different view of her, a different connection point, at any given time, and that's okay, right? That's okay. It has to be okay.

This is what she's turning over in her mind when they pull up to the house and see that Natalie's spot in the driveway has been claimed by a green dumpster. "Oh *shit*," says Natalie. "I forgot all about this. Is it seriously Friday already?"

"Language, Ma," says Scarlett. Mae snorts. Scarlett's comic timing is spot-on.

"It just got real," says Jordan, looking at the green hulk of it, thinking of the piles in the garage. "It just got really real." Soon, this house will no longer be a Shipman house. It will be a for-sale house, and then it will belong to someone else, and then it might not exist at all. Just like that.

IN THE EARLY afternoon, when she's tying Leo's leash to the leg of a chair so he can practice his settling, Mae calls Hal.

"Mae!" He sounds so happy to hear from her that she almost tears up. "I'm really glad to hear your voice."

"Me too," she says, then shakes her head, because that doesn't make sense. She dives right in from there. "I have some bad news," she says. "It's about Leo. He's okay! He's great, actually. But—"

"I know. Leo called me. Leo the person."

"Human Leo."

"Ha! Yes. He told me all about his work situation. He's heartbroken about not being able to keep the dog. We both agree you've made amazing progress with him."

"Thank you," says Mae. "But what—uh, what will happen to Leo? Dog Leo? When I bring him back? Will he have to go back to the shelter?"

"Well, that depends," says Hal. "Would you be interested in keeping him? We could see if the shelter would waive a re-adoption fee, since he's basically been with you the whole time."

Here is the slot in the conversation where Mae could but doesn't want to say *I have no home in which to keep him.* So instead she says, "I'd love to, but I'm not sure how long I'll be staying in Boulder. I might have to make some different plans."

"Ah," says Hal. "Got it." There's a pause, just this side of awkward, and then he says, "I'm sorry to hear that, actually."

She says, "You are?"

"I was hoping you'd be working at Dog On It for the long haul. I have clients who have been asking for you. I posted the videos you sent on the website and on my Instagram account, and the response has been terrific."

She's dumbfounded. She says, "It *has*?"

"One person wanted to know the name of your tattoo artist. But the rest were potential new board-and-train clients. I was thinking you could focus on that aspect of the business, if you'd consider coming back."

"I'm sorry, Hal," she says. "I'd be really sorry to stop working for you. But can I let you know my plans in a day or two? I still have a lot to figure out."

• • •

"I'm going for a swim," Jordan announces. The rain is still coming down.

"Doesn't look much like swimming weather," observes Calvin.

"I don't need sun to swim," says Jordan. "My veins are already part ice." She steals a glance at her father to see if he's grinning at that, and he is, and that's how she knows everything is going to be all right between them.

She walks onto the patio, holding her phone in one hand. She needs to do this now, before she swims. Without listening to the latest voicemail, she closes her eyes, does a ten-second meditation (a length of time recommended by zero meditation experts), and calls Bernadette.

No greeting, but that's typical. "Did you do what I needed you to do?"

"I'm on vacation."

"Screw vacation," says Bernadette. Jordan winces. Bernadette is so harsh. "You know we never really get a vacation in our business. Did you call the reporter?"

"No," says Jordan.

"What?"

"I said no."

"You need to call now."

"No."

"Tomorrow, at the very, very latest."

Jordan says nothing.

Bernadette says, "If you don't call that reporter—"

Jordan knows what Bernadette is going to say, so she says it for her. "Then I'm not going to have a job with you anymore."

"Exactly."

It's time, Jordan thinks. The time is now. She says, "I can't in good conscience call that reporter and say what you want me to say."

There's a long silence. Then: "Why not?"

"Because I'd be lying."

Bernadette says, "*What*?"

"Are you totally forgetting that you sexually harassed me?"

"That I *what?*"

"At the party, Bernadette. On Memorial Day."

"Oh, please, Jordan. Don't flatter yourself. I'm not even gay; how could I *sexually harass* you?"

For an eighth of a second Jordan doubts herself. She'd been

drinking too; is there a chance she false-memoried this? Is she making a mountain out of a molehill?

No. There is no chance. It *is* a mountain. Bernadette is a bully and a liar and a line-crosser. She's excellent at mind games. She will say and do whatever she needs to say and do to make any situation move in her direction.

"You did," she says. "You put your hand on my crotch. You threatened me when I turned you down. I could file a civil claim!"

There's a short pause, enough to let Jordan know that Bernadette is nervous. Not that she'd ever tell Jordan that. Then Bernadette says, "Don't be ridiculous. I was just playing around. If you don't call Samantha and get this taken care of, you can forget what I said about your career. I'll put Irina on the partner track."

There's *no way*, Jordan knows, that Irina is going on the partner track. Irina's work can be sloppy, and her instincts need serious guidance. She doesn't have what it takes to be really good at the job.

"So put Irina on the partner track." Another pause. She has called Bernadette's bluff, and it feels really good. "It doesn't matter to me. I quit."

"You can't quit."

"I just did."

"You have proprietary information about a lot of our clients."

"And?"

"If any of that leaks I'll sue the hell out of you."

"Don't worry about it," says Jordan. "I'm a vault."

Another pause. Jordan can feel Bernadette gathering herself, coiling like a rattlesnake before a strike. "Do you know what your problem is, Jordan?" Bernadette's voice is full of venom.

"What's that?" asks Jordan. She's a little scared, but she's also genuinely curious. What *is* her problem?

"You're good. But you're not nearly as good as you think you are."

"Ha!" Nice one. Jordan readies herself to unleash the zinger of all zingers. She wishes she could say it in person, so she could see Bernadette's expression before turning her back on her and leaving the room. She says, "That's where you're wrong. I'm even better."

She ends the call, puts her phone down, and opens the slider. Across the patio, down the steps, across the sand, and into the angry sea.

She dives under the first wave that comes toward her. It's bracing. No swim in the history of swims has ever felt as good as the one Jordan takes that day, with the rain streaming down and the wind whipping the waves into a frenzy. It's perfect.

After this, she is going to call Samantha Braddock.

• • •

Once she has Caspian down for his nap, Natalie takes a look to see what the ocean is doing.

What the ocean is doing is spitting out Jordan, who is striding up the beach in an extremely fetching athletic two-piece, the kind that confident and fit models wear in surf or yoga catalogs. She has no towel, no cover-up; she's holding no flip-flops that she might have flung carelessly in the sand. No phone. She's just in a full, beautiful stride, muscles popping. Jordan has incredible abs. She has abs that Natalie didn't even know were possible. Jordan's abs have abs.

Jordan is, and always has been, such a badass. Jordan's high school friends had been cool and sophisticated. They weren't the most popular crowd but rather the smart crowd, who were cool enough not to care that they weren't popular because they truly believed they were going to change the world. And many of them are doing it! Clerking for Supreme Court justices or doing big things in big tech. Doctoring without borders. Being Jordan.

"What are you doing?" calls Natalie. She grabbed a rain poncho from one of the hooks in the mudroom and now she has the hood on. The only people left in the water are the serious surfers, the ones who will go out in anything.

Jordan continues to stride up to the patio, where she ushers Natalie under one of the table umbrellas. She says, "I just quit my job."

"You did?"

"I'm shaking, look." She holds out her hand.

"Well, you're freezing. Come in. Let me get you a towel."

"That's the bad news."

"Then what's the good news?"

"The good news is, I'm going to go out on my own, like I told you. And I thought you could be my first clients, you and Austin."

"Us? Jordan, can we go inside?"

"You're in crisis, right? You're having a crisis?"

"We're definitely having a crisis. But I thought you didn't want to help us."

Jordan wrings out her hair. "I didn't," she says. "But I've been thinking a lot about it, and now I do."

"Yeah? So what's your plan?"

"We can figure out what to do about that article. We can reposition you."

Natalie takes off the poncho and says, "Here. You deserve this more than I do." Jordan waves her away. Her eyes are bright and clear, and she looks, in fact, a lot like old photos of Theresa. "Maybe," she says. "But I need it less. You keep it. Listen, Natalie, here's what got me thinking. When you were talking to Mae the other night—"

"And you were eavesdropping?"

"Yes. You were talking about how hard it is to be in your twenties, that space after college but before you've figured your life out? That's the most authentic version of you I've seen in a long time."

Natalie says, "Hey," and looks insulted.

"No, but it's true, though. I think people like you when you're being honest and vulnerable. I think you can reach way more people that way. So what I think would help you and Austin and maybe even your kids is a rebranding."

"A rebranding?"

"Yes. I think you should become someone who's honest about the messy parts of parenting. The ugly parts! People love to see the mess. They want to know what happens when Caspian tries to run away to the milking barn and Scarlett sneaks off with the iPad. They want to know that Cinnamon ate Evangeline's tooth, not that you handmade her tooth pillow."

"I didn't make the tooth pillow," says Natalie.

"You know what I mean. They want to look under the hood, see the streaks on the window glass. You could be the *anti*-tradwife. The messy mom."

Natalie wrinkles her nose. "I don't want to be the messy mom."

"The honest mom, then. The mom who tells the truth. I bet a lot of your sponsors would want to keep you, and those that didn't we could find replacements for."

"But what do I do about my clothes? I have so many clothes!"

"You can still wear them."

Natalie brightens. "I can?"

"Well, maybe not all of them. Maybe skip the gingham."

"I look good in gingham," says Natalie.

"We can negotiate that," says Jordan. She pulls open the slider and drip drip drips into the sunroom, where Natalie finds her the biggest, warmest towel in the whole basket. She's wrapping the towel around Jordan when she hears a familiar voice say, "Helloooo?"

It almost sounds like—

But it can't be—

"Daddy!" comes Scarlett's voice, loud and clear from upstairs, and then Evangeline's voice joins hers, and they come running down the stairs.

Austin is here!

"How is this even possible?" she asks, after the girls have flopped all over Austin; after he has swung Caspian in the air so high Caspian squeals and begs to be put down; after he has opened his arms so wide for Natalie, and then wrapped them around her and whispered, "I'm sorry," into her hair.

Now the kids are in the kitchen getting a snack with Mae and Kara (how anyone can be hungry after a Friendly Toast breakfast is beyond Natalie) and Austin and Natalie are in the sunroom. The rain is still pouring down. "How are you here?" She runs her hands up and down his strong forearms. She knows each muscle in these arms so well.

Austin explains that Shane and Travis, the farmhands, are staying at the farm. Shane's cousin is available too, so they have a third set of hands. Austin will drive back up tomorrow and he'll be home before dark; they'll have to do three milking sessions without him, but they'll be fine. Nobody is about to give birth. Buttercup's mastitis has responded to Dr. George's homeopathic treatment. All is well. "And anyway, the most important thing is that you and I talk, really talk, in person."

"Agreed," she says. "Austin! I'm so happy you're here. I was really scared after our last conversation. You didn't say goodbye. You didn't say I love you."

He looks at her levelly and says, "I was scared too. I still am. Can we go somewhere to talk? Somewhere private?"

She thinks about this. "There's not a lot of privacy in a house this full," she says. Then she remembers. "The Beach Club! We can go to the Beach Club." The week has gone so fast, she hasn't had a chance to get there. That's not really it, though; the staying away has a reason wider and deeper than scheduling. The truth is that nobody wanted to go without Theresa. Certainly nobody—even Mae, Natalie would bet—wanted Calvin to bring Kara there. The place is so full of childhood memories, of ghosts and nostalgia, of Theresa herself.

On a sunny day, they'd walk the mile along the beach, but given the rain, which is coming down even harder now, they drive. Calvin and Kara are more than happy to watch the children, so she and Austin hop into his truck. Natalie doesn't know what to do with herself. She fiddles with the seat belt, her hair, her bracelet. She fiddles with her anger, and her confusion, and her relief.

The parking lot—the most coveted parking in all of Rye, according to some—is mostly empty because of the weather. Natalie checks in with Deb at the front desk. A couple of diehards are swimming laps in the pool, and the cute teenage lifeguards look both bored and ready to blow the whistle at the first sign of lightning.

"Want anything?" Natalie asks, pointing to the snack bar.

"No, thank you. You?"

"Nope. Big breakfast at The Friendly Toast. I may never eat again." She leads him to a table under the canopy, a coveted spot in the sun, really the only option in this rain. They look out at the ocean. They're a couple of hours after high tide and the water is beginning to recede, but the waves are choppy and big.

"Is it possible that the kids grew?" asks Austin.

"Since Sunday?"

"Geez, it's only been since *Sunday* that I haven't seen them?" He shakes his head. "Feels like a month since you left."

"Yeah, to me too," she says. "Where do we start?" She wants to put her hands all over her husband. She wants to anchor him down to make sure he can't go anywhere without her.

"You go first."

"Okay." She's been giving this a *lot* of thought, what she would say when she and Austin had a chance to talk it out. Natalie looks hard at the rock wall along the edge of the building, reinforced after the storm two and a half years ago that wreaked such damage along the shoreline. "I've been thinking a lot about how we got from where we were to here." Deep breath, then the plunge. "I gave up a lot of things, Austin. I gave up a job I loved, a job I was really good at, a city I liked living in, to move up to the farm."

"Yes," says Austin. He takes her hand. "You did. But before that, I gave up my world to try to live in yours. I left Montana, and my family. I moved across the country, Natalie. I'd lived out west my entire life, and I left it behind because that's how much I believed in us."

He doesn't say this with bitterness: it's a fact, like that day's price for milk or the size of a specific milking stall. She clocks the past tense: *believed.* Does he not believe any longer?

"But," she says. She takes a breath, tries to absorb what Austin is saying before moving on to her own point. "I mean, you're right." Pause, breath. "But you're the one who wanted to leave Boston—"

He closes her hand into a fist and squeezes it before letting it go. "We both wanted to leave Boston."

"You first. I liked my job. You hated yours."

"We were both worn out."

"We were. But *you* found the farm, and you wanted it so badly. We moved there for you. And I found a way to make it work, to make it *profitable* even, to help our family. I worked really hard on all of that. That magazine piece was supposed to be a big deal, our first big media hit! You should have known that. But I feel like you spit all over it and you didn't realize. Or care. Even this week, when I tried to tell you, you didn't care."

Austin is perplexed, she can tell by his expression. *It was just a joke*, he'll probably say.

"It was just a joke," he says. Bingo, thinks Natalie. She really does know him so well. "I didn't mean anything by it!"

She casts about in her mind for a Theresa-ism to help her through. The one about asking before you pet a strange dog won't help, nor will a reminder not to put her drink down at a nightclub. She looks around. She was a little kid here, then a bigger kid, then a teenager. When you're sixteen you're allowed on the upper deck. Now the deck has couches but when Natalie was a teenager they made do with old lounge chairs. She feels Theresa, all the dinners they ate here, home-cooked food packed so carefully to enjoy among friends at these tables, bottles of wine poured into plastic goblets. The Third of July parties, the fireworks. Her eyes move over the red geraniums that line the pool. The red geraniums have been a part of the club as long as Natalie has been alive, and they will continue after she's gone. No person is immutable, but these flowers are. She folds her hands on the table.

"Is there any chance," she begins, "that you did know you were doing damage? Like, without one hundred percent consciously realizing it? And that you did it anyway." Austin starts to protest and Natalie raises a finger. "Wait. Think about it, okay? Think about it before you answer. Not so we can fight about it, but so we can figure this out. I know you didn't want that reporter nosing around our home. I know you don't love having our kids on social media. Is there any chance that you knew you were sabotaging the article when you said what you said?"

She watches Austin sit with it. It's hard for Natalie not to fill the silence; it's always her instinct to do that. It's almost impossible to let the quiet live and breathe, to be a black-and-white picture that Austin fills in with his own colors.

"Maybe," he says finally. "Yeah, it's possible."

Natalie sucks in her breath. This is where a real fight could start. The triumphantly wronged party, the retreating of the person who committed the wrong. She makes herself pull back. She thinks about what her parents might have done if faced with a situation of equal import. Theresa and Calvin were married for such a long time; of course they hadn't agreed on everything! But they treated the marriage with respect, no matter how angry they were. She wants that too.

"Why—" she starts to say. Then, "How—" Then, finally, "You . . ." She can't get out a full sentence. So she takes a deep breath, lets it out. Another, then another.

Austin has his wrists resting on the tops of his knees, his hands clasped together. He seems to be considering the space between his feet. When he starts talking, he lifts his eyes to meet Natalie's. "Okay, here it is. Yes, the answer is definitely yes. I did sabotage it, and I think I know why."

"Why?" She wants to know, and she also doesn't want to know.

"You aren't going to want to hear this. But. I feel like you do a lot of what you do for the camera. Like, it's not even real. Like you don't love our life the way you used to. You just love how our life looks to the outside world."

Natalie feels like his words have slapped her. She puts her hand to a cheek, almost expecting to feel some heat there. "*What?* How could you think that? I *love* our life. You know I do!"

Austin shakes his head. "When we started, when we got the farm, I know you did. I mean, I know you sacrificed for it, and it was hard, but you seemed really happy."

"I was," says Natalie.

"But now, now it seems like you're happy with conditions."

"What do you mean?"

"Like, you're happy if this video gets so many likes, or that photo comes out the way you want it, or if the calf is born when the kids are awake so you have a record of them helping. Instead of just being—happy that those things are happening."

"That's not true," she says, too quickly. But then it's her turn to think carefully. She forces herself to do that, letting the thoughts crawl out of their hiding holes, even if it feels uncomfortable to have them out in the open.

Austin goes on. "So if I did anything to ruin your big moment, Nat, it wasn't on a conscious level, I swear. I really thought it was a harmless joke. And I'm sorry that it blew up the way it did. But maybe below the surface, maybe I was trying to blow things up. You were so worked up over that reporter's visit, making sure everything was perfect, worrying so much about someone you didn't even know. It feels like you're *always* worrying about what people you don't know think. And I didn't want that reporter there. I didn't like her. I didn't like how you were around her."

"How was I around her?"

He sighs. "I hate to say this . . ."

"Say it." She squeezes her eyes shut as though that will soften whatever is coming next. "Just go ahead and say it."

"Kind of desperate. Like it was so important to make everything perfect for her instead of concentrating on . . ." His voice trails off.

"Don't say instead of concentrating on you. That's not fair."

He tents his fingers, leans his forehead into them. "Me, sure, but not just me. The kids, the people who love you. But also, Nat, yourself. Instead of making everything a performance."

"Hold on," she says. "A lot of it is real. Most of it. The heart of it, of our family."

"But do you see where I can't always tell the difference?"

She nods slowly. She doesn't want to admit it, but she sees.

"You like the money that comes from what I do," she points out. "You liked being able to renovate the milking barn."

"Of course I did. We have the nicest milking barn in the county."

"And you like the fancy stove."

"*You* like the fancy stove," he says. "*I* like what you make with the stove."

God, Natalie really does love that stove. She misses it the way you miss a person.

"How long have you felt this way?"

"Awhile."

"Why didn't you *say* anything? Why'd you go along with it?"

"Because it was important to you. Because you put so much into it. I didn't want to get in your way."

Natalie realizes that this was a gift and a sacrifice from Austin to her, one she didn't even know he was giving.

"I think we have to decide what we really want," says Austin. "And I hope it's the same thing. Because if it's not, that's where we'll start to have a real problem."

She's so scared to ask the next question: "What do you want, Austin?"

He doesn't answer right away, and she feels the panic all the way in her fingernails. She tries to quiet it by watching the rain hit the sand and the whitecaps beat against the shoreline.

"For me? I want the focus of our lives to be our farm and our family," he says. "Look, it takes a while for new owners to make a farm profitable. But we have a lot in the bank now—mostly because of money you earned. Now that we're in good shape there, I don't feel like we need *more.* I feel peaceful when it's just us and the kids and our cows. I feel happier with a private life. Honestly, Nat, I'd love another baby." She's watching Austin's heart open, display its contents for her to see, and she loves that. "And I'd love for you to be able do something like what you were doing in Boston. If you wanted to."

She says, "You want me to find a tech company in rural Vermont?"

He grins. "Find one, start one, I don't know. Not for me, for you. What do *you* want, Natalie?"

What does she want? "I'd love another baby too." She didn't know this was true until she says it.

His smile is so big then. "You would?"

She nods. "I would. And I think I could be happy with a private life too. Jordan has some ideas for us on repositioning and rebranding, like, me becoming a publicly messy mom instead of a tradwife, and when she brought that up I thought I wanted to do that. But now I don't think that's right."

"You don't?"

She shakes her head. "I don't want to do it in public, but I do want to figure out the next steps for us and our family." She wants to put some muscle into working it out.

"And the cows."

"Definitely the cows."

He takes her hand and faces it palm up, traces little circles on it with three of his fingers. It feels so good, comforting and sexy all at once. She closes her fingers over his and there they sit, watching the rain come down.

"I didn't like that reporter either," admits Natalie. "Did you see the boots she showed up in?"

"Ridiculous," agrees Austin. "Those boots were the worst."

SATURDAY

• • •

"They're predicting a fourteen-foot storm surge at high tide," says Mae on Saturday morning. The rain came down all night for the second night in a row, and it's raining still. Mae took one for the team, walking both dogs while everyone else stayed warm and dry. She played the martyr, but secretly she wanted to do it; she wanted to know if she was up for the challenge of walking them together. She wouldn't even have attempted this a few days ago, but Leo's leash skills have improved remarkably, and the dogs are now BFFs. Well, Fs, anyway.

In the water, she'd seen three intrepid surfers—there are always a few, no matter the weather—but there was nobody on the beach. The wind was picking up, whipping the water into a frenzy, blowing Mae's hair back. The waves were ferocious, and she watched one surfer wipe out and then give up, lugging his surfboard up onto the beach. She kept the dogs on their leashes the whole time, even reliable Cinnamon, because she feared they'd run into the water and get swept away.

Now the family is gathered in the kitchen, where something really exciting is going on. In the garage storeroom the day before, Jordan found an old stainless-steel espresso maker, the kind you use on the stovetop, and she's cleaned it and brought it back to life. Coupled with a battery-powered frothing wand Natalie discovered in the kitchen drawer with the measuring cups, they've got a real coffee bar going.

"*Fourteen*-foot?" says Calvin. "Are you sure it doesn't say *four*-foot?"

"I'm positive," says Mae. "I learned my numbers a long time ago."

"Dad?" asks Natalie, who's loading Caspian into his portable booster. "What time is high tide?"

"Do I look like the tide clock?" asks Calvin, a little grumpy because he doesn't want espresso, and he's trying to decide whether to make a full pot of the regular stuff, but there are so many people in the kitchen that he can't get to the coffeemaker. Austin is tall and broad-shouldered, with big hands and big feet; his arrival, welcome as it is, makes it seem like the number of people in the house has suddenly doubled.

"I got you, Dad," says Jordan. "I'll make a regular pot."

"Austin will drink regular too," says Natalie. "He hates fancy coffee."

"Hate it," Austin agrees pleasantly. He's in an excellent mood because this is the latest he's slept since he and Natalie bought Hillside Haven.

"Good man," says Calvin.

Jordan fills up the old Hamilton Beach with water and measures the coffee. Jordan is rolling her eyes at her father, but only a little, and you have to look closely to see. Has this week softened Jordan? Mae wonders.

"You do look like the tide clock, a little bit, around the eyes," says Mae to her father, and Calvin chuckles. "No, but, for real," she adds. "What time is high tide?" She tried to dry the dogs off but drying two dogs is harder than walking two dogs, and Cinnamon's fur holds a copious amount of water. When Cinnamon shakes, Caspian, who's lower to the ground than anyone else in his booster, gets a full shower. Which he likes.

"I'll look it up," says Natalie. She taps on her phone screen. "Just before one thirty," she reports. "A little over three hours from now. Jordan, can I have a double cappuccino? With an extra shot?"

"So, a triple?"

"Sure. Yes."

"You can just order it that way."

"I thought it sounded more demure my way."

"This thing doesn't really make shots, per se, but I'll estimate." Jordan makes Natalie's drink and serves it in a mug that says *THAT'S VERY NICE BUT I DIDN'T ASK.* She makes a latte for herself. She makes Calvin's regular coffee and another cappuccino for Kara, this one with the equivalent of only two shots. She gives Kara a mug that says *MY BRAIN HAS TOO MANY TABS OPEN.*

Evangeline is deep into *Ivy + Bean*, and Scarlett is sitting in Austin's lap and working on a *Cozy Friends* coloring book that features unlikely groups of animals, like an alligator, a bear, and a duck, doing unlikely activities together. Visiting a nail salon. Watering a garden. Sunbathing on beach towels. They do look cozy, doing all of these things. (But what kind of duck gets a pedicure?)

Even though it's closer to lunch than breakfast Natalie makes effortless pancakes, a big tower of them, and Caspian sits in his chair for a long time, pulling his apart and dropping them onto the floor for the dogs. Mae notices but lets it go, because it's keeping Caspian busy and the dogs at peace. Calvin is staring worriedly at his phone, looking at weather reports on a bunch of different apps. A furrow has popped up between his eyes. He hasn't eaten any of the pancakes Natalie set out for him. He's twisting his watch around on his wrist the way he does when he's nervous.

Calvin's phone rings, and Nikoletta Realtor flashes across the screen. Calvin takes the call in the sunroom, and when he returns he says, "Nikoletta wants me to keep her informed if we get any water in here. Obviously that would affect the open house."

"I'm all for affecting the open house," says Natalie, "but we never get water in here. Right?"

"Not so far."

"That's surprising, with sea levels rising the way they are," offers Austin, and Natalie shoots him a murderous look.

"This beach is so big!" says Mae. "Sometimes you have to walk out forever just to get your ankles wet."

"That's at low tide," points out Jordan.

"Yeah, but—" says Mae.

"They say sea levels will rise twelves inches by 2050," says Austin, and this time Natalie hits him ungently on the thigh.

THEY TRY TO go back to what they're doing—eating, coloring, smearing maple syrup (Caspian)—but the worry has pervaded the kitchen. Calvin keeps leaving to pace the living room, pace the sunroom. Mae and Jordan wash the breakfast dishes while Natalie and Scarlett color in a frog with curlers in its hair. At twelve thirty, Calvin takes a trip out to the patio. He's gone so long that Mae gets worried. She takes a raincoat from the hooks in the mudroom and joins her father. He's wearing his yellow slicker, the one he's had as long as she can remember, the one they used to make fun of him for looking like a fisherman in. Now he looks like a sad, wet fisherman; his hood is up, and the sideways rain is beating at him.

He has to talk loudly to be heard over the wind and the rain. He says, "When I think about your mother's parents buying this house, moving in here, and, I don't know, unpacking their things in the kitchen, hanging curtains—it just really makes me miss your mother. I miss her so much. I hope you girls know that I miss her too. Every day, I miss her."

"I know," says Mae. "We do know, I promise."

"And to think that this house will one day be gone . . . I mean, whether or not we sell today or next week or in two years, any house along here that doesn't get rebuilt will one day be gone."

"I know," says Mae. She thinks about how she doesn't have a lot to give, no money, no home anyone can visit her in, no real-life advice because she herself is still learning. But right now, she can give her father something. "Remember what you said when we first got here?" Calvin shakes his head. "You said, 'A house is just a structure. Family is people.' You were right, Dad."

Calvin puts his hand over Mae's, squeezes it once, lets it go. "Thank you for reminding me of that."

"Does that make me the Favorite Daughter?" asks Mae.

Calvin smiles and says, "No comment." Then he says, "I think we should move to higher ground."

"Like, the mountains?"

"I was thinking more like the second floor."

"UPSTAIRS, GIRLS," NATALIE says. Austin scoops up Caspian, the girls follow Natalie, and everyone else moves into formation behind, dogs too.

"Come in our room," says Kara. "Since we have the deck, and the windows facing the ocean." At the beginning of the week, Mae knows, they would have bristled at the *our* and the *we*. Maybe Jordan and Natalie are bristling still, but if so they're bristling very quietly.

They all crowd in. The slightest hint of Kara's perfume hangs in the air. The bed is made perfectly. Hospital corners, of course. On each nightstand is a glass of water and a book—Malcolm Gladwell for Calvin, Elin Hilderbrand for Kara. Kara is tidy; there are no articles of clothing flung around, no grains of sand tracked in, nothing really personal, nothing that says *We have sexual relations here*, and Mae is very, very glad for that.

Kara turns on both bedside lights because the day has grown dark. Jordan steps out onto the deck, closing the door behind her, and comes immediately back in. "It's so windy," she says. "I felt like I was going to get blown right off."

"I'm scared," says Scarlett, and Natalie tells her, "She didn't really mean she was going to get blown off. We're all safe, you don't need to be scared," but she sounds scared too.

Calvin goes out to the deck next. It takes some effort to close the slider behind him. Mae starts to worry now too: Is Calvin going to blow off the deck? No, he's not. But when he returns his hair is all leaning in one direction and there's an anxious look on his face. He pats his hair down, checks his watch, glances at the kids, and shakes his head. He says, "Almost high tide."

Mae wonders if a storm surge comes exactly on time. She tries for a joke to this effect: "Does it tell you, like an Uber driver, when it's three minutes away?" She looks around; nobody is laughing. The dogs are whining, reacting to the change in atmospheric pressure, walking in circles, unable to settle. They seem like many dogs, not just two, winding around Mae's legs, then Natalie's, then Jordan's. They seem like ten dogs; they seem like a shiver of sharks. Austin puts Caspian on the bed, then Cinnamon leaps up next to him, messing up Kara's careful bed-making.

"Sorry, sorry!" Natalie says. "I'll fix it!"

"Please. Don't worry about it," says Kara. She doesn't say, *That's the least of our worries,* but they're all thinking it. The house shakes from the wind.

Caspian puts his thumb in his mouth and looks at the ceiling. "He's ready for his nap," says Natalie. "Should I take him in the other room?"

"Let's all stay here," says Calvin.

Then Austin does something surprising. He lies down next to Caspian and sings to him, without compunction or embarrassment, a lullaby about sleeping critters and rolling tumbleweeds and long nights under a bright full moon. It's *mesmerizing*, and for several moments they all forget they're in the middle of a coastal storm, and they feel like they're on the ranch or the range.

And then it comes. The ocean comes toward them, and the beach that is normally so wonderfully big, the beach that, sometimes when the Shipman girls were small, seemed so endless it felt impossible to cross, disappears altogether, and all they can see is water. The ocean is *so loud.*

The lights flicker, then hold, then flicker again.

Calvin goes out to the deck again and comes back in immediately, saying, "It's over the wall."

"Maybe it's stopping at the patio," says Mae optimistically.

"I don't think so," says Jordan. "Water doesn't usually respect boundaries."

The lights go out.

WHEN THEY GO downstairs an hour later, when the rain has started to slow, they can't quite comprehend what they're seeing. They stand there, taking it in. In the Shipman living room, the water is several inches high, inches over the baseboard. It's a foot of water or more. Probably more.

"This house has been here for more than sixty years, and there's never been water in it," says Calvin, the first to speak. He crouches down to inspect the walls, and the water sloshes around his pants. He says, "It's starting to recede. But the waterline? It was over the outlets. See that? Those will have to be replaced. Evangeline and Scarlett, don't touch anything."

"*Everything* will have to be replaced," says Jordan. "Look at the furniture! All of Mom's things." There's water halfway up the legs of the coffee table, and past the legs of the couch, and soaking part of the end tables, the plant stand, the cord for the standing lamp.

"Probably the refrigerator and dishwasher too," says Austin from the kitchen. "If the insulation got wet, you're not going to be able to repair."

"And the cabinets," says Kara. "These are oak, right?" Calvin nods.

"I'm going to see how our neighbors did," says Calvin. He goes outside and comes back fifteen minutes later with a full report. The Zimmerman house next door is newer, built to code and FEMA regulations, set higher, with a raised deck instead of a patio. No water. On the other side of them, the Prescotts had gone to see their grandchildren in Maine, inadvertently leaving their slider open by two inches. It's even worse at the Prescotts'. Many of the homes have rocks flung upon the lawns, patio furniture that has blown over.

Calvin's phone rings. It's Nikoletta, on FaceTime. She wants to see how the house is. Calvin walks around with the phone, showing her. "Oh, no. Oh, no," Nikoletta says as Calvin makes the rounds. They hear her say things like *rot* and *wood floors* and *immediate mold remediation*. "We can't sell this," the girls hear her say, and they look at each other, eyes wide. "We cannot sell this home right now. Calvin, while you talk to your insurance, I'm going to make some calls. I'll be in touch." As quickly as she appeared on the screen, she is gone.

"We never finished the storage room," says Mae.

"You never started the storage room," points out Jordan. "Natalie and I did it all."

"True," says Mae, remorselessly.

The Shipman girls troop out to the garage to look at all of the things they had dragged out and organized and never finished dealing with. The three carefully separated piles are now one wet sloppy pile. There will be no donating and no keeping. It will all have to go. Everything will have to go.

• • •

The rain stops. The tide recedes, as it always does eventually. Instead of spending Saturday evening eating dinner out so they can keep the house tidy for the open house, the Shipman family spends early Saturday evening eating dinner out because the first floor still has water in it and they have no power and Calvin has been on hold with the insurance company for what feels like years. Finally he is able to leave a message and is waiting for a call back.

They gate the dogs in the dry upstairs and take two separate cars to Flatbread in Portsmouth, where there is power, and where they order way more pizza than they need, and also the salads with the secret dressing, and beer for Calvin and Kara and Austin, and wine for Jordan, Natalie, and Mae. They order the organic sodas for Scarlett and Evangeline, a *very rare treat indeed*. Caspian has his own sippy cup with the last of the Hillside Haven milk. The mood is somber, but laced with giddy relief. They are all okay; they are here, together, a family without a structure, which is infinitely preferable to a structure without a family.

While they're waiting for their food Calvin's phone rings and he goes outside to take the call. When he returns, he gives them the update. The flood insurance adjusters will be out as soon as possible to assess the damage, but in the meantime the Shipmans should begin the process of throwing out ruined rugs and furniture, removing the wet drywall. "Looking on the bright side, we already have a dumpster."

"A layperson can remove drywall?" Jordan asks. "I can't imagine doing anything in my place, I just call the super."

"Of course," says Natalie. "Drywall isn't a big deal. Right, Austin?" She and Austin have done many things to their house in Hillside Haven over the years (videos available for viewing with the proper search terms). "You just cut it out a foot above the waterline."

"I can't believe you know that," says Jordan. "You are such an enigma!"

Natalie shrugs and takes another piece of pizza.

Calvin pops his new glasses on top of his head and rubs his temples. "We'll have to get contractors in for the floors and the baseboards," he says. "And electrical. And haul out the appliances. It's a lot." He looks tired and a little bit old, sitting in front of his pizza, his beer mostly untouched. "I'm not sure how I'll manage this from Lenox. I'm teaching the summer social sciences program, and Kara is due back at work."

"Maybe I could stay—" Mae begins.

Then Calvin's phone rings again, and Nikoletta Realtor flashes on the screen. "Sorry, excuse me," says Calvin. He steps out once more. They can see him walking back and forth in front of the restaurant, raking his hands through his hair. When he returns, he sits and says, "Okay, everyone. Here's the deal. We need to wait to see what kind of settlement we get from insurance." He takes a deep breath, blows it out slowly. When Natalie drops her napkin and bends to pick it up, she sees that her father and Kara are holding hands under the table. Five days ago this sight would have filled her with an unspeakable rage, but now she's sort of glad that Calvin has someone's hand to hold. "And then. Well. What Nikoletta is suggesting is . . ."

The sisters look at each other, alarmed. Why can't Calvin finish a sentence? Is he having a stroke? "Go ahead," says Jordan.

Calvin clears his throat. "You have to understand that this isn't how I wanted things to go. But Nikoletta suggests that we sell immediately to a developer who will demo to the foundation and rebuild."

Even the kids seem to understand the import of this moment—even Caspian, who is sitting in Austin's lap. He puts down his sippy cup and casts his saucer eyes around the table.

Mae is the first to speak: "But that's so soon. It won't be Mom's house anymore."

"No," agrees Calvin. "No, it won't."

"And we won't be selling to a family," says Mae.

"You knew whoever bought it was probably going to tear it down," Jordan points out.

"Yeah, eventually. But I thought maybe they'd live there for a little bit first. I pictured little girls in our rooms. I know that doesn't make sense. But it's what I pictured. That's what made me feel better about it."

"I pictured little girls too," admits Natalie.

"If I'm being honest," says Calvin, "I did too. But I don't think we have much of a choice here. To remediate flood damage in a house that will only get more destroyed by the next flood—it doesn't make sense."

"It doesn't," agrees Austin, and one by one they join in. *It doesn't. It doesn't. It doesn't.*

The server clears the plates and pizza pans and brings the check. Calvin puts his credit card down, and for a few long moments nobody says anything.

Jordan speaks first. "First thing I would do if I were rebuilding is no more wood floors. I'd do slate in the kitchen, then those faux-wood floors made of ceramic throughout."

"Geez, Jordan," says Mae.

"What?"

"The body isn't even cold."

"There are some fantastic wood alternatives out there," says Austin experimentally, and after a time Natalie joins in. "I always thought a breakfast nook would be nice. You know? Like we have at Hillside. The kids love it."

Mae shoots daggers at Natalie with her eyes, then Kara says, "A raised deck would be lovely. With one of those built-in grills, maybe? An outdoor kitchen?"

They can see all of the emotions cross Mae's face. They watch her come around. The Storm is passing, and they wait for her to speak. Finally, she says, "If I was rebuilding anyway, I'd get one of those walk-in dog bath things. You know, to get the sand off before they track it in the house."

They all agree that this is an *excellent* idea.

THEY ATE SO early that there's plenty of daylight left when they get back, and the Shipman girls want to walk in the direction of the flagpole, just the three of them. Maybe all the way to the Beach Club. It's decided that Calvin and Kara will take the kids for a walk in the other direction, while Austin checks out the water level inside the house.

"Can we look for a whale on the beach?" asks Scarlett.

"I hope you don't find one," says Natalie. "That would be really bad news for the whale. There'd be no way to get it back to sea."

"A dolphin, then," amends Evangeline.

"Same deal."

"Maybe some crabs that can make their way back to the water as soon as they need to," suggests Mae, and they agree that, yes, crabs would be okay; they'll look for crabs.

Kara reaches her hand down, and Caspian stretches his up, and off they go, a funny permutation of a family.

On the way to the Beach Club, there's more detritus, more people examining their homes or picking through what the receding tide left on the beach. The air feels clean and clear, like the bad parts have been swept away with a broom. And there, arching across the sky out over the ocean, as perfectly placed as it would be in a child's painting, is the most beautiful rainbow. They all see it at the same time. Because, as they were instructed their whole lives, they remembered to look at the sky.

"You can't tell me that isn't Mom," says Mae.

"Oh my god," says Natalie. "Never. That's such a cliché. Mom would never come back as a rainbow. She'd come back as, I don't know, like, a sandpiper or a seal or a surfboard or something. Something more interesting."

"Natalie's right," says Jordan. "Mom hated clichés."

"You guys are wrong," says Mae. "That's *our* rainbow. That's Mom."

Mae waves at the rainbow and says, "Hi, Mom." She looks at her sisters expectantly.

"Really?" asks Jordan. Mae nods. "Okay. Fine. Hi, Mom," says Jordan. They both turn to Natalie.

Natalie sighs.

"Go ahead," says Mae.

"Hey, girl," says Natalie, nodding at the rainbow. She feels silly, but she does it for Mae.

"I wish she left us a letter," says Mae.

"What kind of letter?"

"With, like, life advice, the way moms do in a movie."

"We were there when she died," points out Jordan. "Why would she also have written a letter?"

"To remind us not to put our drinks down at the bar."

"Not to dry an untreated stain."

"That thank-you notes are not optional."

"I think we know the advice," says Jordan. "Now we just have to live it." Then she squints down the beach, where a gray blur is visible, running in wild circles, and asks, "Is that Leo?"

"It looks like him. Somebody let him out!" Natalie cries. "Oh, no, I bet it was Austin, he didn't know any better, I'm sorry, Mae!"

"It was probably Kara," says Jordan. Then she says, "Sorry. I forgot I'm nice now. It probably wasn't Kara."

"It's okay," says Mae, although it really isn't okay. If Leo gets in a situation he can't handle, if he finds another dog on the beach and goes after it, if he gets *above threshold*, as Hal would say, thirty seconds could undo all of the hours of careful training Mae has put in over the last week.

She inhales, and on her exhale she yells, "Leo, COME!"

No dog's recall is perfect when the whole world beckons, that's just a fact. Mae learned from Hal that the recall word is not to be overused, because if you let a dog ignore you too many times you have *poisoned the cue* and your dog won't listen when you really need him to.

("Be careful not to poison the cue." —Hal Miller.)

Mae has been so careful with her recall word! She doesn't think she has poisoned the cue, but of course you never know. All you can do is hope.

Always offer something enticing, Hal would say. *Always be the best option.*

She sees Leo's head turn toward her and watches his body still, watches him pause, considering. One way to freedom, but also to uncertainty, unpredictability, possibly danger. The other way to home. Mae calls one more time, and one more time is all it takes for Leo to run toward her as fast as he can, ignoring anything he passes on the way, sliding like a baseball player into the most beautiful sit in front of Mae.

It's a *perfect* recall.

"Good boy, Leo," says Mae. She's so happy she could cry. She takes off her belt and fashions it into a leash to hook around his collar. "Good, good, good boy. The best boy."

They start back. How many times have they walked this beach in the past? So many times. *So many!* They were little girls on this beach, and preteens, and teens, and young adults, and now here they are, the girls from the photos, the girls from the memories, the girls from yesterday and today and tomorrow. Here they are, the Shipman girls.

EPILOGUE

One Year Later

It's Kara who has the tickets for the family for James Taylor's Fourth of July show at Tanglewood. They were a gift from the family of a patient. In all the years they've been Lenox residents, not one of the Shipmans has been to this legendary show! They've always been at the Beach Club for the holiday, or off in their own adult lives.

They have seats on the lawn, and they get there early to spread their picnic blanket out among the other blankets, a giant patchwork quilt as far as the eye can see. Natalie put herself in charge of food, with assists from Kara and Mae. Calvin took on beverages, and Austin assigned himself bathroom duty for Caspian. Caspian is no longer wearing diapers, and they're aware that a break in routine can mean a break in newly formed habits. They decided collectively not to give Jordan any family jobs because she's in the middle of a work crisis. One of her clients, the CEO of a major pharmaceutical company, a married father of four, was recently caught canoodling with someone not his wife on the Jumbotron at a Red Sox game, and to say the clip went viral is an understatement. Jordan has been on her phone nonstop.

This is the first time they've all been together since the previous summer, and the first time they've ever crowded into the house on Galway Court with Kara. (For Christmas, Natalie had hosted Austin's family at the farm, and Mae and Jordan had joined, while Calvin and Kara had gone to visit Kara's mom in Ohio, celebrating her first five months of sobriety. "I hate to say this," Kara told Mae after, "but my mom sober is harder to deal with than my mom drunk.") Scarlett and Evangeline have been sleeping in the basement. Natalie and Austin are in Natalie's old bedroom, and Caspian has taken to sleeping on the floor in Mae's room, next to Leo, who has graduated from the crate. Sometimes Mae wakes and finds both Leo and Caspian in the bed with her, and while she knows only one of these creatures is technically allowed, she pretends she didn't notice a thing. Cinnamon stayed back at the farm with the new farmhand Austin and Natalie hired in the spring, after they added a dozen head to their herd.

When the Shipman girls first got to Galway Court they'd combed the house for changes, for signs that said Theresa's memory was being erased. They'd found the following: new pillows on the living room couch, but same couch. New deck furniture, same deck, right down to the wooden railings that will need to be replaced next summer. Kara has brought Theresa's vegetable garden back to life, and the tomato plants are staked with Theresa's old green stakes, bent like crooked fingers pointing to the sky. Kara, it may be noted, is a better gardener than Theresa was. There's a new comforter on Calvin and Kara's bed, but the bed frame and nightstands are as they were. In the kitchen, a happy surprise, all of the coffee mugs from Ruby on Rye are populating the cabinet near the coffee machine. Today Mae drank out of one that said *YUP, WOKE UP AWESOME AGAIN* and Natalie (decaf) from *I'M THE MIDDLE, I'M THE REASON WE HAVE RULES.*

It's no easy feat for Natalie to lower her seven-month-pregnant self down to the beach chair that Austin has brought for her. Austin holds her elbow and guides her. As soon as she's sitting, Caspian says, "Mommy, I need the bathroom."

"Not it," says Natalie.

"I got you, buddy," says Austin.

"I want Mommy to take me," says Caspian. His lower lip begins to tremble theatrically.

"Oh, no," says Natalie. "No no no. I just got down here. I'm not getting up until at least July eighth."

"I got it," says Austin. He holds his hand out for Caspian's.

Jordan says, "I'm finishing this email and then I'm turning my phone all the way off." Kara and Calvin begin to unpack the coolers. They have so much food! Vegetable tarts with ricotta and pesto spread. Sour cream and onion deviled eggs. Ranch slaw. Roast beef sliders. Strawberries and cream made from organic Hillside Haven cream.

Soon after the storm Nikoletta brokered a deal to sell to a developer who had a vision for a new home that will respect the landscape. It won't be Theresa's home, but it's not going to be as bad as anyone feared. After clearing his debts Calvin had enough to give each Shipman girl ten thousand dollars. Mae had paid back Tony, settled her storage fees and her Afterpay account, and bought the domain name and top-of-the-line equipment for her new business. She's the sole proprietor of Fido in the City, which specializes in training rescue dogs for urban life. She and Leo (and the occasional foster dog, when the foster dog has *literally nowhere else to go*) are living in Jordan's second bedroom on the Upper West Side. Close to the park—a dog's dream! In exchange for rent, Mae is doing admin work for Jordan's crisis comm business. After Samantha Braddock's article came out, many of Bernadette's former clients left her, and now Jordan has more work than she knows what to do with.

On the subject of articles: the previous summer, returning to Hillside Haven after the storm, Natalie had a long talk with her publicist, Bethany, who advised her that the fallout from the article was not nearly as bad as Natalie feared. Her follower numbers were holding steady, and while you could find negative comments if you looked hard enough, you could find negative comments about anything if you looked hard enough. Natalie decided not to look very hard. She had many long talks with Austin, when the kids were in bed and they could sit on the front porch of the farmhouse looking at the stars. She'd gone through several bouts of soul-searching. She'd searched for days, even weeks, and what she'd found there had been her next steps.

She finished out her contracts for sponsorships and affiliates, then she closed her online accounts. She's trying out life as a private person again, to see if it still fits. So far it fits! She has put her money from Calvin into the farm, specifically into investing in wearable tech for cows, which bigger farms have been using to monitor cows' habits and physiological changes for early disease detection and reproductive efficiency. It's a data scientist's dream! Natalie is trying to figure out how to make the investment worthwhile for smaller family farms like those in Vermont. And maybe, just maybe, she can help make them a little cuter. The Ladies work so hard, can they please get some bling on their collars or their ear tags?

In the fall, Scarlett and Evangeline will enter the public school system. They are *beyond* excited, and also a little nervous. They can't stop talking about the school bus, and when they are back home after this trip they're going to go shopping for lunch boxes.

Calvin will teach only one class in the upcoming school year. He and Kara are debating whether to take up pickleball or mahjongg on Kara's days off. Maybe both! Maybe neither!

Now, Austin and Caspian are still picking their way back from the bathroom—the real estate between blankets is at a premium—when James Taylor takes the stage. Natalie sees Austin look around frantically, not sure where to find them.

"Stand up and flag them down," she instructs Mae.

Mae stands up and waves until Austin sees her. He swings Caspian up on his shoulders and finds a path toward them. Before she sits Mae looks toward the horizon, over the people, over the fan-shaped building. She swears she sees a shooting star. It could be an errant early firework. It could be nothing at all—could be her imagination. If she told her sisters, they'd probably tease her, tell her again that it's not Theresa, that their mother would be more original than to show up as a shooting star, that you can't see a shooting star half an hour before sunset (not true, Mae knows—you can). *What a cliché!* they'd say. *Just like the rainbow! Mom would never!* So Mae keeps it to herself. *Hi, Mom. We miss you so much, but we're all okay here.* She sends out those thoughts as Austin and Caspian arrive at their spot, as Austin lowers Caspian to the ground and Caspian somehow manages to step on a deviled egg, as the music, at long last, begins.

THERESA SHIPMAN'S 13 RULES FOR LIFE

1. Don't dry an untreated stain.
2. Never put your drink down at the bar.
3. Take care of your friends.
4. Take care of your sisters.
5. Thank-you notes are not optional.
6. Have the best day.
7. Relax, you have more time than you think you have.
8. Good habits are 90 percent of the battle.
9. Swim in the rain.
10. Dance in the dark.
11. If you're sad, pet a dog.
12. When you need to apologize, do. When you don't, don't.
13. Remember to look at the sky.

ACKNOWLEDGMENTS

I would be nowhere in the book world without my agent, Elisabeth Weed of The Book Group, who listens and guides and supports and is equally brilliant at long-range planning and manuscript edits. I'm so proud to be one of The Book Group's authors! Thanks also to Adi Vildorf for insightful comments on early drafts of this book. At William Morrow, my editor, Liz Stein, is so smart, poised, and efficient that she was able to look at the mess of a first draft I presented her with and draw out things I didn't even know were in there. Thank you also to many others at Morrow: Liate Stehlik, Alexandra Bessette, publicist extraordinaire Julie Paulauski, Amelia Wood, and the salespeople who get the books where they need to go. Karen Richardson, I'm grateful for the careful and thoughtful copyediting. Will Watkins at CAA, thank you for taking me on!

In addition, my gratitude goes to the following people:

Dory Rosati, for talking to me about dog training and being such a great example of dog ownership and training for me with my own dogs, along with all of the staff at Camp K9 (Jenny, Wren, Matt, and Rian especially!). Erin Connolly, for answering my real estate questions. Lizz Reilly, for inviting me to visit her book club full of young mothers to remind me what mothering young kids is like (it's hard!). Alex Herlihy, town historian for the town of Rye, New Hampshire, for taking me through photos of the area through the decades. Meganne Fabrega, for talking to me about the Beach Club, inviting me to visit, sharing old photos and her deep insider's knowledge of the area, gently correcting my errors, and being a smart and valued reader. Ryan Percy of Percy Farm and Megan Mayhew Bergman, for talking to me about dairy farming and Vermont life. Sue Love—we finally got Lenox in a book! Even if Taylor Swift beat us in a song!—for answering my endless questions about her beloved hometown. Derek Hayes, for the valuable info on Boulder. Lisa DeStefano, for architectural insight a second time. Margaret Dunn, for really smart editorial help both big picture and small picture, and for being a BFF (one of two). The Truelove girls, Julie, JoJo, and BFF Jennifer (two of two), for filling my imaginary garage storeroom in memory of their own mother, Jan Truelove. Risa Heller and Nathan Miller, for talking to me about crisis communications.

A few other notes: Jordan's job was inspired by the article "Get Me Risa Heller!" by Shawn McCreesh in the February 14, 2023, issue of *New York Magazine*. The children's book *Bunbun, the Middle One* was not published early enough for Natalie to have read it as a child—but this is where it's handy to be a fiction writer. I pretended that it was. The name for the Realtor in this book came from Nikoletta Tarkan, who bid generously on an auction item for the Newburyport Education Foundation.

I've been writing novels for a long time now, but only in the past couple of years have I made so many new writer friends. A bounty! Better late than never, I say. I worry if I start naming you all I'd leave someone out, but you know who you are, and let's keep hanging out and talking about books and writing. People at my publisher have called Elin Hilderbrand my Fairy Godmother and I think that's quite apt. Thank you, Elin, for years of support and for sending so many of your readers my way. I admire you so much as a writer and as a human. And thank you for introducing to me to Tim Ehrenberg of Tim Talks Books! Mitchell's Book Corner is one of several indie bookstores that threw their support behind *Mansion Beach* last year and brought me many treasured new readers I hope will follow me to this book. Among them: Bank Square Books, Book Love of Pinehills, Books on the Square, The Book Shop of Beverly Farms, Buttonwood Books and Toys, Charter Books, Illume Books, Ink Fish Books, Island Bound Bookstore, Jabberwocky Bookshop, The Purple Couch Bookshop, and Wakefield Books. It feels like we've entered a new era for innovative, lively author events and I'm always honored and delighted to partake.

In my adopted hometown of Newburyport, I'm grateful to the Newburyport Literary Festival and my excellent friend group of amazing women. I'm so lucky!

Most of my books are about families in some way but this one is *really* a close look at one family. I'm so fortunate to have my parents, John and Sara, and my sister, Shannon. My husband, Brian, is an endless source of support, love, and understanding when it comes to writing but also life in general. The Shipman girls aren't real people, and they aren't based on real people, but my three daughters, Addie, Violet, and Josie, have shown me what a delightful, hilarious, different-from-each-other but nonetheless loving triumvirate of sisters can look like. It's been a pleasure and a joy to be in your orbit all these years.

DISCUSSION QUESTIONS

1. The family beach house is a central symbol in the story. What does it represent to each sister, and how does the impending sale of the house reflect their struggles with attachment and loss?

2. The Shipman sisters share a close bond but also experience significant conflict. How do their differing personalities and life choices create tension, and how do they ultimately support one another?

3. Each sister plays a distinct role within the family—Jordan as the responsible one, Natalie as the struggling mother, and Mae as the lost youngest. How do these roles evolve throughout the story?

4. Mae is described as the "most chill" sister but is also struggling with financial instability and a sense of being unmoored. How do her choices reflect her desire for a fresh start, and how does her relationship with her sisters shape her journey?

5. Jordan is often the voice of reason and practicality in the family. How does her role as the eldest sister influence her interactions with Natalie and Mae, and how does her past relationship with Simone add depth to her character?

6. Natalie juggles running a farm, managing a social media empire, and raising three children. How does her struggle to maintain a perfect image impact her relationships with her sisters and her sense of self?

7. The death of the sisters' mother, Theresa, looms large over the family. How does her absence shape the sisters' decisions and their relationships with one another? How do the sisters' respective methods of grieving affect their relationships and their ability to move forward?

8. Calvin's decision to remarry a younger woman, Kara, who was also Theresa's hospice nurse, creates tension within the family. How do the sisters' reactions to Kara reveal their feelings about their father and their mother's memory?

9. The sisters hold on to various objects and traditions that remind them of their mother and their shared past. How do these items and rituals help them cope with loss, and what do they symbolize?

10. By the end of the story, do you think the sisters come to terms with their father's remarriage and the sale of the beach house? What does forgiveness and acceptance look like for each of them?

Meg Mitchell Moore lives in the beautiful coastal town of Newburyport, Massachusetts, with her family. *Down with the Shipmans* is her tenth novel.